THE HADRIAN ENIGMA

A Forbidden History

THE HADRIAN ENIGMA

A Forbidden History

A novel by

GEORGE GARDINER

A GMP EDITIONS publication

Second Edition published in 2010
by GMP Editions
www.MmRomanceNovels.com

ISBN: 978-0-9807469-1-4

Cover :
Bust of Antinous, known as the Antinous of Ecouen.
Courtesy of the Louvre, Paris.

In memory of M.R.

Author's note

THE HADRIAN ENIGMA – A Forbidden History is fiction based upon an incident recorded by historians of the ancient world. It is a novel elaborating on the suspicious death of Antinous, the *favorite* of Caesar Hadrian, emperor of Rome, reported at the River Nile in Egypt in 130CE.

This novel's events, cultural ambience, and characters reflect recorded history. Several characters and circumstances are entirely fictional. Background information and a bibliography are available at:-

www.MmRomanceNovels.com

George Gardiner

".. the noble lover of beauty engages in love
wherever he sees excellence and splendid
natural endowment, without regard for
any difference in physiological detail."

PLUTARCH *Erotikos (Dialogue On Love)* **146**
(Lucius Mestrius Plutarchus,
Greece 46CE-121CE)

"Archer (Eros), son of little Aphrodite,

living at Helikonian Thespiai by the

flowering garden of Narkissos,

be gracious :

receive these spoils of a bear which

Hadrian killed on his horse and gives you,

and in return breathe soberly* on him

from heavenly Aphrodite."

Dedication to Eros at Thespiai by the Emperor Hadrian, c.125CE

(found in Kaibel, *Epigrammata Graeca*, n.811 -

quoted in **PAUSANIUS, GUIDE TO GREECE**, as n.144,

trans. Peter Levi, Penguin UK 1971)

(* breathe soberly = be generous)

PROLOGOS

In the 13th Year of Imperator Caesar Divi Traiani filius Traianus Hadrianus Augustus. (Hadrian, ruled 117-138CE)

Stop now. Cease immediately. You are at risk. If you intend reading this history, take great care. Caesar will not be pleased. Hadrian may exile you to some bleak rocky outcrop dashed by stormy seas if he learns of it. Or worse. Reconsider while yet you may.

However, if juicy morsels of gossip have reached your ears and you cannot help yourself, then be it on your own head. You now share in my own plight.

This saga came to its climax three months ago. Its culmination struck Caesar's traveling Household at the dawn of one of those bleached-out, white hot, stupefying days so common in Egypt. In the molten miasma of liquid heat that morning three months ago his Court's communal bloodstream froze to ice, as they say.

An unexplained death at Court is a sobering matter. The death of a young, vital, handsome *favorite* augurs even greater concern. What is to be made of it, we wondered?

Three months later my anxiety escalates. My head is now forfeit. Hadrian does not forgive my revelations before his Court. They were truly embarrassing. His reputation for machismo as a Roman Imperator was exposed to view for what it really is. Yes, Caesar's *loving tenderness* was revealed. Tenderness is a sentiment an Imperator deems it unwise to disclose.

This is the path of my chronicle's journey. By the grace of *Fortuna*, I hope these words will persuade Hadrian of the integrity of my actions that fateful day. May they fix my head more securely to my body.

Greetings dear reader, whoever you may be.

Your writer is Gaius Suetonius Tranquillus, renowned lawyer and alleged playboy of Rome. 'Alleged' because all Rome assumes I have been notably successful in a Roman male's obligatory career of lively *priapic* endeavor.

However in this thirteenth year of Caesar's rule I will have seen a full sixty winters. This means I am six years older than Hadrian. Being no spring chicken, my alleged priapic activities wane alarmingly.

My *patron* and friend of the past twenty years, Gaius Septicius Clarus, the well-known senator and one-time Prefect of the Praetorian Guard, has kindly assigned me a suite at his luxurious villa at Alexandria. Here on Caesar's behalf I am under house arrest until Hadrian decides what to do with me. As a member of the *eques* class at least I know what my worst fate may be – a swift beheading or permission to suicide somewhat less messily.

In the meantime I gather my thoughts onto paper about the recent journey through Egypt. These thoughts will either save my neck or make it even less secure. While the memory remains fresh I must record the fate and subsequent *apotheosis* of the young man at the center of its most disturbing event, Antinous of Bithynia. To some he was Caesar's beloved companion and *Favorite*; to others a mere catamite, a toyboy, a typical Greek hustler on the make.

I have written several admired histories for the Empire's book copiers and their readers. I am best known for my *Lives of the Caesars*. Perhaps you too know of it? There I show in eight scrolls all I have learned of our first Caesar, Julius, and the following eleven Caesars from Augustus to Domitian. That last monster ruled in my youth at much cost to the lives of members of my family.

In my *Lives* I tried to tell of Rome's rulers as they truly were. It has not always been a pretty picture, dear reader, but as you may perceive,

I am up to the chore. I leave no unsavory stone unturned, no scandal unexplored. If a Caesar proved to be boring, I might even invent a little.

Thirteen years ago on Hadrian's succession to the role of *Princeps* he appointed Septicius to be his Prefect of the Praetorian Guard. I was then appointed to be the Director of imperial correspondence. For five years I was active at the very center of imperial affairs. No letter, official document, edict, or warrant in Latin or Greek went to the far reaches of the Empire without my oversight.

After some time Hadrian's wife, Vibia Sabina *the Augusta*, declared Septicius and I to have insulted her. Sabina is a strong-willed woman, so she cleverly engineered a charge of *laesa majestas* against us and our subsequent dismissal. Hadrian was obliged to agree with his wife's claim for public form's sake.

It's well known no love is lost between the Imperial couple. Nevertheless both show proper conformity to their marital obligations. After all, he is our *Princeps*, the First Citizen, who leads us all by example.

Hadrian leads in most things except perhaps in the matter of whelping progeny to populate the Empire or stock the Legions with fighting sons. He and Sabina have bred no children.

Hadrian wed his arranged bride at the usual age when he was twenty-five. As usual, Sabina was thirteen. They do not sleep together. I doubt they have much in common other than their unlikely coupling by the strategies of the imperial succession.

She has been heard to say her husband is a monster!, though she never defines her meaning. She swears she will never bear him a son. And she hasn't. Nevertheless despite their mutual antagonism the two maintain a prudent public comportment as the *Princeps* and his respectful wife. They are role models for all Romans.

My books of *Lives of the Caesars* focused upon the acquisition of power by the emperors, their uses of that power, and their abuses of power. Of the first twelve Caesars I revealed how only Julius and three of the remaining eleven retained their moral authority.

However, in recording the sexual orientations of all fifteen *Imperators* up to this very day, the tally declines to but two recognized for their common, garden-variety disposition. The remaining thirteen sought opportunities to be erotic innovators of considerable invention, if not outright ingenuity.

The remote province of Bithynia has been a prominent source of this inventiveness. Earlier when I was secretary for two years to Rome's ambassador at this backwoods colony on the edge of the Black Sea, I experienced its wild, exotic culture at close hand.

Bithynia seems a place before memory; a place intoxicated with time's open endlessness. Antique gods, demons, nymphs, or sprites of the forests, waters, skies or inner perceptions seem close to us at Bithynia. They challenge our very sanity. Sacred rites and holy oaths are essential to placate their feverish spirits. Strange, crude, brutal superstitions are veiled behind the token adoration of our sacred Pantheon or the honoring of our Deified Emperors.

Vestiges of customs from some ancient epoch survive beneath today's normality, often undermining its validity. Ordinary assumptions become blurred, diffuse, flexible, shifting the barriers of understanding in unexpected or disturbing ways.

Male and female categories too become malleable, diaphanous, interchangeable, obverse sides of the same coin. In this heady climate the portals of license open wide. Vistas of voluptuous sensuality arise before us. Bithynia disturbs, shocks, and thrills simultaneously.

As you well know, a Roman male's function is to subjugate, dominate, and penetrate. This has always been the victorious Roman way. Romans conquer and subdue compelled by their driven virility. Manhood is defined by the right to have sex – that is, to dominate and penetrate, or in earthier terms, to fuck, if you forgive honest Latin - whether it's with a woman or a man, a mature youth, a slave, an enemy, or a business opponent, though perhaps reluctantly metaphorically in the latter. Some say we Romans have an unimaginative sexual agenda. Others say we are immoral, wanton, crude fornicators.

Subjugation and domination are perceived to be a Roman male's purpose in life. The way of the *phallus* rules. This is our ancient heritage, we proclaim. We despise intimate emotion. It is a sign of weakness. Only the meek, slaves, losers, and girls succumb to such defects. They are to be pitied.

Yet there are times when even I seriously wonder about this?

However in Bithynia, perversely, it is the giving and receiving of pleasure which rules. To this rustic breed pleasure is a two-way exchange at minimum, or every-which-way when inclined. Sex is a leisure activity, play, a game, recreation, an exercise in indulgence, a mode of *luxury*.

Those ancient rulers of Bithynia, the dynasty of her four opulent Nikomedes kings, were lauded across the Middle Sea as dissolute practitioners of this quality of *luxury*. Since Rome's annexation of the province our virile Roman tastes have been infiltrating this Dionysian culture very slowly indeed, if at all.

To Bithynia's social elites sexual appeal is focused upon the *beauty* of the object, a person's visual or moral attraction. This aesthetic ignores class, status, or even gender. The Bithynians are famously gender blind. Human beauty is praised, wooed, and hopefully consummated, regardless of the vehicle.

A century ago that last of the Bithynian kings, the notoriously bawdy Nikomedes IV, happily satisfied this racy itch while entertaining a visiting Roman ambassador. The ambassador was the nineteen year-old Julius Caesar. It seems our handsome future triumphant Roman victor of wars was introduced very personally, very intimately indeed, to the Bithynian mode of *luxury*. Consequently, his Legions later regaled the founder of the dynasty of the Caesars as being *"every woman's husband and every man's wife'*.

Yet today Rome's stolid elders reject such license. To Romans, the Bithynians are soft, decadent, compliant, accommodating, too easily subjugated, too readily penetrated.

I am unsure which of these opposing convictions is the more natural under a philosopher's definition of Nature's Law? Surely if something occurs in Nature it is natural? Read Epicurus or Lucretius of long ago. But try telling that to Rome's austere Stoics or those atheist followers of Chrestus who pester us with their prissy ways while defaming our gods and habits! Their abstemious asceticism chills our blood. It is utterly unRoman.

This leads us inevitably to --- What then is love?

Is love the urgent compulsion to have your way with someone, Roman style? Or is love some more ambiguous sensation, Bithynian style? Our thinkers search exhaustively for the answer. Even today's philosophers Plutarch or Epictetus display uncertainty.

Take Hadrian and Antinous. Was this a love? Was it Roman style or Bithynian style?

Caesar's promotion of his former companion to the status of *Divus* - godlike - positively compels our query.

His edict about the young man's divine nature, as depicted by statues of the muscular stud as a New Apollo which are popping up all over the place, or the commemorative medallions being minted with his chiseled features, or the many reports of miracles attributed to his role as Osiris Resurrected, or the discovery of his new star in the heavens, plus the cult burgeoning everywhere in his name, make debate almost compulsory.

Was the five year liaison of these two a mere bizarre, brazen, delirious debauchery? Or was it a romance to touch our minds and hearts? Was it of Cupid, who Greeks call Eros, or was it of Venus, who they call Aphrodite? It was certainly a striking phenomenon.

Consequently I dedicate these scrolls of A *Forbidden History* to our Great Caesar. With luck they will persuade Hadrian how my revelations before the Court at Egypt three months ago were necessary to his peace of mind. The revelations do not warrant my head being cleaved from my shoulders.

In preparing my chronicle for the public record I have interviewed courtiers at the highest echelons of the *Imperium*. I have searched into times gone by to explore the hidden pasts of key participants.

I and my aide-in-detection, the beguiling Syrian beauty Surisca of Antioch, have probed the Court's incessant gossip mill to weave together this tale's dense tapestry.

Surisca is a captivating *daughter of Aphrodite*. She is a sweet courtesan enchantress of striking charms and superior intelligence whose worldly perception provided sharp insights into these concealed treasons. Surisca became my eyes, my logic, and even my heart.

I will relate these events as I experienced them. I will recount this saga as in a novella or romance by, say, Titus Petronius Niger of long ago. Incorrigible Petronius lived in the days of Caesar Nero and fell victim to that ruler's vile temper. His lively *Satyrica* parodied the truths of that despised tyrant's rule to warn us of the dangers of despotism. He paid the price for his witticism. But my tale is no comical parody. It will communicate the events of the life and death of Antinous as they occurred, plainly.

In this *Forbidden History* I will take a role as a character in the unfolding scenario. I, Gaius Suetonius Tranquillus, an historical biographer, will appear as but a single performer in my saga.

The treason against Hadrian began long ago, Surisca and I discovered. It began a quarter-century ago at the very edge of Europa on its northern frontier of Dacia. This was an entire decade prior to Hadrian's ascendancy as Caesar and five years before Antinous had even been born. At that distant time at least one contender in my saga was compelled to invoke the remainder of this chronicle's savage drama.

But I am ahead of myself. First we must travel back to Middle Egypt three months ago to revisit the climax of these events. This opens the door to all else.

Here my tale begins ----

CHAPTER 1

"Steward! Bring me your latest women!"

The well-groomed gentleman of noble demeanor garbed in a summer toga fragrant with rich perfume clapped his hands and called aloud. The thin wisps of smoky blue fume were striking home at last.

Gaius Suetonius Tranquillus breathed the pungent, fetid scent deep into his nostrils. Once again this fruity vapor channeled the sweet-sour rot of an exotic herb deep into his psyche. Suetonius's crepe-skinned, muscle-sagging features relaxed even further. The small ball of resin had only been burning in its Theban faience bowl for barely a few minutes, yet its strength and pungency were already impacting.

"Only new ones, I say. I've already sampled last week's stock," he proclaimed a little too loudly as he inhaled. His judgment was rapidly drifting off-kilter.

Cadmus, the Steward of Slaves, smiled knowingly. As Suetonius fanned the fumes into his face with both hands he was ingesting deeply for full effect. He waited expectantly for its unique warmth to rise once again deep in his being. Such vapors quieten the thoughts, relax the muscles, and ease the aches of many winters. They provide a waning male a fleeting illusion of the forceful virility which constitutes a Roman male's necessary character.

The herb, if that's what it was, was already providing this illusion to his immense relief. This expensive resin, itself the cost of one of the better girls at the House, was indeed of the best quality. The steward claimed it was from the land of Kush, far away to the south beyond the Nile Cataracts into the Africa hinterland.

Yet perhaps, Suetonius cloudily contemplated, it was merely the scrapings of a fungous residue common to a local Egyptian shrub, and so of no real cost whatsoever. In the East such deceits are commonplace. He sensed he had been the unwitting victim of many.

Suetonius, an elegantly mature, handsome Roman noble of the *equites* educated class, was at the *House of the Blue Lotuses*. This fine establishment was situated in the Street of Pleasures of the city of Hermopolis Magna, capital of the 15th Nome of the Province of Middle Egypt.

It was the first day of the three holy days of the Festival of Isis in the Egyptian month of Akhet. This is the festival celebrated across the Empire in our month of October known as The Isia.

Suetonius was eagerly anticipating a late afternoon's schedule of relaxation as the heady vapors enthralled his senses. His intoxication became evident when he could not finish the sentence he was uttering. Instead, he was stricken smilingly mute, ready and craving for all manner of sensory pleasure. The vapors may have induced heavily leaden limbs and tongue, yet they accompanied this relaxation with enhanced physical yearning. The fumes infuse a rare swooning delight which is good, he determined, very good indeed.

For a man at an age where a firm erection is problematic and seminal secretions modest, this unique resin offers assistance to a Roman to perform the necessary arts of virility. It helps make a man's member stand up properly, and a rigid member gives a Roman confidence in his purpose as a living creature.

At least that is what we Romans say.

Recollections of a once vibrant youthful passion were stirred in Suetonius's memory, though they tended to remain a distant echo. The vapor obliged him to express himself in pointing and gesticulation to negotiate the necessary transactions of pleasure. Suetonius tried to recall his own advice -- *always bargain your prices prior to ingesting intoxicants, not afterwards.*

The day had started well for him. After the morning's sacrifice to the gods at an altar beside his river-ferry accommodation moored close to the west bank of the Nile, his party of six ageing notables carefully divined the entrails of a white dove. The omens for the day were acceptable, if peculiar, the augur explained.

Aristobulus, an astrologer companion of the party and a senior advisor in matters astrological to Hadrian himself, queried the reading of the entrails. He based his doubts on star signs he had calculated. Being the first day of The Isia, it was no ordinary day. Yet he sensed an uncertainty in the stars which caused him professional concern. He frowned a great deal, as expert men of science are prone. Yet the astrological confluence was vague.

Suetonius sensed this was typical of so many claims made by seers and soothsayers who enjoy a bit each way as insurance against the risks of their predictions.

Regardless, he and the more phlegmatic members of the group decided to take advantage of this first day of the Festival. The day sorrowfully mourns the death of the god Osiris. Three days later the Festival celebrates his spiritual rebirth or resurrection into Isis's arms. For a thousand years gloom and doom had been followed by joy and uplift, much to the cheer of the populace and the profit of the various priests or priestesses.

With a retinue of litter bearers to beat their path, Suetonius's gentlemen-of-quality joined the throng of mourners in the dusty streets of Hermopolis. Crowds swirled all round. Chanters and musicians lamented loudly in the lanes and temple forecourts. The air was alive with wailing voices, the scintillance of cymbals, and the shimmering rattle of *systra*. Dancers garbed in mourner's white beat their breasts and cried in grief to Mother Isis as they mimed their ritual search for her husband Osiris's dismembered body. Their hair was strewn with ashes, fabrics were rent, ritual objects were waved.

This year was an Isia of particularly serious supplication to the goddess because of the dismal rise of the Nile's flooding. Since July the river's waters had not swollen to the necessary levels to fully deluge the surrounding flatlands. This was a second year it had risen poorly. A bad harvest was assured for those farmers on higher ground. All were dependent on the flood's black silts to nourish the soil and its crops.

Naturally, the Imperial plantations close to the river were well nurtured. Yet the native Egyptians at the outlying fields wondered what offence had been committed to deserve the punishment of famine by the gods.

Egypt depends on the Nile for its agricultural survival. The two annual harvests would be affected. Deficiency induces famine. Social disturbances may erupt.

Even the city of Rome, far across the Middle Sea, depends on the Nile to nurture the crops. These provide the grain to feed the city's unemployed, impoverished, trouble-making *plebs*. The governing classes may afford to eat well, but Africa's grain is the underlying buttress of Imperial influence in the decrepit alleys and smelly lanes of the Subura at Rome's center teeming with its denizens. And Hadrian, the Senate, the Legions, and Prefect Turbo too know this well.

The charmless, dun-colored cluster of flat-roofed hovels of Hermopolis clustered around the weathered temples at the western bank of the Nile lies two hundred leagues upstream of the Middle Egypt capital of Memphis. This ancient city is the locale of the stupendous Pyramids and its implacable Sphinx.

Caesar Hadrian's ragtag flotilla of boats, barques, and barges of varying types and sizes had meandered the Nile for weeks past taking in all the famous sights. The flotilla was accompanied on land by hundreds of his staff, his guests, a Legion cohort, and his Guard corps.

The emperor's spectacular river barque, *The Dionysus*, accommodated his wife Vibia Sabina and her personal household, while the remainder of the travelers sailed in hired river craft in the great flotilla's wake. Many of his Household traveled with the mule-train of supplies which followed the cortege on land for a whole mile. Soldiers marched the journey in full pack and weaponry. They were usually accompanied on horseback by Hadrian, Antinous, a dozen Companions of the Hunt, and other officers of Caesar's glittering cavalcade.

At places where the Household intends to linger for a few days an expansive portable city of tents, marquees, and pavilions is erected to provide luxury accommodations for his retinue and its camp followers. This mobile palace travels ahead and is erected at carefully chosen landscaped sites.

The hundred marquees are policed by Caesar's personal Horse Guard, the civic Praetorian Guard, and much of a military Legion within a low stockade. The center of the complex being a many-chambered palace in itself, it is graced with silken drapes, fluttering banners, extravagant rugs and furs, travel furnishings from across the Empire, all set on shiny removable marble tiles. Food and water are bullock-driven ahead, with the entire entourage self-sufficient in food, wine, slaves, and potable water. The river provides bathing water.

Suetonius and his five learned scholars had spent the late-October morning playing tourist at the ancient temple precincts of Hermopolis. After several hours of touring, the six decided to refresh themselves at the Baths of Tiberius at the Forum in the city. They bathed, steamed, and took an olive-oil massage while twittering a gossipy conversation suited to senior courtiers.

After having been *strigiled* clean and well kneaded by his body servant, Suetonius took the precaution of ensuring he was sweetly perfumed and garbed in a fresh summer-weight toga. He was now ready to sample the stock at *The House of the Blue Lotuses*.

After the morning's hectic jostle with crowds, he was eager to find solace for the call of his groin while enjoying some pleasurable female conversation. After well-mannered farewells to his companions he retired to the *House* accompanied by a personal slave, five litter-carriers, and a hired much-scarred former-gladiator named Macro to clear his path and protect his person.

Gaius Suetonius Tranquillus is a Roman knight of Umbria at the north of Italy, and a former private secretary to Imperator Caesar Hadrian. He has now reached an age where carefully husbanded wealth plus fame as an historical archivist provides the necessary comforts and interests of life.

He was currently researching his latest book, *Lives of Famous Whores*. This is a work which will certainly find a ready market among the Empire's book copiers. For this reason he had been keen to sample the wares of the many providers of courtesan services which abound in Egypt, especially at Alexandria and nearby Canopus. This offered an opportunity to explore the history of the leading exponents of these arts and their special techniques.

Mind you, Suetonius has long accessed the services of courtesans across the Empire. He can name you each of a hundred of the better houses and their locales, along with their unusual specialties, prices, and possible risks.

For this reason Suetonius had retired to *The House of the Blue Lotuses*, the best in Middle Egypt he was advised.

"Good sir, my master, a leading councilor of the Greek community at Alexandria, has ensured our stock is exemplary," Cadmus opened his sales spiel.

"And expensive ..!" Suetonius contributed jovially from within the burning herb's enveloping fug.

"My master has acquired several of the leading girls of Alexandria, but has also bought fresh purchases from the slave emporia at the Isle of Delos in the Aegean," the steward continued.

"The newest ones are very young and come from exotic places across the Empire. They include some racy Germans with flaxen hair and sluttish habits, a delicate peach-cheeked Briton of very white skin and a shy manner, a pair of Parthian identical twins for dual pleasure, and some fresh professionals from the island of Samos."

Suetonius acknowledged how Samos off the Ionian coast was a major exporter of well-trained girls, along with its knitted lace, deep-sea sponges, sweet wines, olives, and other luxuries.

"If it is to your taste, fine sir, my master has acquired two guaranteed virgins as well as three handsome youths from around the Middle Sea. This includes a white skinned, white haired, pink-eyed albino novelty from Crete."

Cadmus was exultant about the quality of his produce.

The virgins and the youths didn't interest Suetonius. It was likely the 'guaranteed virgins' had not been so for quite some time, but clever surgical arts assisted the illusion. Also for Suetonius they were far too inept to be mixing with men of mature experience. Loose folds of sagging ashen skin, wispy hair pasted across long-balded pates, a few missing teeth, and demanding sexual expectations were prone to distress them. Besides, he recalled, such girls were entirely without conversation. Amusing conversation was at a premium among sex entertainers. It drew good prices.

Separately, the young men rarely enjoyed being ravaged by their clients. They bite their lips in discomfort, and in the provinces are likely to be still untrained in simple intestinal hygiene.

But Suetonius kept the albino slave in mind to mention to Hadrian's master of diversions, Geta the Dacian, to whom he owed a favor or two. Perhaps the albino might meet the emperor's taste, despite Hadrian's known aversion to sex worker slaves.

In the recent words of the philosopher Plutarch, an emperor does not stoop to importune a slave who will have absolutely no rights in the matter, regardless of their admirable looks or unique sexual skills.

Besides, Caesar's long companionship with his Favorite of the past five years, the sweet-natured young man Antinous of Bithynia, had seen him desist from the excesses of his predecessors. This is despite many earlier Caesars being prone to an exuberant intemperance in such things.

Hadrian had a reputation in much earlier life for pursuing beauties. Nevertheless though Suetonius could recall the names of several elite males who had succumbed to Hadrian's seduction, he could not recall any of a member of the opposite gender. An interesting omission he thought, unless Hadrian's marital status precluded such dalliances?

The historian's own taste had contracted over time into an unfashionable focus on women young enough to be his grand-daughter's age. That is, if he had actually bred any children or grandchildren. This included a taste for voluptuous fleshiness in lasses capable of maintaining a breezy conversation. Such qualities recalled his favorite slave-concubine Priscilla, he realized, may the gods bless her long departed soul.

Priscilla died after being his companion for five years. She joined her ancestors while giving birth to a child who may, or may not, have been his. The child too died. Mortality is a constant companion to us all, we know, yet one whose presence inevitably interrupts unexpectedly.

Cadmus, the *House* steward, ushered his Roman client beyond the open public *atrium* of the establishment into a secluded chamber to select his choice of the newer stock.

"Fine sir, please enjoy the comforts of our premiere salon," he encouraged with much Egyptian-style groveling. "We reserve this parlor for only our most important clients."

Suetonius absorbed its distinctive decors with interest.

The chamber was comfortably appointed with cushions and drapes and a reclining couch of quality with a large divan to one side. Witty but tasteful wall paintings portrayed copulating couples or multiples in a variety of elaborately ingenious combinations. They were accompanied by allegories of the Gods in similarly lascivious, comedic entanglements, merrily looking down upon their earthbound mortals.

These amusing images with their prodigiously erect *phalluses* and tortuous contortions conveyed an optimistic tone to the room. They endorsed a cheerful, spicy view of life happily beyond the influence of the Evil Eye or other demonic presence.

The room was redolent with the intense fragrance of bowls of blue lotus blooms, with dried fruits, dates, honey-cakes, and nuts displayed for a client's enjoyment.

Suetonius's servant unclasped the outer garments of his toga and stripped him to the underlying tunic. He poured a goblet of wine for his master and retired to the doorway to await instruction.

Cadmus sent his girls into the suite one by one. Each regaled Suetonius with a jolly smile or a sensual leer. They flashed their bodies from beneath their skimpy outerwear with a spin and a turn, highlighting their best bodily feature. They displayed their genitals forward to arouse his sensuality and check for signs of eczemas, blisters, or infestation.

Each wore a *House* identification slate chalked with their name and place of origin, plus their price. Charges vary according to age, beauty, or special services. Several of the girls had uneven teeth, thin chicken legs, or flat busts, probably reflecting their poor diet since childhood and the poverty of their mothers' similar calling. These influence price. Others were exemplary even by Rome's standards where the cream of the Empire's courtesans flourish.

One dark haired beauty immediately took Suetonius's fancy. Her well-formed limbs, shapely bosom, and intelligently-twinkling eyes caught his attention.

"What is your name, girl?" he asked, hazily reading the name inscribed on her board.

"Surisca, my lord. I am Surisca of Antioch," she responded in a cheery teasing trill.

Suetonius recognized she was from Syria because she spoke Greek with the accent of those whose native tongue is Aramaic, the common language of the farther East. The Syri was probably in her late teens, yet looked older from the rigors of her profession. Her board announced she was a dancer and flautist, hints her gifts included athletic activities and oral skills.

Her long hair bound high in a Syriac headband possessed a well-combed sheen. Her teeth seemed evenly lined, and her limbs were healthily straight but fulsomely feminine. There were no eczemas or signs of lice at her *mount of Venus*. She also wore less face-paint than some of the other girls, which was a definite attraction for him in a sex-worker. Only the faded henna-dye patterns stenciled onto her hands, arms, and forehead told of her ethnicity and implied her mode of livelihood.

She greeted the Roman with a shy deference he found disarming. She whirled and teetered on tip-toe to prominently display her bodily wares. Suetonius preferred her lively approach rather than the lascivious insolence tediously affected by the other girls. In fact Surisca vaguely reminded him of his late concubine Priscilla, which was a pleasing recollection. So he called for the steward and clapped hands on the price, which was trivial.

The steward departed. This left his servant standing discreetly by the door awaiting further instruction. Macro stood guard outside to maintain vigilance against intruders.

Surisca began her contract with Suetonius by taking a cue from the sultry music echoing throbbingly from the main salon beyond his chamber. She performed a distracted, sensually arousing dance before him. This was her sex worker's preliminary routine for a client, leisurely displaying her fleshy showcase of goods and erotic possibilities.

Loosening her hair so it tumbled down her back in a flood of shiny waves, and letting fall all her Damascene veils to the floor, she cheekily tossed her more private vestments into his face with a chuckle and grin. They exuded the scents of roses and the female creature.

Then Surisca slowly undulated and writhed before him in subtle shifting moves matching the echoes of the music, moving ever closer to him with each phrase of its melody. Her body surged and flowed with the rhythms, her full bosom and pink nipples were invitingly prominent, while her shapely configurations revealed every nook and cranny of her flesh, every pore of her skin, every fold of her femininity, just as she intended. The shy smile had now become a remote sensuality as her eyes locked dreamily onto the older man's attention in alluring, if professional, calculation.

Despite the leaden effects of the inhalant's fumes and being over three times Surisca's age, Suetonius felt his blood race into his genitals, incite his lust, and firm his member for action. Well, almost. With very little effort nubile Surisca had aroused the older man with her simple arts, searching eyes, and fleshly rounded curves. He began to melt in readiness for enveloping her in his arms and penetrating that Doorway to Eternity which the female Other holds in perpetual mastery over mere mortals such as he.

As Surisca drew closer to him in rhythmic distraction he could detect the redolence of myrrh and frankincense oil on her skin, while her breath was fragrant with musk and mint. The mixed scents, the impact of the heady inhalant, and the leisurely throb of the music induced a swooning delight.

Of course Surisca had other intentions prior to satisfying Suetonius's increasingly urgent impulses. Like the experienced working girl she was, she intended to prolong his pleasures and titillate his body's nine orifices with other arts of touch, mouth, tongue, and breath. Delay was delicious. Exquisite tension was thrilling excitement. She blew whispers into his ear, she nibbled and sucked at his navel, she fondled and licked his nipples. She explored hidden places of his physique that he himself might not choose to, and she did it with bravado.

He responded clumsily with the vapor's leaden, ineffectual, distraction.

She toyed with his genitals with abandon and stroked his struggling member with delicacy. She knew inherently she had touched some remote part of his psyche and provoked some distant memory of a past liaison. She played with him and his memories in a manner which brought him a marvelously pleasing satisfaction. Yes, she was certainly professional.

But it was to be not to be for long ---

The chamber door burst open with a tumult of voices. Both the steward and Suetonius's manservant tumbled into the chamber genuflecting and groveling profusely before him. Macro, the gladiator, stood with his back to the room with his *gladius* sword unsheathed at the ready, awaiting Suetonius's signal for action.

Surisca clutched up her garments to flee to a corner to cower at the sudden intrusion.

At the door stood a tall senior officer of the Praetorian Guard, the emperor's security police, plus several lesser officers. The Praetorian, spectacularly regaled in his muscular leathern breastplate, ceremonial swathes and tassels, plus a crested helmet with its heroic horse-hair brush typical of the Guard, stepped forward with military precision. He disdainfully brushed the gladiator aside. He snapped the *honor-and-hail* arm-salute at the bare-arsed Roman senior flustering messily on the divan before him.

"Gaius Suetonius Tranquillus? Equestrian knight and former private secretary to the Imperial Court? Hail!" the Praetorian declaimed.

Suetonius stumbled to his feet and clutched his private parts behind his tunic with as much dignity as his clouded state, unsteady gait, and distressed arousal could marshal.

Damn! he thought, *things were just getting really interesting!*

"I am he," he mouthed in his best legal-argument voice trained in earlier years at the Bar of Rome. He had only the faintest nervous tremor in his vowels. "All hail, Praetorian!"

"On the instruction of Imperator Caesar Publius Aelius Hadrian, I convey to you an Imperial Summons."

The officer extended a small furled scroll at arm's length. It was bound in the scarlet silk tie and clay seal of the Imperial Administration which Suetonius instantly recognized from his own years earlier as Private Secretary to Hadrian.

Gathering his composure, he took the scroll and broke the seal to unfurl the small roll beneath. His mind had cleared swiftly and his nerves returned to a steadier flow as the inscrutable Praetorian stood at ease intently observing his responses. The officer would already know what he was about to learn, Suetonius imagined.

He read the epistle silently to himself, trying to ensure his hands weren't trembling. It began with the standard triumphalism.

"Imperator Caesar Trajan Hadrian Augustus, son of the divine Trajan Parthicus, grandson of the divine Nerva, pontifex maximus, tribunican power for the fifteenth time, thrice consul, pater patriae, on this 28th day of October of the thirteenth year of our rule, to Gaius Suetonius Tranquillus, knight and scholar of Rome. Greetings --- !"

"*Greetings*", Suetonius thought, so this was not to be something alarming. Without this word the document would inspire immediate fear in the sturdiest soul. It continued ---

"It is our desire you attend our person immediately on receipt of this summons."

That's all, "attend our person immediately", finalized with the usual politesses.

The Praetorian unlaced his helmet, swept it under his arm, and snapped to attention.

"I am instructed to deliver you immediately into the presence of our lord and master, the *Princeps*, Imperator Caesar Hadrian. Immediately. Now. *Praise be to Caesar!*"

He pronounced his message with the same unemotional tone he probably used when announcing someone's transport to a giddily joyful wedding, or receipt of a glorious military commission, or summons to immediate execution.

"I have a horse at your disposal, and we are instructed to accompany you into Caesar's presence across the River. Now, sir. *Praise be to Caesar!*"

By this time Suetonius had recovered his wits and realized the fellow meant business. He signaled to his attendant to help him gather his belongings.

He waved wanly at Surisca hovering demurely in the corner and tossed a small gold coin in her direction from his belt-purse, a sum far beyond the negotiated price with the steward.

"I'll be back sometime soon, Surisca," he whispered. He made a point of remembering her name.

Turning to the officer he blurted aloud, "But how did you know where to find me?"

Suetonius simply had to ask. How would Praetorians locate someone enjoying the private pleasures of a bordello in an outback town late of a holiday afternoon?

"I am not instructed to converse, sir" said the officer. "We must journey immediately."

Suetonius dismissed his servant and the litter carriers into Macro's protection, disposed of the astounded Cadmus with further silver well above the negotiated prices, bundled his bulky toga into a satchel because it is far too bulky to ride a horse attired in one, and tossed the bag to one of the Praetorians to carry.

"Can you tell me anything, Centurion?" he asked the officer as his horse frisked under its new rider, "…anything at all?"

Suetonius used the most authoritarian *patrician's* vocal timbre he could muster. He was sure it would impact on a soldier's sense of rank and duty. Meanwhile he toyed with his equestrian knight's gold ring on one hand, the symbol of his lofty status in the pecking order of things. But the officer already knew his rank.

The centurion looked Suetonius over to assess the risks. He calculated his likely value as a person of influence at the Imperial Court, an impression to which Surisca's and the steward's coins had added persuasively. He leaned forward out of earshot of his companions.

"Sir, Antinous of Bithynia, Caesar's personal companion and *Favorite*, is dead."

Suetonius sensed he instantly regretted telling him. Suetonius was thunderstruck.

Antinous dead! How? Why? Where? Of what? Healthy twenty-three year-olds at the peak of physical fitness do not die suddenly of good health.

With such questions spinning through his brain, Suetonius and the Guard escort cantered off into the dusk through the town's narrow lanes towards the Nile's shore.

CHAPTER 2

An unexplained death among the Court's inner circle is sobering, Suetonius mused while the Praetorians stabled their horses at a ferry jetty by the Nile's shore. Such deaths often had cryptic features. There might be more to it than immediately met the eye.

The historical biographer had noticed as they cantered through the stony back streets of Hermopolis how the celebrants of Isis were still making a great din with their rites. Shaven-headed priests in leopard skin mantles, linen-garbed acolytes, and simple householders or workers in rags were loudly shaking tambourines or *sistra*, beating drums, and chanting, dancing, or mourning with cheerful abandon. It seemed the first day of The Isia's three days of commemoration would proceed long into the night.

Brazier cauldrons were burning at lane intersections, with countless torches and lamps illuminating the colonnades of food stalls, taverns, traders booths, artisan's cubicles, fortune-teller's tables, and whore-house doorways which lined the town's lanes. These people certainly know how to party, Suetonius thought.

What was it, he wondered, that made the sadness of the death of their god Osiris such a cheerful event? The season's desultory deluge threatened harvest disaster for many whose land lay above the river's customary levels. This should induce fear and trembling, not joy.

After stabling their horses at the jetty the Praetorians commandeered a river ferry captain to cross to the east bank prior to the approaching sunset. Coins were exchanged along with sharp words and manhandled swords.

During the bumpy journey across the river beneath fading light Suetonius asked the ferry captain how long the celebrations would continue into the night. As a swarthy Egyptian in soiled skirt and leather headpiece with all manner of talismans hanging on his neck and arms and ears, the ferryman's Greek was basic. He could only respond to the biographer in a jumble of words of the unfathomable local dialect with a single phrase in Greek, "A miracle! A miracle!"

Suetonius thought this a quaint response as no miracle was immediately evident, unless he was referring to the dubious capacity of his rustic wooden tub to survive a river crossing. A Praetorian based at Alexandria who understood the local dialect spoke up.

"Sir, the ferryman says there's been a miracle today. An important man has been sacrificed to the river. Such a sacrifice joins the gods, becomes godlike, they believe."

"An important man?" Suetonius asked doubtfully. "He becomes a god?"

"Yes, the victim becomes a manifestation of Osiris. He is now Osiris who resurrects in two days time. The river's temper is appeased. That's the drift of the man's words," the trooper said.

The biographer sunk into a thoughtfulness as the creaking tub flexed against the river's churn while its rowers thrashed at the flow. He wondered if the reputed sacrifice had anything to do with the passing of the emperor's favorite, Antinous. Surely not?

So Antinous was dead. The golden youth was no more.

Suetonius wistfully recalled his first sighting of the *Favorite* in the ninth year of Caesar's rule. It was when Hadrian and his cavalcade had returned from a lengthy tour of the Empire. Their journey had included a sojourn at that pivot of all Greek sentiment, the city of Athens in Achaea. Here Hadrian acquired a new consort in the form of the *ephebe* Antinous. Courtiers whispered Caesar was smitten by the young man.

Fired two years earlier from being Hadrian's secretary, Suetonius was awarded a small suite within the huge palace complex being constructed at *The Villa Tiburtina* twenty miles outside Rome. The entire Court withdrew to *The Villa* for Rome's summer. The biographer was encouraged by Hadrian to research his *Lives of the Caesars* in the Villa's new Library. Obliged to attend many of the daily rituals of palace life, his client's duty included attendance at assemblies, religious rites, dining occasions, public audiences, and the Villa's elaborate entertainments.

Hadrian and Sabina were always accompanied by their interminable human *contubernium*, their attached mass of courtiers and families. This Household included wheedling senators, consulting magistrates, clerks, supplicant clients, foreign emissaries, several seers, astrologers, priests, generals of the Legions, a cluster of personal friends of disparate genders, poets, architects, Horse Guards and Praetorians galore, assorted wives, extended families, three dozen fidgeting children of varying ages and relationships, and an array of servants or slaves on tap to provide creature comforts.

This retinue assembled in protocol array in the private garden of the Doric Atrium at *The Villa* at Tibur each morning. An *augur* performed the reading of auspices detected in a fresh-killed offering's liver. Prayers to the gods, for the people and senate of Rome, with a nod to Caesar and his wife, were obligatory.

Suetonius lingered at the edge of this seething mass of vassals to appear to participate without actually being involved. The Imperial couple are obliged to perform their daily duties in such populous company, sharing their dining, bathing, toilet, and enrobing, at each stage of duty from dawn to bedtime. Only secret state business, the discussion of diplomatic correspondence, or sexual relations are exempt from public attention, though suitably reliable slaves might attend in mute invisibility.

Among this congregation Suetonius spied a young man close by Hadrian's side he had never seen in the retinue previously. The fellow followed the imperial couple at a slight distance to one side, attending the occasion yet somewhat abstractly remote from the action at hand. He was tall, though not quite as tall as Hadrian. He was solid bodied in a young athlete's slender-waisted, broad-shouldered, firmly muscled way. He was an utter contrast to the usual run of either decrepitly weedy or obscenely portly courtiers of the imperial retinue.

Further, unlike other males of this company where balded pates predominated, the young man had his own hair. That is except Hadrian himself, who retains a full growth of gray-tinged locks with a close-cropped beard.

The lad's shock of hair was of a strikingly light blond tone. This indeed was a novelty at Court except among the flaxen-locked Germans of the Horse Guards or the occasional Celtic slave. The lad's mop was the color of pale straw whose sheen glinted in the sunlight. Its fulsome bulk tousled around his crown and rolled down his nape in luxurious coils. They signified a young man who hadn't yet trimmed his hair or first beard as maturity's offering to Jupiter. His height, his powerful build, his copious hair, and his obvious youth, coupled with a very un-*patrician* sporty tan, made him stand out among the senior grizzlies who attend Caesar. Most of these are of the short, sallow, Italian or Aegean racial types, and are neither sporty, nor tanned, nor young.

To Suetonius's eye the newcomer was eighteen years of age or older and shone with visible health. Translucency of skin and a peachy flush at his cheeks were set beneath inquisitive blue-gray eyes. Despite the Latin world's prejudice against the pale eyes of barbarians, in Antinous they had an appealing impact. They searched deep into one's spirit with piercing, enquiring but a friendly intensity. A fresh scar across his left cheek was the sole physical blemish in this flawless animal.

Only the newest slaves at Court or students of the Imperial College on assignment as pages, with the occasional son or daughter of a senator, displayed such youth. Even guardsmen are all well into their mid-twenties by the time they are sufficiently proven to warrant duties for the emperor. Amid this motley crew gathered from around the Empire, the sculpted features of the Bithynian were conspicuous to all.

Antinous was attired in a simple white *toga virilis* without status markings, fully slung around his body in the proper manner above a tunic. It revealed muscular shoulders and a crisply defined chest line beneath its under-tunic. The toga's woolen swathe was clasped with a rustic bronze *fibula* brooch of Greek ethnic design, not Roman; the sole indication of the young man's breeding.

There was no ostentation -- no bracelets of precious metal, no jewels, no *kohl* eye-liner in the eastern fashion, no clan or caste tattoos, no evident perfume wafting to engage attention, no overwrought hairstyle augmented with an elegant corona or pierced with inserted décors, and certainly no iron, silver, or gold finger or thumb rings certifying status. There was a solitary blue-stoned ring on one index finger.

This lack of baubles probably endeared him to Caesar's renown undecorated tastes. Hadrian himself displayed no unnecessary frippery.

A simple leather band restrained the lad's mane, accompanied by a thong around his neck with an attached *bulla* locket. In Rome this is the tell-tale sign of a freeborn youth, probably of good birth. It warns the ambitiously promiscuous to keep their damn distance or risk dire consequences at the hands of family!

Gossip whispered how Antinous's manner would be accompanied by the nauseating bravado of those unbearded, spoiled young men who were specially favored at Court by virtue of their youth. There were several readily known and barely tolerated. Yet with Antinous no beard was evident. Perhaps blond tones camouflage whiskers into an invisible downy fluff? As for a privileged swagger, the young man moved with calm discretion and polite modesty which belied the usual posturing of the Court's inner circle.

Suetonius noticed how the bustling retinue surrounding Hadrian unwittingly gave the young man a clear circle of space in unofficial acknowledgement of his status as Caesar's special intimate.

The lad's height was balanced with a slim, sinewy silhouette. Obviously well exercised after a lifetime invested at the *palaestra* in sports and military exercises, his rangy, slinky-hipped figure was typical of those statues of Olympic athletes in bronze or marble wrested impulsively by past emperors from cities across the Aegean or at Olympia itself. These trophies are now displayed in Rome's public gardens for all its citizens to savor.

Mostly nude, such works of the stonemason's craft exhibit the male form in its ideal magnificence. It was a form which Antinous's own chiseled appearance proved was no heroic myth or sculptor's erotic fantasy. It was a physique not often evident among Rome's mélange of gnarled or decrepit denizens except perhaps among the junior military, some sporty patricians, or the arena's fleet-footed gladiators.

Antinous had a lithe and proportioned frame which proclaimed mature muscular power coupled with the animal dynamism of youth. This was a bearing assured to attract the attention of admirers of both genders.

His sharply-cut muscles, defined chest line, orbed abdominals, and triangular upper frame above lean loins and an athletic butt expressed the *alpha male* physique readily recognized by any sexually aware mortal. It proclaimed him as a vital font of virile fertility.

Here was a living, breathing Adonis, or a flesh-and-blood mirror of divine Apollo himself.

Yet other than physical characteristics which shine for but a handful of years, plus sexually-charged contours of a similar ephemerality, one wondered what on earth could appeal to the sophisticated tastes of our imperial aesthete, Hadrian, beyond simple lechery? The young fellow was very appealing in a manly way, but so are many young people of health and shapeliness who may be accessible to an emperor's earthier gratification.

Other than the highly perishable attractions of the flesh, Suetonius wondered what Hadrian saw in the lad that justified such an intimate yet very public attachment? Hadrian had begun to exhibit Antinous at every opportunity in a manner which proclaimed the young man's role as a personal consort almost equal to the status of Vibia Sabina herself.

The biographer had difficulty believing the two men had a great deal in common intellectually or in genuine companionship.

Other than the lively excitements of the hunt, or the camaraderie of bivouacs with the Legions, or youth's wildness in immoderate drinking sessions at men's symposia, plus the bodily enticements of the boudoir while sexual novelty survived, what else could such a fellow offer? He wondered if Antinous possessed depths of character which evaded the biographer's immediate perception.

So there must indeed be something more to the relationship to sustain it than met the eye?

Yet Suetonius had to admit how, beyond his physical attributes, Antinous often conveyed something somewhat more interesting. At first he interpreted the boy's sculpted features to proclaim the petulant self-indulgent and feminized sensuality of a sybarite, or even a dissolute *cinaedus* in the renowned Bithynian style.

These characteristics were suggested by youthful full lips and heavy-lidded eyes cast downwards in pensive introspection. Suetonius interpreted this sulky demeanor to suggest bedroom interests which indicated the self-absorption and narcissism of the *cinaedus's* promiscuous lifestyle. Or so others suggested.

But he came to realize this was mere prejudice about the emperor's supposed plaything or *catamite*. This revelation happened when he first heard the fellow speak.

Antinous's seeming shyness of manner was belied by the calm, thorough, persuasive *timbre* of his voice. Its deep modulation expressed well-studied Latin with an Attic accent, true, but did so with cool assurance and a baritone which communicated intelligence, honesty, warmth, and audible manliness. The youth's voice projected a definite *vir*, not an indulgently frivolous *cinaedus*, let alone a shrill eunuch or pale hermaphrodite. At least to the ear and eye, if not in the privacy of the bedchamber, the fellow was striking in his masculinity.

Suetonius and the Praetorian escort were off-loaded downstream at a jetty adjacent to one of the guard-houses of the Imperial encampment stretching along the east bank. The city of tents sparkled with multiple braziers, torches, or lamps flickering among the date palms in the descending darkness.

The Praetorians led the biographer through a labyrinth of lanes of tents and marquees spreading along the river bank for a hundred paces. The camp conformed to proper Legion practice, with regular fire precautions and defensive barriers. Guards maintained watch at intersections or surveyed the site from low towers.

Suetonius was led to the forecourt of the Imperial complex itself, announced by its prominent military standards, Imperial insignia, and the enormous multi-poled proportions of Caesar's personal marquees.

A bronze lifesize statue of Hadrian stood on a pedestal to one side with an arm upheld in salute while nursing his staff of office in the crook of the other. Hadrian's familiar stance as a heroic commander whose bare-headed thick-cropped curls, close-shaved beard, and embossed cuirass decorated with victor's medallions, gave authority to his mute presence.

His cuirass displayed an image of the goddess Athena of Athens protecting the infants Romulus and Remus of Rome, with a portrait of Antinous's profile embossed on one of his hip lappets. This struck Suetonius as an intriguing statement of the emperor's priorities. It spoke of Greek culture nourishing Roman values while his Greek paramour observed from the close proximity of his hip.

The detachment reached the inner circle of protection for the emperor. He was now to be defended by his Horse Guards. This elite corps of cavalry from across the Roman world serves directly at the emperor's side. The officers are identified by their scarlet cloaks and a high scarlet crest on their helmets, as well as their ethnic variety. Their mixed races display the Empire's true diversity.

Three Horse Guards and two Scythian archers stood shiftily about while a senior officer was seated at a camp table sorting papyrus sheets. As he did so Suetonius became aware of the sound of muffled moans being emitted from within the tent complex. They were the cries of pain usually associated with some unfortunate person having information extracted by due legal process, meaning torture.

Hadrian is not known to wield torture to any degree, though his Prefect at Rome, Marcius Turbo, is readily disposed to its efficacy.

The Horse Guard officer arose to smartly salute. Suetonius and he recognized each other, though the biographer could not recall the German's name. The accompanying Praetorian stood to attention before the more-senior officer and informed him of the summons and delivery as instructed. The German turned and smiled warmly to the biographer.

"Gaius Suetonius Tranquillus, I Scorilo, a Decurion of the Horse Guard, salute you."

At last someone was speaking to the biographer as a human being.

"I am instructed to escort you to the emperor's quarters. Senator Septicius Clarus and others of the Imperial Household await you."

Aha, Suetonius thought, a friendly name at last. Clarus, his *patron*, to whom he owed his entire good fortune and utter allegiance after Caesar himself, will know what this is all about.

The decurion led Suetonius into the marquee complex. It dawned on him the muffled cries coming from somewhere deep in the labyrinth were not those of a torture victim but of someone sorrowfully sobbing. In fact it was a male person weeping in deep anguish.

As they progressed through chamber after chamber, sitting rooms, map rooms, shrine alcoves, armory stores, dining alcoves, small reception halls, and small courtyards, the sobbing grew louder. Suetonius realized the cries were being emitted by a voice he recognized.

The pained voice was that of Hadrian.

Scorilo guided Suetonius into a large reception chamber where several notables were gathered and where the moans were even more pronounced. They were heard from behind nearby drapes.

No one conversed. They stood in clusters staring distractedly at the shiny floor tiles beneath them. The cries had thoroughly intimidated them.

Suetonius spied Septicius Clarus seated at a table littered with uneaten food and empty wine goblets. The grouped individuals included some known to him and others unknown.

To one side hovered the Easterners dressed in *chiton* tunic and slung mantle whose primary language was Greek. These included the Governor of Pannonia, Flavius Arrianus of Bithynia, a personal friend of the emperor. Arrian is a wealthy Greek from Nicomedia. Accompanying him was Phlegon of Tralles, a freed slave historian whose extravagant literary fantasies were popular with Hadrian. Polemo of Smyrna, a sophist and master of heroic speeches, stood beside Aristobulus of Antioch, the court astrologer who had been in Suetonius's party that morning. It was probably Aristobulus who had revealed his whereabouts to the Praetorian messengers.

At another side stood the Latins. Flavius Titianus, Hadrian's appointed Governor of the province of Egypt; Julius Vestinus, a Gaul who was the current Secretary to the emperor; the eunuch Favorinus of Arles, a teacher of rhetoric; and Alcibiades of Nysa, Hadrian's chamberlain who was Greek but who too had been accorded Roman citizenship.

At the table with wine cups before them sat Suetonius's *patron*, Septicius Clarus accompanied by the Praetorian Tribune, Lucius Macedo, commander of the security forces for the Egypt tour. The Praetorian Prefect, Quintus Marcius Turbo, remained at Rome to maintain order at the seat of Empire.

Suetonius reflected on how this modest tented chamber in the desert wilds by the River Nile four hundred miles south of the city of Alexandria contained the cream of Hadrian's inner circle. Except three, that is. These three were his wife, Vibia Sabina *the Augusta*; his factotum Geta the Dacian; and the much-cherished freeborn Bithynian Antinous.

In another corner stood a man whose presence made the hair of Suetonius's neck rise on end.

'Pachrates' was a corrupted name in Greek for an Egyptian priest whose name in the local dialect was unpronounceable. Pachrates or Panchrates was a close translation into Greek. He was one of the shaven-bodied, *kohl*-eyed, leopard-skin swathed, linen-skirted priests of Egypt. The priest is reputed to work miracles, call upon demonic powers, inflict spells, and influence destiny, all for a fee. Preferably a large fee.

Pachrates is of an indiscernible age, seeming eternally old, even very ancient, as befits his profession. His features had his race's distinctive characteristics of a flattish nose, swarthy skin, thick lips, and dark eyes. His eyes penetrate his surroundings with incisive clarity, and project an icy chill. This had always disturbed Suetonius on the few occasions he saw him attending Hadrian's entourage. Yet he had heard how Hadrian and Antinous had found the priest's magical arts to be impressive, if not remarkable.

By Pachrates' side was a younger priest in similar vestments indicating high status. Both were bedecked in beaded chains, amulets, talismans, and bracelets depicting the Eye of Horus, the crucifix ankh, and other exotic symbols. Each wielded an impressive staff of ebony, gold, and ivory. They kept watchfully to themselves while the sobs echoed from within the nearby chamber.

Clarus and Macedo rose to greet Suetonius. He did not kiss Clarus' toga hem as he might at a morning *patron*'s assembly; it might have seemed overly ostentatious in this company. Clarus took his arm in a friendly greeting anyhow. He whispered low to his ear.

"Welcome. Our men found you, yes? As you can hear, we have a crisis on our hands."

Suetonius nodded knowingly, eyes wide in apprehension.

"You've heard the news? Antinous is dead."

Macedo and Clarus looked deeply at the biographer as though he might know something about it.

"Great Caesar is supremely distressed."

This could readily be heard from the nearby chamber.

"I've only just learned of it," Suetonius lied. "May I ask in what manner?" he whispered. "Was it honorable?"

This question poses the primary issue in a Roman death. Is a death noble, is it honorable, is it worthy of the deceased's character? Is a death praiseworthy? Anything less is either an act of spite by the gods or a careless mismanagement of one's fate.

Clarus leaned forward to murmur in his ear.

"The boy was found at the Nile's edge this morning tangled in the reeds. He has apparently drowned. Some fishermen came across him, they say, underneath their boat as they were setting out from their moorings. The tide stream had swept him to the river bank. They raised the alarm. We have them under guard until we sort out what has happened. They will meet torture to test their truthfulness."

It was Suetonius's turn to lean forward to ask the most obvious question. "So how did Antinous come to be in the river in the first place?"

Both Clarus and Macedo glanced towards each other knowingly.

"That might be your chore to find out," Macedo confided.

The sobbing from within ceased. Moments passed in frozen silence as those in the marquee eyed its entrance. Eventually Geta, Hadrian's personal assistant, emerged from within.

"Gentlemen," Geta uttered softly in his barbarian-intonated Latin, "Caesar awaits your company. This moment now might be opportune. Caesar is, is, is … *composed*."

Geta is not Hadrian's secretary nor major-domo, let alone a servant or slave. He fulfills a more important but undefined role. He turned and strode back to the chamber entrance. The four patiently followed.

Beyond a veiled vestibule lay a larger inner chamber where only a single multi-lamp candelabra cast illumination across a dim space. Incense burned in a brazier emitting its lazily wafting coils into the dark cavern. Remote in the gloom, Hadrian was seated upon a chair, doubled over, holding his sides with crossed arms and swaying rhythmically. He was dressed in a crumpled under-tunic furled in a purple cloak trimmed with gilded eaglets.

His hair was disheveled, his feet bare. He was quietly snuffling into the cloak's folds. He had put aside his sobbing for a while. Even in the somber light the five intruders could see he was pale, with red rings beneath his eyes.

Across the chamber within range of the faint glow lay a large open divan. It was enveloped from above by a sheath of gossamer mosquito netting. Water was being finely sprayed onto the nets by a beefy Nubian slave who was simultaneously wafting a voluminous ostrich feather fan at the filmy drape. The fan's faint breeze on the dank net aimed to cool the air around the bed beneath. In the dry, warm Egyptian climate this is sometimes an effective way to cool a sleeping person.

Lying face upwards on the divan was a well-proportioned young man. He was utterly naked as though lazily indulging himself in the hot room of a public bath house. It was Antinous.

He was immobile, yellowingly pallid, crinkle-skinned from water exposure, and quite visibly dead. Even at his distance from the screened bed, Suetonius detected how river parasites may already have devoured the eyeballs beneath the young man's lids and nibbled at the edges of his extremities. His pallor was unusually waxen and drawn.

A depression in the divan indicated where Hadrian had been lying beside his friend, probably weeping. To one side on the tiled floor lay an ornate set of ceremonial armors and weapons. The white enamel inlays of the workmanship reminded Suetonius how their owner had been the Bithynian lad. It was his formal horse parade uniform as a Companion of the Hunt, Caesar's hunting team. Antinous was a championship horseman.

Geta and the four stood before their ruler in silent respect. Hadrian took some time to concede the group's presence. Geta took the initiative.

"May I speak, Caesar? Senator Septicius Clarus, Suetonius Tranquillus, Secretary Vestinus, and Tribune Macedo, are present as instructed," he offered in a low voice.

"I see that, Dacian!" the emperor hissed back.

Geta bowed courteously and moved back a step from the group, undismayed by the reproach.

Hadrian grudgingly looked to the five. He paused to recall his motive for their attendance. He spoke hesitantly. They each wondered at what might transpire.

"Gentlemen, you see before you my hurt. Antinous is no more."

He waved tiredly toward the bed where the Nubian continued to fan the sprayed netting. The five hung their heads in respectful solemnity.

"I don't know what has happened," the emperor continued. "All that is evident is he drowned in the river sometime last night or this morning. Perhaps it is a misadventure? Perhaps a youngster's high-spirited lark? Perhaps something more? No one seems to be able to tell me. *No one!*"

He glanced accusingly at Geta, who stood with head low.

Hadrian rose slowly from his seat, grasping his purple cloak tightly around him. The warm night air flowing through the marquee's overhead vent into the open sky required little additional clothing, yet he distractedly held the cloak close about him. A sea of stars blanketed the black heaven above. Caesar trod slowly in the direction of the divan. The five paced quietly behind.

"It is my instruction to you, gentlemen, to investigate this matter," he muttered as they approached the bed with its immobile figure. As he turned towards the group his voice firmed and rose in greater authority.

"It is my instruction you will explore every avenue of enquiry. It is my demand you will interrogate every person who has been associated with my companion in recent days.

You will check and correlate his movements, his actions, and his conversations with others. You will deduce the precise details of what has happened in the life of my friend, who are his friends, who are his enemies, or if any have reason to engage in foul play."

His voice had returned to its natural command as the Great Caesar of the civilized world.

"You will assemble whatever evidence is necessary to establish the time of death and the manner of his death. But the purpose of your enquiry is to inform me of the *reason* why Antinous of Bithynia has died.

Has there been an ulterior motive for his end? Was his death noble? Was his death base? Did he die a hero's death? Or has his life been usurped by dark forces? Was it by his own hand, or by another's? And you will report back to me with this information in the form of your testimonials, documents, or reasons within two days. Two days only. This is my command."

As Hadrian communicated his commission Suetonius drew closer to the nets suspended over the figure on the bed. He looked closely at the details of the young man's once-fine body and sculpted features. Antinous had certainly been handsome and even in death it was evident.

At least until now. But in the balmy night's air, regardless of the watered nets and the most imperious of an emperor's commands, natural corruption would proceed swiftly.

Soon bloating would be evident. His features would distend, split, erupt, corrupt, and disintegrate before his companion's eyes. Even an emperor cannot command otherwise.

While he listened to Hadrian's instruction Suetonius noted and memorized certain interesting features of the figure. The particularly severe shaggy cut of the youth's hair, the meager outline of a beard with sideburns showing he was no longer a strapping *meirakion* youth, the many scratches around his midriff, a slashed incision evident in his left wrist, and rose-colored blemishes of various sizes at several places across his throat.

Suetonius had never noticed blemishes of any sort on Antinous previously. His skin possessed the clarity of youthful health. He wondered if, in this desert climate, the first blooms of decay were already underway.

Hadrian paused at the bedside to part an opening in the dank netting. He now resumed a Caesar's authority.

"Hear me then, and act accordingly! Item One: This commission will be formalized under Imperial seal immediately by my secretary. That's for you to attend to, Vestinus.

Item Two: Septicius Clarus, you have served me at an earlier time as my Prefect of the Praetorian Guard, my right hand second-in-command. Your record of service had been exemplary, despite serious accusations by the empress Vibia Sabina resulting in your dismissal. It is my will that you assume responsibility as magistrate for this commission to endow it with legal authority.

Three: You will have unrestricted monetary and resources made available to you. That's for you, Vestinus and Macedo, to effect immediately.

Four: Suetonius Tranquillus, in acknowledging your learned experience at the Bar of Rome, I appoint you to the duty of *Special Inspector* of this commission. Also, as my former Chief Secretary, it is my will you retain records of this enquiry and report your results to me within two days.

Five: Clarus and Suetonius, a fee of one hundred thousand *sesterces* will be paid to each of you to perform this commission. This fee will only be paid if you deliver as contracted within the two day limit, at one hour before sunrise precisely.

If you fail to meet this deadline I will re-open the charge against you of the offence of *laesa-majestas* against the empress, a treason and capital offence. Your lives may be forfeit. The investigation starts immediately. That means *now* gentlemen!"

Hadrian dropped his cloak to the floor and parted the nets to look closely at his deceased companion on the bed. The group sensed he was forcefully suppressing a hidden torment deep within.

"However, there are two people you cannot interview. They are myself, your Caesar, and Caesar's wife, Vibia Sabina *Augusta*.

You are permitted to interrogate any member of the Court, Guard, or Sabina's retinue as you see fit, but neither I nor the empress. Sabina is above your station and commission. Besides, you already have that history with her which is impolitic, as you both know. To date we have been lenient about that matter, but be warned."

All five of the group bowed in acknowledgement, possibly with discomfort. Suetonius and Clarus both knew what Hadrian was referring to, so both stomachs churned.

A gleam appeared at one eye. A tear was forming. He grew haggard.

"Clarus and Suetonius, you will want to know why I depend on you after all these years. It is because I trust you, and I trust your forensic skills. Especially, Gaius Suetonius Tranquillus, I trust your capacity for explorative detail, just as you have done in your *Lives of the Caesars*. You appear to seek no favors from anyone, while both of you nowadays are independent from the factions of influence of Court. This may be an essential factor in enquiring into the death of my companion. I rely on you and that independence."

Suetonius coughed modestly at this unexpected flattery and its generosity, with its unofficial title of *"Special Inspector"*. A hundred thousand sesterces would also be a timely contribution to his ramshackle finances, he thought, despite the two-day timeframe and its threat of a fatal indictment. Nevertheless he gathered his wits sufficiently to submit a request of his own.

"My Lord Caesar," Suetonius braved, "may we have access to the body for a physician to inspect to determine the nature or time of death?"

Hadrian's face fell.

"No, not at all!" he declared.

This is a man who knows death very intimately. Yet the notion of an autopsy of his beloved repelled him.

"It is enough we burn the dead, isn't it? In this case I will invite Egyptians to embalm Antinous in their special way so his body and name survive forever. He will live as a pharaoh does, or as King Alexander of Macedon survives in his sarcophagus at Alexandria. The priest Pachrates of Memphis awaits me outside accompanied by the leading master in the land of this art. Antinous will remain incorrupt for all eternity. I command it!"

The emperor was adamant and dismissive, so one prefers not to exceed the limits of protocol in furthering such enquiries, Suetonius contemplated. Pity though. What a wasted opportunity. But Hadrian was understandably emotional, which is an unexpected novelty in a supreme ruler.

Suetonius also wondered if Caesar had some other motive perhaps. Was there something he did not wish to share about the lad's demise?

Another notion entered the *Special Inspector*'s mind. He took the liberty to interject before the group of five was dismissed beyond recall.

"My Lord, if I may? Do you recommend an avenue of approach, or propose key witnesses who should be the subject of interview?"

Suetonius sensed Geta the Dacian freeze at his enquiry.

Hadrian turned slowly toward his former secretary as his brow darkened. It was an expression Suetonius had not seen in the emperor's eyes for almost a decade, and one he would rather not perceive too often aimed in his direction. Had he over-stepped the mark?

"Special Inspector Suetonius, I said you will not interview Caesar himself," Hadrian spat in a whisper. "Nevertheless I rely on your good services as my investigator and feel obliged to offer what little guidance I can to your commission.

Geta here, my worthy factotum, is an intimate of this Household and party to its inner workings. Perhaps Geta will possess perceptions of which I am not familiar? Likewise my Chief Secretary, Julius Vestinus here, or my Chamberlain Alcibiades outside, will have an understanding of those who may be persons-of-interest to you? Others come to mind too.

My friend Arrian of Bithynia could possess details of value? He knew my companion well. You are fortunate that almost anyone who has been involved with my Antinous travels in this Imperial Progress along the Nile. But for myself I would like to know more about Antinous's own personal household.

His young fellow-Bithynian Lysias, for example? Or the woman, Thais of Cyrene? I am sure Julia Balbilla too, the travelling companion of my wife, will have an opinion worth hearing. Explore broadly, *Special Inspector*. But return in no more than two days at one hour before sunrise, or forfeit your *sesterces*. Then Turbo's agents will seek you out. There is no where in the Empire to hide from my chief-of-security Turbo."

Suetonius sensed it was Macedo's turn to stiffen.

"Enough!" Hadrian called. "Away with you! I must have privacy."

His voice cracked with bottomless despair as he dismissed the group. He turned to the divan and, with a bodily surge forward, tore apart the watered nets, tugged off his cloak and tunic, and fell naked onto the bed beside the cadaver. Sobs welled up from deep within him in an intensity which compelled the five to urgently withdraw.

As they were shuffling backwards in deference to his might-and-majesty, the emperor grasped the flaccid figure and lay gently kissing Antinous's gray lips. Again, his pitiful moans began to arise within the chamber. The Nubian silently continued the rhythmic fanning and spraying.

The five drew back bowing continuously as they retreated. The Imperial audience had concluded. They had received their commission. It was time to act, there was no time to waste. One hundred thousand *sesterces* were at stake as well as Caesar's patronage. Otherwise two heads were at risk.

In the vestibule between the bedchamber and the reception room where others of Caesar's retinue waited, Clarus halted the group.

"He weeps as does a woman," he whispered gruffly, "and this in a man who commands Legions from Britain to Parthia. What to make of it all?"

Vestinus spoke.

"Whatever your sentiments, it is our duty to fulfill his instruction," he murmured. "You don't have long to complete this work, my friends."

Suetonius responded conspiratorially but firmly.

"Vestinus, I will need your best scribes skilled in speed notation in both Latin and Greek. They will be assigned to us for the duration. Bring papyrus, wax pads, and writing styluses. We must record everything in detail as we proceed for comparative analysis.

Macedo, I will need your most intelligent agents for investigative work, and access to troops, horses, couriers, and services when required.

Vestinus, tell Chamberlain Alcibiades I will require immediate access to workspace within the Imperial complex with living quarters attached. It must be well provisioned for a team of investigators for several days. Intelligent slaves to service this team would be useful, too.

Clarus, you and I must determine a list of associates of the deceased to be interviewed. Who to interrogate, in what order, and who to ignore in such a brief time span."

Praetorian commander Macedo volunteered the style of services a security specialist would likely consider necessary.

"Will you require torturers? I have three public slaves skilled at the arena at Leptis Magna. They work as a team. They possess extensive experience in all manner of interrogations and terminations. They come highly recommended."

"Thank you for your kind thoughts Lucius Macedo," Suetonius opined as sweetly as he could muster, "but not only would the sight of instruments of torture put the fear of Hades into our subjects and freeze their tongues with fright, but almost all will be citizens of Rome and so legally beyond such persuasion. Besides, as we well know, if you break a few bones and knock out a few teeth you can easily persuade people to confess to being Jupiter Himself."

Tribune Macedo was responsible for policing and security issues for the Egypt tour. He linked into the Empire-wide network of spies and informers maintained by his superior, Prefect Marcius Turbo at Rome. Turbo has proven to be a master of the espionage and political manipulation arts, Suetonius recalled, and his informers reached far across the Empire on behalf of his ruler, Hadrian.

A very useful thought popped into Suetonius's mind.

"Vestinus and Macedo, we should have a personal attendant for our more human enquiries as well. Someone who knows something of the local culture and languages, because we don't do we?

There is a young lass called Surisca who is on the staff at the *House of the Blue Lotuses* across the river at Hermopolis. She's no slave; she's a Syri from Antioch who has fluent Greek, Aramaic, some Latin, and the local Egyptian dialect too. She is very familiar with Egyptian customs and ways, very familiar indeed, which might be a useful skill for us.

Have someone hire her fulltime for several days. Pay any price, don't bargain. Deliver her to the quarters you will be providing. And soon! Tell her to dress for public wear, not her professional duties. And you might arrange it tonight, as a priority, if the moon is bright enough to permit travel on the river."

Vestinus and the others looked askance at the biographer in that querulous way people do, ever so politely, when they have a query they're reluctant to articulate to a person's face. But the Chief Secretary realized how Caesar's instruction was immutable, and Suetonius was to receive whatever he requested. Clarus simply smiled wanly at his *client*'s audacity.

The *Special Inspector* turned to Geta who had followed the other four from the chamber.

"Geta of Dacia, you will already know much more about this affair than we ourselves will have the opportunity to explore. You are close to the Imperial Household. You are cognizant of the details of Lord Caesar's relationship with Antinous of Bithynia. You observe the daily interactions of the Household, and must be aware of the political ebb and flow of things?"

"Yes, yes, *Special Inspector*," he replied in gravel-accented Latin.

Suetonius recalled how Geta's abduction from Dacia as a child after Trajan's victory almost twenty-five years earlier remained evident in his pronunciation. The Dacian spoke in the short, terse statements of his native tongue, a primitive barbarian language of the Getae peoples, which gave his spoken words a fierce strength and surprising power. Suetonius continued.

"Geta, my good fellow, perhaps Clarus, Vestinus, and I should sit with you to explore your views of Antinous's place in the Household, once the basic arrangements are in order with our colleagues? Is that possible?"

The biographer-cum-investigator tried to be as unthreatening as possible. He used his most persuasive bargainer's smile which risked displaying his three missing lower teeth.

Hadrian conceded Geta would be a storehouse of gossip from inside the Imperial Household who would already know things which could take months of enquiry to discern. He will know who is friend to whom, who is doing what with who, and who seeks benefit, lust, influence, or sheer revenge.

He might also know something of Antinous's own activities or ambitions in the hothouse of Court intrigue and ever-shifting amorous dalliances.

"I am at your disposal," Geta offered with a faintly sly glance. Something about the gesture communicated uncertainty within Suetonius.

"I suppose our first chore, gentlemen, will be to construct a consistent pattern of enquiry with our subjects?" Suetonius offered. "You know, an interrogative grid we apply to each interview for a parallel comparison of actions, timescales, and opinions of this matter."

Clarus, ever the pragmatist, interjected. "But what particular matter, Suetonius? A river accident? A suicide? A murder? Or some other phenomenon?"

Vestinus, Macedo, and Geta looked to the biographer.

"All four, my good Clarus," he responded. "At heart Caesar wants us to identify *why* his companion died, not simply merely how or by what method. *Why* is more demanding than *how*, is it not? Of course the *who* will be an important facet of the *why*, agreed?"

The five nodded affirmatively at Suetonius, but with expressions of uncertainty.

"And Macedo might do us the favor of delivering to us the fishermen who discovered the body of the Bithynian. Preferably undamaged, all in one piece, please Lucius. Their testimony might be of greater use that way."

Tribune Macedo grimaced weakly, saluted the group in his brisk military fashion, and they entered the reception chamber where the other members of the Court patiently awaited Hadrian's pleasure.

But Suetonius still had Geta the Dacian on his mind. Geta was something of a mystery to him, despite his role at Hadrian's side over many years.

The *Special Inspector* recalled how ten years earlier he had reason to take testimony from a commander of cavalry in the Balkans – the Roman officer Tiberius Claudius Maximus – who knew a great deal about Geta's early years.

This officer who, in Trajan's campaign against the murderous *Decebelus*, king of Dacia, fifteen years even earlier, had been an *explorator* of cavalry auxiliaries, was obliged to provide an archive record of how Geta had been captured. During that Dacian campaign, Maximus had witnessed the *Decebelus's* death. He then delivered the king's son as a war hostage into Rome's protection under Hadrian's personal *aegis*.

Tiberius Claudius Maximus's recollections were a dark tale which conveyed a great deal about the character of the young Dacian. It was a chilling story which had remained in Suetonius's memory ever since.

Those events of twenty-five years ago now returned to haunt him.

CHAPTER 3

"'By the great god Zalmoxis, may blessing be upon you! Wait for me in the god's Underworld, woman. I am soon to join you,' the warrior king whispered into her ear."

Maximus was detailing the events which occurred during the campaign at Dacia.

"Diurapneus, the proud Daci Wolf, held his wife close to his chest to embrace her as tears welled to his eyes. He leaned her head back gently with one hand and drew the thin blade across her throat with the other. He turned her to one side as she emitted a rasped rattle when the crimson flood rushed.

Diurapneus gripped her firmly as her body shuddered, her furs splashed in scarlet, her life racing to Zalmoxis. He lowered her gently, tenderly, to the earth as she quivered into her final stillness. His wife's autumnal furs were sprinkled with the king's tears amid splashes of blood.

The Daci Wolf King had not shed tears for a long time. Today was a day for tears. The mother of his two children, who once he had killed three men in fierce combat to possess, had journeyed to the Underworld of Zalmoxis. Zalmoxis was the Great God of her ancestors of Getae blood. She would patiently await Diurapneus there, he knew.

Dacia's warrior king, honored by all as *Decebelus*, 'The Heroic One', felt less valiant as he looked towards the two small children sitting on the edge of the wagon cart. Their eyes were on their prostrate mother engulfed behind ample autumn furs and crumpled embroideries, twitching sporadically in a widening pool of gore amid mottled leaves. Their eyes, too, were on their father's hooked hip dagger. Neither uttered a sound.

'Save yourselves, Wolf Brothers! Go! It's time for you to go!' Diurapneus shouted at his mounted bodyguards listing anxiously about. Their stallions frisked, jostled, and hoofed at the earth as their foaming sweat flicked around.

'The Iron People are upon us! The chase is over! Save yourselves so one day you can revenge me! Revenge me, the Daci Wolf, my brothers! By the god Zalmoxis, revenge me! Swear it by the Great God!'

The Wolf Warriors, six royal bodyguards arrayed in grimy furs and slimed leathers with hair braids greased in sheep fat dyed blue, saluted their master and cried aloud from behind faces strewn with rough-stabbed tattoos. In a single voice they proclaimed their holy oath.

'By Zalmoxis we swear!' they shouted, their tattoos stretching in lewd display.

The greater the number of tattoos, the larger number of heads they had taken in combat. The more refined their markings, the higher their status as *Tarabostes* aristocrats of the Getae people of Dacia.

'By the great priest Dicineus, my father, I swear it!' one of the refined horsemen bellowed.

While they shouted gruff obscenities of high honor, the riders charged down the muddy trail bravely flailing bill-hooked *falx* swords against malevolent forces, forest ghouls, sky demons, or the abiding presence of the omniscient Evil Eye itself.

Diurapneus searched back down the earthen track through the woodland towards distant Sarmizegethusa. Until only two days ago that rocky peak had been his capital and his fortress. Splashes of light flashed off the armor of the approaching Iron People on their chargers. Iron weaponry glinted through the forest pines. The enemy was closing in. The Daci Wolf's audacious, duplicitous, game-plan had failed. The king of the Iron People with his iron-shielded army had prevailed.

Sarmizegethusa would now be bestowed as spoils by the god of war upon the Iron People victors.

'The city fort's clans of Wolf Warriors, my children, will have thrown themselves into the Night of Zalmoxis,' he announced exultant with pride. 'They will laugh heartedly at their attackers!'

He neglected to add it would be laughter laden with the maniacal exhilaration of the utterly defeated.

'Come to me, my children,' the tired warrior king called, searching his mind for an adequate response to his situation. Diurapneus was alone now with his son and daughter. The enemy horsemen would be upon them soon. Seven-year-old Prince Dromichaetes and his twin sister Princess Estia sat at the wagon's lip unmoved by their predicament. To Diurapneus all the boy's titles of honor and his future promise now seemed so futile.

Prince Dromichaetes, a *Tarabostes* aristocrat of the Getae Peoples, was the only son of Dacia's king of all the lands and tribes of the Daci Confederation. He was King Diurapneus's heir to the vast forests, ranges, and plains stretching from the Carpathian Mountains to the Rivers Tyros and Danube. He was of a line of warrior kings stretching back to the god Zalmoxis himself. Dromichaetes' very blood was sacred.

The three circle tattoos on his face across each cheekbone told of his stature in the eyes of the god. His blue-fatted hair told of his inborn status before his fellow warriors. His destiny was foretold to lead the Wolves' Brotherhood to glory against the Iron People' king. His destiny was to seal the attacking king's doom with the cunning of a stalking wolf.

Diurapneus wondered what to do with his two children. Kill them to avoid some cruel outrage at the hands of the Iron People? The enemy were known to use the young to satisfy their earthier appetites. Or herd the two into the forest's vastness to wander alone and die of hunger or be eaten by forest creatures? Leave them to face alone the forest's night demons, sprites, and ghouls? Or let them live to take their chances at the mercy of the enemy until Zalmoxis himself steals them to his Underworld some later day?

When the riders with their crested helmets and lances came glinting closer to view Diurapneus now knew how retreat to the Land Of Death was the most honorable path to a warrior's glory. The shame of capture and being ceremoniously strangled at Rome before the Iron People masses was not an option.

He kissed the young prince and his sister farewell, and blessed them in the name of God Zalmoxis. He leaned close to his son's ear and whispered ancient oaths. He swore the child to fulfill his princely destiny in the name of Zalmoxis by revenging his father and mother's death. He extracted an oath of honor from the wide-eyed shivering boy as his sister listened close-by. The princeling uttered the oath loudly for all the trees and leaves of the forest to hear and record forever among the swirling winds and rustling leaves of Nature.

'By the great god Zalmoxis and his sacred lineage of kings, I Dromichaetes, Prince of the Getae, swear to take revenge upon the King of the Iron People. I swear to kill his loved ones before his very eyes, just as my father's loved one has died. I seal this oath among the leaves and winds of the forest by my own sacred blood!' the little boy called aloud in a wavering voice into the wooded density around him.

'Farewell my children until we meet again before Zalmoxis himself!' the elder proclaimed with gusto.

Diurapneus grasped his bill-hooked dagger and rent at his own throat in a single slash. Streaming gore burst over the moldy bark of the fallen trunk of a forest tree trunk with the force of a stallion's piss. His body fell beside his wife, their blood soaking fallen leaves.

'Father! Father!' the princeling called again and again.

His sister buried her face into the furs enveloping the boy's bony frame.

The children had seen such sprays of scarlet many times before when the womenfolk of the Wolf Warriors tormented and slaughtered captives of the Iron People. The prisoners were trussed like sheep. They sawed off the heads of the squirming, squawking captives to offer victory sacrifice to their God.

From communal cups they would sip the warm salty blood of their enemies and lick blood-tipped fingers. They shelved the cut heads around the forest altar of the god and poured the victims' life-blood over their own faces as a food for the deity. The Wolf Warriors laughed aloud at the ironies of life and death. They danced ecstatically to the throb of tambours of human skin and the strum of stretched gut.

'The tyrant has deceived us! The coward has taken his own life!'

The lead rider of the Iron People troop, cavalry captain Tiberius Claudius Maximus of the *ala II Pannoniorum* auxiliaries, was angered by the king's too easy escape to his Underworld of Zalmoxis. In his mind Maximus could hear Diurapneus laughing at him from the Beyond.

He stripped the king's body of its weapons, furs, jewels, and gold medallions, severed the dead man's head with his own hooked sword, and tore off his bejeweled right arm. Each would be proof of the Dacian's destruction for the Iron King himself, Caesar Trajan, and his senior commander Hadrian.

The seven-year-old princeling probably thought the same fate would occur to his sister and himself, but he was proved wrong.

'What have we here? A royal princeling and his sister? Well that's something of value perhaps!' Maximus called to the troop of *Iron People* legionaries.

The two children were thrust into a wooden cage on wooden wheels intended for securing the captured *Decebelus,* and trundled laboriously overland to the Roman forces. It took two days to return to Trajan's encampment beneath the smoldering ruin of the fortress at stony Sarmizegethusa.

Dromichaetes and Estia were put on display to the troops. The two clung to each other secured behind the cage's sturdy timbers while the Roman soldiers in iron armor bearing iron weapons shouted harsh words at them and cast handfuls of wet animal dung at the cage.

'A sweet lad. Weedy but sturdy,' Trajan declared to his officers, 'and sufficiently young to educate in our ways. As a prince of his race a portion of his father's treasure is to be endowed to his upkeep and training. He will be a hostage ward of the State assigned to a noble family. He will blossom, and may have value in some future strategy of state. Hadrian enjoys mentoring young men. Allocate the Dacian prince to my commander.'

Trajan ignored Dromichaetes' sister, Estia, who possessed only marital value between contending communities. Yet the antagonism against the children ceased from that moment and their protection and sustenance improved greatly.

The captured high priest of Zalmoxis, old Dicineus of the blue-fatted braids and the elegant tattoos curling into deep facial creases, whispered to the young ones how they were safe for the time being.

Dicineus, an advisor of their father's, understood the Roman speech and the Roman ways. Dicineus was the architect of the Daci Wolf's policy. It was also he who, with his family members and children, officiated in the sacrifice of Roman captives. He knew his days were numbered with his Roman captors. Zalmoxis now beckoned him too. Security for his own offspring was his immediate priority after attending to the Decebelus's progeny.

'My Lord and Lady, children of the *Decebelus*, I bring good news to you. Your fate is well favored. The Iron People's king, Caesar Trajan, has cast his grace upon you,' the old man rasped. 'You will not be sent to the Underworld to join your ancestors, as others of us may. You'll be taken under the protection of his commander and friend, the Roman general Publius Aelius Hadrianus, who is an important senator and *praetor* at Rome.'

'Tell me Priest Dicineus, who is this commander Hadrianus? Is he worthy of us?' the boy prince demanded of his aged advisor and tutor in the imperious style of a true aristocrat.

'You will shortly see, my Prince,' Dicineus replied with a deeply deferential bow to the seven-year old. 'But be assured, this is a gesture to your advantage and to your sister Estia's advantage. Take my advice, my child. Welcome this opportunity. See where it may lead. It has possibilities.'

Hadrian looked down upon Dromichaetes from his high seat. It was the very same throne from which Diurapneus, the boy's father, had until recently pronounced rule upon the Getae. With Dicineus as the translator, the Roman commander questioned the boy.

'Tell him to proclaim his pedigree, Priest. Let him tell me of his quality in his own words,' Hadrian instructed. He then sat back to observe the boy's responses and manner.

The muddied, soil-clothed, disheveled princeling stood steadily before his interrogator to call out in his reedy voice a well-rehearsed litany of names, titles, honorifics, and tribal clan relationships. He did it with shrill gusto. They were proclaimed in the hard guttural consonants of his native language in the proud manner the boy had heard his father declaim similar lists of honor.

'This boy has a noble's manner, Priest. He deserves watching, in more ways than one,' the Roman commander offered.

Hadrian was actually moved by the child's courage and dignity. He smiled at the miniature warrior standing before him and nodded approvingly to Dicineus.

'The lad, as a barbarian, possesses a paler skin than we Romans. I assume the tattoos on each cheek with three circles proclaim his supposed bloodline from your cruel god, yes?

He's also a hand or so taller than a seven year old of our Mediterranean world, even though generally you Dacians are not a physically imposing people. Your breeding, your diet, your angular bodily shape, your bad teeth, your lack of common cleanliness or baths, and your barbarous habits all lack the finesse of the Empire's subjects. Yet this wiry princeling displays promise of future merit.'

'I am pleased that my captor approves of the child,' Dicineus dissembled with much bowing. 'I too have children who carry my seed and the sacred blood of Zalmoxis. Perhaps I and my family have found favor in the commander's eyes as well? Children, at least, deserve to live.'

Hadrian smiled patiently but enigmatically.

'Begin the boy's instruction in spoken Latin. He is to be prepared for display at Caesar's victory Triumph at Rome.'

After the winter snows abated Prince Dromichaetes and Estia were brought from the rugged ranges of their homeland to the warmer climate of Italy far away to the south.

Princess Estia was taken one night into separate protection elsewhere, unexplained to the princeling. Her brother never saw her again and his pride demanded he wouldn't ask.

Now in his eighth year, Dromichaetes walked on his short child's legs behind Trajan's grand chariot with its spirited chargers along the Sacred Way of Rome. The emperor's Triumph paraded amid the raucous crowds of the great city.

The lad was awed at the spectacle of high stone structures, sweeping flights of staircases, wide avenues, marble columns, and whole buildings of red brick and white marble. It was so contrasting to the rough-cut stony ramparts, timbered palisades, or muddy daub and straw-roofed huts of his Dacia homeland.

He was chained in fine golden bonds to an officer's wrist. Two other aristocrat captives of the Getae were shackled in hard iron together. The traitor of the Dacians, Bicilis, once the king's best friend who turned to the Romans to reveal the hiding place of a vast treasure cleverly buried beneath a river's bed, along with Dicineus the priest, were tethered side-by-side for display to the city.

As Trajan's Triumph progressed through the avenues, arches, and circuses of the great city amid the roar of the crowds, the two tried to raise the boy's spirits with jokes and smiles and heroic bravado. His little legs tried to keep up with the officer's restrained pace. He stumbled to the flagstones again and again but scrambled nimbly to his feet each time. His wolf-fur cloak, tattoos, and blue-tinted braids conveyed to the Roman crowd's eyes a portrait of a typical barbarian enemy, but in amusingly miniature, unthreatening dimensions.

Following after the emperor's chariot marched cohorts of the Roman Legions of the Dacian campaign. Officers and troops of the fourteen Legions progressed proudly through the crowded Circus Maximus to the Sacred Way, past the high arches of the colossal Flavian Amphitheatre, and on to the ancient Forum, the official centre of the Empire.

They chanted ribald marching rhymes accusing their beloved emperor of lusty obscenities and vivid sexual excesses, the plausible priapic tokens of his proven gift for victory and booty. Their saucy limericks spared no reputed peccadillo.

The Legions were followed by fifty wagons of captured treasures or weapons and chained rows of captives. Ten thousand prisoners of fighting age shuffled sullen and subdued, tethered together in hemp and shackles, amid the catcalls of the *plebs* of Rome.

The cavalry captain Tiberius Claudius Maximus rode a charger holding the brine-pickled skull of the *Decebelus* aloft atop a *pilum* spear. An aide paraded with his severed right arm impaled on a captured wolf-tail lance. These crumbling remnants of the vanquished king were held high so Roman citizens could savor his defeat, witness his shame, and celebrate his submission to Rome's virile dominance. They shook rude gestures with their fists and shouted obscenities as the desiccated remains passed by.

Later when wine and feasting had loosened the city's manners, the pickled head was ceremoniously flung down the city's sacred staircase, the *Scalae Gemoniae,* as a formal insult from the Senate and People of Rome to a crushed enemy.

The skull lobbed and slipped and bounced down the majestic flight into a sewer's gutter at the bottom. Then it was cast into the turbulence of the River Tiber racing through embankments close by.

Dicineus and Bicilis were taken to the same staircase, pressed to their knees, and slowly garroted by sturdy men wielding thin nooses. Their broken bodies too were cast into the Tiber. The crowds and assembled patricians of Rome cheered themselves hoarse at their public humiliation.

But Dromichaetes was not harmed in the Triumph celebrations despite him being of the same blood as the enemy. Nevertheless the boy's declining status as a prince of the Getae was slowly becoming apparent to him. No one was bowing to him anymore.

Hadrian encouraged the boy to be receptive to friendliness. The lad learned quickly.

However, the young Wolf Warrior's names and titles were difficult to pronounce in Latin. Hadrian abbreviated the name into something more easily pronounced. Among the florid list of attributes Dromichaetes proclaimed in the Greek *patois* of his native tongue was the name for the Daci Tribes of his homeland. This word was "Getae". Hadrian identified these two repeated syllables in the staccato flow of consonants and gutturals babbled by the princeling but which no longer possessed any consequence in the new era ruled by Rome.

'Getae? Yes, so I will call you Geta,' he said with ready satisfaction to the child chained at his feet. 'You are of The Getae, so I will call you Geta.'

This leading senator, general, praetor, and tribune of Rome inaugurated his personal beckoning call for the stripling chained at his feet. It was to be "Geta". The list of privileges and distinctions forged in ancient wars by the boy's father and his father's fathers before him, were now compressed into these two tight syllables. Eventually Dromichaetes came to understand the symbolism perfectly.

But his oath to Zalmoxis on behalf of his father also continued to ring through his mind night-by-night, day-by-day, month-by-month. His father's shame was seared deep into his very heart.

'Revenge me, my son!' resounded through his mind. 'By Zalmoxis, kill the Iron People King's loved ones just as his soldiers killed me and mine! Kill his loved ones too, in honor's revenge, my son!'

Geta had begun to adapt to his new world and his new status in life as well as his new name. Yet a single memory lingered. It was an image of that bony orb shedding flecks of decayed flesh as it bobbed and bounced and skidded down the steep incline of the *Scalae Gemoniae*. He could hear the surrounding throng shout and cheer and hiss as it descended.

One day, the boy mused to himself, he too would find an opportunity to deprive the Iron People's king of a loved one. Then the oath to Zalmoxis would be fulfilled and his father's honor appeased for all eternity ---."

Tiberius Claudius Maximus's report sent a chill through Suetonius and his staff at the Imperial Secretariat. In the gloomy high-columned marble arcades of the Secretariat flanking the Palatine slope at Rome the cavalier's tale was deemed worthy of storing against future eventualities. But that was many years ago.

Now in Egypt as Caesar's *Special Inspector*, Suetonius recalled the testimony and its covert threat. He wondered at its relevance a quarter century later in understanding today's Geta of Dacia, who is now a grown man in his thirties? How much of that threat has survived so long a period, he wondered?

CHAPTER 4

Julius Vestinus's chambers were dressed in the stately style expected of the emperor's primary secretary. Busts of his patron Hadrian, the empress Sabina, the former emperor Trajan, various ancient philosophers of Greece or heroes of Rome, along with plaster face masks of Vestinus's own ancestors, cluttered the space.

Vestinus was a generation in age beneath Suetonius, yet already the pressures of his job were evident in his features. Vestinus was the second incumbent as Hadrian's secretary since Suetonius's dismissal eight years earlier, so the biographer could easily appreciate the rigors of his chores. He would be a busy fellow at all sorts of hours and not always thanked for it.

Vestinus would also be party to numberless details about the management of the Empire, its ever-drifting politics, who was currently in favor, who was on a slippery slope out, and who might be absolutely doomed.

But it also crossed Suetonius's mind how Julius Vestinus could already know more about Antinous' death than it would be politic to disclose? Suetonius sized up his target and began the investigative journey as he sipped some wine.

"I say, Julius, this is a good drop you have here. Falernian, yes? I'm surprised it's traveled so well. Here we are in the Egyptian desert miles from any real civilization, and we have the pleasure of real Falernian."

Suetonius could see Vestinus was flattered by the comment, as he expected. The biographer knew how power and influence are sometimes expressed more impressively by discreet gesture than by grandiose display.

"Was Antinous much of a drinker himself, do you think?" he added perfunctorily, hoping to widen a door on this subject. "Did wine have anything to do with his death, I wonder?"

Vestinus paused for a considered moment

"Not that I was aware of, Suetonius. He seemed to enjoy wine, but I don't recall him ever being drunk. It's often wiser to drink wine than risk local water when traveling. I only occasionally saw him tipsy, yes, but never drunk. Not in my presence, anyway. He was very sporty, so I think he tried to keep a clear head for the hunt or for his athletics. He was young and lively after all."

Vestinus had loosened up a little. Falernian, even when watered, moves tongues swiftly.

"Well, what do you think has happened here, Julius?" Suetonius asked as casually and innocently as he could manage.

Vestinus firmed up on him.

"Well, that's for you to find out, isn't it Tranquillus. I haven't a clue. Try someone else."

He had shut down. Clarus interceded.

"But you must have an opinion, Julius? You've been close to Caesar and the lad for several years now, you must intuit something about this unhappy event?"

Vestinus shuffled from boot to boot.

"I think things haven't been going well for the boy, really," he advanced distractedly. "You know, he's not a *meirakion* anymore, is he? They've been together now for almost five years, isn't it? He was approaching his twenty-fourth birthday, though you'd never know it to look at him. It was next month, I believe. But he's reached the age where that relationship is no longer tenable. At least not in the way such liaisons are supposed to proceed in the Greek custom. The mentor-cum-mentored balance was rapidly becoming one of two seniors. The convention deplores that. The accusation of *cinaedus* was on the horizon."

Suetonius and Clarus looked to each other at the ease of information now flowing, Falernian assisted. Vestinus continued.

"For example, if you look closely at the young man you can see he has a light down on his cheeks. Because he is so fair-haired it is barely noticeable. But it's already a beard really, and I guess he shaves it quietly on the sly. Sometime soon, even in a blond, it will be an obvious beard, obvious to everyone."

Vestinus paused to see what effect these observations were having.

"It's never been discussed in my presence," he continued, "but I'd say Hadrian believes it's not appropriate for a Caesar to be partner to someone who has entered full manhood. Perhaps he thinks it's not seemly? It suggests something about the nature of the relationship that breaches the code of honor. It is one thing for a mature man to be attracted to a handsome youngster, but it's questionable for the same man to be attracted to another mature man. Especially a Caesar. Though Rome has enough such partnerships. I have spoken too much already ---." Vestinus trailed off.

"But what are you suggesting?" Suetonius dared to continue. "Do you think Antinous committed suicide because his time as Caesar's lover was up? But why? Being the emperor's Favorite would be a marvelous way to enter maturity. Think of the influence and connections and wealth the lad has acquired in his years with Caesar."

"Perhaps that's not how Antinous saw it? I suppose the boy knew Hadrian could never adopt him as his official son, even though the relationship seemed a father-and-son sort of thing some of the time. Neither the Senate, nor the Army, nor the people, would ever accept a non-Roman candidate despite his popularity .. especially someone they believe is fundamentally Caesar's catamite. That's where the '*Western Favorite*' comes in ...."

Vestinus innocently sipped his wine and picked at a fig or two after his quietly catapulted incendiary device had lobbed.

Suetonius had to quickly find a way back into his opinions.

"*Catamite* is a bit hard, isn't it, Julius? Trajan had dozens of similar liaisons, and he was applauded. The relationship isn't one of those castrated marriages of Nero's or incestuous couplings of Caligula. It's even been of four years duration, good grief! There's a definite affection between them that fits the classic Greek custom, so the boy's no cheap gigolo or harlot on-the-make. By Jupiter, they've been together longer than many legal marriages manage these days! Even Sabina approves of the lad. It's the height of respectability! So what's this about a 'Western Favorite'?"

"I think at Rome Hadrian had been seeing a great deal of Commodus again recently before this tour. That's Senator Lucius Ceionius Commodus, the well-known playboy aristocrat," the secretary offered. "Surely you know of him? Some colleagues joke he's Hadrian's *western* Empire favorite, while Antinous is the *eastern* favorite," the Secretary offered.

"Senator Commodus is rather profligate, sybaritic, and hopelessly spoiled, but still very good-looking. I think he brings a dash of wildness and frenzy into Caesar's staid sense of duty. Hadrian's relationship with Antinous is more measured, more composed, less frenetic. Yet Commodus is also five years older than Antinous, which contradicts the convention. He's no real match in the looks department, either. Antinous is a classic who becomes more striking with each passing month. Until today, that is, I suppose. Commodus also has the bloodlines, wealth, status, and connections for political advancement, if not the necessary talent."

"So you are suggesting Antinous might have had good reason to suicide?" Suetonius tried to clarify. Vestinus was offering far more than they had expected.

"I don't know if the boy would suicide, or if some other malevolence was at play? Perhaps he simply went for a night-time swim in the river and got into trouble. It happens. The Nile is not a bath-house pool, you know. People drown in it every day. Yet there've been many odd things happening in recent times which make one wonder."

Vestinus ceased suddenly. He realized he might have overstepped an imaginary line somewhere. Suetonius tried to respond as nonchalantly as possible, as though it was impromptu.

"Odd things? What sort of odd things, Julius?" he chanced.

Clarus shifted forward to hear. Vestinus mulled his words carefully.

"Well, there's been a lot going on. There's the competition from the Western Favorite, which I'm sure the lad found intimidating. Then there are people in his own circle who I wonder about. Lysias of Bithynia, for example, his friend of his own age. Does he have reason to be jealous of Antinous? Or that young courtesan Thais, if that's what she is? Or the woman Julia Balbilla who travels with Sabina? Or ---?

Then there's the business with Pachrates, the Egyptian priest we saw earlier. Both Caesar and the lad took a close interest in this charlatan and seem utterly entranced by him. All I see is a clever trickster with a bag of magical trinkets and a line in fast-talk. *'Beware priests selling religion'*, I say.

Then there's the Nile itself. The river has had a bad season since July; it hasn't risen to the necessary height for large harvests, so the locals are claiming it's the emperor's fault. Too much water or too little are equal disasters in this strange land.

Apparently emperors and pharaohs are not supposed to travel on the Nile during its flood season, it's a bad omen. It brings bad luck. These people are very superstitious. They see omens everywhere, even more than we Romans. And then of course there's Caesar's cough too ---"

Vestinus fell silent abruptly. He had said too much.

"Caesar's cough?" the biographer asked as casually as his racing mind could manage. "What about Caesar's cough? Hadrian has long had a mild chest or throat complaint; it's nothing important, is it?"

Vestinus measured his words carefully.

"I am unsure of that, Tranquillus; I am unsure of that indeed. Nowadays he coughs up spots of blood. We are forbidden to talk of it, but it's true. Even his physicians are concerned. But we must not go down that path, Tranquillus, it's forbidden. It gives ambitious discontents big ideas, ideas usually with a huge cost in human life attached."

Much scuffling was heard down the tent corridors. Guards shouting loudly in Latin and Greek alternated by rough accents in the local Demotic dialect sounded nearby. Tribune Macedo stomped into the chamber followed by guards manhandling two peasants struggling with wooden leg shackles.

Macedo's men pushed the two Egyptians to the floor and stood over them. The frightened peasants in their rags, reed sandals, and tattered leather jerkins, looked around the marquee at the ageing men in togas. Macedo saluted.

"The are the two peasants who found the body of Antinous this morning."

Clarus, Vestinus, and Suetonius looked over the duo. They weren't promising material, but at least they were unharmed.

"Does anyone here speak their language," the Special Inspector asked. One of the attending Praetorians stepped forward and saluted.

"Centurion Quintus Urbicus, sir. I am based at Alexandria with Governor Flavius Titianus as an officer of his Guard. I was born at Lambaesis in Numidia and have served with Prefect Turbo in Mauretania. So I know a little of the old languages of Africa and Egypt," he stated with military precision.

"Well, you might translate for us, if you can," Suetonius said. "First, tell them we must have the truth from them or else all sorts of horrible things could happen to them. They'll believe that, I'm sure!"

Praetorian Urbicus spoke in a stumbling way to the Egyptians. From watching their faces carefully reading his lips to follow his misshapen version of the local dialect, it was clear they nevertheless understood what he was saying. They blanched suitably.

Vestinus called quickly to his steward nearby. He explained.

"This man's name is Strabon, my freedman secretary. Strabon specializes in speed dictation. He records testimony verbatim in his special code onto wax notebooks. He later transcribes these in ink onto papyrus. He's good, and he's fast."

Suetonius posed his first questions as Strabon readied with his stylus and waxpad. Urbicus attempted a simple translation, shaping his words hesitantly to be reasonably faithful to his speakers.

"Ask them, Centurion --- What are your names? Where are you from? What is your trade? Who is your master?" Suetonius demanded in his best authoritative tone. The Praetorian's translation followed the peasant's responses closely.

"We have no master, great lords," Urbicus interpreted. "We are free tenants of temple land. We are registered by law to our Nome at Besa. My name is Ani; his name is Hetu. We are catchers of fishes and netters of birds. We are cousins. We live with our families in a hut outside the town wall of Besa. Besa is the village near to this city of great palaces. We are worshippers of the god Asar, so we are Asar's servants."

Urbicus added as an aside, "The god they call Asar is the one we call Osiris, the husband of Isis."

"Tell us how you found the body," Suetonius asked. Urbicus translated.

"At dawn of this first day of The Festival of Isis, great lords, we went to the river's edge to untie our fishing boats, as we do every day. It was first light, so early indeed only one other boat was on the river. We were intending to catch red-billed ibis from nests in the river wetlands, but certainly not sacred ibis which is forbidden. Red-billed ibis are good eating. Today, the first day, is the day when Asar dies. In two days time Asar will be reborn. There will be many pilgrims who mourn and praise Asar's death over these days, so the ibis will fetch good prices for the feasting on the day of Asar's resurrection."

Ani paused to assess his effect on his listeners. Hetu was quaking in fear and stricken mute.

"Yet when we untied our boat we found we couldn't release it from the bank. Something was stopping it. We looked into the water and could see a man's hand caught in river grasses under the boat.

We thought it was a river demon beneath the boat. He was either a demon of the Underworld, or he was a drowned man. Then we could see he was actually a god. A god was caught beneath the boat. We tried to pull the god from the water, but his robes were water-logged and heavy because he was dressed in precious silver and gold and white jewels.

We knew he was a deity because he had drowned in Mother Nile on the first day of the Isia. To drown in the Nile at the Isia is to become divine. He had frightening white hair, white skin, and strange clothes. Even his face was fleshed in silver. We saw he had the special armor and sword which Pharaoh's soldiers wield.

So we pulled him onto the bank from beneath our boat, and Hetu started calling for help. It was some time before anyone came to us, but soon many people came.

There was much shouting because everyone could see he was a god. Then Pharaoh's soldiers came and took us away. I thought we would receive many coins for our discovery, but we have been locked-up like thieves instead. We are not thieves, great lords!"

Clarus and Suetonius exchanged glances. "Pharaoh" was obviously Caesar. They could see from their simple faces and open expressions the fishermen were probably telling the truth, at least as they saw it.

"What does he mean 'his face was fleshed in silver'?" Suetonius asked.

Vestinus contributed a response.

"Among Antinous's armory is a cavalry parade-mask of beaten silver. He only wears it on ceremonial occasions where formal cavalry kit is expected. He receives gifts of armors from Caesar for every occasion, but wore his 'silver-and-whites' with its mask only at official ceremonies as a Companion of the Hunt. But why he was wearing it last night is unknown," the secretary explained. "It was among the items stripped from his body piled on the floor in Hadrian's chambers."

"How do you think this 'god' came to be in the river?" Suetonius asked the fishermen through the Praetorian translator. He wondered if they might possess an opinion of interest. They responded with their own questions.

"We do not know. Is he a river god? Is he a demon? Is he Asar himself dying again? Is he a gift to Mother Nile from the priests?" the trembling Hetu managed to stammer.

"What does he mean, '*a gift to Mother Nile*'?" Suetonius furthered. Hetu braved the response.

"The first day of the Isia tells us of the death of Asar. Asar went down to the Underworld, and Isis the goddess of waters and moistures prayed, and three days later Asar was reborn, brought back to life. It was a miracle! It is the promise by the gods how the sun will be reborn too after the shortening days of winter. The sun will return and the river will flood another year to bring prosperity to all. He who drowns in the Nile on the day of Asar's death becomes Asar. He is divine. He will be reborn on the third day. It is a miracle!"

Superstition again, Suetonius thought. "And what about a *gift to Mother Nile?*" he repeated. Urbicus translated.

"We are told how if the river rises too high the dikes will be destroyed. If it's too low the peasants at the edge of the desert will starve. Then the *fellahin* will riot. They will have nothing to eat. So the priests will have to throw someone into the river to appease the gods to make it flow as we need. That person becomes Asar. It is a great honor," Hetu explained with cheery enthusiasm.

"You mean you *sacrifice* a human to the gods?" Suetonius had to confirm. The fishermen nodded brightly. Clarus spoke at last to one side.

"You see where this might be leading, Suetonius? Antinous dies on the same day as Osiris in the annual Isis festival. He dies in a year when the Nile has not properly performed its annual inundation. It's the second year in a row which threatens famine to many folk. Is there a connection? Don't you think it's a bit too convenient by half?"

"Hmm," Suetonius murmured. He had one more question to put to the fishermen through Urbicus.

"Was there any other boat on the river so early in the day? Another fisherman perhaps? Or was it still too dark?" he asked as Clarus, Vestinus, and Macedo looked querulously at him. Urbicus again translated Ani's reply.

"Yes, great lord. There was a stranger's boat. It was barely at first light. We know all the fishermen and ferrymen at this place. We know their vessels and their daily habits. We all know everyone here well. Even though it was some distance away, we could see this craft was a different sort of boat to local boats, with strangers onboard."

"Describe it. Why was it a stranger's boat?"

Urbicus paused as he tried to translate the fisherman's terms.

"It was a strong wooden *felucca* of quality, sir, well made and costly, not a boat of bundled reeds, tied leathers, or palm fronds."

"And who would own such a boat at Besa or Hermopolis?" Suetonius asked.

"I did not know either this boat or the two boatmen," Ani replied. "It could have been a new boat from Shmun across the river we had not seen before, but I would still know the two crew. Perhaps it was a boat sailed by priests from upstream for The Isia, or a boat belonging to Pharaoh's people," Ani said.

Urbicus added an aside.

"Shmun is the native name for the city of Hermopolis across the river."

"Did the boat have any identifying features? Would you recognize it again?" the Special Inspector queried. Urbicus translated the question with careful emphasis.

"Yes. The *felucca* was painted the color of the sky, and was marked with the ever-watching Eye of Horus at the prow," Ani responded. Urbicus translated hesitantly. "The sail had no insignia."

"I see. Thank you, my good fellows," Suetonius gestured. "I think we can let these fellows go home, but we should note how we can locate them if we need them again," Suetonius suggested to Macedo's dismay.

The security chief looked to Clarus and Vestinus with concern. He was not used to releasing prisoners in his grasp, especially peasants, foreigners, or slaves, without a little rough violence to pass the time of day and impress respect of their betters upon them.

"I think Suetonius is right, Tribune," Clarus nodded, "they merely retrieved the body from the river. Release them."

Macedo reluctantly snapped to attention as Suetonius reached for his belt-purse and found a few small coins to toss to the fishermen.

"Here's something for your day's labors."

The two fishermen fell avidly upon the trove.

"Urbicus," Suetonius asked the trooper, "what do you make of this tale?"

Looking to Macedo for permission to speak, who nodded grudgingly, Urbicus responded.

"I was one of the Praetorians who brought both the body and the two fishermen back to the camp. When we arrived at the river and saw who it was, we were amazed and alarmed. We had all come to know Antinous quite well one way or another over the past few months, and he was well liked.

We carefully drained the body of waters and removed his armors, partly to search his flesh for wounds or other indications of the cause of death. We simply could not understand what Caesar's companion was doing in the river in full parade armor, which is far too heavy in water.

We wondered if he had tried to swim in the river in his regalia for a drunken bet or some other lark. Had he fallen overboard while he risked crossing the river at night in a reed canoe? Had he been attacked and thrown into the river by robbers? There were many unknowns. Especially, we wondered, why he was dressed in his formal uniform on a night when the entire imperial retinue was partying and no parade for Caesar was scheduled anyhow? Also, it seems noone felt compelled to report him missing."

"What about the incision in his left wrist?" Suetonius asked to test the officer's competence. Urbicus was amazed.

"How did you know about that! You have seen it? We saw it too," he stammered. "But we didn't mention it to anyone, because it makes even less sense to us. Why would Antinous have a slit wrist? It raises a prospect which we have no authority to comment upon. It would be idle speculation. We decided such comments must await a proper inspection by Caesar's physician. It implies death by suicide."

"Centurion Quintus Urbicus, _we are_ the investigating team," Clarus announced with stentorian authority. "Would you agree the incision was consistent with Antinous slicing his wrist with his own weapon?"

"As an accident or as an act of suicide, my lord?" Urbicus daringly responded.

"Whatever, soldier," the senator snapped.

"There may be many ways someone might slice their left wrist, accidental or not."

"There is a problem with that proposal, Clarus," Vestinus interrupted. "To my knowledge Antinous was by nature left handed. He dressed his weapons at his right hip for left-hand use. If he was to slash a wrist in suicide, I guess it would more likely be his right wrist, not his left wrist, he would slice. Make of that what you will, gentlemen."

Suetonius, Clarus, and Macedo, looked to each other. Suetonius considered the situation.

"An accident? A suicide? Some sort of assault? Each is one possibility among several. There must surely be other options yet to be detected? But who should be next to interview who may offer fresh insight? Who will possess sufficient understanding of Antinous's circumstances to throw light on this mystery?"

"I think, gentlemen," Clarus called, "it is time to visit the inner sanctum of the deceased himself, to see for ourselves."

"His living quarters?" Suetonius asked.

"Yes. I visited his apartments in this tent complex when we were camped at Arsinoe a few weeks ago. The general layout of the camp remain similar. Follow me, I think I can find his section!"

Macedo and his Praetorians including Urbicus stalled behind.

"We will attend to releasing the prisoners, as you request," the Tribune muttered grudgingly.

"I too will return to my duties," Vestinus excused himself. "But remember, your time is fast elapsing, gentlemen,".

"Follow me then, those who remain," Clarus proclaimed.

CHAPTER 5

Senator Clarus led Suetonius and the scribe Strabon through a maze of tented passages in the labyrinthine complex. They passed Horse Guard or Praetorian sentries posted at intervals who simply nodded knowing recognition as they passed. Familiar faces wearing togas are sufficient password for some.

Eventually the trio arrived at a vestibule entrance bedecked in a particularly idiosyncratic way redolent of a students' quarters at a *palaestra*. The entrance was wittily marked with whimsical decorations of ratty, used, young men's loin-cloths tied in improbable patterns, a blazon of knitted Egyptian palm fronds supporting a mummified cat with an attached moustache, and two oversized priapic dildos of carved wood pointing to the entrance into quarters of special significance.

"We are here, I think," Clarus offered. They gingerly entered the chambers.

"Lysias of Bithynia? Thais of Cyrene? Staff? Anyone?" Clarus called, clapping his hands for prompt slave service. There was no response.

"Anybody home?"

The two toga-garbed Romans entered the large darkened space within, followed closely by their Greek scribe.

"Yes, this is where the Bithynian was accommodated, along with his friends and household. I was here once before in the company of Caesar to inspect the young man's grazes and scratches after his brush with a wounded lion outside Alexandria."

Lamps burned low in the night's gloom. Tired wisps of incense drifted from occasional bowls. Ripples of bell notes from a suspended wind chime tinkled lazily in the desert breeze. There was no sign of anyone, including the serving slaves of the household.

Clarus peered into each of three openings leading to further chambers. He turned and beckoned Suetonius and Strabon, pointing into one of the darkest spaces.

The two followed him into a larger space beyond a vestibule offering concealed privacy. It dawned on the three they were entering Antinous's personal sleeping quarters. They glanced to each other in wonder. They were setting foot in the intimate domain of the *'infamous catamite'* himself, as puritan elders at Rome often decried.

This new chamber was the private boudoir of the tall, blond-maned, muscular figure who had graced the inner circle of Caesar Hadrian's retinue for almost five years. The presence of the Bithynian youth at the emperor's side, it had been noted, was more ubiquitous than that of the empress.

Many at Court quietly appreciated how Hadrian's impulsive and acerbic nature, his searching restlessness, or his intimidating capacity to dominate and control everything or everyone, seemed to be placated in the presence of his laid-back, easy-going paramour.

Nevertheless regardless of the Court's more spiteful wits, Antinous was not a substitute 'wife' in all things except law. This was despite the wide assumption his sexual role was likely to be a *bottom* by definition. A Caesar is by convention assertive. Yet even the most passive *cinaedus* may feign believable machismo in public.

Cinaedi behavior arouses the Roman prejudice against ambiguous sensuality, despite its widespread frequency across the Empire. Rather, Antinous was athletic, hardy, and masculine. Nevertheless there were those who crudely saw the lad as being the emperor's bugger-boy, *catamite*, or common toyboy. To many at Rome the relationship was founded on some very basic urges of a notorious earthiness. After all, *what do they do?*.

Hadrian's reputed short-term liaisons with a string of freeborn favorites, patrician's sons, and rising officers in the military had been legend. Yet these were never as legendary as the colorful exuberance of his predecessor, the much-adored Trajan.

The offence of committing *stupra* under the ancient law code of the *Lex Scantinia* can theoretically invite social censure, at least at the western end of the Empire if not in the east. But those ascetic attitudes withered generations ago. Today an irrepressible sexual playfulness prevails among the elites, much to the vexation of Rome's prim, if usually hypocritical, elders who slyly forget their own youthful indiscretions.

Suetonius's celebrated biographies of the first twelve Caesars showed how the pressing compulsions of sex consumed each one. Their appetites had been capricious without apology. They showed how sex makes fools of each of us, even lofty *Imperators*.

Yet today's absolute master of the civilized world restrains these impulses. The one man whose status can entice any maiden or youth, can outbid the market competition for any beauteous slave, can impose his will on any woman or man reliant on imperial patronage, or can afford to assemble a private seraglio of assorted slaves or concubines in the manner of several notables of his own Court, nevertheless limits himself to a single wife and a single young man as his consorts. Though others of his retinue ostentatiously maintain assorted slaves for their bodily entertainments, Hadrian is conspicuous in his restraint.

"Importuning a slave, freedman, or *client* --," Clarus announced, "-- even if they're willing partners so as to advance their fortunes, appears to be beyond the role he perceives for himself as Rome's champion of social responsibility. He deigns it beneath an emperor, just as the philosopher Plutarch recently counseled. Plutarch sneers at those who impose upon a slave, who has no rights in the matter. Hadrian soberly presents himself to his subjects as an exponent of sexual right-mindedness rather than indulge himself without limit."

"Yet do not forget, Clarus my friend, how Caesar may also be in love with his companion. Restraint may have other origins than public probity," Suetonius added sagely, "it may be sensitive to his companion's deeper needs."

The three moved cautiously into Antinous's sleeping chamber. The tenting was open to the night sky and its blaze of stars. A solitary lamp was slowly exhausting its final drops of oil, casting long flickering shadows into the gloom. Stale incense hung in the air while another wind-chime tinkled randomly.

Filling much of the chamber was a low bed which could sleep five. It was draped in tribal Greek rugs. Crumpled cushions lay about. Empty goblets had fallen to their sides across the floor-tiles beside the bed, leaking droplets of russet stain onto the tiles.

Strabon noticed a wax-block notebook and writing stylus folded closed on a side table. He drew the other's attention to it. Clarus was nearest so he picked it up and opened its cover.

"Well, does it say anything?" Suetonius asked.

"It's in Greek. I think it's expressed in an archaic mode of Greek, not today's common Greek. It's being very *historic* or poetic. If I'm not wrong it translates as:

> 'WHEN THE KING OF LIONS
> PLAYS WITH THE LION CUB
> NO MORE
> IT IS TIME FOR THE CUB
> TO LOCATE ITS OWN PRIDE.'"

The weak pun on 'pride' might have been intentional, if artless, Suetonius thought. All three of the group grasped its basic message, though there was no way to know if it was in Antinous's own hand or another's.

"Strabon, keep this wax-pad safe and away from heat until we can identify the writer," Suetonius instructed. The scribe wrapped the tablets in a cloth and placed it securely within his shoulder basket of tools and pads.

Clarus then turned to one of the other entrance portals. He heard a sound beyond. The others followed as he tentatively moved through another vestibule outside Antinous's bedchamber. A further smaller bedchamber extended beyond the vestibule.

They entered hesitantly. Lying close to the tented wall in the shadows lay a curled figure. It had its back to the visitors. The figure was quietly heaving, huddled against the felts.

Strabon raised the chamber's single lamp and played its light onto the bundle of fabric. The bundle realized there was company present and slowly turned towards them, wiping its eyes as it did so. Once again they had intruded into the private space of someone displaying eyes red from weeping.

It was Lysias of Bithynia, the school-chum friend of Antinous.

Lysias was already a man. At twenty-four years of age he displayed manhood's razored bristles, a sturdy athlete's body, pronounced bone structure, and bright intelligent eyes showing the benefit of well-nourished ancestors. Nevertheless, where many men his age were already senior officers in the Legions slaughtering barbarians at the frontiers or hunting down and crucifying gangs of Judaean bandits in Palaestina, here was this sturdy youth lying curled against a tent wall with his eyes red from weeping.

"Come, come, come, lad," Suetonius called, half in rebuke, half in sympathy, "this is no way for a man of honor to act. Lysias of Bithynia, I believe?"

They awaited a response. After a few moments the figure turned towards them, wiping his eyes as he shuffled upright. The fellow stumbled clumsily to his feet.

"Lysias, son of Lysander of Claudiopolis at Bithynia-Pontus. I travel under the patronage of Antinous, son of Telemachus of Claudiopolis, who is the special companion of Caesar Hadrian. I am a freeborn member of the landholding class of Bithynia and a captain of the Claudiopolis Militia. At your service."

He spoke Latin with only a hint of a Greek accent, the audible outcome of a good education at both Nicomedia and at Athens.

"Your tears, I assume, are for your former *patron* Antinous?" Clarus probed, perhaps somewhat unnecessarily. Lysias's lip trembled.

"Yes," he said simply.

"We are Senator Septicius Clarus, a magistrate to the Imperial Household, while I am Suetonius Tranquillus, Special Inspector into the death of Antinous. It is our duty under the seal of Caesar to investigate the circumstances of the Bithynian's death."

"On behalf of Caesar?!" the youth declaimed daringly. "You mean Lord Caesar does not know?!"

Clarus and Suetonius were startled by the provocation.

"Caesar has delegated this enquiry to us. We are obliged to interview you on the matter, as we are to interview all those involved with the deceased who might know something of the manner and reason for the youth's death. We possess the authority of law and its instruments of interrogation."

Clarus was hinting not so delicately at the range of options open to their investigation, without actually mentioning the fiercest possibility. Suetonius coughed politely, to distract them from any mood of threat which might arise. Not formally being a citizen of Rome, Lysias was potentially subject to the more brutal forms of interrogation.

Suetonius interceded. "I understand you are -- you were --boyhood friends together?"

"Antinous and I have known each other since early childhood; we have known each other all our lives. We are *friends*."

Lysias uttered this claim with its special emphasis on *friends* in a loaded manner. Suetonius mentally filed this comment for later exploration.

Glancing around the chamber, he realized how Antinous's apartments were probably not the place to interview Lysias.

"Gentlemen, I think we should retire to Secretary Vestinus' chambers to conduct this interview, don't you think?"

He looked at Clarus with an eyebrow raised. "Besides, there'll be food and wine to enjoy," he added. "We are keen, Lysias, to learn more about your remarkable friend Antinous. I'm sure you will know many things about the youth which may assist us in determining the manner of the lad's death?"

He was interested to learn more about the dead youth's relationships and activities and where Caesar fitted-in to that. Separately, what was the precise nature of their relationship? Was Lysias an alternative lover of Antinous?

Suetonius thought something provocative might be a useful opener.

"Tell us, did Antinous sleep with others in this bedroom?"

Strabon lurched urgently to his writing tools and began fluttering a stylus across a notepad's wax surface.

"No, not at all," the young Greek responded firmly. "Antinous sleeps in this bed with none other than Caesar. He was Caesar's *Companion*. That was their compact. When Caesar was disposed elsewhere, Antinous slept here alone. And I can assure you it was not because he was without petitioners. Half the Court and even the eunuchs seemed eager to hop into bed with him."

Suetonius was surprised to learn of this fidelity.

"Did you sleep close by last night, Lysias, the night of Antinous's drowning?" Clarus asked. "Or did you sleep elsewhere?"

Lysias paused thoughtfully. His eyes flashed momentary pain.

"I remained on my bed next to this chamber all night."

"Then you will know what times Antinous came and went through the night or morning? You will know something of his movements?" Clarus contributed.

Lysias paused again to consider his response. Strabon's stylus paused its fluttering.

"Antinous did not sleep in his chamber at all last night," Lysias said at last with increasing emotion.

Clarus, Strabon, and Suetonius looked questioningly to each other. So Antinous had been elsewhere throughout the entire night?

"Where then, Lysias, do you think Antinous had been?" Suetonius asked.

"Elsewhere, I would assume," he offered obliquely.

"Elsewhere? With Caesar?"

"I do not know," was the simple reply.

Clarus cut across this line of questioning. Anything of proximity to Caesar made him uncomfortable. Caesar was not under investigation.

"It's time to return to our assigned apartments," Clarus demanded. "And it's time to take a formal record from this young man."

"Join us, Lysias of Bithynia. We wish to take testimony from you."

CHAPTER 6

Secretary Vestinus's tents were buzzing with activity and ablaze with light.

Chamberlain Alcibiades had returned with two slaves for the investigative team's service. Vestinus had assigned a further top-notch scribe to support Strabon in the wax-pad transcription chores, while the Praetorian Tribune Macedo had delegated the Alexandrian Centurion Quintus Urbicus to be an investigative agent to the team, accompanied by two troops.

Urbicus's translation skill had already proven useful with the fishermen. He seemed a sharp fellow suited to Suetonius's temper.

Standing in the background behind the two guards under Macedo's command was a further figure draped in a hooded travelling cloak and carrying a large carpetbag. When the figure dropped back its head cowl it revealed a mound of auburn hair dressed in the high woven style worn by ladies of fashion. Suetonius realized it was Surisca, the young entertainer from the *House of the Blue Lotuses*. His heart leapt a beat. His pulse raced. His groin stirred.

"The woman Surisca of Antioch," announced Macedo. "Delivered as demanded after considerable effort. It needed a team of twenty Guards and six ferrymen to traverse the Nile at night with flares, torches, and special skills to collect this female from her place of employ, negotiate a fee, and repeat the journey back to this encampment, at very considerable expense and danger to all."

He was rubbing it in, probably justifiably.

"My officers had to buy out the fee for her client tonight, and a double fee for each day until we return her to her contractor, plus a large inconvenience fee. She wasn't cheap."

Macedo announced this in Latin. He was certain Latin would not be her first language so it might pass her by. From the restraint expressed across her features, Suetonius suspected she clearly understood his words.

Surisca stood regally at the doorway to the rooms. She wore her bearing with unexpected dignity. She glanced around at the elegant luxury of this itinerant, fabric-built metropolis. Her eyes settled upon Suetonius across the chamber and, on recognizing him from only that very afternoon, smiled in a sweetly shy way that one wouldn't usually expect of an entertainer. Perhaps she had no idea who her purchaser had been, and was relieved to see a familiar face.

She was taller than Suetonius remembered and wasn't painted with her bordello colors. Her hair was held high by a Syriac headband and combs, but still folding down her back. She wore simple vestments more suited to the Forum than her whore-house duties, and with her ample bosom taped fulsomely in the Syrian way she looked more her real age of the high teens.

Her earlier skimpy costume, face paints, and tart's frivolous manner had added five years to her appearance at Hermopolis. Without the professional decors she presented a wholesomely healthy look, Suetonius mused. She was both more natural and more appealing to him at the same time. He spied Clarus, Vestinus, and Urbicus giving her a good looking over, and could sense their unspoken approval, perhaps even envy.

"Surisca, my dear!," he called as warmly as possible in Greek amid this nest of Latins, sounding as though the two had known each other for decades. "Welcome to the Imperial Household!"

He tried to offer reassurance in these unfamiliar surroundings. She would have no idea of what was expected of her in this all-male environment of people far above her class. Perhaps she thought she was going to have to perform sexually for a whole gang of Roman party-goers, or worse?

"I said this afternoon I would be seeing you soon, but I had no idea it would this soon. Please come and be seated among us. Are you thirsty or hungry? Would you enjoy some refreshments?"

Surisca entered the chamber hesitantly and accepted the invitation to take a seat.

For a sex worker to be seated among her class superiors and receive their hospitality was a marvel in itself. This was indeed an unexpected turn of events for a woman of her trade. She lifted back her demure headscarf and dropped it to her shoulders to reveal the full sheen of her auburn locks. Such a public display of a woman's hair before strangers was a novelty in itself.

Suetonius waved at the two service-slaves to find something to eat and drink, and they quickly disappeared into the complex. It was then that he identified a familiar waft of the faint fragrance of myrrh or frankincense oils emanating from her skin. These had impinged on his mood so effectively earlier that afternoon.

"You have been contracted, my dear, to give my companions here and myself advice on the customs of the local inhabitants and to help translate for us. We also hope you may provide some other guidance as we embark upon an urgent project on behalf of Great Caesar," the biographer explained. "It will take several days to complete. But, as my personal assistant, you will endeavor to stay close to me throughout. You will sleep in my bedroom for the period too, if you understand my meaning?"

Instead of expressing surprise, Surisca visibly relaxed. The final notion and Suetonius's politeness had reassured her how she hadn't been hired to be available to all-comers without limit, as can occur at men's drinking parties. Yet Suetonius wasn't deceiving anyone, either.

The staff arrived with dried fruits, cheese, nuts, and bean-mash pastes with fried bread to dip. Honey pastries and crushed almond halva followed. They were laid on a low table for self-service as required. The wine from Vestinus's larder was now a simple local Fayum wine of drinkable quality.

Surisca rose and delicately helped herself to the foods. She was hungry, though the professional entertainer in her saw her select tidbits and morsels arranged on a platter accompanied by a knife, which she brought to Suetonius. She then poured the Fayum in a 50/50 watered mix into cups for each of them.

Suetonius thought silently to himself, oh yes, my impulsive demand is going to work quite well. The others probably wondered why they hadn't thought of it themselves.

They each knew it was unusual for a woman to be in the company of strangers unaccompanied by a protector, husband, brother, or eldest son. Women of the elites across the East, and very often at Rome too, are secluded within the home and only appear in public in the company of male guardians.

Yet considering Surisca's trade including being a foreign non-citizen, this fact did not apply in this circumstance. Due to the Special Inspector's interest, perhaps she automatically assumed a role as an 'honorary male' for the immediate duration.

She had barely uttered a word thus far. But when she did respond to her benefactor's queries, the quality of her voice was a surprise. Unlike the shrill, mischievous harlot he recalled from the *House of the Blue Lotuses*, Suetonius realized she unexpectedly possessed a much lower vocal register which communicated an extremely level-headed quality. This raised Suetonius's pulse another beat or two.

The earlier harlot's voice could well have been a merchandising ploy from a sex worker's grab-bag of seductive tools. Suetonius appreciated he was in the company of more than an expensive trollop who you wouldn't trust with your purse.

But attention now returned to Lysias.

"Lysias, we are to question you on aspects of your relationship with the deceased, Antinous. Your personal testimony will be recorded for report to Lord Caesar," Clarus opened the formal interviews. "Please remember we possess the authority of an inquisitional Court, so you are obliged to tell the complete truth on these matters at penalty of severe imposition."

Macedo and Vestinus had departed the chamber and left the central team to their chores. This lightened the atmosphere no end. Clarus initiated the interview.

"You will begin with an oath of truth, then state your full name and origins, your status in relationship to the Imperial Household, and then describe under what circumstances you met and know of the deceased. On completion of these details, you will await further questions."

Lysias had uneasily taken his seat in the centre of the chamber. He looked towards the eager faces confronting him. He began hesitantly.

"In the name of Apollo Alexikakos, son of Zeus, healer of heaven, and Apollo Kourotrophos, protector of youth; as well as Artemis, who Romans call Diana, twin sister of Apollo, protector of hunters, I swear fidelity to the truth.

As a clan servant of these deities at the cult in Bithynia, may my oath be true, and may their arrows strike me down if I speak untruth."

Lysias began, sitting to his full height before the group while fingering the *bulla* locket around his neck. Suetonius assumed the *bulla* contained prayers or a talisman.

"I am Lysias of Bithynia, son of Lysander of Claudiopolis, born at my father's house at Nicomedia in March of the eighth year of the rule of Caesar Trajan. I turned age twenty-four this year. I travel with Caesar's retinue by invitation under the protection of Antinous of Bithynia, companion to Caesar. I have known Antinous since childhood."

Lysias paused for the next question. Suetonius took the reins.

"Because Antinous cannot speak for himself, tell us what you know of the deceased's origins too," Suetonius asked. A dewy drop was appearing at the *ephebe*'s eye.

"Antinous, son of Telemachus of Claudiopolis, was born eight months after me at Mantinium, upland from Claudiopolis near the border, in the ninth year of Caesar Trajan's rule. He too would turn twenty-four, if he was alive, next month.

Since entering the older age-class of *meirakia* youths five years ago, we were registered as *Companions of the Hunt* with the Imperial Household."

"Tell us, Lysias, how did you two fellows come to be enrolled in Caesar's retinue?"

"We were both appointed by Great Caesar when Antinous fell under Caesar's eye during his tour of Bithynia," Lysias explained. "Caesar proposed to Antinous's father, Telemachus. He wished to fulfill the role of *erastes* to Antinous under the terms of the custom of the Hellenes. Both father and son acceded to the request. I was present at this very consultation and heard it discussed between the family members.

Antinous has remained Caesar's *eromenos* until very recent times. At least that's how Antinous saw it."

"What were the circumstances in which you both fell under Caesar's eye? How did this happen?"

"It is a lengthy story, my lords. It would take time," Lysias offered.

"We have a little time, young man," Suetonius reassured. "It is important to hear about the nature of your relationship with the deceased. We need to know the details so we can take a bearing on the issues involved. Everything, Lysias, everything."

Lysias thoughtfully sipped his mug of wine and looked moodily to the floor tiles.

"I can recall the very first time we two discussed the issue of being an *eromenos*," he said. "After qualifying for the *meirakion* age-class where we train with the heavier, more dangerous weapons of the *palaestra*, we must consider how to locate an experienced trainer. A trainer must teach us effective fighting skills and practice long hours with us. It's very time consuming.

Antinous and I talked about such things between ourselves when we journeyed on hunting expeditions. Antinous was a keen hunter. Five years ago we always shared experiences, we were inseparable friends. The *eromenos* issue arose during one particular hunt in the Pontine Ranges to track a herd of horses we had been told were running wild …."

The Greek gathered his thoughts to recall the occasion. He spoke with a shimmering emotion. The group of listeners sat in quiet attention.

"It was the fall of that year. In Bithynia winter descends quickly. We and our mountain ponies were ranging the lower slopes of the Pontine Ranges. We had spent two days searching for the herd ---."

CHAPTER 7

"Antinous braced his pony Tiny cautiously," Lysias recollected. "He pressed his calf and thigh muscles, gripped the horse's bony flank with both knees through the backcloth, and gently tapped its neck with the loose end of the reins. The pony moved forward slowly. Antinous then carefully lifted his hips and butt from Tiny's spine to take a peep over the edge of the ridge ahead of him.

His eyes revealed what both of our ears had sensed. There they were, fourteen of them, all quietly grazing. The Imperial Post courier had reported accurately of the number and type of horses, though the pack had moved a mile or so since the courier's sighting. It had taken two full days for us to find them.

Antinous beckoned back towards me following close behind. He held a finger across his lips to hush an urge to make voice, and then point-marked towards the gentle slope falling away beneath the ridge.

I approached carefully on my pony, Blaze, drawing to Antinous's side. I looked over the ridge at the grassy slope below. We soothed Tiny's and Blaze's tension with calming strokes and whispers.

'Great Zeus!' I heard myself hiss. 'It's a whole herd!'

'Fourteen of them,' Antinous whispered. 'Running feral. Mostly Turkomans. Small grays. The two foals and their mares look healthy still, but they haven't faced a winter yet. They'll be a good catch if we can corral them before the snows arrive.'

'Where are they from? Their crests are cropped, so they're domesticated.'

'Their tails are docked too in the barbarian style, see,' Antinous pointed. 'Maybe they've escaped from a brigand's hideaway, possibly after a run-in with a Militia? Or perhaps they've wandered off from a roaming tribe of Alans nomads and crossed the border into our territory? The Alans were too afraid to come after them or the Legions would crucify them. I can't see any of our usual branding or ear nips, and I certainly don't recognize the stock from trading meets, do you? So they're not local.'

I agreed. 'But where are we, what's their position? We'll have to note where we are, to come back for them. There's too many for us to capture.'

Antinous considered the options.

'It'll take six riders with hounds to round them up and rope them one by one. We're about a mile due west of the trapper's hut in the valley under the south side of Vulcan's Peak. The grazing is good, so they'll move on very slowly. They can't go higher into the range, the grazing runs out and there's no water.

We'll have to come back within a few days with our best riders to round them up, or they'll melt away. The two foals and the colts would make good breeding stock. Father says we need fresh blood badly, we inter-breed too often. If the colts can be ridden they'll give good service. The mule looks like it has farm work to spare. If not, it's meat and leather time for them all. They're a good find, Lys. We're very lucky.'

We slowly backed our steeds away from the grazing herd's sight. With our broad-brimmed sunhats strapped to our backs over woolen mantles and tunics torn short for riding, we were full of youthful health and spunk. We willingly displayed our muscled forearms, thighs, and trim torsos in our recent status as *meirakia* grown youths. We were proud athletes moving rapidly into full manhood. We were both very aware of our developing powers and our bodies. I especially was sensitive to these things.

Our fiercer weapons were stoked across our horse's backcloth while quivers of arrows and carry-bags were looped around each pony's neck within reach. Only hip daggers offered emergency defense against the possibility of a roaming bandit or an unseasonable wolf in the lower ranges of the Pontine Mountains. But we were trained to handle such risks.

Carefully drawing our ponies back, we returned to the woodland track behind us.

'It's getting late,' Antinous said. 'Sunset is in an hour. It's time to hunt us some hare or fowl and find a protected camp site. There was a creek back-a-bit with a clearing nearby. That'll do for the night. We don't want to alarm the herd with fire light, or they'll haul off.'

'Well, what'd you think of the news, Lys?!' Antinous called to me as he swung off Tiny's back.

I once again perceived how my friend made the leap off his pony's spine with light-speed energy and grace. I could discern the animal power and tight body coordination of his rapidly evolving physicality. It was an athleticism which already drew nodding respect from our peers and elders at the *palaestra*. It drew similar regard from me too.

I had watched my blond-haired, pale skinned friend grow from childhood pal into a sleek, sinewy youth in the space of a few years. It was accompanied by a growth in personal confidence and a broadening of a very appealing, impertinent toothy grin. We had shared the same deity, the same clan and caste, the same tutors, the same peer group, and the same life adventures as each other since before we could even remember. Antinous was an extension of myself. I was perhaps more conscious of his body than I was of my own.

'What news?' I asked, pretending not to know where the conversation was heading. Antinous was buzzing with boyish enthusiasm again after the serious business of identifying the valuable cache of ownerless horseflesh open to a profitable grab. My less outgoing nature secretly admired my friend's liveliness.

I was already tethering my pony to a tree while holding a fat range eagle chick impaled on an arrow tucked under one arm. Of hares there were none to be seen; so a new season's eagle chick pierced at its cliff-face crag was to be the day's fireside meal. It was a chicken large enough to feed four.

'Lord Arrian's trading steward has told Father how Caesar and the Imperial party will be arriving next week! At last! They've told the councilors at *Polis* to organize the celebration events, and to do it well!'

'What sort of events, Ant?' I responded using the abbreviated familiar name common among our generation. I raised my *chiton* tunic to relieve an urgently pressed bladder in a steaming stream against the tree trunk. The day's scouting for the wild ponies had delayed a well-needed piss. But now the herd had been sighted grazing within two-day's reach of our hometown, Claudiopolis. With their position noted, it was time to relax and enjoy our hunting trek's return home journey.

Antinous and I regularly mounted hunts into the ranges around Claudiopolis – *"Polis"* being the local nickname for our town protected on its hilltop in the secure walled Roman manner. We brought back rabbits, hares, other wild rodents, young boars, assorted fowl, river fish, any fruit or berry visibly edible, plus the occasional orphaned bear to nurture, to the fireside hearths of our family compounds.

'You know what I mean, Lys -- a welcome celebration for the Emperor, grand speeches, the sacrifice of a steer to the Gods,' Antinous spelled out, "with a public feast, dances for Apollo, music competitions, youth athletics at the *palaestra*, all that sort of thing. Everything we do well in the provinces, they say. Even freeborn girls will be allowed to attend events, with suitable guardians.'

Antinous was now also relieving himself against the tree trunk.

'But *Polis* has been preparing for all that for months now,' I reminded us. 'We had the tour's probable dates a year ago.'

Hadrian has been travelling with his Household for two years, so the Province Legate had sent scouts ahead to inform us long ago. The Household had departed Antioch four months earlier, all four hundred of them plus most of a Legion. We were one of the last provinces in his tour of the Empire, with only the Troas and mainland Greece to follow.

'So who told you that?' Antinous queried as we prepared a campfire of rocks and dry branches for the night's warmth.

I glanced over my younger friend covered in brush dust, pine needles, and the slick of the day's sweaty exertions. It was difficult not to notice, however, how my school chum's slender musculature had advanced yet another step in shapely power since such issues last crossed my mind, which was often. Antinous didn't have my beefiness, but he had a fine rangy physical line which grew more sculpted with each passing month.

'Arrian himself told us. He stayed overnight with us at the compound a few weeks ago on his way back to Nicomedia from his border inspection,' I confirmed.

But Antinous couldn't let that piece of one-upmanship pass by unchallenged.

'Yes, I know, he stayed with Father at our compound on his way out,' Antinous replied. 'He checks the border barbarians every few months. He's worried about the increasing incursion of the Alans tribes. They're searching for places to settle, and there are a lot of them.

I like Arrian. He's very direct and no-nonsense about things. That's probably his military training. He likes me too, I guess. He was keen to congratulate Father and my Elder Brother on our public duty in repairing the old Baths of Claudius and its *palaestra* training yard. At last we younger ones at *Polis* have a *palaestra* worthy of the pain of the practice.

Arrian said Caesar has offered to do the opening ceremony while he's here, which everyone immediately accepted. It's a great honor for Father. It might even be worth the huge cost to the family.'

Despite the autumn chill, we stripped off our sweated tunics and splashed around in the bracing mountain waters of a rivulet tumbling down the slope by our bivouac site. We noisily body-washed after several days' soiling. We scrubbed all over with handfuls of wet sand and scoured each other's hard-to-reach parts for thorough cleanliness.

'Arrian is now a citizen of Rome, you know?' I continued as we splashed. 'He says they're gradually adding Greeks to the citizen roll under Hadrian's influence, but only if you earn it. Caesar is said to honor Greek life and Greek ways. Even some of his equestrian- class advisors at Rome are said to be Hellenes now. The times are changing, Ant.'

'But Romans still don't trust us, Father says privately. At war we are only allowed to fight as auxiliaries or as expendable front line fodder, while the Legions remain firmly Roman,' Antinous mused aloud as he rinsed the sands off his skin's glistening surfaces.

I have to admit how being so close to my friend in his natural state is inclined to introduce a sensual glow to my being. Like most of the guys I know, we find bodily exposure induces an unexpected surge of energy – erotic energy. It is a very pleasing sensation. In fact I sensed my private parts were displaying signs of arousal, just as they did during close body contact sports at the *palaestra*. More than once I have found I have developed a discernable erection while tussling at close quarters with a wrestling partner or while watching others compete. Many of the boys do. It's natural, I guess.

Antinous had long realized I was prone to being aroused when we tangled as wrestlers. This wasn't too surprising to lads at a time of life when our groins sought urgent, irrepressible, self-relief several times a day. Antinous laughed at my heightened state of enthusiasm amid the rivulet's chill that evening. He flicked water at my crotch to dampen my fun. He only ceased laughing when he realized he too was displaying similar signs.

'Local gossip says Lord Arrian might have been an intimate friend of Hadrian's long ago, even his lover perhaps, in Caesar's wilder days before becoming emperor," I confided. "He might even have been his *eromenos* at the time of the Dacian Wars. That's the rumor anyway. But that was very long ago.'

I spoke hesitantly as we toweled ourselves with our loincloths by the warming campfire. These are sensitive matters for young men to discuss between them at their time of life. By then the eagle chick had been plucked and gutted, and was roasting on struts above the campfire's flicker.

'Nowadays they remain just good friends, it's said. In private they're social equals who share similar tastes and experiences. That often happens between an *eromenos* and his *erastes*, doesn't it?' I concluded knowingly.

I had raised the issue which all youths of the Bithynian upper classes must address through their maturing years. Until our full beard is evident are we supposed to remain celibate until our wedding day, or are we to sow youthful oats? But how, where, and with who?

In lieu of the availability of girls of our own class, whose virginity is securely protected from all males until matrimony, are we to depend on the erotic services of expensive *hetaerae* consorts, or importune our household slaves, or common sex workers, or other women or males of available inclination? Alternatively, were we to take a more senior guy as our *erastes* mentor, weapons trainer, social network guide, companion, and sex partner?

'What events will your household pay prizes to?' I asked Antinous as I tore the roasted chick in two to offer his portion. The campfire flames danced before our eyes. Night had swiftly fallen, so deep swigs from a shared wineskin washed the fowl flesh down. The sweet dark wine was our respective vineyards' own drop. It helped warm our insides now our dried loincloths and tunics warmed our exteriors.

'Will you offer money or food when Caesar is here? And what will you compete in yourself, Ant? Foot races, of course.'

I was envious of my friend's sprinting skills, especially in full-dress heavy *hoplite* armor. He had far greater stamina than I. But my body-weight was useful in wrestling matches, even when age-matched.

'Father says he'll fund major prizes as usual, and I'll enter the wrestling bouts in our age group even though I'm not fully in condition," Antinous offered with a knowing grin. "With luck, you and I will draw lots to wrestle again, eh, Lys? It's my turn to take you down this time. Those recently-bearded ones at the *palaestra* who watch us both so closely must be missing their regular dose of naked flesh to letch over. You and I haven't grappled nude in front of them since the meet at Heraclea in July, so they'll be hot for it I guess? But I'm already training for the javelin cast and sprint races too, so you should enter the wrestle challenge at least.'

We both devoured our roasted flesh noisily as we talked. Then Antinous became thoughtful for a few moments.

'I've a very good chance in the sprint-in-armor in my age group, and I'm a possible for the *pentathlon*. You can't win everything, you know Lys, but I'll sure give it a try. This isn't the Olympics or the Pythians where hard cash goes to a winner. These are show matches for Caesar! Greek *arete* is on show!'

As *meirakia* young men, Antinous and I were mature enough to train with the heavier, more dangerous weapons of the *palaestra*. We were senior cadets in the *Polis* Militia and no longer fell under the guardianship of our family's *paidagogoi*, the chaperone slave who keeps older, hassling-with-intent men at a proper distance from us.

Antinous's family line proudly derived of Hellene origin from Mantinea in Arcadia at the Peloponnese, and provided warriors as auxiliaries to Rome's legions in combat at Dacia, Pannonia, Parthia, and Armenia. I'm told Antinous was a late pregnancy to his mother, who died in childbirth. Perhaps he was a 'happy accident', considering ten years separated him from his first-born brother. It was said his father had North Land maternal blood, so both his sons and an intermediate daughter possess hints of the fair hair, blue-gray doe eyes, and clear complexion of the Rus tribes of the Far Frozen Quarter. It's an appealing look.

His father Telemachus was still living then, but was infirm due to old war wounds. Antinous's married Elder Brother managed their estates, plantations, and timber businesses. They traded in hardwood timbers harvested from the Pontine Mountains for the ship-building workshops at Nicomedia and across the Aegean Sea, often in partnership with Lord Arrian to share costs and risks.

I am the son of Lysander of Claudiopolis, born at my father's townhouse at Nicomedia, capital of Bithynia-Pontus I had already turned eighteen in March that year, so I was already a *meirakion*. My clan too was of Greek warrior origin from the city of Mantinea at Arcadia. They migrated to Bithynia many generations ago. My father was of the landowning nobility of Bithynia who fought with the Greek cavalry auxiliaries of the Legions under Trajan. He was wounded and died of his injuries after battle against the barbarians at Pannonia a month before my birth. My family under my Elder Brother's inheritance as *paterfamilias* possesses estates dealing in grain, sheep, horses, leather, and timber.

Antinous and I are related by clan as officiates of the cult of Apollo, Healer of Heaven. This gives us wide contacts in the province. We had shared tutors together as children; played and sported together with other children of our caste; and spent our *palaestra* years in countless wrestling bouts, archery matches, swordplay, athletics, and other competitive games. Above all, we enjoyed each other's company. But the time was approaching for us to complete our education in Athens, far from home across the Aegean Seas.

'Do you still think about Athens, Ant?' I asked as he stoked the fire and added extra brushwood to keep the heat going. 'Are we going to do it?'

I was sitting close by Antinous to maintain body warmth in the increasing chill of night. We shared warming squirts from the carved-bone nozzle of one of the two leather wine bladders our ponies had carried around their necks into the Pontine ranges.

'Father says he's willing to cough up the costs for finishing my education, so I guess it's going to be alright,' Antinous offered while staring distractedly into the flames. 'He says we should think about making the journey early after winter in the new year. Perhaps in March at the beginning of the sailing season, he says. He's willing to pay for a whole year's stay at Athens, including schooling and gymnasium fees.'

'My Elder Brother says if I accompany a cargo of timber to Piraeus near Athens, the family can justify the expenses for the remainder of the year. Isn't that exciting?' I enthused.

'Father has already made enquiries through Arrian with letters to a former cavalry companion at Athens named Herodes,' Antinous continued as we intently studied the inner patterns of the flickering flames before us. 'Herodes is Bithynia's *proxenos* at Athens as well as being Prefect of the Free Ports of the East, Father says.

The man has a son of the same name, Herodes, who's been contracted to seek living quarters, servants, horses, and all that on our behalf. He's also applied for entry to the School of Secundus at Athens to complete our education. Secundus is a highly-regarded teacher of rhetoric and philosophy. His school is Stoic, but of the older moderate Stoics not one of those new puritans who suppress emotions. Father says these new Stoics are extremists who rail against all pleasures, even sex itself unless it's strictly done for baby making. They demand restraint to the point of abstinence.

Neither Father nor my tutors accept the new puritans. We'd all have to become celibate or, alternatively, we'd end up with too many mouths to feed. Then we'd have to dispose of all the unwanted ones. No one agrees with killing babies. But celibacy isn't the answer, at least not for hot bloods like us. So it's all happening, Lys.'

After a few more wine-sack passes, we had mellowed to a mood for approaching sleep. While the two mountain ponies lightly grazed nearby with an occasional snort and snuffle, we two crawled together under our shared horse backcloths. We stayed close by the fire to keep warm. With my tongue now loosened by wine, I had a provocative question to ask my friend.

'Tell me, Ant, is it true that the *ephebe* captain of the town militia, Phaenius, the guy who won the *pentathlon* at Nicomedia two years ago, has propositioned you to be his *eromenos*?'

I immediately clammed shut when I realized I'd asked more than I was entitled to ask. Antinous was ominously silent for a few moments.

'How did you find out?' he eventually asked.

'It was all the talk of the *palaestra* a week ago.'

'The truth is, Lys, I didn't know anything about it at the time. But the guy is obviously a blabber-mouth. He asked Father for the permission rather than ask me. I knew he had his eye upon me around the *palaestra* yard and in the baths over the past year, but the old *gymnasiarch* kept moving him on. I didn't take him seriously. I bet he had his eye on the other unattached guys too, probably including you, Lys.

It seems every older boy who sports chin fuzz wants to get into your groin these days? That's unless they already have a companion of their own to fuck around with.

But Phaenius formally asked Father for me to be his *eromenos*, Father told me later. It's very flattering but it's a damn stupid thing to ask. Father would always have asked me first. So instead Father said 'No, go ask Antinous.'

My friend with the disheveled blond hair and wine dribbling down his chin remained thoughtful for a few moments before continuing.

'I guess he sensed he had no chance with me. Yet I suppose he's a good catch for somebody, yes, Lys? He's a top athlete and militia man, he's good with weapons, he's from a wealthy family, and has good contacts with Romans. His physique has its admirers too, he's very trim.

But he's also up himself. He thinks he's really special. Besides, Lys, he's not my type, if I have a type, that is? I told Father I was still very unsure about the *eromenos/erastes* thing anyway. He understands. I don't think I want someone I don't respect trying to mount me, Lys. I'm not that desperate.'

After a moment I took my opportunity at last. 'So, what is your type then, Ant?'

I think my query was somewhat transparent to Antinous. He sensed how perhaps I secretly aspired to be his *erastes* myself. Antinous considered his reply carefully amid the mellow haze of the wine. We both knew each other so well, and shared so many values and experiences, that the idea of being confirmed as a 'couple' until our maturity as bearded *ephebes* wasn't necessarily an outlandish one.

In Bithynia same-age couples are not typical but not unknown, as long as it wasn't a *cinaedus* style of relationship, whatever that really means. But there would always be the problem of deciding who was mentor and who the mentored?

This led to the sensitive issue of who imposed on who if sex was to be a facet of the relationship. And the issue of who *tops* and who *bottoms* would quickly surface for lads like us. Sex was at the very forefront of our being and existence.

You probably appreciate, gentlemen, from your own youthful days, how Bithynians in their sexually-charged *meirakion* years fulfill a 'boys will be boys' role. That's despite the fine sentiments of ancient philosophers or religious crackpots. They expect their pals to do good things for each other, but with some restraint rather than abandon. I'm not too sure if much restraint is actually practiced though. Sex makes its own rules in a guy's life.

Yet we also both also understood it is customary for the *erastes* to provide gifts of armor or weaponry to his *eromenos*, to teach advanced fighting skills in continual practice, to provide mutual public protection, and to join drinking parties to share wild times and possibly sex with other young aristocrats or enjoying the services of slaves or sex workers. Ultimately it is important the *erastes* introduce his *eromenos* to new social connections among our peers. This also provides networking opportunities for later life in the military, in trade, or in government.

The usual reciprocal exchange for these gestures, as well as the glue to their rapport, is obviously going to be sex. After a lifetime of observing strict emotional distance from the senior males of our lives, we were at an age where closeness takes a priority in our affairs.

'What's my type, Lys? I'm duty-bound by Father to enter a marriage contract with Deianira, a cousin on my deceased mother's side of the family, when she comes of age and her dowry matures. This is my 'type' and destiny, Lys,' Antinous affirmed. 'It is my Father's command. Yet Deianira is still a wee babe. Even menarche is five years away.'

At Bithynia, gentlemen, we and our caste understand how the postponement of marriage with its expenses in child-rearing or providing housing is a valuable by-product of the *pedagogy* system. This delay helps control the birth-rate, limits family expenditures, and constrains a dividing of inheritances among land owners. This is especially necessary with such limited arable soil where continuing division may lead to uneconomic fragmentation.

'My type?' Antinous repeated. 'I don't know if I have a type, Lys. Of all the guys at the *palaestra* hankering to smooth-talk me into sex, few inspire me to return the gesture let alone waggle my tail at them. In fact, except for you and our personal rat pack, I don't feel any desire to share the company, let alone the flesh, of those guys.

I feel misused by the ones who eye us too saucily, Lys, regardless of their high status or superior fighting skills or fine physiques. So I wish they'd stop staring at me and my private parts when we're training or competing. It's very flattering, but it distracts me.'

Through the warm fug of wine I felt obliged to reassure him.

'They're probably just appreciating your form, Ant. You're developing very well, you know, in all things,' I heard myself offering. 'I overhear the whispers about you after wrestling bouts or watching you sprinting or casting javelin. They admire your shape plus your personal cool. Many secretly fancy you, and some not so secretly.'

'No, Lys,' Antinous corrected me, 'they're just checking out your flesh, your privates, or your butt. They're also fantasizing whether you *go-off* like a broody mare on heat and scream 'have me, have me!' I've already seen lewd ditties scratched on walls in *Polis* about me, Lys, cruel ones, ones which insult my lineage. They were probably scrawled by the fool Phaenius after Father said 'No!'

They're insulting limericks claiming I'm a no-good fuck who's happy to go with anyone for money, while my mother's a whore and my Father's a *cinaedus* reprobate.

We both know none of that is true, Lys! I've never done it with anyone, not even you my best friend, despite our jerk-off competitions sometimes. Mother died long ago and Father is certainly no *cinaedus*! So I had to sneak out after dark with a brace of slaves to protect me against night goons to whitewash the graffiti away.'

The flames in the campfire had reduced to a comforting glow. The occasional consoling snort of a pony and the distant cry of a night bird added to the wine-mellow mood of the night. The moon shone hazily behind racing autumn clouds. Honesty was now on the agenda.

'I could never prostitute myself, Lys, nor could you,' Antinous declared. 'We're too choosy, and it's beneath us anyway. We both know our names would be erased from the city roll and we'd never hold our heads high among our people again. Civic Law would prohibit us from serving on the town council or ever voting in the Assembly, because we might sell our vote just as we sold our body.

Father would then disown me utterly or have me killed outright, and I wouldn't blame him. My inheritance, for what it's worth as a second son, would be forfeit. And my betrothed bride Deianira, the baby cousin I've only met once, would have the dowry oath cancelled. It would be as death to me!'

My friend with his fading summer tan of golden skin and his shock of blond hair protested aloud. Silence prevailed for some moments while the flames crackled and snapped.

'Lys, tell me, is it really important to have an *erastes*?' Antinous muttered moodily. 'Am I missing something? Do you feel you need an *erastes* in your life?'

There was another long pause. I wasn't sure of the answer, but in this brooding fireside exchange approaching sleep now hovered languorously in the air.

'It depends on who it is, I suppose,' I replied reluctantly. 'Most of our rat-pack have already paired-off with some guy with good connections or fighting skills who has been approved by their father. Others have done so on the sly with fuck-buddies because the approval might not be forthcoming for the guy they're keen on. The rest of the lads are still playing around, showing-off their pecs and abs at the *palaestra*, or flirting with anyone who takes their fancy.

But being with your own *erastes* has its advantages, I guess? It gives a fellow real status. At least you can walk the street hand-in-hand proudly with a true friend,' I offered chirpily. 'Not only are you viewed as the *alpha* males of your generation, you're quietly getting your rocks off together while everyone pretends not to notice. Girls-for-pay are no ongoing substitute, they have no conversation, they've never been taught to read or write, they know nothing of a man's world, their trade obliges them to be unfaithful, and they're probably lice-ridden or poxed to boot. Their last customer was probably your worst enemy at the *palaestra*, so you're probably swimming in that guy's pool. Yuck!'

'Yet I sometimes feel a loss not having someone close, Lys,' Antinous reckoned. 'My family, our tutors, our slaves, our school chums are all good company, including you too Lys. I love you all, but being really close to someone special would be different. Even closer than we are. And it's not just about sex or status. It's about having a *friend*. Even something more than a friend. Someone really special. Someone who returns your concerns, who knows you well, who shares your life just as you do theirs.'

My schoolchum trailed off thoughtfully.

'Isn't that what they say your wife will be when she eventually gets to know you, even if it takes ten years?' I suggested. 'Yet if one of us does take an *erastes*, Ant, surely it should be someone we feel at ease with, don't you think? Someone you can rely on. Someone who's there for you,' I concluded, inserting a barely veiled plea for my own cause. But it didn't wash with him.

He had turned away from the fire and tucked himself beneath the mantles and horse back-cloths to lie curled for body warmth. He gave no reply as daydreams and ambitions swept both our minds. My eyelids too now drifted closed as we pressed together for warmth. The fire's glow ebbed low as the chill in the air deepened. Sleep rapidly descended.

From here on I must speak chivalrously, gentlemen. You can make of it what you will. Yes, I am proud of my ardor, of my passion, of my intensity. I too am flesh and blood. So I will speak honestly to you.

To achieve warmth against the mountain air I found myself pressing closer to Ant's dozing trunk. I huddled close against his warm flesh and his thick mane of honey-pale hair. My arms arced around him to bind him closer. Yes, I could sense the hard tissues beneath his tunic, feel the places where bone meets bone, where bone meets skin, and where rounded flesh melds into one's own contours. It is a pleasing, comforting sensation.

I could study by the light of the flickering fire the shadowy outline of the nape of his neck with its graceful downward flow and blond mane. To me his shoulders' breadth, his neck muscles, and even his nape's hairline had a sculpted beauty all their own.

I could smell the residue of olive-oil rub lingering on his skin while the hunter's sweat smarted saltily from his tunic. His body had its own fresh scents which I long ago identified and recognized for the special aroma which is *him*.

While holding fast to him for warmth in the chill, I was close enough to savor his pulsing heart. I could match my breathing rhythm with his inhalations. To be so closely intertwined with flesh and blood you respect, you greatly admire, is deeply satisfying. His natural honesty and clarity of insight added to the appeal of his sleek form and tight muscularity.

It soon dawned on me how an unanticipated erection pressing against his frame was matched by his own member nudging my fist furled lazily by his crutch. In our sleepy, wined state we both delayed horny action, I guess, purely to enjoy the treat of being bound so close to each other's flesh. Do I need to remind you, gentlemen, what an intoxicating sensation it is to be so intimate with someone you idolize?

Sometime during the course of the night, propelled by vivid dreams and arousing imagery, a discharge of moisture was implanted excitedly between one set of crossed thighs. A surge of the Elixir of Eros accompanied by ecstatic shudders and sighs was ejected onto a thigh's flesh at a tunic's hem. It followed an extended, unhurried, period of grasping togetherness. The thrilling emission induced swooning calm. Yes, gentlemen, it felt pretty good. I'm sure you know what I mean?"

The group including Surisca heard-out Lysias's account in rapt silence.

"Later, the other companion was patiently, lovingly, coaxed to emit a similarly elated discharge. Rapid breathing and suppressed moans accompanied the heady rush of fulfillment. Yes, our natural appetites had been satisfied. Youth's driven sensuality had been shared between two friends in honor, gentlemen. I for one cherish only pride and strength in this.

The night's silence then fell once more as the campfire's flickers declined to dawn's drifting wisps.

Guys will be guys, we all know sirs. After all, Antinous and I were the closest of friends. We were *companions*. I for one found my buddy to be utterly *unselfish* in sharing his body's needs and favors.

You see, our hunter's trek into the forests of the Pontine Ranges delivered more than a herd of renegade horses or a harvest of extra edibles to augment a season's limited diet. Our journeys cemented an unspoken, bodily bond between we two *Sons of Apollo*."

Lysias lapsed at last into silence and stared broodily at the floor while toying at a rug with his foot.

The group watched on silently, transfixed by the candor of his testimony. Each of the men recalled long-forgotten episodes from days of old when their lives seemed more audacious in their possibilities.

The woman Surisca had heard nothing new at all.

CHAPTER 8

"We too should be thinking about sleep," Clarus muttered at last. "We must prepare ourselves for the morrow's interviews. Then we should continue our interrogation of Lysias, followed by a select list of others. More than half a day of Hadrian's two-day allowance will have passed by dawn."

Secretary Vestinus had quietly rejoined the group during Lysias's testimony.

Suetonius looked around at his companions. They were visibly tired already, except perhaps the lovely Surisca seated silently behind him. She seemed as bright-eyed as ever, probably due to her youth and because her professional duties would normally run late into night.

The Praetorian officer Quintus Urbicus remained standing at attention while his two junior officers stood at ease by one of the chamber entrances.

Vestinus spoke. He was long experienced in working late into the night on his master's bidding.

"I have cleared four chambers in apartments immediately beyond these offices to accommodate your staff, Clarus," he stated in proper protocol to the most senior of the investigation.

"They're not especially glamorous due to being workrooms or storerooms until only hours ago, but I've had folding beds delivered to each chamber along with some basic furniture. I suggest Suetonius shares the largest with you, Clarus, as sleeping quarters, with the remaining team scattered among the other three.

The four chambers open onto a communal space which you may wish to utilize as an interview room, or whatever. It's not grandiose, but it's convenient."

"You are most kind, Julius Vestinus," Suetonius soothed as smoothly as he could, "but I might prefer to share one of the bedchambers with my personal assistant, Surisca of Antioch. I don't mind which room, Julius, any will do. Perhaps Senator Clarus will take the larger chamber for himself?"

He made a point of deferring to his honored *patron* while at the same time putting his tag on Surisca for the duration. He deceived no one.

"Whatever, whatever, Special Inspector," Vestinus muttered with a raised eyebrow. Clarus politely confirmed the arrangement with a tired nod.

"All I need is sleep," he announced wearily. "It's been a long day, and tomorrow will be even longer. We should consider, Suetonius, the list to be interviewed and what chores to pursue in the interim."

Suetonius turned to the Praetorian, Urbicus.

"You heard from the two fishermen earlier how they saw a vessel sailing the Nile at first light. They said it was neither a local vessel nor river folk they recognized. I require, Praetorian, that you return to the fishermen at tomorrow's first light to take them on a search of the moorings at Besa to locate this mysterious vessel. They will recognize it, I'm sure. I want to know whose boat it was and who were its sailors so early at dawn on the day of the lad's death? However, Praetorian, neither the owner of the craft nor its sailors are to know of our enquiry; it is to remain secret at this time. I want this information within three hours of dawn."

Urbicus nodded, saluted briskly, and was preparing to depart with his two officers. Suetonius guessed they would probably take a nap before their dawn duties, but he could see Urbicus was intent on prosecuting his search promptly.

Surisca raised a finger to politely interject.

"Master," she whispered deferentially, "may I speak?"

The assembled group was startled by her lapse of protocol, but Suetonius found himself nodding approval to her under Clarus's glare.

"Forgive my presumption, master, but do you have a description of the boat or its boatmen? Did the fishermen describe the craft?" she asked softly.

Suetonius confirmed her voice had a much deeper, more somber tone than the flighty girlish trills displayed at *The House of the Blue Lotuses*. The transformation had definite appeal.

Surisca continued.

"If it is not a vessel known to fishermen at Besa and Hermopolis, it could be one known to those of us elsewhere on the Nile. I have travelled widely on the river, and most of the worthier craft possess owner's markings for easy identification. Disputes over theft and ownership are commonplace."

Unprompted, Strabon immediately began rummaging through the large basket whose folded waxpad notebooks were secured in its bowl. He pulled one from the pile, opened its covers, and scanned his notation scratches.

"The fisherman Ani said --- 'it was a strong timber vessel, well made and costly,' Strabon read aloud, '--- perhaps it was a boat sailed by priests from upstream for The Isia, or a boat belonging to Pharaoh's .. that is, .. Caesar's people. It was *painted the color of the sky and possessed the Eye Of Horus upon its prow.*"

"*Painted the color of the sky and possessing the Eye Of Horus...,*" Surisca repeated. "If I'm not mistaken this describes a craft belonging to the priests of Amun at Memphis. I have performed at Memphis on many occasions and sailed the river nearby often. The priests of the Old Religion, who are thought very wealthy, have been my clients. They pay well, but are not gracious in their behavior. Amun has temples on both banks of the Nile at Memphis and elsewhere, so the priests do much sailing to communicate between their properties.

At Memphis they paint their boat and mule carts, and even the gates of their compound, sky-blue to ward off evil, and are marked with the Eye Of Horus to denote their ownership. At Thebes upstream from here their possessions are white, but with the same Horus marking. I'd say the boat described here belongs to Amun's priests at Memphis."

Suetonius's mind tried to comprehend Surisca's term *'performed at Memphis'* in its possibilities, but he recalled how Surisca was also a dancer and flautist so he desisted. Her profession was her own business, though clients who were not *'gracious'* had a prurient interest.

"And here at Besa or Hermopolis? Where do they congregate?" the Praetorian Urbicus asked.

Suetonius let this further protocol lapse pass because it was the next logical question anyway. Urbicus's prompt initiative boded well for the investigation's time-pressured enquiry. Heads turned towards Surisca for her reply.

"Amun does not have much property at either Besa on the east bank, or Hermopolis on the western, because the Old Religion is deemed heretical and idolatrous by the devotees of the Greek cults. At Hermopolis, a town the locals call Shmun, they favor Serapis. Their fanatical followers will fight to the death between themselves. They will kill each other and eat the other's livers and hearts to argue a fine point of doctrine," Surisca said.

"They ruled this land at the time of the Old Pharaohs. They had the ancient rulers under their thumbs. Their god Amun was the major deity before the Greeks and Romans came. Their riches are still very great but carefully hidden.

When Caesar Augustus took Egypt from the last Greek ruler, Queen Cleopatra, and confiscated the best river land as his own property, Amun's wealth and influence declined, I've been told. They lost most of their best plantations, their source of wealth, but retained their temple compounds with their influence over the peasants but costly upkeep.

However since the violent expulsion of rebellious Judaeans at Alexandria in the days of the previous Caesar, Trajan --- I am told Judaeans were once a quarter of the city's population --- these priests have been buying up available property at cut-rate prices. They're hungry for political influence to re-establish their cult, so owning property is the best path to wealth and influence.

Nowadays in Besa they reside at the small, very ancient temple outside the town by the riverside. The temple lies on high ground above an inlet adjacent to where Caesar's two barques are moored. It's hard to find, it is so well hidden in the palms."

"Where did you learn all this history, woman?" Clarus enquired with astonishment.

Surisca hung her head demurely, as befits a mere woman.

"The wisest of my trade keep an eye of such matters, my lord. We must be prudent stewards of our own hard-earned wealth, and so we follow such things," Surisca replied.

Urbicus looked to the group for new instructions.

"Centurion Quintus Urbicus," Suetonius commanded, "search for such a vessel with the two fishermen. If you find the vessel, confirm the boat's owner and report on who was sailing this craft on the night or morning of Antinous's death. Report to me no later than three hours after sunrise tomorrow.

And, Praetorian, do not wear your Guard uniforms, dress in more informal clothes which will not arouse suspicion. Blend with the lower orders, Centurion."

Urbicus saluted and swept away accompanied by his two troops.

"Thank you, Surisca," Suetonius proffered as graciously as he could. "You've earned your keep already."

The courtesan smiled weakly at this unlikely prospect.

"Julius Vestinus," Suetonius called, "your staff will be in a position to make contact tonight with each of the following list of people to make them available to us at hourly intervals tomorrow for interview. They should be in the following order ---

First, Lysias immediately after sunrise. Perhaps Geta the Dacian at one hour after sunrise. Senator Arrian of Bithynia at two hours after sunrise, and the slave Thais of Cyrene at three hours after sunrise, so we can get a grasp on the entire situation. Other names are likely to arise in the course of our interviews. This should give us coverage of the important people in Antinous's life, and perhaps even his death.

Julia Balbilla of the empress's household at *The Dionysus* moored offshore can join us at high sun, with the Master of the Hunt, Salvius Julianus, or the Egyptian miracle-worker Pachrates waiting until soon after. We will probably have others to follow, but we must move speedily."

Surisca once again raised a timorous hand. The biographer nodded.

"Did you say *Pachrates* the Egyptian priest, master?" she asked hesitantly.

"Yes, Surisca, I did," Suetonius said. By acknowledging her familiar name he had tacitly acknowledged she was now a *person,* not a functionary of no status or particular gender.

"Why, my dear? Do you know something of this priest?"

"I know things about him, master, from my trade," she replied. But then she became silent.

"Tell us, my dear," Suetonius prompted, "what do you wish to say?"

It seemed Surisca had resiled abruptly from making a comment about Pachrates.

"Come on, my dear. Feel free to talk."

"I am mistaken, my lord, I confused the name with another. Please forgive me, master."

But Suetonius didn't think she was deceiving anyone in the chamber. They each realized she was hiding something of interest. Clarus interjected.

"Woman, if you have something to tell us, then tell us. Otherwise hold your tongue or do not speak," he commanded in his booming magisterial tone.

Clarus was likely to consider Surisca an uneducated foreigner of zero social status, plus a mere woman at that, who offended the proper pecking order of knowledge.

"We'll talk later," Suetonius said to Surisca with an evasive wink to ease the rebuff.

Lysias began to rise from his chair.

"Am I to be discharged, my lords, from further interview tonight?" he asked politely. Suetonius shook his head.

"No, Bithynian. We have barely begun. We must continue your interview to learn all we can about your deceased friend. Time presses upon us."

Clarus and Vestinus heaved sighs of regret. Suetonius continued.

"We have only two days to discover how and why Antinous has died. So be seated, lad. You still have not told us how Caesar came to be involved with you two fellows. We need to know. Yes, you have told us of your mutual thoughts about the *erastes/eromenos* custom, and of your personal friendship, but you haven't told us how you caught Caesar's eye. Explain it to us!"

Lysias drew himself back into his seat and fumbled distractedly with clothing items.

"It is an involved story, sirs. Two weeks after our hunting trek into the Pontines, Antinous and I competed in games at *Polis* in honor of Great Caesar's visit. We wrestled, we sprinted in armor, we cast javelin. Both Ant and I were victors in various games before Caesar's eyes.

Some days later we were summoned by Caesar's marshals to attend an Imperial Hunt being held at Councilor Arrian's estates outside Nicomedia. This was a very great honor, so we took to the opportunity with relish. I can recall that day and night well, yet we had several questions about our participation."

Lysias shifted once again into reminiscence mode and began his recollections.

"I wonder why there'll be only five or six of us?" Antinous asked me as our two ponies Tiny and Blaze ambled along a dusty road outside Nicomedia.

We were followed by our wagon stacked with provisions drawn by donkeys, and four walking servants, two spare colts in tow, plus the mule recently snared in the Pontine forests.

"Surely an Imperial Hunt would attract guys from all over the province, wouldn't it? Keen hunters would appear from everywhere," Antinous added. I too wondered about this.

"Maybe today's hunt is strictly for some special purpose? Lord Arrian said it was an occasion that should make us proud. Arrian seems to know all these things," I proposed. "Arrian and my family Elder said our *palaestra* wins before Caesar were the deciding factor. Caesar's assessment of the winners in their events was crucial. I beat you in the wrestle-bout as usual, Ant, and you won your javelin and armored sprint event outright, so maybe Caesar has summoned the has summoned the key victors for a special celebration?"

"Yet not a single one of the other victors at the *Polis* games has been invited, Lys. Just we two, plus several others from across the province who didn't even compete in our games. There must be some other reason we don't yet know?"

We turned a corner of the trail where the landscape ahead opened out.

"*Great Apollo*, Lys! We're there! There it is!" I recall Antinous gasping.

Our party arrived at Arrian's countryside complex of stud farm, vineyards, and vegetable gardens around a palatial villa. It lies a few miles inland from the port of Nicomedia by the Sea of Marmara. The farm was the essential acreage necessary to provision Arrian's lifestyle.

But beyond the cultivated gardens and grazing paddocks lay a vast assembly of tents, pavilions, and marquees. It was the touring Imperial Household. It was the first time Ant and I had seen Caesar's famous portable palace. The massed array of tents was defended by troops bristling with armor and weapons which glistened in the morning sun. It was a spectacle of fluttering pennants, high vaulted marquees, and busy workers.

"It's Hadrian's travelling Palatine itself! *Holy Zeus,* Lys!" he yelped.

"I don't know what we did at the boy's games at *Polis*, but obviously Caesar thought we were worth seeing more of!" I found myself spluttering aloud to all.

Our party was greeted by a welcoming cohort of the Guard cavalry. We were escorted into the stockaded tent complex and ambled along its central avenue to its parade ground before a massive Imperial Marquee. It faced a long plain before the tents. This plain extended beyond the pavilions towards low hills.

The plain's rocky scrubland had been netted at the sides by attendants and slaves, with the nets extending into the far distance. It seemed the Hunt was to be held within a controlled funnel of netting, just as the huntsmen of *Polis* construct when trying to entrap a bear or boar to sell unhurt to dealers in animals for the arenas.

Without noticeable ceremony, Caesar Hadrian followed by Lord Arrian and other officials appeared from within the Marquee to greet our two parties. Both men were casually dressed in the long *chiton* tunics and loose *himation* swathes common to the Greek East, not the bulky Roman togas of the west of the Empire.

Hadrian seemed to be somewhat taller in this environment than he had seemed at the show-games the previous fortnight. While the youth of *Polis* were competing naked in the various events in their separate age and weighting grades, Antinous and I – along with all the other lads, youths, and men of the town – craned our necks to have a closer view of the Great Caesar, Hadrian, in our midst.

As you know, no women attend naked sports events, so this was a once-in-a-lifetime opportunity for the men of *Polis* to see their emperor at close hand. At that event Caesar's tall height and military bearing, coupled with his close-cropped beard topped by hair combed forward across his head, may have been camouflaged by his fulsome purple toga with its glittering embroideries of gilt eagles. But now, dressed in a simple Greek tunic, his tall height was evident beside the lesser stature of Arrian and other Greek notables.

To our eyes, Hadrian was lean for his age. He was in his forties somewhere, Ant and I determined, but in very good trim. His features still displayed something of the renowned good looks of his reputation as a playboy prior to becoming *Princeps*. His frame retained the muscle tone of the professional soldier he had been since his youth, as well as displaying several cicatrices earned at the business end of an enemy sharp. Yet his countenance had a quality whose precise years were difficult to estimate.

His attachment to his troops of the twenty-eight Legions around the Empire was said to be expressed by a lifestyle matching the austerities and hardships of a Legionnaire's training and diet. Whatever his legions could do, he could do. His daily regimen included the necessary exercises to ensure bodily condition, with marches in full pack, simple diet, and regularly assisting in digging stockade gutters or even latrine ditches. These shared disciplines endear him to the Legions. It earns their total allegiance.

Hadrian was nonchalantly chewing on a piece of fruit as we dismounted our ponies. He seemed genuinely pleased at our arrival. He and Arrian beamed at our group with broad grins whose informality jolted we youngsters while absolutely astonishing our stewards and slaves into rigidity. How are you supposed to respond when your emperor smiles at you?

"Welcome, fellow Bithynians," Arrian called to us. "You are well on time, friends."

Our entire group automatically fell to our right knees and bowed our heads. "Hail Caesar!" we proclaimed in muddy unison with a salute.

"Greetings, Antinous and Lysias of Claudiopolis," Hadrian called back. "It's a pleasure you should be with us today to enjoy our Hunt. My friend Arrian speaks well of your families and your service to the Empire. I myself commend you on your victories in the sports events of your town," he called as he took a bite from his apple. "Your accomplishments were well noted, I assure you. We hope you settle-in happily here at the quarters provided for your comfort.

Prepare yourselves too to join us at the sixth hour at the start line of the Hunt when the sun reaches full height. Our Hunt promises to be challenging, so use your most effective accessories. Ask my friend the Master of the Hunt, Tribune Julianus, for any details you need. He is your commander today. And don't forget, we will enjoy a feast and symposium at sunset to celebrate the victors of today's chase."

Caesar clapped his hands once and called loudly, "Geta!"

I saw a tall, lean, pale-skinned man of foreign extraction with a close-cut black beard and slicked long black tresses plaited in a barbarian's style step forward to respond smartly.

"Here, Caesar!"

To my eye the fellow was in his late twenties. He had faded tattoo circles across each cheek. He was dressed in an eclectic mix of short Greek tunic, barbarian leggings, Roman open-weave boots, and a looped mantle which was slung across his frame pinioned with an antique *fibula*. Nothing suggested he was of the slave class because of his attire's evident quality and jeweled rings of visible costliness. Nevertheless he responded to Caesar's call with the immediate response of a servant.

"Geta, direct these visitors to their stables and sleeping quarters," Hadrian commanded. "Ensure they receive every service needed for grooming, feeding, and watering their mounts. Also assign staff to provide them refreshments."

"It shall be done, Caesar," Geta replied as he waved us to follow him down a side track of the tent complex.

This was the first Antinous and I ever saw of Geta. We soon came to know him well. And it was our first impression of the emperor himself.

"Your victim today, men," Tribune Salvius Julianus informed us with an injection of respect as adults, or at least mature *meirakia* youths, "will be a young boar."

The various groups of youths and their staff murmured appreciatively if apprehensively. Julianus was Hadrian's Master of the Hunt who was also an advisor in the Law of Rome.

"The beast was trapped two weeks ago in the scrubland of the Troas near the site of legendary Troy," the Master of the Hunt continued. "Perhaps it holds the soul of the warriors Ajax or Hector? It is a junior from a herd of adults whose feistier members were caged for shipment to the arenas at Rome where wild game is in high demand. So your target is smaller than a full size beast.

You should be told the creature has had its tusks filed to a dull edge to protect you against accident or misadventure. Caesar doesn't want to send one of you men home to your family hearths with body damage.

Being a boar, you are to prosecute the Hunt with whatever mount and weapons you see fit for the challenge," Julianus continued. "No hounds are permitted; you will be obliged to rely on your own detection and hunting skills. The victim will be loosed into a netted funnel to ensure its eventual capture. But Caesar hopes members of the Hunt will corral and destroy the creature long prior to its entrapment. It's up to you, men."

Antinous murmured quietly to me. "It's lucky, Lys, we brought our own ponies for this event, mounts who already know our weight, purchase, and signals, plus who trust us. I expected the Hunt victim to be a deer or something more elegant than a boar. Boars are eccentric targets. It'll need deft footwork and daring. This won't be easy without mastiffs, either."

I had to nod in agreement.

"If we work together as a team, Lys, as in the Pontines, maybe we'll manage it," Antinous whispered back.

Instead of the usual workaday back-cloths for bareback riding, we had brought our family's new-fangled four-horned saddles. The saddles' four corner pummels and seat are secured by a belly strap under the horse. This permits a better seat leverage than a back blanket, so a rider can more effectively brace himself to hurl a range of missiles. But only barely.

For weapons we assessed between lightweight short-javelins, throwing axes, bows-and-arrows, or even slingshot stones, none of which are to be disparaged. Both of us were well experienced in attacking with lightweight counter-weighted short-stave javelins projecting five-inch iron pierces for horseback hunting. Neither of our ponies, Blaze nor Tiny, nor we ourselves possessed the body-weight and expertly-braced riding seat necessary for wielding the long, heavy *pilum* spear used by cavalrymen. The *pilum* demands a large charger with a rider of a beefier body build than a *meirakion* carries.

Despite our physical strengths which, since childhood competitive wrestling, sprint racing in armor, javelin casting, stone discus tossing, and the other athletics of the *palaestra* had built, we still had a little distance to go before our body weight could anchor the heftier battle weapons.

Nevertheless each of we six youngsters were already eligible for entry into military life, as our own fathers had done at the same age. We knew how a commission in the military was the speediest path to public advancement if we survived battle action, scrapes and wounds, foul camp water, disease, or other military perils.

Fortunately, Antinous and I had each brought five plumb-balanced dart javelins in their riding quivers, as well as our family's antique stiff-leather hunting cuirasses, battered helmets, and chipped shin greaves to wear with our hip-length rider's tunics.

The six youngsters appeared a rag-tag mob compared to the richly outfitted officers of the Guard in their service uniforms, or the barbarian costumes in dragon-scale chain-mail of the Scythian archers whose fidgety ponies paced nervously about. We learned how Scythian archers are the precision marksmen of Rome's forces, with the most expert hired by Hadrian's Praetorian Prefect, Turbo, for the special protection of Caesar.

This was the day we first learned of the rule how an Imperial Hunt is one of the few occasions when people around Caesar are entitled to be armed. Except for his Guard, weapons are generally forbidden in Caesar's presence for security reasons.

Meanwhile Hadrian was dressed simply in hunting leathers, helmet, and side-weapons, mounted on a four-pummel saddle strapped atop a high, golden chestnut Nisaean stallion. This exotic stallion was unlike any animal we had ever previously seen. Its gilded pelt shone in the thin midday sun, and it hoofed the ground with spirited life. He was named *Persepolis* after his origin in the wilds of Parthia. To our eyes, *Persepolis* was the perfection of horse flesh.

When the sun reached mid-sky Julianus raised his whip of office to signal to his beaters to sound the display. A *cornu* intoned darkly, drums rattled, and without further ado a cage was flied-open ahead of us.

A squat, hairy, nimble, black ball of furious darting energy was released onto the open plain. The Hunt was on! A dozen horses and their riders of varying sizes, uniforms, and ages leapt forward as one after the beast. The wild boar, all bustle and speed, hurtled forward into the scrub without a moment's hesitation.

Despite the slight incline of the ground and the low rocky scrub, the beast slipped speedily out of sight behind rocks and foliage. The hunting pack had no idea if it was galloping non-stop towards the net funnel far away, or whether it was stalled somewhere beneath our very hooves out of sight. It was obviously canny enough to know when to move out of range, and when to stay still to hide.

Without hounds to smell it out or bark at sight, the creature was the master of the chase, denying we pursuers easy scouting.

Antinous and I, with our plucky ponies at the ready, had lurched forward first, followed by the entire Hunt with much noisy cheering, guffaws, and obscene shouts. Caesar was the third to crash forward on his golden-sheened Nisaean, but no one deferred to his status except the plait-haired barbarian with the tattooed face, Geta.

Each of the young men moved sweepingly across the course, around obstacles, into undergrowth, to seek it out. We each searched carefully for a glimpse of its hairy haunches and upright tail, speeding or stationary.

Now and then one of the boys would excitedly shout a sighting, but then decline the claim as it proved false. This ad hoc approach to tracing the beast didn't appeal to Antinous and I. It lacked method. Half an hour elapsed as the teams eased carefully through the undergrowth searching for any signs of the quarry or its recent path.

Hadrian, the boys perceived, seemed to be in no urgent hurry to prosecute the chase, but ambled watchfully close behind the lads on his Nisaean giant.

Antinous and I followed a strategy we used in our hunts outside *Polis*. We cross-referenced our scanning of the scrub so, as a duo, we applied a methodical stepped sweep to our search. Mind you, using mastiffs makes such hunting far easier. In lieu of dogs, signs of tracks, fresh droppings, broken scrub, hidden shadowy shapes, even smells were to be factored into the possible location or direction of the beast. This process was time consuming but offered a better chance of spotting the creature than mere guesswork. The boar wouldn't appear in our sight simply because we wished it to appear.

Now and then I would silently signal to Antinous with a gesture towards a shape lurking behind a rock, so both of us would arc cautiously towards the site. Again and again, nothing.

On one occasion Antinous quietly point-marked a puddle of still-steaming pig's piss which even Tiny and Blaze found noxious to the nostrils. Yet the boar had moved on. The direction seemed northwards, so we both guided our mounts in parallel in the same direction. Our ponies were as tense as we ourselves.

The other four lads seemed to be captivated by a separate search a hundred yards westwards, each a solitary searcher. The senior members of the hunt ambled lazily in the background, amused by our youthful intensity.

Suddenly with a rustle of foliage, a rasping grunt and cough, a fat furry bewhiskered blob snarling curled tusks leapt forward from a hidden nook and raced helter-skelter northwards. The beast grunted and rasped with each bound, bounce, or sideways dash. Tiny and Blaze lurched forward promptly at speed with a matched swing, sway, and swerve.

Antinous gripped his pony's four-horn saddle firmly with his knees by sheer force of balance. His legs, thighs, and ankles pressed close to Tiny's sides to steady his body weight to support a hold on the reins while his left hand balanced a javelin dart in readiness. Antinous was left-handed, you know. Tiny responded well to his knee pressures and hip sways as it danced through the scrub in speedy dives left then right, following the swerves of the boar with precision.

The wiry pony, all gristle and bone flecked with foamy sweat, knew the name of the game. He took it upon himself to keep close to the prey. The horse was as excited by the hunt as its rider.

Antinous's body swayed smoothly with each shift in direction in a natural flow. Every muscle-fiber danced in a finely-tuned flexed response to the situation's urgency. Yet he retained a firm balance, steady seat, and high stature in readiness for casting the dart.

His speeding reflexes had well absorbed his many years straddling ponies on the forested ranges beyond our hometown's ramparts. Boars and game were regular targets of the hunt at *Polis*. Hunting and trapping was the local recreation which afforded special delicacies for feast days to honor solemn Artemis of the Hunt and her brother, beautiful Apollo, Healer of Heaven.

Yet only the boar knew the next instant's hurtling direction, racing this way and then that, sensing the full danger of the situation and the grim intent of its pursuers.

Hadrian followed close behind, crashing through the scrub on his Nisaean. The eighteen year-olds arced in close proximity. Arrian was followed by Julianus and then Geta the Dacian. Two Praetorians cantered unevenly behind with two dark Scythian archers in close formation. The Praetorians were sullen bodyguards who protected the emperor's person, while the archers were insurance against an unexpected danger.

The wily beast had been bolting hell-bent towards a landfall up ahead camouflaged behind a tangle of surrounding scrub. Antinous raced and scrapped and darted after it, keeping one eye on the grotesque bulk of the creature while marshalling all his reflexive senses into his javelin arm's nerves to respond with precision. With extra dart-javelins in the quiver strapped to his pony's neck if the initial cast failed to bring down the creature, his first attack would nevertheless need to be decisive.

However, in the speed of the hunt Antinous had not noticed the low cave entrance looming ahead, a refuge the pig may have calculated into its rapidly declining options.

I kept my eyes on Antinous as well as the emperor close behind as my own pony Blaze stumbled through the undergrowth somewhat less felicitously than my friend's. I remained a distance behind by necessity of my mount's less focused skill. I was close enough to the emperor to perceive the manner in which Hadrian cast his eye strategically over the victim's narrowing chances.

I perceived the emperor's elegant signal with his left arm to his thudding followers to arc around for a better encirclement of the beast. As his golden Nisaean bounded through the undergrowth with meticulous footwork and a fiery zest typical of the quality breeds, I detected Hadrian smiling to himself at the audacity of the young man racing ahead of him.

Antinous ignored Caesar's *droit de seigneur* of first chance at the kill. Antinous's daring was accompanied by the audacity to lurch into the hunt with heroic, if reckless, even ill-considered, abandon.

I had always appreciated this 'strike first' quality in Antinous. I found it to be a challenging facet of his character and one which gained him many victors' points on the *palaestra's* wrestling sands. But a sense of diplomacy and the unspoken protocol of the occasion restrained my urges --- not that Blaze gave me much opportunity for anything better. I remember asking myself, was I simply less feisty than my young friend? Antinous becomes fiercely tenacious under pressure.

From the short distance behind Tiny, I could see how Hadrian was closely observing Antinous's every action. My blond friend's excited tensions of musculature in neck, arms, shoulders, and thighs displayed their much-exercised tone as his entire physique poured forward from his saddle towards the urgent resolution of the hunt.

I discerned how Hadrian eyed the flecked fair hair streaming from beneath the rusty helmet, the occasional splash of sweat spraying behind, and the straining arm balancing the raised javelin for a powerful discharge.

As a friend who had known Antinous since earliest childhood I could appreciate the flowing line of his distended neck and its delineated nape of strands of coiled blond locks. His upper-body triangle of broad shoulders encased in an heirloom cuirass tapering to a slender waist projected those sinuous contours which only an agile young man's slender hips, lean thighs, and tight butt proclaim to the world. These were coupled with a roseate flush of excitement on high cheekbones as he focused on the issue at hand.

I readily recalled observing these engaging qualities in Antinous many times during the hurly-burly of wrestling bouts or sprint races at the *palaestra*, where men practice naked and women are not permitted. I was certainly not the only member of the gymnasium crowd, old or young, to appreciate my friend's rapidly developing features. In those days I overheard many flattering tributes among the shared whispers of spectators whose eyes lingered on my friend's natural symmetries.

In the past year Antinous's athleticism and condition had bloomed in a sharply defined way which, even though I was almost a year older, matched or exceeded my own shape.

All the young men's anatomies were rapidly achieving the cut delineation of those sinuous Olympic champions' statues which studded the gymnasium at *Polis*, and which were our icons of manly attributes. Such bodily powers announce a youth's real entry into the company of adults and the true beginning of life. Yet I already suspected Antinous would peak even further into a striking handsomeness, perhaps even a vigorous manly beauty, as athletic people often do.

The *gymnasiarch* at *Polis*, the controller of discipline at the *palaestra*, seemed to give Antinous and I special heed in shooing away older obsequious flatterers among the gym's bearded generations. Lewd comments and provocative whistles at the naked, smoothly hairless young men were commonplace. But flattery or not, Antinous always seemed completely unaware of this brazen prurience. Perhaps he simply ignored it.

In those days I recalled how my early choice of boyhood pal had been a shrewd if unaware investment in a friendship which now was bearing unanticipated fruit. We had met simply because we were distantly related by clan, while our age-groups and land owning social status had us participate in the same liturgical functions each year at the sacred festivals of Apollo. Our social background, personal interests, schooling, and neighborly contact coincided. Besides, as kids we simply always had good fun together.

But that was before the onrush of puberty. In our fourteenth year when we were endowed by our elders with the coming-of-age necklet holding a *phallus* talisman celebrating our attainment of virility, we realized it was none too soon as we became urgently, hotly sexual. Unprovoked erections arose spontaneously. Night emissions followed astonishingly lurid dreams.

When racy imaginings excited us, which was often, we could ejaculate barely at a touch, like randy mastiffs spraying. Self-relief became a daily obsession, repeatedly. Our anatomies brought us pleasures we had never anticipated. We then became conscious of the intimate nature of the bonding alliances which were discreetly forming among other youths around us. Our peers were quietly pairing off one-by-one with others more senior. Persistent flattery, knowing winks, and audacious touches made their intended impact on susceptible lusts.

On occasion I had been spied by Antinous intently watching him from a distance at weapons practice or sports training admiring his person and physique. My gaze lingered on him on the pretext of studying his strategic maneuvers. It kidded no one, especially not Antinous.

Sometimes he and I would blush in unison when our eyes met after an intense body-contact bout which stirred surprising emotions and their unexpected bodily expression. The *palaestra* onlookers would grin knowingly and pass winking glances to each other.

Our friendship now became sensitive to the other's innermost needs, thoughts, and emotions, while at the same time being too shy to be too bold in our presumptions. But we began to tacitly understand that if either of us were obliged to form a liaison with another guy it would probably be with each other, not an older youth of higher social status or greater sports prestige. At least that's what I hoped.

When our pubic hair had concluded sprouting and our voices had deepened, our sex drives commandeered our lives. On occasions Antinous and I playfully teased and toyed with each other's bodily sensuality during respites in our hunting and trapping excursions. It is a period of a young man's life when sexual hunger and its triggers seem to be so irrepressibly insistent. We fed that hunger. But it could never be fully sated.

We now began to understand the true nature of our Homeric heroes' friendly liaisons which we had previously misconceived. Those warrior's friendships were based on a spiritual rapport, yes, as the classic tales tell, but they were bodily expressed through an openly carnal one. It was what the ancient poets had praised and ancient custom had sanctioned, but we had never understood. Our companionship now assumed a new dimension of intensity.

We found how the simple pleasures of being in each other's company, or sharing the other's small victories or pains, or brushing each other's flesh in rough-and-tumble games, or comparing the cut muscularity of height, jaw line, chest ridge, stomach grid, line of thighs or butt, now stirred a vibrant energy between us. A mutually heartfelt longing descended.

I recall our tutors told us how other peoples than the Hellenes prohibit these sensations between men. They claim it is immoral, shameful, unmanly, and an abomination in the eyes of their gods. They base these beliefs on antique texts from foreign philosophers of the dusty East promoting strange, arcane beliefs. Their credulity makes we Greeks smile.

Young Bithynians are taught how in ancient times the Hellenes formed whole armies of these companionable warriors. Their intimacy was considered sacred. Celebrated tales of warrior couples or armies like the Sacred Band of Thebes began to make sense to us at last. Our teachers of philosophy and rhetoric, who are scholars from across the Greek half of the Roman world, induct into their students this time-honored code.

The tales and heroes of Homer, the erotic adventures of the gods, the poetry and plays of many classic writers, all attest to the nobility of male friendship. Notable tyrant killers, victorious commanders of armies, or victors at the Olympic or Pythian Games, litter our race memory with praises. Even recent poets of Rome and several past Caesars applaud these sentiments.

Only dry-as-dust metaphysicians with an ageing sex drive, most of who were either obsessed puritans or proven hypocrites, challenge this dimension of life. It's the proper and natural thing for those hearts are open to it, we in the Greek hemisphere believe. Lesser races might find other ways to regulate youth's sexual exuberance, but for us it is an honorable observance.

At the Imperial Hunt I could perceive how the sight of my blond pal's outward form in full-flight pursuit of the young boar was giving Hadrian moments of reflection too.

As I followed close behind stumbling through the undergrowth astride Blaze, I discerned how the emperor displayed his rugged working soldier's muscular condition. His body, arms, and thighs projected the hardened tissue of a professional warrior. I, being an eighteen year-old with military aspirations, envied the emperor's condition as an adult commander. I hoped that I too would exhibit such a fine figure at a similar time of life. Only Caesar's occasional gray hairs and, I perceived, an occasional cough, highlighted his maturity.

I wondered if Caesar saw in my friend's eager chase a distant reflection of an earlier Hadrian, a carefree Hadrian, who had existed long before the obligations of being a commander of Legions or succeeding to the office of *Princeps*? Hadrian has long had a reputation for youthful wildness. But the immediate urgency of the chase swamped these observations.

A crisis point had been reached. Lifting as high as Tiny's skillful maneuvering permitted, Antinous stretched himself above his saddle between pressed knees as the horse gyrated and hoofed the earth, to steadily calculate the trajectory of a javelin cast. Every nerve-end and muscle fiber was fine-tuned for accuracy. Shouting an excited warrior's cry, he flung the iron-tipped shaft at a point into the low brow of the cave entrance. The shrill squeals of a stuck pig followed.

Antinous swung off his mount, swiftly drew another short lance from his quiver, and sped towards the cave as we other horsemen surged to a halt close by. The excited hunter had grabbed a second dart because the beast, full half his size and body weight though still young, thrashed in the dust with the first lance pierced deep into its throat. It sliced its breast nailing it to the cave floor. It spurted thin squirts of blood but not sufficient discharge to indicate a fatal blow.

Antinous aimed and flung the second weapon at its writhing hulk, but the point deflected sharply off its weathered spine onto nearby rocks with a hollow clatter. Leaping forward and grasping the original pike to press down on its staff to maintain its bite on the pinioned creature, while simultaneously fumbling for his hunting knife at his belt for a more intimate kill, he found he was immediately fixed in place by the sheer writhing vigor of the beast.

Though the animal's tusks had been blunted as a safety precaution, its snarling fangs and fear-foamed nozzle could nevertheless do serious damage to human flesh or bone. Hadrian's instructions to his hunt master had taken into account the inexperience of his young hunters, not wishing to distress his provincial families with a hunting accident. Yet no one had advised the boar of this precaution.

Antinous found himself in an untenable position. If he released the hold on his spear as he drew his knife for a proper kill he risked the animal lashing out at his legs and thighs. Regardless of the greaves protecting his shins, the creature could still lacerate. While he applied his full body weight to the spear the boar was temporarily disabled. Yet as it writhed from side to side he realized the light wooden shaft of the lance was likely to splinter under its struggle.

Instantly those arriving at the scene saw his dire bodily peril should the shaft disintegrate. Fevered blood raced through every artery, vein, and membrane. I immediately leapt from my pony, lance in hand, ready to strike at the first opportunity to subdue the creature.

With a silken whistle, flash, followed by a solid thud, the beast dropped to earth. A gleaming short-sword blade had arced through the air with a deadly whisper to pierce directly into the boar's skull. It impaled deep into its bony cranium above its brow.

The boar instantly tumbled to earth with only occasional muscle spasms and twitches, the blade firmly embedded in its broad head. The throw, a field soldier's expert knifing from a distance, resolved the dilemma of the pinioned creature as the two Scythian archers speedily positioned themselves on their steeds for similarly decisive action. The blade had shimmered into its target's skull within spare inches of Antinous's own limbs and flesh.

Antinous, still excitedly grasping the lance shaft, looked back to see which of his companions had made the decisive blow.

Hadrian grinned broadly as he dismounted from his Nisaean and casually approached. He scanned and interpreted the hunter's adrenalin shining wildly in Antinous's eyes. He read his tensed muscles, flaked dry mouth, and frozen hand-grip.

Gently taking hold of the two clasped hands around the original javelin, the emperor calmly and methodically started peeling the rigid fingers away from its upright shaft.

'Found yourself in trouble here, lad?' he asked with laconic dryness. He realized Antinous was frozen to the lance in a race of excited fear and crazed victory by the hunt's sudden conclusion. He was stricken speechless by his predicament.

'You rode well, lad,' Hadrian offered. 'But perhaps your risk assessment skills leave something to be desired, eh?'

While he patiently unfurled my friend's digits one by one, the master of the civilized world smiled knowingly at those gathered around as we all realized Antinous was projecting the hump of an excited combatant's erection from beneath his tunic's pleats. Young men are very easily aroused, even by life's less erotic occasions. My profusely perspiring friend slowly regained his senses and his civil tongue.

'It seems so, my Lord,' he muttered. He could feel his hands being pried loose from the pikestaff and visibly welcomed the restoration of movement flowing back into frozen extremities. The emperor's hands had carefully plucked each frozen finger from its grip.

Antinous's eyes were firmly on the countenance of his rescuer, wide in apprehension. He was struck by the gentleness of the man's firm hold and his generous intentions, while he stammered to find suitable words to respond.

Geta the Barbarian too had noted the gesture with considerable interest. Arrian and Julianus seemed equally charmed by the situation. I was electrified.

Then we, the gathered hunters, broke into a spontaneous applause of cheers and whistles of approval, a gesture which unlatched the tensions of the chase. Smiles flashed all round and helmets came off as the boys, men, and attendants dismounted to recover their relaxed ways.

I clasped Antinous around the shoulders and gave him a big hero's hug, coupled with deep relief that the hunt's outcome had been so propitious.

Hadrian took Antinous' right arm in a firm Legion greeting clasp.

'Bravo Antinous, son of Telemachus of Claudiopolis. The hunt is yours! Hail to the Victor!'

He raised his arm high, just as they had seen gladiators do in the arena at Byzantium after a win. Then he glanced knowingly at his comrades Arrian, Julianus, and Geta with a sly grin.

'But tell me, young man, do you know the story of Hermolaus? Do they teach you these things in Bithynia?' he asked loudly enough for all to hear.

Hadrian glanced to Arrian, and both Antinous and I detected a flicker of a wink pass between them. I saw Antinous slowly beginning to blush to a deep crimson.

I could not recall a 'Hermolaus' story from my studies, though the name was vaguely familiar. I wondered if I had misinterpreted Caesar's accent of Latin-colored Greek. However Antinous seemed very aware of the name. It visibly troubled him. His eyes fell shyly to earth as the hunt support staff arrived to bind the boar for transport.

Hadrian spoke.

'As my friend Arrian can tell us, who is a very great authority on these things, Hermolaus was a page in the service of *Basileus Alexandros*. King Alexander of Macedon was on a boar hunt in Persia with boys from his retinue, and this one lad – Hermolaus – struck at the chased boar which Alexander himself prized to kill. Hermolaus killed it instead.'

Caesar looked around at the group as everyone's eyes narrowed with rising concern.

'Alexander was so outraged at being denied the strike he had the boy thrashed before his fellow pages and confiscated his horse,' he added.

A hush settled on the group, and despite Arrian's knowing smile everyone feared for Antinous's comfort. Was Caesar being cruel? Was this another side to Caesar?

Antinous caught his breath and stood straight to his full height, which was already almost level to Caesar's, to look the emperor directly in the eye. The emperor waited patiently for a response with the barest hint of a smile. Antinous's cheeks flushed.

'My Lord Caesar, sir," he began in a formal tone with a salutary dip of his head, "May I speak?' The emperor nodded. Antinous responded.

'Hermolaus, son of Sopolis, committed far worse than steal a hunter's kill. He was involved, if I recall correctly, in the tragedy of a plot against Alexander the Great, and many of the pages paid dearly for it. Justly so, we in Asia believe, such was the degree of the treason. The Roman historian Curtius Rufus of the days of Caesar Nero records the tale at length.'

He paused to measure his effect in case he was stepping beyond the boundaries of protocol. But it seemed he wasn't.

'We Hellenes read the story of Alexander with pride because he is one of us, though we read the Curtius text in Latin with its parallel Greek translation for our schooling. But we also read King Ptolemy's version of these tales of Alexander in their archaic Attic Greek, along with the historian Aristobulus and the other romance tales of Alexander,' Antinous offered with scholarly seriousness. He had regained his tongue.

Hadrian was taken aback by this schoolroom history lesson. So too were Arrian, Julianus, Geta, and the others, who raised approving eyebrows. Even the two Praetorian Guardsmen seemed impressed behind their professionally sullen demeanor. The emperor nodded agreement but then, after another conspiratorial glance to Arrian, his countenance became stern. He posed a further question.

'Tell me, Antinous of Claudiopolis, what else do you know of Alexander? Who was Alexander's most important comrade? Name some of his Companions.'

The question seemed to both Antinous and I to be a further simple schoolboy's test.

'His strategic comrades, my Lord, were great heroes,' Antinous proposed. 'Lysias, my friend here, and I would probably name from among his Companions his general Cleitus as his worthiest comrade. He saved Alexander's life at the Battle of Issus and always spoke the truth, despite the king's eventual drunken murder of him.'

I was hugely flattered to be included by Antinous in this erudite summary. Yet Antinous continued.

'But for me, of course, it was his Commander of the Companions and fellow prince, Hephaestion, who was most important. Their great friendship sings across the ages and enters our hearts even today, my Lord.'

Antinous is a fond admirer of the Greek heroic classics. Unlike Alexander he doesn't keep a copy of *The Iliad* under his pillow, but he has several precious scrolls of such books in his personal chest.

Hadrian and Arrian shared a further meeting of eyes. It contained a coded message beyond our understanding. Hadrian then changed the subject.

'Where did you two lads learn to cleave to mountain ponies with such mastery? You must teach us your skills,' he stated with perhaps excessive flattery. 'It was a sight to behold. Your mounts are unique creatures and deserve their own reward. Tonight you and your friends here can serve us your hunt victim grilled on a spit to celebrate your victory. My household will provide the entertainments, and we will dedicate the spoils to the Goddess Artemis herself.'

'But my Lord, if I may speak,' Antinous interjected. He had recovered his civil tongue at last, but spoke out of turn without permission. 'It was not I but you who brought down the beast. I was merely your attendant-at-arms, your page. The actual kill was certainly yours.'

Antinous had retrieved sufficient of his senses to offer this polite diplomacy. I guess Hadrian and Arrian noticed it was expressed without any of the cloying deference of a courtier, which was probably a novelty for them.

'That's very modest of you, lad,' Hadrian offered, 'I praise your tact. But in truth I merely fulfilled its destiny, a destiny resolved by your good scouting, chase, and strike. You deserve your award for your skill and courage. Tonight we will assign you its ears and snout as tokens of your victory. Be proud of your feat, my boy. Each of us here are proud on your behalf, and we rejoice in the day's adventure with you.

Antinous blushed deeply again. I think I blushed too.

Hadrian then turned to Arrian, Julianus, Geta, the Praetorians, and the others who had assembled. He regaled us with a message we grew to appreciate later.

'There's fine talent here among these Greeklings in Bithynia, I see. We must inspect their credentials more closely. If this province is to have a new generation of trained statesmen and administrators, or military officers and governors, we must seek out those worthy of the honor with diligence. Perhaps tonight we will test their quality?'

The assembled hunters slapped their swords against their breastplates in noisy accord while we youngsters looked around to each other with swelling pride.

I noticed Arrian smiling calmly to himself in a manner which suggested he was very pleased indeed with the day's work."

Lysias ceased his recollection and reached for his goblet to sip some wine. He looked reflectively to the floor tiles and shuffled his feet. He had disappeared into a private reverie.

CHAPTER 9

"So, did something unusual happen at the celebration feast?" Suetonius asked.

"Yes, there were intimations of what was to follow," Lysias responded.

"Then tell us about it. But remember, time is passing."

"We six *meirakia* guys with our attendants were freshly spruced and dressed in our finest attire," Lysias began. "Our status as the guests of honor heartened us sufficiently to cope with so intimidating a social event. After all, it was an Imperial Symposium.

Were we expected to engage in learned displays of rhetoric or philosophical debate? Would it be an ordeal in classical education or a test of scholarly knowledge? Or would it be a wild drunken revel matching our own young men's monthly gatherings in our respective communities?

The hunt victim had been skinned, gutted, cleansed of vermin, dowsed in olive oil and *garam* sauce, scattered with herbs, plugged with garlic, and slung straddled on a roasting spit above hot coals to be rotated in splashes of basting juices and wine.

When we had assembled at our dining couches, each with an attendant in tow, a horn sounded a fanfare. The barbarian Geta led a column of men from within the marquee into a handsomely gardened dining arena. Hadrian was last in the procession, taking his place at his central couch and adjusting his garments to recline as a signal to everyone to relax. He was again attired in a simple Greek tunic and mantle.

Incense fumes drifted languidly across the dining arc of a dozen or so couches as Arrian saluted Caesar in the crisp manner befitting a senior commander. He had been delegated by Caesar, the host, to be the Leader of the Symposium.

He stepped forward to the centre of the amphitheatre's podium. He took his position as two young girl flautists and a tambourine-thumping boy intoned the opening chords of the symposium's formal prologue. The chords silenced the enthralled assembly of courtiers, we *ephebes*, the various attendants, and officers of the Guard.

'*Hail Caesar*! And welcome honorable guests,' Arrian declaimed. 'In this year of the one hundred and fifty-sixth anniversary of the victory at Actium by Caesar Augustus against the enemies of Rome, we salute you.

On behalf of the People and Senate of Rome we celebrate that victory tonight. We regale among us the descendents of our Greek allies of Mantinea now resident at Bithynia who fought at Actium with Augustus in that triumph. In remembrance of Augustus's victory over his enemies by his appeal to Apollo as his special god, we offer praise too to *Apollo Paean* for that decisive conquest.'

It was now Caesar's cue to participate. Hadrian strode briskly from his couch to the sacrificial altar to one side of the podium. A priest of Apollo in ceremonial garb topped with a fresh laurel-leaf diadem raised a platter piled with the primary organs of the boar killed earlier in the day. As Hadrian intoned the offering in a declamatory style the priest tossed handfuls of laurel, the special favorite of Apollo, and pieces of the flesh into the altar's flames. The mixed smokes rose up to please the god in the heavens.

The melding odors of musky incense, burning laurel, and roasting flesh drifted across the garden arena in a mouth-watering haze. Servants delivered a basket piled high with laurel wreaths interlaced with sprays of wild grasses to adorn each celebrant, accompanied by garlands of blossoms to drape around the shoulders.

Hadrian's clear voice silenced the assembly. He intoned the awarding prayer.

'*Blessed siblings, Apollo and Artemis, Our golden Lord of Healing and the Lady of the Hunt, receive these spoils of a choice young boar which Antinous of Claudiopolis killed in your honor. Hail to the victor, Antinous!* --- And now bring out the food and wine!'

Stewards and slaves appeared from surrounding marquees with goblets, *rhytons,* large mixing *kraters,* jugs of wine or water, platters of olives, dried fruits, nuts, figs, wild herbs, and local cheeses.

'Antinous of Claudiopolis, hero of the hunt, as victor you are inducted to do us the honor of mixing our wine!' Hadrian announced to everyone's surprise, especially Ant and I.

Three senior servants approached Antinous offering separate jugs of wine and water for a ceremonial blending into a larger *krater* bowl. Antinous was utterly startled by this unexpected duty. No one had warned him he would be obliged to perform the ceremony.

We other boys were glad it was not us who had to perform this rite before such distinguished company. Not one of us was ready for the prospect.

The ritual is perceived to be a demanding trial of a person's presentation skills. A command of personal composure, vocal declamation, poetic skill, and understated ritual gesture was on show. Restraint and confidence coupled with a degree of drama was the desired effect. I recalled how we had seen our elders perform the rite at public celebrations many times, but it demands nerves of iron and a steady hand coupled with a solemn sense of theater.

Antinous bravely stepped forward from his couch, adjusted his *chiton* nervously, and ceremoniously guided each steward with the rite's token gestures towards a 30/70 mix of water with the wine into the *krater.* He then studiously spooned-in a pot of honey. He performed the ceremony with the studied intensity expected of an honored ritual.

He boldly proclaimed the traditional prayer of the poet Alkaeus in a firm voice, just as we had heard his father and our elder brothers intone at *palaestra* parties, family feasts, or public sacrifices.

The assembly shouted a cheery agreement to Alkaeus's call for Dionysus's great gift of the vine to man as the mixed jars were poured liberally around. I saw Hadrian, Arrian, Julianus, and others glanced towards each other meaningfully just as they did at the Hunt. They had approving smiles.

It dawned on us both how Antinous might be the centre of attention in more ways than he had considered, though we could not be sure what that attention might be.

Other than the strips of roasted boar flesh and the free flowing wines, the precise courses of food served that evening is a foggy memory. They were many, and included victuals we had never eaten previously.

Antinous and I cautiously ate oysters from the Sea of Marmara for the first time, plus out-of-season fruits pickled in honey syrup. We tasted tiny spiced game birds of an unknown breed but delicious to the taste, and sipped prized Falernian and Setian wines from Italy for the very first time.

A schedule of entertainments began. It was devised, we suspected, to amuse youngsters. Comic actors and mime artists imported from Byzantium performed amusingly vulgar excerpts from classic comedy with many rude fart jokes and eunuch jibes. They were received with howls of laughter.

Jugglers and acrobats from Mauritania performed ingenious human contortions, while barbaric dancers with lithe bodies from Gades in Hispania surged and whirled to wild drummers.

An Egyptian wizard in quaint priestly garb amazed us with inexplicable acts of plucking objects from thin air and then manipulating their utter disappearance in an instant.

A gravel-voiced bard striking a resonant lyre chanted well-known stanzas of *The Iliad*'s battle scenes telling of bone-crushing violence and the death of heroes at Troy. Our audience chanted along with him in the more familiar citations from Homer.

Lord Arrian took the podium to read aloud a short chapter from his writings of *A History of Alexander*. This is his own work-in-progress, we were told, a biography of the Macedonian king describing his remarkable military strategy for victory at Issus against the Persians. We, his audience, well appreciated the intricacies of the ancient *hoplite* phalanx with its long *sarissa*-pike charge which accompanied Alexander's cavalry to victory. We applauded our national hero rousingly.

As the evening progressed and the wine warmed the blood, a silver-voiced Syrian lad whose elegant attire and fine-boned features suggested he was a member of the aristocracy not a slave or low-class entertainer, sung erotic poems by ancient Theognis of Megara. He appeared to address his songs towards the emperor.

These words shifted the mood of the occasion into a mellow place. At one point both Antinous and I wondered if there was more than laurel burning on the altar or steeped in the wine because the occasion took on a richly affective afterglow. Warm delight soothed anxious brows; we were at our ease in a place of balmy delight. It was all very agreeable.

At another time Antinous strung his trophy boar's ears and snout into an arc across his head, wearing the animal's remnants like a silly hat giving him the appearance of having piggy ears. He danced about on his couch in a comical fashion portraying the beast dying under Hadrian's knife cast. This jovial routine amused everyone heartily. Antinous had been tipsy before, but perhaps never quite as tipsy as this night, I recall. At least he was a happy drunk and yet he seemed to retain his senses nevertheless..

Thaletas, a rich man's son from Byzantium who had cavalry aspirations, found himself attracted to one of the pretty slave girl flautists. He chatted her up and had her reclining beside him on his couch feeding him wine and morsels from platters. At some point they disappeared from the party and returned after a while with Thaletas visibly disheveled but grinning from ear to ear. He had obviously enjoyed something more bodily than wine.

Another guy who was the son of an important councilor at Nicomedia had arrived with a strapping fellow a few years his senior who we all assumed was a family bodyguard. He had stood all evening behind the lad's dining couch in a protective way, though they often shared the food and drink from a common plate. As the evening progressed the two became observably friendlier to each other. When they shifted into lying side by side on the couch and being tactile with each other it dawned on the other diners that they were in fact an item.

Whispers circulated how the older guy was of quality birth, a respected *ephebe* captain of the Nicomedia militia, and had been the approved *erastes* to his younger *eromenos* for the previous year.

It crossed our minds how any of the younger slaves or musicians of either gender who might appeal to us were available for similar diversions. But both Antinous and I remained discreetly aloof from any lascivious behavior to ensure we didn't infringe an unspoken rule of manners in such august company.

Geta the Dacian joined me at one point to engage in idle talk while pouring generous dollops of Falernian into each other's *rhytons* in the rowdy, boozy, drunken Greek manner. I was sober enough, however, to recognize how Geta cleverly inserted into the conversation questions exploring the details of my relationship with Antinous. He searched to discover if Antinous and I were committed as *erastes* and *eromenos*, as mentor and pupil, lover and beloved. This was despite us being of a similar age in contradiction of the usual custom.

I neglected to reveal to Geta how, as the proposed leading partner in the mentoring role by virtue of my few months extra age, I didn't have the courage to put the proposition to Antinous. But I knew I would be devastated if Ant rejected me. If it transpired he agreed however, as I expected there was a chance he might, then I wouldn't have had the courage to approach his father for his authority too.

As the evening drew on it became apparent Caesar was calling each of the boys to his couch, one by one, for a personal chat. A secretary had delivered a small chest containing tight-rolled scrolls in ivory encasements. These were purple ribboned and bound with the small *bulla* seal of official documents.

Each of the six *meirakia* young men was summoned by Geta, and as each departed Caesar's couch after a five-minute conversation it was evident the fellow was smiling with satisfaction at what had transpired.

'Caesar awaits you, Lysias of Claudiopolis,' Geta said formally to me, throwing his glance back towards the emperor's couch. I arose and joined Caesar's company, nodding an excited grin at Antinous as I passed by.

Hadrian was relaxed and friendly.

'Tell me, Lysias of Claudiopolis, have you enjoyed yourself today?' he asked while the most senior steward filled both our *rhytons*. 'It's been a most engaging occasion, don't you think?'

'Indeed, sir! This has been a remarkable occasion following a wonderful day's events. I will remember it all my life.'

I was certainly not being dishonest in my claim.

'In my travels, Lysias, I don't meet very many young people,' Hadrian confided. 'I am attended by all manner of people of all ages, and even many children at the Court, and so on, but I have to make a point of going out of my way to meet those who are up-and-coming in my domains and have something fresh to offer Rome. So an occasion like this is rare for me too. I'd forgotten how lively and entertaining young people can be when they're together as a group.'

'I can appreciate that, sir,' I offered as supportively as I could muster.

'I am especially impressed with you Bithynians, Lysias. I can see how the Hellenes in Bithynia are holding closely to their traditional ways, especially among the sons of your nobility.

For example, watching you and Antinous wrestle together in the antique style at your *palaestra* at Claudiopolis a week ago, and also realizing how the hunt is still a feature of a young Bithynian's life, I'm sure that the great traditions of war training are alive and well here. It's been a great joy to see this age-old heritage flourish in its natural habitat, because it's been lost in much of its native homeland.'

I could discern from Hadrian's manner of speaking how he was actually quite sober, or else he held his drink very well.

'Tell me, Lysias, how do you expect to proceed in your life? What are your ambitions? I am told you are the second son of a father who died serving under my own command of the *II Adiutrix* at Pannonia when I was Governor in that chilly place many years ago?'

'It was eighteen years ago, sir. I was born that same year, my Lord.'

I assure you, gentlemen, I was taken aback by his question and by Caesar's obvious knowledge of my family circumstances. I was proud of how our emperor knew of my father's death in combat with Legion auxiliaries.

'As a second son, my Lord,' I added, 'I am obliged to seek my fortune apart from dividing my family's estates or wealth.'

Hadrian would well know how second sons are expected to make their own way in life by entering the military or the province Legate's service, or make a career in law and the magistracy, or even in foreign trade as an adjunct to his family's entrepreneurial activities.

'My Elder Brother, sir, expects me to complete my education at an academy in Athens. Then I'll explore the opportunities open to me. We have good connections in both Bithynia and Athens and the gods seem to favor us, so I expect my path will become clear to me as time passes, the Fates permitting.'

Hadrian nodded thoughtfully and reached over to the box which lay at his couch side table to lift out one of the scrolls. It had my name formally inscribed on its identification tag.

'It is my pleasure, Lysias of Bithynia, to award you with this token of our regard for you and your family, as well as for your deceased veteran father,' Hadrian said.

My inner heart screamed with delight, but hopefully it was suppressed by better manners in Caesar's presence.

'Should I read it in your company, my Lord?' I asked with a quivering hand. What could the scroll possibly contain; I was asking myself, barely managing to restrain my impatience.

'Take it back to your couch, and give much thought to its contents, m'boy. You need not respond until you have spoken with your Elder,' Caesar suggested. 'Go now, and be proud of yourself in the name of Rome and your father's honor.'

I backed away towards my own couch, bowing and scraping before Caesar in an almost obscenely obsequious manner. I did so until I passed Antinous.

He leaned cheerily backwards towards me to intercept me as I passed.

'Well? What was that all about?' he hissed from the side of his mouth. But before I could reply Geta approached him and beckoned him too to Caesar's couch.

I greedily unfurled the scroll from its clay seal and ribbons and read its contents. It was inscribed in Latin which I stumbled through clumsily under my breath:-

"Under the seal of the Imperial Household on behalf of Imperator Caesar Publius Aelius Hadrianus, Greetings! This letter endows Lysias of Claudiopolis, Son of Lysander of Claudiopolis at Bithynia (Corporal of the Bithynian Cavalry Auxiliary, deceased), an Imperial Scholarship to The Palatine College of Provincial Administration at Rome for a period of two years.

Presentation of this letter to the Office of the Legate Governor of the Province of Bithynia-Pontus will enact the scholarship and its attributes, which includes an endowment of all costs for the duration of the scholarship within an approved schedule, including transport via the Imperial Courier Service, all necessary security protections, accommodations, clothing, food allowance, servant allowance, and other expenses as outlined in the schedule.

Signed under Imperial Seal, L. Julius Vestinus, Ab Epistulus" etc.

A scholarship to the Palatine College in Rome is a hugely important step towards progress in the civil service in either Italy or the provinces, and an assured route to financial gain and social status. It has many civic advantages. Even the possibility of Roman citizenship was one.

While this scholarship to Rome still ricocheted around my mind, I noted how Antinous was faring at Caesar's couch.

I observed how they engaged in light banter for some minutes with many nods and smiles, and I could sense that my friend's joy was slowly rising in happy expectation. I watched as Hadrian again reached into his box for the final rolled scroll and presented it to Antinous.

I wondered if it too offered a similar scholarship to the Palatine College, which would be a wonderful opportunity for us both. I lip-read Hadrian using similar words to the words he used with the other boys, though he permitted Antinous to break the seal and open his scroll.

I watched as Antinous read the contents with his face brightening. I could see how he too had received happy news.

However, Caesar then leaned forward towards him, resting one hand on his knee in a familiar manner, and spoke words directly close to his ear. They were apparently words of an intimate or private nature because I could see something akin to surprise register on my friend's face.

He drew quickly back and was rendered speechless for some seconds. My awareness of Antinous's moods and needs told me a matter had transpired which either shocked or amazed him.

Antinous paused, seated at the edge of Caesar's couch. Both looked seriously toward each other for some suspended moments. Then I saw Antinous slowly, shyly, demurely smile in a somewhat fazed manner and nod affirmatively. He was agreeing to something.

Antinous deeply bowed acknowledgement, withdrew slowly from the couch, but instead of duplicating the earlier stumbling obsequiousness of the other boys, he simply strode thoughtfully back to his own couch. It was now my turn to enquire.

'Well? How did you go? What was in the scroll?'

Antinous looked to me in an oddly remote way. It was an expression I had never seen in him previously. Then he brightened.

'Caesar has awarded me a scholarship to the Palatine College in Rome.' Distraction then returned to his features.

'Me too, Ant! Will your Father agree? He will, surely?'

Antinous paused for a moment to think about it and looked beyond me towards some distant horizon.

'Agree? I don't know. I'll have to see, Lys.'

'What else did Caesar say?'

I simply couldn't resist asking. Some other matter had transpired at the couch. Once again Antinous assumed his trance-like gaze.

'I don't know. I'll have to wait and see.'

CHAPTER 10

Lysias continued his testimony before his hearers. They were entranced by his tale.

"We bunked down that night in our assigned marquee on clean straw still dressed in our wine-splashed symposium garb. Antinous and I made sure we slept under separate cloaks so as not to generate gossip among the servants. Personally, I wanted to hug him close in anticipation of the remarkable times we would be having some day soon at the Palatine College in Rome.

Except for the peeps of pleasure emitted by Thaletas lying with his girl flautist, or the muffled moans from the councilor's son from Nicomedia with his militia officer, we fell to sleep quickly. It had been a long, exciting day.

I was awakened by whispered voices and accompanying shuffling. Without shifting from beneath my cloak facing away from the source of the disturbance, I sensed I heard Antinous rise in the darkness from his bedding accompanied by some other person.

Perhaps, I thought, Antinous was heading for the latrine to relieve himself, except he was heading in the wrong direction for that. After a moment or two I sluggishly turned to face the direction of the action only to witness his cloaked outline and another hooded figure disappearing into the night through the marquee flaps.

From the stature of the other person with his beard revealed fleetingly in the moonlight I realized the other person was Geta, Caesar's assistant.

I thought this was a curious turn of events, especially as I didn't expect Antinous to be especially interested in Geta. He wasn't his 'type', I'd gathered from conversations over the years. Not that Antinous's 'type' was ever clearly articulated. So I too quietly arose and, wrapping myself in my cloak, followed both figures a dozen paces distant out of the tent into the chill night air. Antinous and Geta were bustling speedily towards the Imperial Marquee and its gardened amphitheater.

Though darkness prevailed, the occasional bright moonlight and some sporadic torches lit the camp's paths. However no sentinels or duty-guards were apparent, which struck me as odd in an Imperial encampment.

Nevertheless I followed the two figures at sufficient distance not to be detected. I lingered in passing shadows and took refuge beside tent walls or the plinth of a statue. But both figures were businesslike in their speed towards the Marquee.

At the site of the evening's symposium where the couches and much of the paraphernalia of the celebration remained in place beneath the moon's gray pallor, the two figures halted to exchange words. Because of the concave of the arena before the draperies of the Imperial complex, I could catch reflected snatches of their voices.

I felt ashamed to be so sneakily eavesdropping on my dear friend in this manner, it was not our style of friendship. But I was intrigued by the situation and its clandestine nature. I wondered what, by Hades, was going on?

At the end of their journey two Horse Guards were slumped snoozing at their watch by the Marquee's entrance, which I was certain was a serious military offence deserving of penalty. They were slumped close to a single brazier casting barely enough light to illume a cupboard. Geta halted Antinous at the Marquee's entrance. Neither had noticed their follower, me, slipping furtively through the shadows.

'Wait here, Bithynian, until further notice,' Geta instructed in a hushed voice which resonated across the amphitheater. He then slapped each guard smartly around the head with his studded glove to waken them, and the three figures disappeared together into the Marquee's dark interior.

From where I had taken refuge I could readily observe Antinous standing silently by one of the stripped dining couches facing the tents. His tall slim figure was shrouded by his cloak wrapped around his body and swathed over his head against the chill. He was bathed in drifting silvery moonlight as clouds raced the autumn sky.

Several minutes elapsed. Standing in solitude patiently before the Marquee, Antinous was motionless. Slowly it dawned on me another figure had silently appeared from the dimness within the Marquee into the moonlight's haze at the entrance. Even in the dismal glow I could recognize by height, stature, comportment, and beard it was Caesar.

He too was swathed in a cloak to ward off the cool night air. He had no guards or other retinue. Moments elapsed as the two figures stood silently facing each other.

'You came, lad, after all?' Caesar eventually asked. He strolled towards my friend. 'I thought my invitation might frighten the heart out of you and deter you? You have courage, young man.'

The words reached me in muffled but adequately audible tones.

After a formal bow of deference, Antinous deliberated for some moments uncertain of what might be an appropriate response to the query. He shuffled where he stood.

Hadrian unfurled his cloak to reveal he was standing in a rough woolen legionnaire's sleeping tunic which hung loosely from his upper torso displaying the spare, campaign-hardened tissues of a professional soldier.

For a man somewhere in his forties, the emperor presented an image in the moonlight which did honor to his decades as a Commander of the Legions, the *Imperator,* the officer who shared in his troop's training, their engineering fieldwork, road building, stockade construction, crude diet, and other military disciplines. Despite the occasional mild cough, his bodily stature and sheer physical presence were strikingly worthy of the appellation *Caesar.*

'You asked that I should come, my lord,' Antinous responded politely. 'I did not think I had reason to be afraid. Should I be, sir?'

His voice was quite unthreatened by his circumstance. By Zeus, I had to admire his confidence!

'Afraid? Do you wish to be afraid, lad?' Caesar responded with a teasing grin. 'It was a personal request, my boy, a friendly invitation, not your Caesar's command. Yet I must admit I would have been disappointed by your absence,' Hadrian uttered candidly. 'I too know how an emperor can seem intimidating to a young fellow from my own predecessor Trajan's days."

Antinous was unsure what to reply.

'If Caesar invites, surely it is a citizen's duty to respond?' he offered diplomatically. But then he dared to shift into a presumptive tone.

'Besides, if I hadn't come I wouldn't have had this opportunity to share in Caesar's company so intimately, my lord. Would I?'

I perceived Caesar was somewhat taken aback by this courteous response. Antinous continued in a similar vein.

'I cannot deny I am, to be honest, excited by this opportunity, my lord,' he added with a touch of studied bravado. They stood silently together for a few moments.

'Let me look at you in better light, lad. Come closer,' Hadrian summoned as he reached to back-flip Antinous's full-body mantle from the top of his head onto his shoulders. My friend was still wearing the embroidered tunic beneath his cloak he wore at the symposium, with the wilted boar's ears pinned by a *fibula* to his upper chest while strands of laurel wreath and wild grass remained stuck in his hair.

Moonlight fell sharply across his features displaying in relief the sculpted cheekbones, broad forehead, and the thick mane of shag-cut locks which hung down his nape. I again had to admit to myself Antinous was indeed a good-looking guy.

'Ah, yes,' Hadrian sighed, scanning my friend's face approvingly. 'Yes. Perfect. Quite perfect. When I perceive so perfect a creature I wonder if such perfection can be mine.'

I pondered how it was that Hadrian possessed a persona which projected in public an aura of absolute command while in private his character displayed a gentility and geniality not anticipated in so illustrious a Roman. Nevertheless his talk of 'mine' and of possession struck me as speech about the material ownership of a prize stallion, a hunting hound, or a fine suit of arms, not a person. I imagine both Antinous and I simultaneously perceived this comment to possess a sense of enslavement, a concept utterly fearful to the mind and honor of a freeborn Greek.

The risk of enslavement by victorious enemies has always been a daunting possibility among the warring Greeks of antiquity, and its residual fear lingered among Greeks across the Empire. Defeat always meant slavery or death. Death was often the preferred choice.

My friend painfully searched for an appropriate mode of response. He took a daring tack.

'It flatters me, sir, that you find me so agreeable,' he offered. 'I am pleased that the most honorable of nobles should consider me worthy of their company, my lord. But what could lead you to think that this *'perfect creature'*, as you call me, does not find its admirer an even more engaging, even more magnificent entity? It is I, sir, who detect a superior perfection before me.'

I could detect a hint of not-unexpected quavering in his voice. Yet Caesar seemed faintly amused by his calculated diplomacy. I myself would have been absolutely transfixed with fear or awe if I found myself in such a challenging predicament. Caesar is not simply another man, another mere mortal, is he?

Antinous may be a strongly self-possessed fellow but he was not readily familiar with midnight chats under the moonlight with the emperor of the known world. Caesar's single raised finger can mean life, death, glory, or absolute ignominy. Antinous was testing this prospect precipitously.

'My boy, for all you know I could be a cruel tyrant who has his way with attractive people at will,' Caesar hinted menacingly. 'Many of my predecessors have done so, and even I myself have been known to enjoy an occasional opportunity in earlier times. I could simply enroll you into my traveling *gynaeceum* of both sexes for my more basic pleasures at my leisure,' the emperor brazenly proposed. 'Not that I actually possess such a seraglio, unlike several others in my retinue.'

'My lord, if this was Caesar's will,' Antinous declared with a conspiratorial smile, 'I am sure I would not be standing before you here in fearful anticipation. I would probably already be inducted for duty. Possibly flat on my belly, if that is the usual *modus operandi* of these things?'

'You seem to already be familiar with such activities, my boy? Should I do so, then?' Hadrian teased, suppressing half a smile at the wryness of his young subject in guiding the conversation in such risqué directions. Listening from a distance, I was alarmed at my buddy's boldness.

'Would that be a proposition, my lord?' Antinous ventured further, cheekily matching the quip and upping the ante. 'If so, I must feign a respectful fear for my honor.'

Despite the flippancy of the response, I could detect a tremor in Antinous's voice which belied the jocularity. I doubted Hadrian had missed it either. Then Antinous took a less provocative tone.

'But in truth, sir, I am not at all familiar with those activities. I possess little personal experience of love or sex worth talking of, and certainly none at all of any real notoriety. My schooling commends me to the path of marriage, or alternatively to the style of Patrocles' legendary friendship with his devoted *eromenos* Achilles, at least as described by ancient Aeschylus. But my schooling also abhors the fierce abduction by Olympian Zeus of the Trojan prince Ganymede, who Romans call *Catamitus*. One is a willing engagement, sir, embedded in honor and mutuality, the latter is enforced,' Antinous added. 'It is mere rape. I am no compliant Ganymede or *Catamitus* I hope, my lord, and nor do I willingly invite rape.'

Surprised, Caesar smoothed the rising intensity of this exchange.

'Antinous, my friend, relax. Cool down. Take it easy. I am not going to impose anything upon you wouldn't wish yourself,' he reassured. 'I do not tyrannize my companions. So come over here,' he added, taking Antinous by the shoulders in a sociable way and guiding him to the nearest of the dining couches to take seat. The two had moved into a space of clear moonlight which made my observation all the more easier.

Even though Hadrian sat on the lip of the couch, Antinous stood stiffly at military attention in the formal *hoplite* pose of his training. He was facing Hadrian in deference to age, status, or *arete* and the ingrained habits of the military.

'You have spirit, lad. But it is not the wild spirit of the reckless, I detect. You are also tempered by humor and some charm. The humor has natural confidence and a quick wit. It is my will to get to know you, Antinous of Bithynia,' Caesar declared plainly.

'I need someone of spirit in my life again, my boy. I need a young man's vitality at my side for a refreshment of my vision. I need the optimism of the young to reinvigorate my veins, instilled in me through the energy of the companionship of a respectable *ephebe* of good character and personable appeal.

I desire such a person to be in my life again to restore to me values and virtues which differ substantially from our prosaic Roman ones, let alone the cynicism of politics or the venality of my Court.

Your Bithynian enthusiasms for your antique Hellene culture - several of my retinue claim it's an *antiquated* Hellene culture - and your uninhibited engagement with its pedagogical tradition inspires you towards values of great formative power,' he announced with obvious ardor.

Hadrian drew Antinous closer to him by the tip of a finger at his elbow, and even from my distance I could observe how Antinous trembled with apprehension.

'You are still young, Antinous, so I have a great deal to teach you, all to your personal advantage. Though I've been noting youngsters like you here at Bithynia and elsewhere, I will concede you have singularly captivated me. Truly, when you enter my sight, Antinous of Bithynia, I find delight enters my heart at the same time.

Despite your youth you possess a solemnly mature charisma, you display cool charm and sly Greek wiles, while you project the innate dynamism of youth. These bode well for you, my boy. Besides, you are spoken of with honor in your own community, and I am told of your descent from ancient Hellenes of good family and proven warrior stock.

You speak well in your native Greek, and I have been told your Latin shows promise if exposed to regular conversation. These are a sign of intelligence.

Your wrestling skill at the *palaestra* games indicated excellent coordination and a good strategic sense, with a fierce will to win despite your beefier opponent's weight. Your evasive defense throughout was a pleasure to observe.

In the foot races you sprint well with the manly gait of a true athlete. The races in armor prove your high stamina. Your horsemanship at our hunt today was exemplary, perhaps unique even, and you assess and take risks swiftly. I sense you will become adept at hunting all manner of game, large and small, which is a priority of my leisure time.

These things bode well for you to someday receive a commission with a cavalry unit of prestige. Or better. These are telling things about your quality, my boy,' Hadrian offered flatteringly. Antinous was stricken quite dumb by this shower of compliments.

'Yet you also exhibit a natural animal grace and motion, young man, with finely defined limbs and a well-modeled body. Your physical symmetries are indeed well balanced. Your oiled and dusted nakedness while wrestling at the *palaestra* displayed a most pleasing line, widely commented upon with favor by those around, I perceived.

I must be frank with you to say you have loins of proportions which will attract many an eye, young fellow, male or female. I believe this is the Bithynian way? Your compatriots admire the comeliness of youth's perfection and its bodily vigor, accompanied by the magnetism of youth's latent potential. Such perfections can incite a man to seek to couple with such extraordinary beauty. Their earthier impulses may erupt beyond decency.

So you must appreciate the homage of my carnal ambitions towards you. You should be flattered when I say your contours, your silhouette, your cut definition, and your sleek loins compellingly invite playfulness, my friend. Many would agree with me, I assure you. Some philosophers say this bodily perfection echoes an ultimate universe of ideal forms. And it is a perfection I deduce of both mind as well as body.'

Antinous visibly, and I less visibly in hiding, were disturbed by this well-meaning but indelicate shower of flatteries. I am sure they would have alarmed him.

To talk of being the emperor's 'friend' in the same phrases as references to his body and loins is to infringe the unspoken code of honor-and-shame ruling men's relationships. It proclaims a discourse of domination and penetration. To talk carelessly of horseplay is one thing, but to vocalize the prospect of being buggered is something else altogether!

In the years since that night at Nicomedia I have learned how at Rome they call this imposition a *stuprum,* an offence against a freeborn maiden or youth which insults civic honor and may invoke legal reprisal.

A mature Roman's urge to penetrate an attractive younger person might be gender blind, as people say, but the license to do so extends only to targets without Roman citizen's rights, such as slaves or foreigners. Freeborn Romans are securely fenced off from behavior which impugns their status as future citizens. But a freeborn person of foreign origin is a permissible goal.

Nevertheless, in my later travels I was to witness how at Rome the edict about acts of *stupra* against the freeborn is honored far, far more in the breach than in the keeping."

Lysias paused momentarily to sip his wine. His observers waited patiently for him to return to his testimony.

It crossed Suetonius's mind how Greek philosophers since Aristotle, Zeno, Plato or even Epicurus argued that in an ideal city state citizens should restrain their itch to enjoy exuberant sexuality because it diverts from the proper goal of civic mindedness, which is baby-making. But these were not popular sentiments among most Greeks. In a land where too many mouths to feed can impoverish, baby-making becomes a restrained urge in one's sexual repertoire. Less procreative bodily pleasures are preferred.

Worryingly, the later works of ancient Plato propound how even '*total abstinence maketh the man*' because young men who act otherwise '*risk becoming girlish cinaedi*'. Such philosopher's calls to celibacy are not widely regarded sentiments, however, especially among the young who are driven in their sexuality.

These abstemious ways of the philosophers influence all manner of strange cults and new gods.

That notoriously obsessive Judaean advocate of his Savior God *Chrestus*, Paulus of Tarsus, was laughed out of both Ephesus and Athens in Nero's time when he foolishly encouraged celibacy among those cities' unabashed sexual athletes. The fellow's ascetical devotees possess rites and rules for every daily act. They sniff out *fornication* and *abomination* among us everywhere to condemn even the simplest pleasures.

Lysias continued with his testimony.

"Talk of penetration of an *eromenos* by his *erastes* is considered bad form. Yet what may occur between an *erastes* and *eromenos* in private or with others at drinking parties is entirely their own affair.

Both Antinous and I knew of many liaisons among our peers where screwing, *fellatio*, and other raunchy pleasures were the norm, with happy abandon. Lewd graffiti joyfully displayed on public walls about many couples makes that visible to see. Hot blood will simply have its bawdy way regardless of rules and conventions or the solemnities of ancient philosophers.

Yet to have heard the prospect of penetration voiced to his face by Hadrian would have disturbed Antinous. Nevertheless the emperor's proposition moved onwards.

'Antinous,' Hadrian continued, 'in Rome at your age you would already have been accorded the *toga virilis*, the dress code saying this lad is no longer a child but is now fecund, produces seed, and can attain peak arousal. He is a *vir* of marriageable age for the breeding of legal sons. Mind you, an actual marriage contract might still be ten years off.

Rome encourages breeding among its citizens. A Roman wife is expected to deliver many sons to stock the Legions. So everything always leads to marriage.

Yet even though you have entered the mature age-class of a *meirakion* - the age where I had already served several year's military service under my uncle Trajan - you are still part-formed as a man. Your physique proclaims the approach of man's fullest estate, you can produce fertile seed to make strong sons, yet your experience lacks substance and skill.

So, Antinous, a special part of me yearns to be a teacher of life to you, as demanded of your tradition. To my eye you display the promise of a worthy challenge, and I aspire to that role in your life as your *erastes*.'

Antinous stood motionless beneath the moonlight, utterly silenced by Caesar's monologue.

'You blush, I see? Hadrian continued. 'In truth, Antinous, you arouse the most admirable urges in a suitor which are at the same time intellectual, sociable, filial, and carnal. So I must speak plainly to you as your proposing *erastes*.'

Hadrian reached out to grasp my friend's hand as he softly spoke.

'Yes, Antinous, I wish to expand your horizons as your mentor in life, in battle, in the hunt, in philosophy, in the arts, in the sciences, in wealth-making, and in companionship. Just between us here, I desire to bring you the fullest enhancement of life as well as the fullest pleasure of sexual satisfaction. It would please me greatly to heighten your mind's achievement and to enhance your body's sensual enjoyment in the manner your custom sanctions.

This is – frankly – to live with you, to sport with you, to make you my close companion by day and my body's intimate by night,' Caesar concluded. 'Yes, that includes enjoying sex with you. So tell me honestly, Antinous, what is your immediate response to my submission? I wish your response to be entirely of your own free will, without penalty. I do not demand it of you as your ruler.'

Hadrian then paused at last to assess his effect on my friend.

Antinous was evidently startled by the audacity of Hadrian's proposal. I could see he was smitten with anxiety. Hadrian sensed this reserve and aimed to prompt him more encouragingly.

'I, Caesar, possess the desire and the means to favor this potential in a worthy fellow like yourself,' Hadrian entreated. 'I am an admirer of the Greek system of education of a younger man by a maturer one. I admire the way this system has produced great writers, great poets, architects, philosophers, political leaders, and commanders of armies over the ages,' he continued. 'However, for myself, I have not to this day focused my affections on a single chosen companion in this manner. You are the first to enter my life in this way, Antinous.'

Hadrian paused thoughtfully as the focus of his dissertation stood ramrod straight before him. Caesar renewed his presentation.

'There is, perhaps, a less obvious dimension to my proposal – but maybe the most important factor. I am ruler of the world yet I have no one to love, Antinous. I am ruler of the world yet no one is my lover. My station impedes the free flow of affection between me and others, except at the level of Imperial State allegiance. I am seen as a figurehead, not a human heart.

So I seek once again to have love in my life. I seek once again to be fond of a single particular person, not a multitude. Yet a multitude is my fate. My closest family has now passed away. Those of my blood I long loved are no more. You, Antinous, bring light into my heart, and though much of that light shines from your animal beauty, it is your nature, and vigor, and potential which attracts my favor.'

I could see my schoolchum was smitten with dismay by these confessions. I could also sense his interest had been fortified by their unexpected sincerity. Hadrian continued.

'As *Princeps* it is now politic for me to bind myself to a relationship in the accepted Greek way with one single young man. I am married to a dutiful wife, Vibia Sabina *Augusta*, though she has borne me no children. I take no paramours even though I am in a position to do whatever I wish. Perhaps in my wilder days I did so, just as my predecessor Trajan had.

Instead, to conform to lawful behavior as the Empire's pre-eminent citizen and its model of probity, it obliges me to be married to my single wife and now to retain a single young man as my consorts.'

Antinous was frozen in place and frozen in tongue. His ears were ringing, I am sure.

Hadrian continued.

'Because I have no sons, Antinous, I will eventually legally adopt a *patrician* of Rome whose credentials are patently eligible to succeed me on that day when I too journey to my ancestors. Imperial succession-by-adoption has proven to be a safeguard against the defects of bloodline succession. It is a more mindful decision about eligibility than the accidents of dynastic birthright. The *Imperium* has had several bad experiences with bloodline succession, and very few good ones.

But my successor will certainly not be you, Antinous of Bithynia, because in our Roman way it cannot be someone of Greek descent. You must realize I have no intention of adopting you as my heir. If I did so you would be dead within a month, I'd say,' Hadrian confirmed.

'Yet I wish to locate a fitting companion to share my private life and my private bed for the years until, in accordance with the custom, my consort's beard matures. I will then offer praises to Jupiter on that day when he trims his full beard sufficiently to sacrifice its cuttings, and so the consort relationship will cease. This is likely to be several years away for you, Antinous. In the meantime I have much to offer my chosen companion.'

Caesar rested his case for some moments.

'I sense someone of your background is himself on a quest for his *erastes*? He seeks a companion-of-quality who will induct him into adult life? This companion will encourage his acquisition of wealth and property. He will fight side-by-side in his friend's battles or blood feuds and support him in legal disputes. He will be Best Man at his wedding. He will be godfather and sworn protector to his friend's children. And he will avenge his friend if malevolence befalls him. Above all, he will possess a special affection for his friend.

And I, young man, as an aspiring *erastes* am seeking a suitable *eromenos* to allow me full rein to express the Hellene side of my own nature. You, Antinous, are my chosen contender for this role.'

Antinous remained stiffly upright in the pale moonlight, rigid with wonderment if not sheer visceral terror. I am sure he had no idea his nocturnal meeting would lead to such a daunting proposition. He was now standing almost knee-to-knee to Hadrian.

Caesar continued.

'I, Caesar, am *Princeps*, the First Citizen. I command the Empire's citizens. I shape the world's future. I make nations create themselves anew. I endow the Empire with tax money and public works to encourage it to become better than it has ever been. I have consolidated the borders with the barbarian races so the *Pax Romana* prevails to our benefit and our wealth grows unhindered by war or rebellion.

I bring Roman civilization to every corner of the Middle Sea and beyond. Rome brings law and order, we punish robbers and pirates, we guarantee the food supply despite famine, we build useful roads, aqueducts, public facilities, bath houses, sanitation, ensure clean water, provide games and festivals, protect safe travel and trade, and even secure justice for foreigners, debtors, widows, or slaves as well as Romans. I am the bringer of justice and the giver of justice.

To be engaged with me as Caesar is to be engaged with the mightiest of men in action of great honor. No Zeus with his Ganymede, no Apollo with his Hyacinth, no Patrocles with his Achilles, no Socrates with his Alcibiades, no Hephaestion with his Alexander, has ever been an *erastes* of the quality of your Caesar. I am the ultimate *erastes* to his chosen *eromenos*, Antinous. All this I offer you, and I offer you alone.

I could woo you with baubles and trinkets, fine clothes and perfumes, palaces, slaves, weapons, or a magnificent horse or two. They say everyone has their price. But I would think less of you if you conceded easily in this way. My informants tell me you would think less of me too.

No, I want your full-hearted commitment without coercion. I wish you of your own free will to accept my proposal, to invite me into your life as your *erastes* under the terms of the custom. I wish you to announce fearlessly to me : *Yes Caesar, I am yours!* Nothing less.

If the answer is *No*, for reasons of your own or your father's, then I will send you safely on your way with sufficient reward to thank you for your attentiveness. This, Antinous, is my submission.'

Hadrian shut-up at last and waited for a reply. I am sure Antinous and I were both convinced Caesar rarely patiently awaits a response from his subjects, yet here in the moonlit calm of a deserted garden amphitheater outside Nicomedia he did so. Eventually Antinous found the presence of mind with a sufficiently emotion-rasped voice to speak.

'Forgive me, sir,' I heard him say in a challenge which alarmed me, 'but I am certainly no prostitute. I am proudly born of a clan and a father who would disown me immediately, my lord, if it was believed I had sold my body for money or possessions or position. My honor among my peers would be permanently impugned. For the remainder of my days I'd be labeled as someone whose body, mind, and tongue are purchasable. I'd be denied society by my peers or a future role in our governing councils. This would be as death to me, my lord, and my father would be in his rights to kill me for it, as some do.

Yet your proposal has appeal, sir, I must confess. I am dismayed but truly flattered to be deemed so worthy. It leads me to ask: why me, sir? I am just a country boy, and there are finer lads in Bithynia with smoother talk or whiter skins who are equipped with a courtier's wit or are expert in the boudoir's special practices. I am not trained in the wiles of the Court, my lord, let alone the arts and speech of love or sex.'

I recall Antinous paused uneasily for a while to measure Caesar's response to his hesitancy. Hadrian replied in low tones I could barely hear.

'Antinous, I could offer you or your father a great deal of money or property, but yes, that would be prostitution. I'm fairly sure that such a transaction is probably outside the code of your caste, yes?

As you probably realize, Antinous, I can take my pick of the most excellent slaves of all types available at market, and then some. I can buy whatever fits my desires, or simply seize that which is un-buyable. I am Caesar, after all. Yet I am a law abiding Caesar.

Importuning a slave is beneath me, no matter how beautiful or desirable. It is an abuse inflicted by mediocrities. As Plutarch has recently written, a wise ruler does not solicit people who ultimately have no choice in the matter. My rule as Caesar has seen the codification of the legal rights of slaves for their safety and justice, so I must be consistent in these things.

My goal instead is to engage with a freeborn companion; a *willing* freeborn companion; a friend of good family, of a suitable class, of intelligence, of an appropriate education and potential, and of great natural beauty, yet who is not Roman. It is my duty as the protector of the law and an exponent of the law.

I have been searching for this person for more than two years, but I've found only one or two who are even barely equipped for the role.

For example, you have seen Glaucon of Syria? He was the sweet-voiced singer of ancient love songs at the symposium tonight. He is the son of a leading Syri aristocrat at Damascus who aspires to Roman citizenship and entering the Senate, so he is cultivating my favor expensively. It is clear the father has thrown his son at me as a down payment on his project.

Glaucon is quite appealing in a sensual, even feminine, sort of way and is most congenial in his sexual accomplishments, I assure you. I have reason to know.

But he is not a person to be at my side as my consort at Court, at a military parade, at a religious sacrifice, in the company of rugged soldiers, on a Legion bivouac, at audience in the presence of my wife Sabina, or before the baying *plebs* at Rome's amphitheaters. He is not someone whose very presence adds *gravitas* to my official comportment beyond his feline beauty, of which one tires quickly. An emperor requires the companionship of someone who possesses visible *substance*, someone who displays self-evident *quality*, not merely delicate bones, a silver voice, a slim waist, wears silk well, or offers eager orifices to my amusement. He also does not inspire delight in my heart as you do.'

Hadrian paused to measure the impact of his words on his young confidante. They were strikingly, brutally candid, if ultimately flattering.

'But tell me now, Antinous, what do you yourself seek in your life?' he asked.

From my hiding place I wondered how my pal would respond.

'Sir, I do not know how to reply,' I heard Antinous utter in dismay. 'As a second son I am obliged to make my own way in the world. I am ruled by honor and my search for my contribution to my community, my elders, and my peers. As typified by the condemned gladiators of the arena, I wish my death to be noble, heroic, fearless, an event worthy of my life's living.

I am on a quest for my life's meaning, sir. My Father tells me I must take the actions necessary to fulfill my quest, they will not arrive of their own volition. I seek opportunities for engagement which fulfill this quest.

Yet in honesty, Caesar, I do not know if I possess the gifts you seek. I am unsure of what you expect of me. I might disappoint you, particularly among your courtiers or in your bedroom. I do not know if I possess *gravitas* before my seniors, or can perform inventive sexual novelties. I am entirely inexperienced in these things and am protective of my *arete*.

Fear of shame and the pursuit of honor are my guardians. So it's my hope and desire that until the day of my betrothal my Father will permit me to enter schooling at Athens. This will be prior to taking up your gesture of a scholarship to the Palatine College at Rome.

At Athens I aspire to learn something more of life, of philosophy or rhetoric, to read the classics, to study the new sciences, to hear the debates of today's thinkers, to take initiation into the Mysteries, to attend the *gymnasia* and *palaestrae* to refine my body or improve my technique with weapons and sports. Perhaps, too, to experience love or lust with a worthy companion, whoever he or she may be.

But I do not feel I am equipped to provide you with the satisfactions of a proper *eromenos*, especially an *eromenos* worthy of Great Caesar.'

He fell silent with his eyes downcast in shame.

'Antinous, lad, all this and more may happen. Do not be at a loss,' Hadrian interceded. 'You are young, so another year's education in a major centre of culture like Athens will do you no harm. Your body has entered manhood so extra training in armor, or casting javelin and discus, or refining riding on proper-sized chargers, will help you achieve it swiftly. You are well on your way. But I must add, the guidance of an experienced cavalry officer and exponent of hunting who is also familiar with the ways of love can complete it. That, Antinous, would be my contribution.

I am sure your father will be pleased with your decision if you decide to become my companion. You only have to ask him.'

Both Antinous and I immediately intuited Hadrian might already know of Telemachus's response. Hadrian may have made separate contact.

'I am grateful for your patience, sir,' Antinous responded hesitantly, beginning to find his tongue at last. 'Yet I must confess I possess only limited experience of sex. My body makes demands of me I myself cannot fulfill, let alone provide readily to another.

Surely there are many other freeborn youths in Bithynia who already know the arts of love, who are experienced as an *eromenos*, and who are familiar with a courtesan's skills or a slave's duties? I'm sure they may satisfy your desires with greater accomplishment than I ever could? I fear I'm not equipped with the aptitudes you require, my lord.'

Antinous assumed that shy downcast-looking gesture which was quite familiar to me when he was insecure in a situation. Caesar now grew more assertive.

'Let us test that aptitude, young man. Step closer, Antinous,' Hadrian instructed.

Antinous hesitantly moved a half-step nearer the couch.

'This will be the extent of my demand upon you at first,' he added, 'the rest may prove equally as engaging some later day.'

Hadrian leaned forward and tenderly brushed my friend's lips with a kiss. Antinous was startled but did not withdraw. Caesar's fingertip gently raised his chin to search into his eyes while the other hand reached down towards his groin. Patiently, calmly, deliberately, Hadrian, the ruler of the known world with thirty Legions at his beck-and-call plus twenty-thousand slaves, reached to the lower hem of my friend's tunic lying tucked behind his furled cloak. Ant reacted with a reflex shift of body weight but didn't overtly respond to the provocation. In fact his body was surprisingly impassive, I thought.

Hadrian lifted the tunic's hem away from his groin with one hand, and then gently, purposefully, teasingly, searched with the other into the binding folds of the loin-clothed mound lying close against Ant's crotch.

My recollections of my friend's threshold of sexual arousal indicated an immediate response by his generative organ; after all each of us was at the age where self-relief was a thrice-daily necessity to satisfy the demands of hyperactive genitalia and their wantonly lurid fantasies. We used to joke about it. Our organs certainly had a mind of their own which simply ignored our better judgment.

Hadrian obviously understood these things. Silently fussing about for a moment he playfully withdrew Antinous's already firmed member from behind the folds of the flannel. Antinous flexed bolt upright in astonishment while remaining available to Caesar's touch. Even at my distance from the scene I recognized how Antinous was fully aroused in a manner familiar to me. He had firmed despite the chill air.

He breathing was accelerating. I sensed he was powerfully turned on by his extraordinary predicament. Antinous has a comfortably sized organ, though nothing to gloat over as some owners do when on display in the public baths. Yet his erection is nothing to be ashamed of either. Perhaps he was no roadside priapic Herm with its extravagant *phallus* to defend a house from intruders by its sheer enormity, yet he was adequately built for pleasing action.

He stood motionless before Caesar, immovable, stricken, mesmerized, thrilled, but goose-fleshed. His erection and his scrotum were exposed from beneath his tunic in heightened arousal. His mouth gaped open, galvanized in amazement.

Hadrian calmly spat into one hand a few times and then applied his saliva to Antinous's package projecting from its foreskin. He worked the spittle into every nerve-end and sensory nodule of his member while his other hand methodically fondled the testicles. Both received intense, languid, voluptuous attention. Due to my friend's pelvic thrust projecting from beneath his tunic, I guessed Hadrian might have been fingering his anus with his other hand.

Shifting closer to look intently into Antinous's eyes, Caesar savored his intoxicated responses as he kneaded and stroked his parts. I thought I detected half a smile wash across Hadrian's face; a smile which combined teasing whimsy with some form of victory. It was entirely without sleazy prurience; it was quite *generous* in its intent. It was affectionate, even loving. Yet it was knowing.

Antinous simply stared wide-eyed back at Hadrian. He was uprightly entranced with astonishment verging on sensory swoon.

A few protracted moments elapsed until, with a faint gasp, half-closed fluttering eyelids, and a writhed undulation at the hips, he quivered ecstatically as he flung back his head in cathartic release. His bright shaggy hair bounced in the moonlight as he emitted a strangulated cry, an animal yowl of agonized rapture. I guessed he had ejaculated charges of semen directly into his paramour's fondling palm, just as I had seen him forcefully expel on those occasions of our jerk-off competitions under the stars by a wilderness fireside. Young men are fascinated by the extraordinary demands of their sex drive and its uncontrollable bodily manifestations.

Hadrian, bemused but determined, teasingly rolled the ejaculate around Antinous's penis to intensify his sensitivities, causing him to squirm in feigned hurt in a burst of nervous laughter. He then calmly wiped his palm on the flannel of Ant's loincloth while grinning into his companion's shining eyes.

The episode complete, he took Antinous's cranium in both hands to fondly buss him on the forehead, each eyelid, the tip of the nose, his lips, and bat a final brotherly tap to the butt.

'Young men are so hasty,' I heard Hadrian mutter in amusement, 'they don't wait around, do they?'

'Can I do something pleasing for you too, my lord?' I heard Antinous ask limply.

I suddenly realized how such reciprocation could lead in embarrassing directions; directions I might not wish to witness or even know about. The prospect of being obliged to avert my eyes from watching my best friend being butt-fucked by Rome's great emperor in an artificial garden by pale moonlight rose to mind. But I was immediately rescued from this prospect. Hadrian responded.

'You have already done enough,' he replied. 'But there'll be time for those things some other day, Antinous. We are going to part now, so you can return to your friends. I have other matters to address. But I hope my message came through to you? If you speak to your father for his permission, and if it is given, I would welcome you with your friend

Lysias and your servants too, at Athens in the spring. You could join me for the Festival of Dionysus celebrations. That is, if it is your father's will. Farewell until then. I hope we meet again, Antinous. I look forward to it.'

Hadrian began to wind his cloak around himself in readiness to depart.

'Hadrian,' I heard Antinous murmur, halting the emperor in his move away from the couch with a presumptuous tug at his sleeve.

Caesar froze at this lapse of protocol as Antinous searched into his eyes. He had used the emperor's name in a familiar manner, while the tug at the sleeve was not a subject's approved kiss of a cloak hem. As we all know, a Caesar may engage in familiarity without permission, but a citizen should not do the same at risk of a lethal response from the Guard.

Hadrian scanned the garden to flick his head in a subtle negative shake. It immediately made me wonder if he expected hidden guards to be monitoring the occasion from somewhere nearby. If so, they were not evident to me, thankfully.

Antinous stumbled out his words. He was quaking with emotion.

'When next we meet, and with my Father's endorsement, I hope to be able to say to you '*Yes Caesar, I am yours*', if this remains your desire,' he said softly but clearly.

Hadrian smiled.

'Prepare yourself well, Antinous of Bithynia. Your true life is about to begin. You will fulfill your destiny to your heart's desire. Until Athens, farewell.'

Caesar rewound himself in his cloak and swept back into the Marquee's dark interior. Once again Antinous was standing alone in the moonlight, disheveled, cold, while fumbling to adjust his loincloth and re-furl his cloak.

But then I perceived how, besides myself beneath the pale gray moon, another concealed observer had seen these events. Both of us had witnessed the inauguration of something which proved to be momentous for our generation."

"An observer, you say?" Suetonius interjected.

"Yes. I began to back away from my place of concealment. I withdrew into the shadows to return to the lanes leading back to our sleeping quarters. I moved quickly to ensure I returned ahead of

Antinous. I knew Antinous would feel his honor had been impugned if he realized I had observed the exchange with Caesar.

As I moved into the shadows I noticed another figure flit through the darkness ahead of me, someone who too had been concealed. Startled but evasive, I caught the image of this figure from the corner of my eye silently emerging through the moonlight and again disappearing into darkness. It happened momentarily. This figure must surely have seen me too concealed up ahead. He too had probably been a witness to the transaction between Hadrian and Ant. I perceived the shadowy figure's height, breadth, and body type to have been similar to someone like Arrian.

It dawned on me how the absence of Horse Guards or Praetorian protectors at the site of the rendezvous was intentional to permit the night's events to proceed unhindered. The emperor's assignation with my friend was arranged to be entirely private and personal.

I then moved swiftly through the tent city's lanes to be ahead of my school friend's return."

The four listeners heard out Lysias's reminiscence with fascination. The graphic details of Caesar's adventure with his Bithynian subject concentrated their minds wonderfully. Lysias returned to silence while sipping at his wine.

CHAPTER 11

"So? What happened next?" Suetonius asked.

Lysias sat upright to begin his testimony again.

"On returning to our sleeping quarters I was confronted with another surprise. Our staff was standing around staring in dismay at the places where Antinous and I were supposed to be asleep. Squatted atop Antinous's bed of piled straw a pace from my own stack was a human figure reclining in a nonchalant manner.

She was a young woman of striking pertness, delicacy, and shining with a copper-colored complexion. Her dark hair was bound high on her head in the fashionable style of gentlewomen of quality at Rome, pinned with needles of ivory. She was dressed in the fine, sheer raiment and silken mantle of a member of the Imperial Court adorned with drop earrings and a necklet of filigree gold. Her eyes were outlined in thin black lines of *kohl, a* striking fashion affected at the eastern half of the Empire.

She had a travelling sack bulging with possessions lying beside her, and as I approached I realized she also had a sheathed *gladius* short-sword lying on the blanket before her. The weapon's matching hip dagger and its finely-crafted belt-strap were immediately-recognizable. It was the knife which had brought down the boar earlier in the day. Hadrian's knife. It was accompanied by an Imperial scroll tied in scarlet silk and sealed with a clay *bulla*.

'Antinous of Bithynia?' she asked brightly as I came near.

'No, I am Lysias, his friend,' I responded. 'Who are you? What do you want with Antinous, young lady?'

'Oh,' she said firmly, 'I am instructed to speak only with Antinous of Bithynia.'

At that moment Antinous entered the marquee, only to be surprised to find everyone awake and standing forlornly around his bedding place. It was occupied by the dark eyed interloper seated between her various possessions. He glanced around the motley group facing him.

'What the …?' he gasped.

The lithe young beauty arose from her seat with a supple dexterity and a delicate feminine grace I have rarely seen expressed so effectively in a single human bodily movement. I realized the delightful creature in the resplendent attire with her supple elegance was perhaps one of the dancers from the evening's entertainments, or some other nubile attendant to the Imperial Household.

She met eye-to-eye with Antinous and immediately understood how this blond haired, tall-statured youth with the gilded suntan was her mission's objective. Someone had told her Antinous would be the very good looking fellow of our group.

'Antinous of Bithynia, victor of the Hunt, greetings!' she proclaimed gaily. 'I am instructed by my master to deliver these gifts to you and ensure their purpose is understood.'

With a nod of the head gesturing to the sword and dagger at her feet while proffering the official scroll, she continued trippingly.

'These are awards from Great Caesar to be delivered directly into the hands of Antinous of Bithynia. I am also instructed to deliver myself into your household's service as well,' she said with a teasing flash of the eyes. She rose to her full height barely up to Antinous's chest and offered the *gladius*, dagger, belt, and scroll, accompanied by a small kidskin pouch knobbled with bulges. It suggested many coins within.

'Yes, I am Antinous of Bithynia, young lady,' he confirmed with formality before the eyes of all. 'So who are you?'

Antinous scanned his grooms and steward for an explanatory response.

'The young lady was escorted to our tent by two of Caesar's soldiers,' his steward said. 'They departed just before you arrived. She is unaccompanied.'

Antinous glanced at me questioningly but then took the sword belt with its attached scabbard and dagger in his hands and unsheathed the well-wrought polished blade. The gleam of quality metal and fine craftsmanship shone beneath the lamp-light while the white enameled inlays and silver decoration announced its costliness. Antinous looked to me as we both immediately recognized its origin and owner.

'It's the blade which killed the boar today. It's Caesar's.'

Antinous developed a growing blush as its implication dawned on both of us at the same time. '*A small hunting kill, a fine weapon, or a drinking vessel*', the classic definition of admissible suitor's gifts to an *eromenos* which did not imply bribery, let alone prostitution.

'My master has instructed me to say you will understand what this gift represents,' the petite birdlike woman confirmed in wide-eyed innocence.

The nutty russet of her skin, her straight line of white teeth shining from a beaming face, her whiter-than-white eyeballs with their piercingly dark pupils, the painted *kohl* around her eyes, and the slenderness of her figure told us this pretty creature was a foreigner of neither Hellene nor Asia Minor origin. Yet her spoken Greek was without accent.

Antinous nodded acknowledgement and took the scroll and sack of coins in curiosity. He broke the scroll's clay seal and unwound the papyrus. Glancing to me and the others from time to time, he began to softly enunciate the message within.

'*Antinous of Bithynia, son of Telemachus of Claudiopolis, greetings! I, Imperator Caesar Publius Aelius Hadrianus, as a token of my friendship, regard, and affection, bestow your person with this gift of a finely wrought sword of best Syracuse workmanship. This sword was once the property of King Nikomedes IV of Bithynia, being a part of the treasure endowed by his estate to the SPQR at the time of Caesar Augustus. You will recall this sword's efficacy in our Imperial Hunt this day, and comprehend its intended message as a gesture of my regard. Respect the beauty and quality of this rare artifact just as I respect the equivalent character of its human recipient.*

Accompanying this gift is an endowment of a specially selected slave acquired at market at the Isle of Delos, the holy abode of our divine Apollo, for your personal service. THAIS is her name. She is fifteen years of age, and a native of Cyrene at Roman Africa. She is trained in all domestic duties, household stewardship, finances, is a body servant or lady's companion, and is a dancer and singer of talent.

However, more importantly, she is also schooled in Palatine Latin, Koine Greek, plus Syrian Aramaic to a high standard for your continuing language instruction. She reads and writes in all three scripts. This bestowal of ownership with its documents is supported with a purse of coins to pay for upkeep of her services for at least a year. Future annual upkeep is subject to your continuing demand of her services. Yours in friendship, etc."

Antinous and I stared with amazement at this gift of living flesh standing demurely before us. Antinous peeped into the pouch. His eyes widened as he poured the contents of the purse onto the cloth before him.

A pile of coins of deep yellow gold lay before him, to the audible gasp of the surrounding household attendants. There was enough gold in the pouch to purchase several slaves of quality and provide their upkeep for years. Antinous didn't think anyone of the group, including him, had ever before seen so much gold in one place.

The assembly looked to the human acquisition before them in wonderment. She looked back to Antinous with an open expression of disingenuous delight and a brightly twinkling smile.

'Hello Master. My name is Thais,' she volunteered without permission, 'I am trained as an educated servant for a master or mistress of quality. I was born of a slave mother at Cyrene, capital of Cyrenaica in Africa, and raised in the household of the Imperial Prefect of the province at Cyrene and Ptolemais. My mother was Lais of Canopus, the concubine favorite of the Prefect. I am competent in the duties necessary for managing a household of quality such as the Prefect's two palaces in Cyrenaica.

At age fifteen on my maturity I was sold in the specialist slave emporium at Delos in the Aegean Sea. I was offered by my master, the Prefect, on the understanding I was to be sold only to masters or mistresses of honor, and not to traders in virgins or courtesans. I am told my price was subsidized by my master to ensure a select placement. However, due to my language skills and proficiencies in the service of the Prefect and his wife, I was acquired by the Imperial Administration on behalf of the emperor's Household, possibly on the Prefect's recommendation.'

Thais paused to observe and assess her audience's reactions. She then continued.

'Among my duties, I am intended as a live-in tutor of spoken languages and of courtly comportment. I am an instructor in manners in the Imperial mode to special students assigned by the Imperial Administration. I am charged by my former master that you, Antinous of Bithynia, are to receive my services,' the delicately boned waif with the hugely bright eyes and winning, if presumptuous, manner announced with lively enthusiasm.

Antinous and I shared a querulous expression and then burst into laughter.

'Well,' said Antinous after studied consideration, 'I see. Welcome to our service, Slave Thais of Cyrene. Make yourself useful to my steward and ourselves until such a time as I confirm your acquisition with the elders of my household.'

'I am desirous, Master, of performing well in your service,' she responded with a courteous, if slightly too obsequious, genuflection. Her response was spoken in pure Latin. It possessed an exacting pronunciation redolent of a native speaker of the *patrician* class. No Bithynian intonation was evident.

'May I take the liberty of offering this first lesson in conversational Latin, master?' Thais said with a tinkling laugh.

It was uttered with a lively gaiety which brought a smile to everyone's lips despite her faintly patronizing tone and a worrying lack of proper servility. It seemed Slave Thais had learned the habits and lifestyles of her masters too well at the Prefect's palace at Cyrene.

Antinous and I realized at last it had been a most unusual day and night.

CHAPTER 12

"So does it end there?" Clarus asked, yawning. It was now very late and the seniors of the group were inclined to catch some sleep. Only Surisca and Lysias seemed fully awake.

"No, not at all, my lord," Lysias uttered brightly. "There was then the matter of Ant's father learning of Caesar's desire to be *erastes* to his son."

"I see. So?" Suetonius asked, "What did his father have to say about it?"

The group settled back in their seats to continue hearing the testimony. Lysias again sipped wine before returning to his reminiscences.

"As his best friend, I accompanied Antinous to his family villa at *Polis*. The interview was held in the portico atrium where the men of the family meet for consultation. Antinous was obliged to formally seek paternal permission from his Father for the proposal."

"And ---?" the *Special Inspector* enquired. "What did his father say?"

"I sensed some ambivalence in Telemachus, so the occasion proved to be very memorable.

'My son, Antinous,' Telemachus opened in his rasping voice, 'the time has come for you to go out into the world to complete your education and weapons training now you have entered the older age-class of a *meirakion* warrior.'

This wiry old soldier with gray skin, grayer hair, and dulled eyes announced it in a breathy voice. He carried his left arm as a crook; his muscles stiffened due to a war wound long ago. His speech too was slightly afflicted. Telemachus was probably much younger than his visible years conveyed, but some war infirmity had aged him prematurely. He had served Rome well in the many campaigns of his youth.

I, with Antinous's elder brother and the senior steward of the House, stood impassively before their *paterfamilias* seated upright in his high chair in the atrium court. I was always a welcome guest at Ant's home, always.

'As the head of our House I, with your elder brother here as well as your deceased mother too I'm sure -- if she were here, *bless her shade!* -- with your extended family across Bithynia, your community, your tutors, and many others of good will, all encourage you on your journey. We will watch your progress from afar, and make regular sacrifice to Apollo and to his virgin sister Artemis to defend you from harm.

My son Antinous, you have received from us the blessings of a provident upbringing, proper discipline and tutoring, plus the foundation of a healthy body. You have been inducted into the code of honor which guides Hellenes to noble deeds to bring glory to our House, and brings dishonor, defeat, and death to our enemies.

You have displayed your worth as a member of our family, clan, and to our city council. You display the courage and martial skills expected of a future member of the town's militia, where you are likely to receive a commission on return from your studies.

You must now complete your education and advance to full adulthood. Someday soon you will sacrifice your first beard cuttings to Zeus as proof of your maturity. It will then be time for you to assume the joys and obligations of matrimony. In this too we will offer our supports, and we trust you will breed sons to project our seed, our *arete*, into the distant future to deliver our lineage to future generations. You must be the master of your own fate in this matter.

Lysias too, on behalf of your deceased father Lysander, I offer the same advice to you. Your mother has asked me advise you.

You both are now to go out into the world to drink of life at the font of Hellene culture at Athens. Letters of introduction and financial arrangements have been completed through the offices of Bithynia's *proxenos* ambassador at Athens by Arrian of Nicomedia.

Provision has been made for your and Lysias's education under the tutorship of the Academy of Secundus of Athens, whose school is renown. Accommodations at Athens and membership of the Kynosarges Gymnasium have been negotiated on your behalf.

You have received awards of scholarships to the College of Imperial Administration, generously endowed by your admirer Imperator Caesar Hadrian. *Praise be to Caesar!* This gesture in honoring you both is a token of your worthiness in the eyes of others. It is a remarkable boon. This now brings me to a matter of very great consequence.

A private letter conveyed to me by Caesar's Proconsul to Asia, Serenius Granianus, has enquired if I as your Father offer my authority for your special engagement, Antinous, with the Imperial Household in the station of *Friend to Caesar* until your maturity.

The role of 'Friend' is outlined under the terms of the traditional *Erastes/Eromenos* relationship of the Hellenes. It is for your further education in Greek and Roman customs, in the Latin language, courtly manners, and the procedures of Roman Law. It is for mastering the hunt and the prosecution of warfare, while sharing the companionable society of distinguished men of the *Imperium*. It means you would enter within the Imperial Household under the emperor's protection for its duration. You are entitled to include friends such as Lysias within your personal household under Caesar's patronage.

This is an extraordinary honor for a young man's advancement. Are you aware, my son, of the munificence of this endowment to a Greek of non-Roman origin? Also, son, are you aware of the implications of the role as *eromenos* to such a noble supplicant?

I am obliged to respond promptly to the Proconsul with my opinion. But importantly, my son, do you yourself accept these terms? You must think upon this and respond to me here today prior to my permission. I will be guided by your desires.'

Telemachus paused for breath, took a sip of wine from a chalice, and observed his son's response with keen intent. The previously dulled, ageing eyes glinted with the intelligence and confidence of the man at an earlier period of life. Antinous took his time to reply in the hushed chamber.

'Father, I believe I do,' Antinous responded cautiously. 'My tutors and companions have long prepared me for the prospect of a role as an *eromenos*. Among my friends, including Lysias here, we have discussed such matters often since childhood. But I had not expected a suitor to be one as noble as Great Caesar.'

I noticed Telemachus shifting uneasily in his seat.

'To receive the favor of the emperor is a remarkable boon,' Telemachus continued, 'but it has obligations to be carefully weighed. In addition to your exposure to the uppermost echelon of Roman life, the role of 'Friend' in Caesar's private *contubernium* possesses remarkable opportunities. However, it also has equally remarkable obligations.

Do you appreciate the extent of the demands to be made upon you by Caesar as your *erastes*, Antinous? I do not wish to give my permission to you unless it is your firm desire to become a *Friend of Caesar* and to freely accept such a notable mentor.'

The older man scrutinized his son with some intensity, I recall. He continued his queries.

'I am your father, Antinous. You are the fruit of my seed and, along with your elder brother, carry the seed of this House and our line into the future. I wish to ensure your well-being, son, with your personal confirmation of this proposal if it suits your temper.

It may surprise you to learn how in recent times I have received two submissions from suitors of quality for the honor of being *erastes* to you. Though they were newly-bearded, unmarried young fellows of the land-owning class a few years older than you who are probably known to you from the *palaestra* yard, I nevertheless rejected their proposals. They were petitioners of an unsatisfactory quality for my son. I did this even without discussing them with you.

However, Antinous, a proposal from Caesar seems an exemplary opportunity to your benefit, and one in which I have difficulty detecting fault. Do you agree?'

There was a thoughtful pause.

'I am proud and flattered, Father,' Antinous uttered with not a little calculation, "that Caesar has taken an interest in my character and welfare. My single day's exposure to his company at Nicomedia proved our *Princeps* to be a most generous gentleman. He was very attentive to those of us there, and to me especially, with openness I found disarming in so great a noble.

Nevertheless I request your opinion, Father, of his proposal and your advice on what you expect of me? I request your instruction about the terms of this relationship, as a father expects of a dutiful son.'

Telemachus again shifted uneasily in his seat.

'You and your friend Lysias are very young men, Antinous, barely out of childhood though already of a military age," he said. "At your age I was already serving as a junior officer with the Greek auxiliaries to Trajan's legions at Dacia.

Over the coming few years both you and Lysias will mature towards man's complete status. You will learn what it is to be a man who takes initiatives in life, who possesses focused drive and consummates his ambition by effective action in a warrior's way. It is the dynamism of being male, both physically and spiritually. It is training in a way of life which separates us of the Hellene elites from the craven races beyond the Black Sea and our borders. They are slaves to their masters.'

As he continued his brow darkened. Telemachus drew himself forward towards the four men standing before him.

'Among the Hellenes the optimum virtue is *arête*, the pursuit of excellence. In Homer or Socrates or Aristotle it is *arête* which infuses the Greek view of life. *Arete* is goodness, *arete* is achievement, *arête* is manly excellence, *arête* is when our actions rise above the conflicts of life and we achieve high honor. *Arête* propels our Olympic Games. *Arête* drives Greeks to Victory! *Arête* is life! The spirit of *arête* is the most important facet of the training of youths to full manhood,' the ageing soldier and farmer proclaimed with intensifying emotion.

'In days long ago our forefathers told that a man's masculine power, his *arête*, is carried in his life fluids. His living blood, sweat, and semen convey the masculine energies. Especially, they said, his semen, which is the source of his regenerative powers. Semen propels the seed of life of a man, and conveys within it a man's domination of his world. Our physicians say a man's semen, when sown into the body of a woman, nurtures and ripens and grows in her nourishing moistures until it blooms and fruits into a newborn child. Preferably a son.

Likewise, those ancients said, when it is planted in the body of a youth it nurtures and grows spiritually. The *arête* ripens into masculine traits worthy of participating in the society of mature men, for deeds of courage, honor and decisiveness.

The ancients said a student, an *eromenos*, partakes of his trainer's - the *erastes'* - male energy by ritually absorbing his vital spirit and vital fluid. By intimately relating to his *erastes* over time, the *eromenos* is imbued with the *erastes'* gift of the power to pursue excellence, to achieve victory, to be a leader of his people, and also in the breeding of straight-limbed sons. He learns how to act like a man in the competitive arena of life.

In return the younger man shares his friendship and his body's perfection with his *erastes* in both spiritual and physical ways. This has long been the way of the Hellene elites, my son. It has a noble pedigree over many generations.'

His listeners were deathly silent.

Antinous fumbled for an appropriate response. He was made apprehensive by such a candid exposition of the *eromenos'* role.

'I think I understand, sir, and I salute the heritage,' he waffled. 'But, Father, I humbly seek your advice on an aspect of this matter which concerns me and remains barely spoken among my tutors and peers. It is a clouded matter. It is this. Women and even young girls who have attained menarche are said to enjoy and delight in the reception of the male seed from a worthy partner, their husband. We are told their bodies are created to desire their husband's dominion and penetration so as to nurture his seed into living offspring, our sons.

They display a Nature-given satisfaction with his lust, just as we see among all the farmyard and forest creatures around us. But does an *eromenos* seek and enjoy penetration by his *erastes?* Is this the understanding of the tradition? In truth, Father, I do not think I would enjoy such an imposition upon my body or willingly succumb to another man's domination readily -- even so great and noble a man as Caesar! What is your advice on this issue? It is a concern for me.'

Telemachus sat impassively for some moments, his eyes resting upon his troubled son.

'Yes, this is certainly a question for a worthy *eromenos*,' he said. 'You are correct to raise the matter, to be frank. It's an area where polite fictions may prevail.

Yet you already know how it is natural for men to be driven by Aphrodite's urging or her child Eros's impulses? It is natural and proper for men to be hot blooded and lustful, especially the young. The urge to inject seed is common to all male creatures. The urge to receive seed by a male is less obvious, though it too exists among many creatures around us. We see it in the farmyard or forest more often than we recall, and there are many among us disposed by temperament to its appeal. However, for an *erastes* and his *eromenos* there is a subtle dispensation about the matter.

In the times since our forefathers it has been held how receipt of an *erastes'* semen need not be bodily, Antinous, it need not penetrate the body physically. Several ancient philosophers of the Hellenes have even proposed it should be entirely spiritual, not a bodily invasion aroused in the heat of lust. But 'spirituality' is an ambiguous term of uncertain meaning.

For the mutual expression of Eros among the wellborn a mode of intimate friction between the thighs has been given the tacit sanction of the Greeks. It is not talked of readily. As an *eromenos* you need not have your body's integrity and your personal honor compromised, if this is how you view such relations. Personal regard and intimacy can be shared without abject submission or penetration. You both retain your pride and there is no shame to either you or your relationship, meanwhile an *erastes'* and an *eromenos'* satisfaction can be gratified. Do you understand?'

'I see, Father,' Antinous said with lingering doubt. Telemachus continued.

'In this way the elites of the Greek world have reconciled their suitor's passion yet found ardor and solace with honor,' the old soldier continued. 'Think of Achilles and Patrocles, or the heroic tyrant-killers Aristogeiton and Harmodius, or King Alexander of Macedon and his Prince Hephaestion, where no shame is known, only glory. Yet it's also true how fierce emotion too can erupt between friends under certain circumstances, with its fulfillment consummated vehemently. Eros toys with us interminably, while we mortals are only flesh and blood.'

The four men stood silently immobile lost in wonder.

'For example I recall, Antinous, my own great friendship when two years prior to your age while serving in Dacia with an *erastes* companion of noble bearing and toughened military skills. His name was

Hippothales of Nicaea. He shared his fighter's spirit and his *arete* with me, a callow youth from the wilderness back blocks of Bithynia. We shared pains, joys, sweat, spittle, blood, and each other's body in close encounter often. Yes, Antinous.

He died bravely at Salinae in Dacia while defending me from a fierce barbarian ambush. We each here today should be eternally thankful, *thanks be to Apollo Protector.* I often pray for the comfort of Hippothales' shade and make offerings or pour libations of wine to his great honor.

Some years later when my beard had matured and my fighting skills were far better-honed, I became an *erastes* successively to two younger *ephebes.* This was prior to my marriage to your mother, Antinous. It was through a long, hard campaign fought on the plains of Pannonia.

It may come as a surprise to you to learn how Lysias's father, our heroic Lysander of Claudiopolis, was the second of these two *meirakia* young men. Our mutual friendship of that time has been the source of the close bond between our two houses long after Lysander's death at Pannonia.'

Telemachus then turned to me standing by Antinous. I was instantly alerted, even alarmed, at what might follow.

'Your father Lysander,' he announced to my astonishment, 'who was my greatest friend ever and four years my junior, died in brave combat with front line Greek auxiliaries of the *Legion II Adiutrix* under the command of Hadrian himself. This was many years before Hadrian's elevation to the purple after Trajan's death.

Lysander was cruelly overcome by three Sarmatian Jazyges madmen warriors, one of who he destroyed with his *pilum* lance while the other two fell to my blade. But the damage was already done. Lysander was mortally wounded. He took two days to die despite my every care and precaution against corruption in his wounds.

Your father's death, Lysias, was a calamity for me from which there has been no recovery. Ever. After all, at that time I was the noble and handsome Lysander's *erastes.* I was his friend-in-arms, his weapons trainer, his advisor, his protector, and his true *companion.* We were a team. We covered each other's back in battle. We fought side by side in drunken brawls. We bound each other's scrapes and wounds. We shared food. We often slept for body warmth beneath the same blanket. We talked together of our future families at *Polis* and of the sons to come. Your father knew me better than I know myself, Lysias.

After that fatal battle it was I who retrieved Lysander's body from the communal pyre for the dead to bury him with proper military honor in a field at Pannonia. It was I who dug his grave deep beyond the reach of carrion creatures, who sewed his wounds so his body was of one piece again, who licked the blood from his torn flesh to cleanse him and to absorb his *arete*.

It was I who anointed his well-formed shape with sweet oils, and who wrapped his nakedness in my own best cloak for burial. It was a nakedness well known to me.

It was I who placed Charon's coin in his mouth, who poured libations to the gods over his grave's tumulus, who burnt incense to the heavenly domains, and who screamed loud paeans of praise to his heroism while shedding bitter tears into that long, pained, rainy night on the freezing Pannonia plain.

It was I who carried back to your mother's hearth his battered armors and weapons which still hang high on display in your family's *andron*. It was I who cut the bloodied lock of hair from your father's scalp which your mother wears to this day in a locket around her neck, and which I too retain enclosed in a niche of my sword belt. Your father, Lysias, was my greatest friend ever.

Yet regardless that it is I who privately commemorates Lysander's death each anniversary with proper ceremony, and knows intimately of his courage and nobility of character, it is you - Lysias his son - who projects his seed forward into time. This is your responsibility as a son.'

Telemachus sunk back into his chair exhausted.

I was absolutely shaken by this speech. Not one of we four had heard this story in the past, though a moment's deeper reflection could have realized its possibility. Telemachus resumed his address. His features now grew magisterial.

'In a man's world of fierce war, in hard training, in labor at the battle encampment, or on a forced march, rare human beauty shines in bold relief against a warrior's harsh realm. There are men who will be captivated by, aroused to ardor for, actively entice, and lustfully pursue to consummation such a paragon in whatever guise it manifests. Many men will be indifferent to the gender of their enchanter.

The extraordinary bloom of youth and the urge to entwine with it bodily before it passes away into time becomes an obsession for warriors daily facing fearful danger and imminent death. A beardless *ephebe* crossing over the short bridge into full manhood may discover how sharing the friendship of such a man can be both gratifying as well as protective. And its pleasures may be found by surprise to be reciprocal.'

The chamber was utterly silent.

'I think I see, Father,' Antinous offered hesitantly, politely, if uncertainly. 'All this was unknown to me, so I rely on your guidance.'

Telemachus brightened.

'But enough of this inconsequentia! Basically, what transpires between honorable men in private is their own affair. We do not snoop. So let us now explore Caesar's proposition, my son, seeing you appear to be reconciled to the role of a *Friend of Caesar*. I will repeat my query to you, do you accept Caesar's proposition, yes or no?'

All eyes turned to Antinous.

'If it is with your permission and blessing, I do Father,' he replied with renewed confidence.

'Then let it be recorded here before us: I provide my approval on behalf of our Household,' Telemachus intoned. 'I will write to Hadrian's Proconsul immediately.'

"The hour is late, Suetonius. We need sleep to be fresh for tomorrow's interviews. We should continue the Bithynian's interview in the morning," Clarus tiredly whined.

Lysias at last rose from his seat to depart.

"Am I discharged from further interview tonight?" he asked politely. Suetonius nodded.

"Yet we require you to attend us again just after sunrise. Do we send for you with *lictors* and the Guard, or will you arrive of your own volition?" Clarus asked sternly.

"On my honor, I will be prompt in attendance without escort," he confirmed. Lysias departed.

Clarus was about to dismiss Strabon and his assistant until the morning but Secretary Vestinus interrupted.

"Something of interest has come up," he announced quietly. "Caesar has released the body of the dead Bithynian into the hands of the

Egyptian priests," he announced. "They have taken the cadaver to a special pavilion by the riverside. I am told they are preparing to perform their arts upon the corpse to defeat decay. It occurred to me you might wish to inspect the youth and his condition before they damage his tissues?"

The group looked to each other with immediate interest.

"Certainly. Lead on!" Suetonius called. "Sleep will wait!"

CHAPTER 13

Secretary Vestinus led the four through the camp's labyrinth of tented corridors and lanes. From behind felt walls cheery gales of laughter and muffled conversations echoed, while the rhythms of drummers or the heavy sighs of lovemaking were emitted elsewhere. Suetonius's early-to-bed generation had forgotten how younger folk engage in pleasurable activity late into the night.

They arrived at a pavilion erected in the Egyptian style close by the Nile's shore. Suetonius, Clarus, Vestinus, Surisca, and Strabon noted how it was signposted with a blue-painted Egyptian cartouche inscribed with the Eye of Horus symbol. A large-bodied, armed Nubian guard plus an imperial Horse Guard of German stock maintained watch by the pavilion's entrance. Both obstructed their approach with their weapons.

"We demand entrance in the name of Caesar!" Vestinus proclaimed.

The guards deferred to Vestinus. The Nubian disappeared into the pavilion to seek permission for their entrance. He reappeared accompanied by the priest who had been in the company of Pachrates earlier at Hadrian's reception chamber.

On sighting the four men and a woman he genuflected deeply before them in a spectacularly deferential manner, accompanied by a tinkling of bracelets, necklets, earrings, and golden chains as he bowed.

"My lords," the priest uttered in broken, accented Greek, "I am at your service."

"Egyptian, you have the cadaver of the dead youth Antinous within?" Clarus declared bluntly. "We are here to inspect the body."

Despite his priestly eyes drifting over the scarlet stripes of the togas of the two senior men with a visible calculation of their status, the Egyptian waffled his response.

"I am at your humble service, my lords, but I am presently engaged in the holy process of preparing the body of the deceased for rites of death on behalf of Great Caesar," he pleaded. "The preparation is underway, and is most displeasing to view, my lords."

"Displeasing?" Clarus asked in a stentorian tone. "We are familiar with the realities of death, Egyptian!"

Clarus was uttering a truism if ever Suetonius had heard one.

"Give us entrance immediately!"

"I bow deep in humility, great lord, before your noble stations, but do you possess the written authority of Pachrates, the high priest of Amun? I am only under the instruction of my master, Priest Pachrates," he said somewhat riskily, "and may not take orders from others. This pavilion is consecrated to the god Amun for the purpose of our rites. Only celebrants of the god are permitted entry into this sacred space, my lords. Otherwise Amun will be offended and bad omens could be invoked. "

The large Nubian was toying with his hip dagger and flexing his small wicker shield in readiness for action, unsure of the nature of this confrontation and awaiting the priest's signal for a response. He did so with some trepidation in the presence of three mature-age Romans in formal togas.

It is at times such as this that Clarus performs best, Suetonius recalled. With a sharp hiss through clenched teeth, the magistrate swept the priest and the Nubian aside with one arm and lunged through the pavilion's flaps. The others including Surisca swiftly followed through the opening.

In the gloom of the pavilion's interior the four could see several Egyptian workers hovering around a worktable lit by blazing torches shimmering their fumes through a vent into the night sky. The bench appeared to hold the bodily remains of the drowned youth laid out for the worker's attentions. An intense charge of cloying incense perfumed the chamber to mask the atmosphere, but the underlying sickly-sweet odor of decay cut through the fragrance nonetheless.

A separate table stood nearby with another body's shape lying under a covering. It was attended by two other workers, one of whom wore Greek not Egyptian attire. As the four entered the pavilion Suetonius noted how a covering cloth was quickly flung across the figure on the second table to obscure its features.

Jars of varying sizes and instruments of a surgical nature were laid on other tables, while *amphorae* of fluids stood in their racks to one side. Strips of linen were piled into several baskets nearby. The group gingerly approached the worktables as the Egyptians ceased their activities and turned to confront the intruders. They had been splashing scoops of river water over the table to sluice its surface.

Antinous lay stretched atop the table, held up by wooden braces under his neck and hip.

The workers were evacuating the innards from his cadaver with surgical hooks. They drew the guts from an incision in the intestinal area and slid the slimy entrails onto a large wicker tray. The perforated wicker allowed the waters to rinse detritus away while the intestinal tissues remained behind.

Streaks of coagulated blood, mucus, and fecal matter from the innards was rinsed away but left the fleshy tissues undamaged. The five intruders immediately drew the folds of their robes to cover their faces against the odors.

"What is going on here, Egyptian, what is this process?" Clarus demanded. "It seems sacrilegious."

"We are preparing the body of the Worthiness for public display, great lord," the priest groveled before his betters. "It is not sacrilegious, it is performed with the prayers and rites suited to a god.

We must cleanse the inner cavities of the deceased of all putrefying organs before they pollute his Great Worthiness. The brain is especially difficult to recover without damaging his features. A body left in its natural state will emit polluting miasmas which quickly corrupt the flesh. Already a day has passed. Bloating and infestation are underway. By removing his organs into pickling jars and packing his cavity with linens drenched in cedar oil, as well as painting protective wax onto the skin, we delay corruption for a few days. But only a few days, lords, no longer. Decay is unavoidable unless we engage in proper Royal Embalming."

Clarus spoke sharply to the priest.

"I am told, Egyptian, you possess arts which will preserve a body indefinitely, not just a few days? I have been shown such miracles at Memphis."

"My lords, Great Caesar has demanded his companion be displayed in two morning's time. Special ceremonies are planned. Caesar requires his young friend to be ready for public showing on that occasion. Royal Embalming takes two months to achieve, not two days," he intoned with unctuous servility but evident honesty. "He would be bathed in special salts for a full month, just to begin."

"What do you do with his innards?" Suetonius asked. "Are these dispensed with?"

"We wash and oil them carefully, my lord, to protect them, and store them in canopic jars in protective lotions to await Holy Divination," the priest informed us. "They are accorded great respect, my lord, as is to be expected of such a Special Worthiness as this noble youth."

"Holy Divination?" Suetonius asked, "what is 'holy divination'?"

"Sirs, I am instructed that the entrails of Caesar's companion are to be prepared for divination. Their occult message is to be interpreted by the great priest Pachrates, Servant of Amun from Memphis," he soothed in a reverential tone. "My master awaits our delivery of the necessary elements as soon as they are prepared."

"Where are you to deliver the entrails?" Clarus demanded. "To whom and where?"

The priest looked anxiously at his workers and the Romans with their solitary female. He hesitated.

"Well?" said Clarus sharply.

"To the Temple of Amun beyond Besa on this east bank," he murmured reluctantly.

"And to whom?" Clarus added.

"To my master, the priest of Amun, Pachrates, my lords – but in the presence of Great Caesar himself," he stated with subtle emphasis on the emperor's name.

"In the presence of Caesar?" Suetonius and Clarus voiced in unison. Suddenly, it occurred to each of the group they had stumbled onto a project which might have been better left unknown.

"May I proceed then with my duties, my lords?" the priest oozed with a glint of victory.

The mention of Caesar was his masterstroke, he believed. But Suetonius felt there was now much more to be known.

"What is beneath the cloth of the other table?" he demanded.

A body shape was clearly evident beneath the folds. Was another corpse being eviscerated here, he wondered? Is there another death involved here?

"It is nothing, my lord, it is not to be considered," the priest fumbled.

Suetonius took the Clarus approach to simply walk to the table to flip the covering away from its contents. The priest cried "No, no, my lord!"

The Greek workman and his Egyptian assistant stood back smartly as the object beneath was revealed.

A figure of a human body carved into a single log of softwood was lying on the table. Its lower limbs were apparently still incomplete in mid-carve. Tools, chisels, and fine-edged razors lay nearby along with pots of paints and brushes.

The shape of the body conformed closely to the proportions of the figure of Antinous lying on the other bench. The head and facial features were already at an advanced stage of sculpting into a likeness of the Bithynian's face. Flesh-tone color had been applied to its surface.

"What is happening here, Greek?" Suetonius demanded. "I am an investigator commissioned by the emperor, Caesar Hadrian. Who are you, and what is this effigy? Name yourself and your status."

The Greek trembled before the man in the toga.

"I am Cronon of the Fayum, sir, registered in my *nome* as a freeborn artisan" he pleaded in Greek accented with the local guttural Egyptian dialect. "I am a painter of images of the living and the dead, my lord. I prepare coffins with portraits of their inhabitants so the Land Of The Dead can identify the owners throughout posterity. It is my trade, my lord. I have been hired to create an exact portrait of his Great Worthiness, the god Antinous."

The man was obviously a local born tradesman of Greek immigrant descent. Suetonius had seen such portraits of the Greeks and Romans of the Fayum Oasis and at Canopus in their prime of life which are painted onto coffins in anticipation of the day of their funeral. Many people retain these portraits instead of sculpted busts because they are very realistic likenesses. They are displayed in their homes as a record of their appearance at an earlier time of life.

"But what is it you are performing here? This is an effigy, not a painted image," the biographer blurted. The man bowed and offered obeisance in an especially demeaning way for a Greek. He had acculturated well to Egyptian values, Suetonius thought.

"My lord, we are preparing an exact likeness of the god. It, it, it ---" he replied, but trailed away uncertainly. The priest interrupted.

"Sirs, Great Caesar and Priest Pachrates have commanded we possess a copy of the cadaver should the god decay beyond acceptance," he said. "We are creating a true likeness of Antinous of Bithynia. It is done in materials which will sustain exposure to the elements without decomposition. The likeness will be very accurate, my lord. It will be substituted for the fleshly body should spoiling overtake the god."

"Oh," Suetonius responded somewhat dismayed, "I see. You are taking precautions against decay?" But somehow Suetonius was not entirely persuaded by these responses. Something was not ringing true. He waved to his companions to gather close out of earshot of the Egyptians.

"Does any of this make sense to us?" he asked, "We have a corpse being eviscerated for priestly divination of its entrails. We have a wooden copy being prepared for its apparent replacement if decay sets in. And we have this magician Pachrates taking full control of the funeral rites in an antique Egyptian ceremony. I recall how Caesar was aghast at the prospect of any form of autopsy! Yet here we have a full-scale disemboweling underway? There's no consistency in this."

Clarus raised a question.

"Can someone tell me, what they are on about when they talk about 'the god Antinous'?" he asked. "In what way is Caesar's *catamite* a god?"

"Masters," Surisca quietly interjected, "with your permission, may I speak?"

They nodded grumpily in unison as people do when there's no alternative offering.

"It was today's street gossip at Hermopolis and among the ferrymen when I was traveling to your tent city how a marvelous omen had occurred. A true miracle of The Isia was being touted by the priests. I was told a special sacrifice had been made to the divinities. A very special man had drowned in the River Nile today, the first day of The Isia.

They say someone who drowns in the Nile as a sacrifice to Osiris during The Isia becomes Osiris Himself. It is a tradition. The sacrifice is a miracle which will protect against a poor flood next year. Osiris will protect us in exchange for the life of the sacrificed man.

Is it right to say that your dead friend might be the special sacrifice, the drowned man? If so, he has become the god Osiris on this auspicious day of The Isia."

The four men glanced from one to the other. None articulated a word, yet each knew what the other was thinking. What is going on here? The coincidences are now becoming too obvious. The Nile floods badly; a sacrifice is called for. On the first day of The Isia Antinous conveniently drowns; etcetera. How much of this is accidental, they were asking themselves?

"May I now continue with my duties, great lords?" the priest asked. "We must work at speed to combat decay, and my master awaits delivery of the sacred tissues."

"I have two matters to address with the body, Egyptian," Suetonius stated firmly, "and I have a single question to ask of you and your workers. Firstly, I wish to inspect the wrists and neck of the deceased."

Suetonius stepped closer to the cadaver of the youth lying askew on the table awash with waters and bodily residues. He pointed to the wrists of both hands.

The nearest worker lifted Antinous's arms for his inspection so he could achieve a closer view of each wrist. Clarus too moved nearer to view the wrists. Neither was marked or damaged. There was no incision. Yet Suetonius was convinced he had seen an incision when the same corpse lay on Hadrian's divan in his tents only seven or eight hours previously. The Praetorian Urbicus had confirmed the incision when he and his troops first retrieved the youth's body from its fishermen finders.

Suetonius looked across to Clarus who was equally as wide-eyed at the lack of an incision.

The Egyptian priest observed the two with some apparent concern but made no comment.

"Show me the lad's neck," Suetonius demanded. "Surisca, come closer," he asked his honorary male associate.

She stepped forward to the table. "I want you to see these markings and tell me what they are," he asked, quite clearly recalling the several hickey-like bruises or decay blooms on the youth's throat from the earlier viewing.

Once again a worker lifted Antinous's head from the supporting woodblock pillow beneath his cranium. Again Clarus, Surisca, and Suetonius peered at the throat and neck of the youth. The markings which were clearly seen only hours earlier were no longer evident.

"What markings, master?" she asked.

Again, Clarus and Suetonius were wide-eyed. The workers were silent. Neither the wrist incision nor the roseate blemishes were visible.

"Egyptian," Suetonius proclaimed in exasperation, "we are dismayed. There were certain markings on this body only hours ago. And I'm not talking about the faint scar across the lad's left cheek."

The priest simply smiled apologetically in feigned humility.

Surisca had an idea.

"May I, master?" she asked the biographer with her eyes firmly on the youth's neck, "I think I have an answer."

The courtesan with the full bosom, the luscious flood of hair, and the well-modulated voice wiped a single index finger across Antinous's throat. After checking her fingertip she held it up for the group to view. The tip was covered in a thin slime of pink-tinted fat. His throat was painted with a cosmetic in a fleshy color and dusted with powders to present a natural appearance.

Surisca then took a kerchief from her sash and wiped it carefully over Antinous's neck. A thin line of make-up paint wiped off revealing a streak of yellowed cadaver flesh beneath. It exposed several rosy blemishes.

These were the marks Suetonius recalled, but now the hickeys were no longer pale pink blazons on his throat, they were blue-gray bruises seeping into his tissue. Each was edged in a thin yellow rim. Perhaps corruption was underway?

Surisca continued to swab the paint and reveal the full extent of the bruising. She uncovered four love-bites on the upper left side of his throat, and three on the lower alternate side, in two differing sizes. Suetonius looked directly at the Egyptian.

"Why didn't you tell us you had painted the marks, priest?" he demanded.

"You did not ask, sir," was the inadequate reply.

Surisca now applied her cloth to one of the wrists. As she lifted the left arm and wiped her napkin on its inner side a small lump fell to the tabletop. The priest leapt forward and sharply cried "No!" trying to halt the procedure, but Clarus pushed him back.

Surisca continued with her inspection of the fallen item and held it up for the group to view. It was a small wedge of wax embedded with fine pins of ivory. Surisca had bumped a slender molding of wax fitted with pins which had fallen from a deep incision on Antinous's left wrist. The incision had not been simply sewn together as one does with the cut limbs of warriors; it had been packed with wax to conceal its very existence. Surisca checked the right wrist but found no similar incision.

"Seven bruises and a slash into the left wrist," Clarus confirmed. "Is there anything else we should note before these people destroy the cadaver entirely? Are there other hidden wounds, I wonder?"

Suetonius took the initiative. "Priest, one further question."

"Yes," the Egyptian responded coolly. To date he had not been especially eager to meet requests in a helpful manner.

"How long had your team been assembled at Besa to attend to this preservation of the body?" Suetonius asked, looking him directly into the eye to detect any shiftiness.

"Sir, we are residents of Besa at the Temple Of Amun. We are already here," he offered as Suetonius sensed a half-smiled quickness to his response. "We assembled only yesterday by instruction of Priest Pachrates on behalf of Great Caesar."

"I see," Suetonius said. He took a more audacious path.

"Tell me Greek ---," he addressed the painter of pictures from the Fayum, "when were you summoned to this place from your home city?"

The priest sharply interrupted the Greek's reply. He sensed the drift of the query.

"This is irregular, my lord!", he called.

Clarus simply replied, "Shut up, priest!"

The Greek artisan, a quiet sensitive man who would not have been aware of the nature of the interrogations underway but who was fully aware of the status and powers of the men before him in russet-striped white togas, muttered his hesitant response.

"I was instructed to be at Besa before the first day of The Isia, my lord," he said plainly.

"By whom?" Suetonius asked as sweetly as possible.

"I was contracted by Priest Kenamun's servants, my lord," he responded cautiously, nodding towards the Egyptian priest before them. The priest, now known to the team to be named Kenamun, seethed with suppressed anger.

"And when was that?" the Roman finalized. "When were you asked to come to Besa?"

"Six weeks ago, sir," he continued. "Priest Kenamun's servant contracted me at The Fayum six weeks ago. It takes at least three weeks by mule and sail to reach Besa from The Fayum, my lords, where I am a well known painter of portraits for funerals."

Suetonius looked across at the Egyptian. His brow was furrowed. Clarus, Vestinus, and Suetonius realized they had uncovered something unexpected. Surisca understood the situation as well.

"Six weeks ago? That's long before the death of your client, isn't it," Suetonius offered graciously. "This is such remarkable prescience of mind. Please continue with your duties, gentlemen."

Outside the pavilion in the balmy night air the group of four took stock of the situation.

"Gentlemen," Suetonius said, incidentally acknowledging Surisca as a token male, "we have here a circumstance where Caesar's companion has seven love bites to his throat. This may indicate his last day or night was a time of intimate passion?

His left wrist possesses a deep incision sufficient to bleed fatally, despite his death seeming to be by drowning only a day ago. And yet a specialist painter of funerary portraits was contracted many weeks ago before the lad's death to fulfill a mission to prepare an effigy of the dead youth. I might also add, the Greek artisan was contracted by a priest who dissembles about the concealment of wounds on a corpse. These might be seen to be a suspicious set of circumstances? What do we make of it?"

They were each silent for a period. Surisca spoke politely again.

"With permission, masters, may I offer an opinion about the marks of his neck?"

Even Clarus now was coming around to an acceptance of the young woman's contribution to their investigation, though with *patrician* reluctance.

"Speak."

"The marks upon the young man's neck? I have seen many such markings in my time," she offered in a manner which received little dispute from her hearers.

"To my eye, they are the loving attentions of two people. A woman and a man."

"What on earth makes you think that?" asked Clarus, surprised. A male was to be assumed. But a female was less expected. Surisca continued in her matter-of-fact way.

"The hickeys at the far right side of his neck are higher up and are of a large size, while the ones to the left of his neck are lower down and smaller in size. The positions of the lower small ones makes me think they indicate a partner who is shorter than the dead youth, and therefore possibly female. The higher large ones suggest a male partner. Also, the female bites were placed several hours earlier than the male ones."

"Why do you say they were implanted some hours apart, woman?" Clarus queried.

"It has been my observation how hickeys change their coloring over a very short period of time," she explained. "At first they appear as pale pink blemishes, but over the hours their color changes to a deeper hue and eventually go from rosy to gray with a fine yellow rim. It takes almost a day for a hickey to develop the yellow rim.

The two sets of love bites on your friend's neck show a distinct difference in color. The smaller ones already possess a graying color and a thin yellow rim, while the larger ones are still at the rose stage. I've seen it often on the necks of my colleagues and noted it, too, on my own."

When they thought about it, they felt Surisca had a point. There was no issue with the young man's diverse choice of partners, Suetonius acknowledged to himself. Yet Antinous was known by all to be the emotional property of Caesar for the previous five years, so it would be a brave man or woman indeed who would be so unwise as to engage in intimacy with the emperor's recent *Favorite*.

"What about the incision in his wrist?" Suetonius asked. "It was deep enough to sever all vital veins. This was no accident. If it were done before his drowning, he would have bled to death long before he drowned. If it were done after his drowning, it would be pointless. Did he do it himself? Or was it done to him? And when? So, is this suicide or murder?"

"Yet I understand Antinous was left-handed?" Clarus reminded. "In wielding a weapon Antinous would logically use his left hand to cut at his right wrist, not at his left wrist. But the incision was in his left wrist. What do we make of this?"

"I have seen the youth playing ball games and casting javelin," the Special Inspector offered, "and from recall he was adept at utilizing both right and left hands. He often drank from his cups with his left hand, while he also reclined at his dining couch on his left side as is normal. Nevertheless he wore his weapons to his right side. So perhaps he was ambidextrous?"

"That indeed it seems," said Clarus with irony, alluding to Surisca's theory of the hickeys. "And despite these issues not one of us knew of Caesar's appointment with the magician Pachrates and his 'holy divination' ceremony?" Clarus forwarded. "Is this what our two day deadline is all about?"

"I admit it is not the sort of thing I would have thought Caesar would contemplate. After all, only a few hours ago he was utterly distraught at his companion's demise. I can't see how an occult reading of the lad's exposed innards fits my picture of his mood at this time."

Suetonius scratched his head. "There's something missing from our understanding of the situation. Hadrian is not a cruel-minded Caligula nor a rapacious Nero, is he? So what could our *Princeps* hope to gain from such a disrespectful augury?"

"Gentlemen, and the lady Surisca, I'd say it is time for each of us to sleep," Clarus declared. He was exhausted.

Suetonius was surprised to hear his *patron* acknowledge his assistant as a 'Lady'. Perhaps she had earned her acknowledgement in his eyes by her contributions.

"I agree, my good Clarus," he responded. "I too wish to sleep on the day's adventures and digest its meaning. Tomorrow will be a very busy day."

His eyes lingered upon the shapely proportions of his Honorary Male companion, Surisca. Her post-midnight pleasurable potentials skated through his imagination. Perhaps, he considered, it was time the activities rudely interrupted at the *House of the Blue Lotus* were fulfilled?

CHAPTER 14

Suetonius looked around the chamber. Vestinus had arranged the space for Surisca and him to share. Two simple traveling beds adorned the chamber. Each was dressed with a thin mattress and a linen sheet accompanied by a simple pillow. Considering how Suetonius had been slumming-it in a rented Nile ferry with five antiquarian notables of Alexandria, the encampment chamber was luxuriously appointed.

A single net tumbled from a high pole as protection from the airborne creatures buzzing around. Suetonius instructed a slave to drag the two beds together side by side for Surisca and he to share, despite a central separating ridge. It was as good as excuse as any, he thought, to encourage intimacy for the night.

Surisca retired to a camp washhouse guided by a slave to complete her toilet. Suetonius presumed she would also perform whatever precautionary arts a woman of her profession uses to avoid pregnancy. He guessed it might be something more artful than an Egyptian crocodile dung pessary or other traditional native contraceptive.

She returned to their chamber dressed in one of her beguilingly translucent nightgowns of Kos lace tied in the high bosomed Syrian style fashionable in the East. Her hair was now fully loosed in a feminine flourish while her increasingly-excited client detected the sweet aura of oil of roses exuding from her skin. Her gown revealed more of her flesh than any woman dared display in public or before a stranger, yet still veiled her limbs and feminine curves beneath layers of obscuring gossamer.

Surisca delicately crossed the chamber to extinguish several of the lamps to dim the light to a soft glow. She brought two goblets of watered wine to the edge of the double-bed arrangement. She sat very close beside Suetonius where he could catch the sweet scents from her body. Her thigh and one of her knees glanced across his leg thrillingly.

They sipped their cups so closely each was touching at the brim and their eyes were only inches apart. The biographer, ever a considerate seducer, ordained to torture his enlarging enthusiasm by introducing conversation to break the ice and restrain his impatience.

"Tell me, Surisca my young beauty, how old are you?" he asked.

"Master, my mother told me I was born at Edessa near the border to the Kingdom of Parthia in the fifth last year of the previous Caesar's reign. I think this means I am eighteen years of age. Other than that, I do not know," she replied.

"So Surisca, tell me something of yourself," he invited. "You have so many hidden talents, I have difficulty knowing which Surisca is the real Surisca. I notice how even with your Syrian accent you speak good street Greek and you handle everyday Latin to an acceptable degree. You appear to have a smattering of the old pharaonic language of Egypt, while your mother tongue is Aramaic, the major language of the East. Do you read or write in these languages, my dear?"

"Master," she responded openly, "I do not read at all except some words of Greek, a few Latin words, and the simplest of Aramaic words. But I cannot write in any of these for myself, except my own name. I am not a fine scholar like yourself, master."

"How did you come to your profession, young lady?" Suetonius posed with polite interest, despite the burden of slumber increasingly making its presence felt.

"I was born to it, my lord," Surisca responded. "My mother was bonded to the mistress of a troupe of entertainers at the city of Zeugma on the border of the Parthian Empire before the previous Caesar defeated Parthia in battle. She and her mistress's household fled back to the safety of Edessa in the north of King Abgar's land, where I was born. My mother, of course, did not know who my father was. It was one of her many clients, so I am known simply as Surisca, with no fatherly patronymic."

Surisca paused to check if her client's attention had wandered or if such talk of the lower orders offended the noble patrician's sensibilities. It hadn't, she realized.

Suetonius was observing Surisca enthuse about her past with a keen gleam in her eyes. This had an agreeable charm all its own, he thought. He assumed very few of her clients were interested in her life story.

"I am told too how, in the year when Trajan put down the Judaean rebels across the East, I turned five years of age," she continued. "Because of those wars my mother's mistress was caught up in the movements of people trapped by the upheavals. Temples were destroyed, cities were put to the sword, and many people killed. Then the Legions killed the Judaean, Lucuas, and fiercely put down the rebellion, I am told.

But my mother had accumulated sufficient coins in her trade to buy her freedom from her mistress before my birth. This means I was a freeborn child, not her former mistress's property.

It is the tradition in our profession to retain some female children to learn the trade to support us in our later years. Clients become less interested as you age, so one or two children are raised to become our breadwinners. I am such a one."

Suetonius acknowledged to himself how Surisca had the checkered career typical of her caste. Here was a young woman of the world, he contemplated, who is engaged in the most insecure of trades yet who also seemed to possess her own mind to a high degree. Her strengths were attractive. They incited his bloodstream to race to his privates as his imagination conjured the warm touch of her flesh and the all-encompassing folds of her body. He felt a deep longing descend upon him.

Things then shifted unexpectedly.

Suetonius didn't recall the precise details, the memory was a little hazy, but he later guessed he had simply fallen dead asleep during Surisca's explanations. He slowly crumpled head first into the basin of her lace-garbed lap, mid-sentence. Here was a warm, comforting, secure place redolent with floral fragrances which, in his drowsiness, reminded him of his concubine Priscilla's intimate nooks-and-crannies long ago. Or was it his mother at some even earlier era?

In fact, ageing years and the call of rest had finally consumed the Special Inspector. He fell into deep slumber and its pleasing reminiscences.

"Master! Master!" a close voice cried. "Wake, master, the hour is late!"

The biographer revived from his fuddled reverie to perceive Surisca was looking down at him with an expression of great concern. It was a long time since a woman had expressed concern over Suetonius and looked into his face so closely and seemed to mean it.

"Good grief," he mumbled, "I must have drifted off. Please forgive me."

"My lord, it is time to rise. The Watch has already called the hour before dawn," she announced.

"An hour before dawn? Is that possible?!"

"You've been asleep for more than four hours, master," she said. "You have appointments immediately at dawn. I heard you demand it of your companions last night."

Suetonius sat up in the bed and looked around, his wispy hair askew.

Surisca and he were lying close together on the side-by-side traveling beds. He was scantily attired in his under-tunic and cloths. Surisca was almost naked with her long hair falling fulsomely around her shoulders. He realized she must have undressed him of his tunic and belts once he had fallen asleep, and put him to bed like a babe, though he had no recollection of that happy occasion.

A chamber slave clapped her hands from her sleeping post beyond the entrance for permission to enter. Suetonius stammered approval as she entered and bowed.

"Master, His Excellency, Secretary Julius Vestinus awaits you outside."

He nodded acknowledgement and dismissed the girl.

"My dear Surisca," he offered to his young hireling, "I must wash and dress. We have a busy day ahead of us. You too should prepare yourself for the day's chores, and make yourself presentable."

On second thoughts it occurred to him, however, how she was quite presentable just as she was. A query crossed his mind.

"But one question, my dear. Um, did we, er, make love last night? --- or this morning?" he asked in a very small voice in case his memory of the joyful event had somehow evaded him by. He had been known to be forgetful of a night-time, especially after wine.

Surisca looked to the ground in the manner servants or slaves pretend when they are being scolded for their slackness in performing duties and a beating might be on the horizon.

"No, master, we have not. Have I given you bad service, master?" she replied, as any conscientious service provider would do.

"Oh, I just wondered. That's all," he responded half-heartedly. He had hoped he might have had some simple, delicious pleasure, yet had merely lost recall.

"Before we both address our morning toilet, Surisca my dear, one or two questions arose to mind in my sleep, my dear," he continued. "You remember yesterday at the embalmer's pavilion you commented upon the love bites on the neck of the corpse of Antinous on the table? You said you believed they were implanted by two different people, one set low at the front and another set higher on the throat stem? Are you sure in that opinion, my dear?"

Surisca crumpled her features in a girlish manner displaying a struggle for certainty.

"Master, I am not expert in understanding such things --- especially upon the dead, who quickly develop all manner of blemishes. Nevertheless, the marks on your young friend's neck looked to me to be about a day in age. I am rash enough to estimate that the hickeys imposed by the male companion were more recent than the smaller ones with the yellow rim. Those appeared older. They could have been acquired some hours apart, possibly as much as half a day. This is my humble opinion, my lord," she concluded.

Well, Suetonius thought, a true professional had spoken. So it seemed the boy was not as absolutely faithful to his *erastes*, Caesar, as common gossip would have it?

As countless impetuous paramours discovered in the reign of past emperors, it would be a risky itch indeed to indulge oneself with Caesar's wife, favorite, or other bed partners. Such behavior could possess fatal consequences. In the past this itch had rapidly propelled offenders to lifetime exile at some far away barren desert. Alternatively, they could find themselves upon a funerary pyre following an inexplicable misadventure upon a sword or unexpected fall from a high place.

Yet the prospect of Antinous having a concealed bit of fluff in his life was a prospect which might, or might not, possess value in fulfilling Caesar's commission, Suetonius considered. Perhaps jealousy and duplicity are involved in the young man's death, or some other commonplace passion?

The launch of the second but final day and night of Hadrian's assigned allotment for investigation possessed interesting promise.

CHAPTER 15

'*Hail, Gaius Suetonius Tranquillus!* Welcome to Day Two of your assignment as Special Inspector!" Julius Vestinus was as efficient as ever despite the early hour.

"My staff has arranged the list of interviews you ordered, by the hour every hour. The only person on your list who has not been located is the youngest member of Antinous's retinue, the language tutor Thais of Cyrene. I have instructed Tribune Macedo to assign soldiers to search for the woman on your behalf. In fact I've had Macedo issue a warrant to that effect under Caesar's seal in case the young lady has met with some misadventure or is being purposely evasive."

"Thank you, Vestinus."

"For your convenience, you are set up in the courtyard close-by. Your scribe Strabon and his assistant are waiting for you there now, as well as your Praetorian centurion Quintus Urbicus with his two sidekicks."

"Once again, you've thought of everything, Vestinus," Suetonius acknowledged.

Centurion Quintus Urbicus and his men were standing in the early morning light of the courtyard. They were dressed in local Egyptian habits instead of their Praetorian uniforms. The three were unkempt and their clothing was oddly stained. Perhaps their costumes were undercover disguises in the style of the local customs? In the crook of one arm Urbicus carried a bulky, stained, rag-cloth bundle.

The three snapped to attention with Praetorian precision as Suetonius arrived to take his place in the center chair at a long bench. Senator Clarus and the scribes were already in place at either end of the table, with a separate chair for Surisca placed a few feet behind the Special Inspector.

"*Hail in the name of Caesar!*" Urbicus proclaimed as the three Praetorians saluted on Suetonius's arrival.

"*All hail!*" the Special Inspector responded in as military a manner as he could muster.

Strabon and his assistant had their writing tools ready for action. Clarus, being the legal magistrate hearing the interviews, had now arranged for a court *lictor* to attend the sessions. This sturdy young man in a simple tunic emblazoned with its Imperial eagle insignia and carrying his *fasces* baton of punishment-rods bound around a sharp axe-blade stood impassively to one side. He was wearing the regulation-issue po-face of a court officer. A *lictor*'s official duties often include witnessing the execution of punishment upon offenders. Clarus, in his role as supervising magistrate, had decided the presence of a *lictor* during interviews might give the panel greater *gravitas*.

"Report, Centurion Quintus Urbicus!" Suetonius commanded with military bluster.

Urbicus snapped to attention, stepped forward a few paces, and placed the large cloth-bound bundle on the tabletop before him.

"Special Inspector, sir, as you have instructed, my troop searched for and located the two fishermen who Your Honors interviewed yesterday," Urbicus recounted. "The men are known to live in a nest of huts with their extended families by the river's bank outside the village of Besa. The men are well known in the town, so it was not difficult to locate them.

On your instructions, we were to accompany them to identify a river vessel which fits the description they provided, and to determine who may have been sailing this craft upon the Nile at dawn yesterday. However, we were too late to locate the men. Other unknown persons had made contact with them earlier. They inflicted bodily harm."

"Inflicted harm? Bodily harm?!" Clarus croaked. "What sort of harm?"

Suetonius and the others leaned forward to hear.

Urbicus placed the wet-stained cloth bundle onto the tabletop into a streak of sunlight falling across the bench, and began unwinding its cloths.

Suetonius sat back in uncomfortable apprehension.

Ani the Egyptian fisherman's severed head, still recognizable from the previous day's interrogation but somewhat battered and bloody, toppled out and rolled across the table top. His cranium's heavy weight rolled to reveal the bloody serrated neck flesh facing upwards, a mass of all chopped veins and flesh with serrated bone. The incisions seemed to have been hacked crudely with a chopper rather than sliced by sword at a swift stroke.

"The fisherman Ani, who spoke with us yesterday, was dead," Urbicus explained. "He had been killed by persons unknown. The other fisherman Hetu who spoke less yesterday had either run away or been killed elsewhere. Their families were in a state of great distress at their losses. It seems a team of hooded men attacked the family's huts after dusk yesterday, only an hour or so after the fishermen departed us here.

They dragged Ani into the open and killed him, and then chased Hetu away to an unknown fate. We have brought proof of the former's destiny for your confirmation," he concluded with military precision.

Urbicus adjusted the head's position to reveal to the group Ani's sagging-mouth, distantly distracted eyes, and yellowed waxen flesh. Suetonius sensed Surisca drawing her veil across her eyes behind him. Clarus and Vestinus raised themselves from their seats to more closely inspect and confirm the identity of the relic.

"What hooded men?" Clarus demanded. "Who were they? What was their origin?"

"I do not know, sir," Centurion Urbicus responded, smartly snapping again to attention. "The family said the offenders were fully shrouded so they could not identify their features, and they did not speak so they could not hear their language to determine their origin. They could be men of any community at Besa. Egyptian, Nubian, Greek, Jew, or even Roman.

I was told they galloped up to the huts after dark, hunted down the two fishermen, and immediately beheaded one with knives while the other ran off into the night. The killers then followed in the same direction. I retrieved the severed head from the family when we ourselves arrived some time later. I bring it to you as proof of the death. They want it returned, of course, for burial ceremonies today. They will sew the head back to the body, so the man goes to their Underworld in one piece."

"What does this mean?" Clarus turned to Suetonius. "Why would anyone want two humble fisher folk dead?" The two subsided into their seats.

"I'd say the sailors of that river craft emblazoned with the Eye Of Horus might not want to be identified?" the biographer suggested forlornly. He moved closer to Clarus to add a further observation in a low whisper.

"But it also seems, my good friend, that someone among us here has communicated our desire to identify that river craft to some other party with an interest in this matter," he murmured low. "That other party wanted those two witnesses out of the way promptly."

Clarus paused thoughtfully.

"But who in this godforsaken place, Suetonius," the ageing senator murmured, "has the authority or soldiery to prosecute such an attack? They were mounted on horses! Whose horses? Who has the power to organize a cohort of riders to kill two mere fishermen? Neither Caesar nor his officers have issued such orders, to our knowledge. Nor why should they? Who else here has such authority?"

"Unless those priests of Amun are more combative than we imagined," Suetonius rationalized, "or there are local bandits involved somewhere? There aren't many options really. The local town militia is a scruffy ragbag of imported Nubians, but they keep well out of Rome's way. The local nobility are few and far between. This then leaves only our own people."

Suetonius shifted closer to the senator so only Clarus, Surisca, and the scribe could hear his conjecture.

"Are Governor Titianus and his Alexandrians on a private mission? Or, have some of Tribune Macedo's Praetorians gone feral? Are there disaffected Horse Guards around Caesar, unknown to anyone? Yet who traveling with us has the authority to instruct soldiers or cavalry independently of Caesar's commanders? But then, why should they murder simple fishermen? Is it because they were the only known witnesses to that suspect vessel on the river yesterday?"

Suetonius gave Centurion Urbicus new orders.

"The death of the fishermen affects our enquiry greatly, Praetorian. Even if they have both been killed, it doesn't change our need. In fact, it makes it more necessary. We must discover who was sailing the craft emblazoned with the Eye of Horus. Who? To where? And why? This is your primary duty, Praetorian," he affirmed. "And we need the details by high sun today. Perhaps their families know of other fisher folk who can assist you?"

Urbicus cleared his throat.

"We've taken the liberty, sir, to do a preliminary search at first light of the riverside by the Temple of Amun. There is a craft fitting the Egyptian's description moored nearby. But we have yet to discover who was sailing this craft yesterday," he explained.

"Then find out, Quintus Urbicus, by high sun. You might have to consult one of the priests and take them into security," Suetonius instructed. "Our uncertainties about the Bithynian's death now grow with each hour."

Urbicus raised a clenched salute and announced, "It will be done, sir! "

A trooper rewrapped Ani's butchered head. He wiped-up the moist stain on the bench-top where it had dribbled juices, and then marched off with his colleagues.

Suetonius looked at the stain on the table and decided he didn't feel especially hungry for breakfast. Surisca developed a similar lack of appetite. Clarus returned to devouring his platter of victuals and signaled a slave to pour wine.

"Where is the Bithynian youth Lysias? He is due here now! He's late!" Clarus called.

"He is not to be found, gentlemen," an oddly-accented voice unexpectedly interrupted.

Geta the Dacian had arrived at the courtyard accompanied by one of Caesar's Horse Guards.

"I have been to visit Lysias at Antinous's apartments to summons the lad to attend Caesar, only to learn he is not to be found," Geta repeated. "The chamber slave says he hasn't seen the Bithynian since late last night. The youth slipped away somewhere in the night, the slave told me. I had hoped he might be here with you already?"

Geta scanned the clustered team gathered around the long bench. His eyes fell upon Surisca and lingered momentarily. He displayed surprise. Surisca returned the gaze, only to then lower it demurely to the ground. Suetonius noted this interesting exchange.

"What of the language tutor, the slave Thais?" Suetonius added.

"I am told she too is not to be found," Geta stated.

Clarus reacted angrily.

"What? Have these two absconded? Have we been deceived by the Bithynian?!" he clamored. "Issue a warrant to apprehend them both!"

The *lictor* departed briskly to his new commission.

"My good Septicius, to where can they abscond?" Suetonius posed. "Beyond this encampment lie irrigated fields of grain and then a wilderness of desert. There's nowhere to go, my friend." He turned to Geta. "You know these people well, Dacian," the biographer queried Geta. "Where will they have gone?".

The man with the faint blue circles tattooed across his cheekbones hesitated.

"I have no idea, Suetonius Tranquillus. You are the Special Inspector, not I."

His eyes drifted back towards the Syrian female standing nearby with lowered eyes.

"What does this mean?" Clarus called rhetorically. "Two witnesses are killed, two others disappear into the night, while the hours pass quickly towards our deadline. And our heads are at stake!"

The biographer avoided response by making a formal introduction of the Syri entertainer to the Dacian.

"You have met the lady Surisca of Antioch, Prince Geta of Dacia?" Suetonius asked in his best silkily polite manner. He was offering an unlikely social gesture to two people of impossibly unequal status. He followed their interaction closely as Surisca dipped a suitable curtsy.

"Just Geta, Special Inspector," the Dacian responded with unexpected modesty. "I am a simple man of little consequence. Yet I am pleased to acknowledge the lady Surisca of Antioch."

Suetonius sensed the two already knew each other regardless of his genteel introduction. It occurred to him their meeting may have been of a professional nature it might not be polite to explore.

"Dacian," Clarus proclaimed, "it's time you gave us your opinions of the death of Antinous. You probably know things we don't? You have lived close-by the lad daily. You knew him over several years."

"I am at your disposal, gentlemen, though I must also attend to my duties shortly," Geta responded evasively. "Feel free to ask what you will."

His eyes barely departed Surisca.

"Strabon, our scribe will record your words. We have several questions to put to you, so take a seat," Suetonius intoned. "This is a legal statement, a deposition, Geta, as Caesar commanded us. State you name and titles, your age and place of birth, and your functions in the Imperial Household. Remember, you are under oath to your titular deity."

"Under oath? I, Geta, am being interrogated?" he asked with dismay. He sat against the edge of the bench table, not in the chair provided, implying only brief participation. Strabon's stylus was poised ready to flutter. Geta gathered himself reluctantly.

"This is unexpected, gentlemen, but I'll try. By Sacred Zalmoxis of the Dacians, I am known among Romans simply as Geta. This is a mistaken *praenomen* given to simplify my proper titles in my mother tongue. My true name is Dromichaetes, a *tarabostes* prince of the royal house of The Getae," he announced with quiet pride. "I was born at Sarmizegethusa in the year when Palma Frontonianus and Sosius Senecio were consuls at Rome, I'm told. Caesar Trajan was ruler. I was taken hostage as a child after the wars against my father, the king of the Dacians known as *Decebelus*.

Rome's victory against my father saw me assigned into the care of Hadrian when he was a commander of Legions. I remain even today under Hadrian's protection in his household. Yet I possess my own independent wealth endowed from my father's treasures. *Hail Caesar!*" the Dacian added diplomatically.

"What do you know about the death of Antinous?" Suetonius continued. "Tell us what you know or have heard. The Household gossip mill must be running riot?"

"I have no special knowledge, gentlemen," Geta stated plainly. "Like you, I'm appalled at the tragedy. I can only imagine he fell into the river two nights ago? How, or where, or of what misadventure, I do not know. Perhaps he had taken too much wine? Perhaps he foolishly tried to swim while armored? Who knows? Perhaps he was dealt cruelly by some enemy? It is a waste of a young man's life, and a serious hurt to our Caesar. Hadrian has taken it very badly, as you saw."

"Do you believe the youth may have taken his own life? If so, why would he do so? Or was he a victim of treachery?" Clarus contributed.

Geta considered thoughtfully before responding.

"At Court there is always the possibility of foul play. There are many eddies of conflict at Court, political or romantic or financial. Some of them are dangerous, even life threatening. Others are trivial.

Yet Antinous was not caught up in factions or politics. He seemed quite apolitical, perhaps intentionally. He simply brought Hadrian great pleasure and relaxation from the ordeals of government. He was like a lively son, a frisky hound, or a well-loved horse. And we've come to realize Caesar's affection was more than skin deep.

It strikes me the death benefits no one, so no political goal is achieved. It has caused Caesar great pain. Great pain. Perhaps this was the purpose of the death? Regarding the boy taking his own life, I cannot see why Antinous would do such a thing."

"You say *there is the possibility of foul play*? Explain," Suetonius probed. "We've already seen how unknown forces are willing to kill innocent people to impede our enquiry. Others disappear suddenly who were known to us as people of repute. Foul play is already among us."

Geta drew breath before responding. His eyes flitted to Surisca again and again.

"Gentlemen, you are men of the world. You will appreciate there may be many forces at work in the life of the Household. Some of these forces take power and wealth very seriously. Issues of State are at stake. Personal ambitions are forged in the furnace of this Court. Great wealth can be achieved or lost. Shifts in political goals are fought with tenacity.

Even affairs of the heart become matters of intrigue. It's not all ceremony, feasting, and games, you are aware. What more can I say?"

He dismissed the query with a shrug of the shoulders.

"You can say much more, good fellow," Suetonius clarified. "For example, you will have an opinion of the nature of the current issues at Court which impact on these conflicts. Tell us of your perceptions of such things. We need to know."

Suetonius wondered at Geta's glib manner. It seemed strangely remote from the issues.

"There are many undercurrents at Court," Geta conceded. "I am not sure I understand all of them myself. Of those pertaining to the dead boy, I suppose issues of the succession are uppermost."

"What issues, Dacian? He was no candidate for the role."

"Well, once again *the Western Favorite* has resumed his place at Caesar's side."

"Lucius Ceionius Commodus, the young senator?" Suetonius asked.

"Yes," Geta continued. "Senator Commodus arrived from Rome at Alexandria only a month ago. Antinous has been staying out of sight because Commodus and he have a bad history together. Commodus is reputed to have inflicted that scar on Antinous's left cheek some years ago. Commodus cleverly knows how Caesar abhors imperfections or mutilation. He is perceived to be the leading claimant to the imperial succession. Yet there are other claimants to the succession whose noses will be out-of-joint about Commodus's recent return to Caesar's favor.

But Commodus is now a married man, he's no *meirakion* young man open to a role as an *eromenos*. In fact his wife is with child. Yet he remains high in Caesar's esteem. Many believe Caesar is planning to adopt the senator as his son. And soon. If so, Commodus will be first in line to be Caesar after Hadrian's passing. Mind you, Hadrian is also amused by the fellow's uninhibited manners and clever wit. The fellow is irrepressible."

"Does Commodus sleep with Caesar? Has the young senator displaced Antinous in his bed?" Clarus asked provocatively.

"My lords, it is not for one such as I to offer comment on such things! I am not authorized to report the private habits of --- ."

"Yes or no?!"

"I think it may be Yes," Geta murmured. "Well, on one occasion that I know of. I do not think it was especially successful, but I do not monitor Caesar's sleeping arrangements, gentlemen. These are Caesar's own affair. I am not at liberty to ---"

Clarus interrupted again.

"Would this be grounds for suicide by the boy?"

"Suicide from despair? It might be," the Dacian murmured weakly. "But I think Antinous is much hardier than that. Besides, Antinous may have had other issues to address."

"Surely, with Antinous out of the way, claimants to the succession can consolidate their influence on Caesar to enhance their chances?" Suetonius proposed.

"It is possible, my lords. There are many possibilities," Geta muddied the discussion.

"Are you suggesting Antinous was murdered to get him out of the way so *the Western Favorite* could consolidate adoption?" Suetonius probed.

"Many things are possible, my lord," Geta replied evasively. "But I must not slander my fellow courtiers. They too may one day be my *patrons* and protectors."

"What else could influence the death of the young Bithynian, Geta of Dacia?"

"If we are being so candid, my lords, perhaps you should consider the influence of the Egyptian priest known as Pachrates," Geta responded. "He possesses a hold over both the emperor and Antinous."

"A *hold?* What do you mean?"

"Well, at Alexandria and then again at Memphis on this river journey, this priest gave displays of magic and wizardry which impressed them both. Egypt contains many mysteries. The priest Pachrates is said to be its greatest exponent of sorcery. I have seen him do things I cannot explain," Geta intimated in too-breathless a reverential hush.

"What sort of things, Dacian? Magical tricks and illusions?" Suetonius proposed.

Geta leaned forward conspiratorially.

"I have witnessed marvelous things. I have seen him and his assistants transform a wild cheetah on a leash into a bridled horse in flashes of fire and thunder. Both were living creatures who moved, spat, snarled, or snorted --- they were no illusion, my friends.

Most of all, I have seen his assistants behead a condemned criminal, who bled across the stones of the courtyard just as in an arena. Then with a race of curtains, much drumming, colored smoke, and cries of magical formulae, he restored the same beheaded man to life again. He was returned to life all in one piece. It was an extraordinary achievement!

Pachrates has spells for all occasions and purposes. Egypt is in his thrall, and much of Egypt is willing to pay well for his services," the Dacian enthused. "Our own astrologer Aristobulus and the mystical poet Julia Balbilla are attracted by the priest's skills. I believe even the empress, Julia Vibia Sabina, follows his arts."

"Doesn't the *Augusta* Sabina follow the cult of the Roman priestess Anna Perenna, the wife of Governor Titianus? At least so I've been told?" Clarus asked. "Surely she prefers Roman magic to foreign sorcery?"

Geta was startled by the comment.

"Anna Perenna? The Grandmother of Time? Is this who you mean?" he asked.

"*Grandmother of Time?* More like *Queen of the Witches!*" Clarus challenged.

"She's the woman the Prefect Governor Titianus treats as a wife, though she's not his wife," Geta confirmed. "She travels with the Governor on his barque *The Alexandros* which follows close behind the empress's *Dionysus*. Anna Perenna has her own chamber aboard his vessel, I am told. Yet as a priestess she is well regarded by the women of the Court. She has panaceas for all manner of women's matters. But this is the science of an apothecary, not a sorceress or witch ---"

"I assume she's a master poisoner too?" Clarus added. "In what way does the Egyptian magician or this Roman priestess reflect upon the death of the Bithynian, Dacian?"

Geta thought carefully before responding.

"It's to do with Caesar's condition. Many are worried at it. It's his cough."

"His cough? We have been told it is not improving?"

"Worse, it grows. I have seen days when Caesar coughs up light sprays of blood. He complains his chest is on fire. His features become ruddy and inflamed. He lies down for long periods to alleviate its severity. The physicians are reluctant to treat him. They sense the matter is serious and do not wish to be attached to so exalted a medical failure. We are not to discuss it in public. It impinges on issues of the State, and that's forbidden," Geta murmured as the group subsided into thoughtfulness..

"How do this priest or the priestess fit into this matter?" Suetonius asked.

"Well, if Pachrates and his like can bring beheaded criminals back to life and rejoin them into a single piece again, perhaps this priest of Amun can cure an emperor's cough?"

"Oh," the biographer returned, "you mean Priest Pachrates should perform his magic upon Caesar? Cure his coughing sickness?"

"Of course. At least that's what some people have been asking," Geta surmised, "especially Antinous some weeks ago at Memphis. However I've observed how Pachrates can talk up many things, but he carefully talks down his skill with cures. He always seemed to have a good reason for avoiding the subject in Caesar's and Antinous's company --- even when the boy put it plainly to him recently.

Antinous wears an Abrasax jewel on his finger. It was a special gift from Hadrian. Abrasax is a deity of infinity and eternal life, they say, capable of great magic. Antinous wanted Pachrates to use the ring, which was said to belong to Basileus Alexandros long ago, to restore Hadrian to full health.

Pachrates claimed he only knew the magic of Amun, not of other gods. He doesn't know the magic of Abrasax. So he slipped out from under again."

Suetonius filed the matter of the Abrasax ring to his mental notes. Where was the ring? It was not seen upon the cadaver in Caesar's sleeping quarters, and nor was it upon the corpse on the embalmer's table. Where was the blue jewel? Had it been stolen?

"So why should we explore this avenue of investigation, Geta?" Suetonius asked.

"Because Pachrates knows something he's not telling us. I don't know what it is, but I wouldn't be surprised if it didn't have something to do with Antinous's death. That's all," the Dacian rounded off. "But I must leave you now and rejoin Caesar."

He finalized his interview with the authority of someone with far more important issues to address.

"No, Dacian, you may not!" Clarus intoned with his magistrate's authority. "We have other matters to discuss with you. You claim *the Western Favorite* is an enemy of the dead youth?"

"Yes," Geta murmured quietly, "but you must tread with care on the matter."

"Why? What has transpired between them which makes them enemies? Speak plainly to us. We want to know."

The Dacian rested impatiently back onto the table's edge and glanced furtively between Surisca and his interrogators. He was not happy at this turn of events.

"It is a nettlesome story, gentlemen. It occurred four years ago when the Household was passing through Athens. It was after a long tour of the Empire. Antinous had been introduced to Caesar briefly at Bithynia, where they found each other's company highly agreeable. Antinous and his chum Lysias, accompanied by their Latin instructor Thais of Cyrene, traveled to Achaea to complete their education at Athens.

As usual I was travelling with Caesar's Household, so I was a witness to the events which transpired, or heard of them from others. Later I heard greater detail from Antinous or Lysias themselves over shared wine. I also garnered some private details from slaves who report to me. I follow such things closely on Caesar's behalf.

Athens was Caesar's priority destination for that tour. He had been appointed President of the spring festival of the Great Dionysia, events which bring Hadrian great satisfaction. Their arrival at Athens was to be a pleasure to both Caesar and the Bithynian, so the sojourn was highly anticipated by all, including me. It proved to be an important, if unexpected, conjunction of personalities.

Antinous and his party had sailed from Nicomedia accompanying a shipload of his family's commercial cargo. They travelled on Senator Arrian's huge sea-freighter *The Bithynian*. The seven day journey of island-hopping across the Aegean Sea had tested the youths' sea-worthiness. They later told me so over many jugs of wine. "

"Fine, but tell us how it involves *the Western Favorite*..." Suetonius interjected. "Is there something we should know for our investigation?"

CHAPTER 16

"As it was told to me by the two lads, on that sea journey's seventh day Arrian's freighter roiled past the temple-topped promontory of Cape Sunium south of Athens and slew across the Bay of Salamis towards the city. Antinous's party was sailing to Piraeus, Athens' major harbor. This approach reveals the distant metropolis as a strip of structures glistening brightly in the sunlight.

From the deck of their ship plowing through the Aegean chop it seemed to Antinous, Lysias, and Thais how their destination was the knobby line of white buildings lining the coastline. As *The Bithynian* drew closer, this mere sliver transformed into a spectacle of high-pillared temples and shrines in stone and marble, lofty castellated defensive towers, or meandering walls and courtyards, warehouses, private villas, and tenements. Our two provincials had never seen such a panoply of urban structures before. Athens is far larger than Nicomedia.

Equally impressive were the number of vessels and fishing craft thronging the city's two harbors. An occasional sturdy Roman war trireme braced the sea too, with their rows of oars sweeping in rhythmic unison attacking the waves. A hundred other vessels were anchored at the shore's moorings. All this was very new to them.

However, as *The Bithynian*'s captain pointed out, the buildings they had been viewing were merely Athens' waterfront suburb of Piraeus. The metropolis itself was several miles inland from the port. Later, this then proved to be an even more spectacular vision. After a lifetime's ambition they were at last to arrive at the very heart of their Hellene world, the city of Athens.

Once berthed, they transferred their personal baggage to an oxen wagon and trundled inland to the great city awaiting them. It was the most exciting event of their lives, they said.

As they drew closer to its walls and gates, the city's presence proclaimed itself by impacting on their nostrils. As any large city is prone, the comforting odors of potter's kilns, baker's ovens, and a multitude of family hearths melded contrastingly with the fetid sweetness of sewer residues, tanner's or fuller's soaks, public latrines, plus the fragrance of the conical pines of Achaea. All joined to proclaim the city's human, animal, and industrial immensity. Perhaps a quarter of a million people live in this legendary city, they realized. Athens was truly a large metropolis.

To strangers, this ripeness of atmosphere is matched by a similarly earthy visual display. Garish effigies of the randy god Priapus adorn cottages and villas. His prodigiously erect *phallus* protects against the Evil Eye and threatens a likely rude fate for unwanted trespassers. Wittily obscene graffiti, crude insults, and lewd limericks litter all vacant wall spaces with droll texts, comic scenes, and bawdy pictures. Their jovial vulgarity offers few concessions to a polite sensibility. Athens conveys the impression, they realized, of being a city happily ruled by rampant sex in its many differing varieties or configurations. Each was more comical than the last, aiming to ward off malign spiritual influences while providing pleasing gaiety to the heart.

On their journey through the lanes to the Agora market-place their wagon trundled past a forest of statues of Olympian gods, ancient philosophers, hardy warriors, or victorious athletes frozen dramatically in mid-action. Wall niches holding devotional figures, shrines, chapels, sanctuaries, and pillared temples graced street corners and lane intersections. The debris of candle stubs, exhausted lamps, and crumbled shards inscribed with petitions to the Fates attested to the piety of the citizens in praising their gods and their heroes.

Antinous spied the side-by-side statues of the city's much admired tyrant-killers Harmodius and Aristogiton, an *eromenos* and his *erastes* of six centuries earlier, as the wagon ambled through the Agora gateway. These ancient bronzes had been abducted to Rome by the city's conqueror Sulla two hundred years ago, but had been recently restored to the Agora on Hadrian's command. Hadrian's respect for all things Greek earned him the favor of the city's voluble population.

First impressions can be persuasive. Antinous and Lysias, guided by Thais's perceptive eye, noted how Athenians dressed themselves with more refinement than Bithynians. Except for the rabble of slaves who throng the narrow lanes, mature Athenian citizens and their matrons wore finer jewelry and fancier fabrics in brighter dyes or weaves than worn by elders at Bithynia. Even the men of Athens seemed to be fashion conscious. Respectable women, however, were fully veiled from view behind gauzes.

There were far more women in the streets going about their business than one would see at Nicomedia, let alone in conservative regional Claudiopolis. Some seemed to be without a male guardian or a watchful slave, and were garbed in a less veiled manner than other citizens.

Unaccompanied females in public are perceived a provocation at Claudiopolis. It could lead to damaged reputation, public insult, or worse. Athens seemed more relaxed with its women.

The trio even spied a few young girls of marriageable age among the throng without hair coverings to proclaim their maidenly modesty. Perhaps they were foreigners, courtesans, or common street harlots? It seemed the women of Athens were less secluded and more open to public life than their equals in the provinces, yet they also noted how women of the elites traveled in well-guarded litters carefully screened from prying eyes.

Younger males were dressed in the regular Greek *chiton* tunic and *himation* swathe, but the fabrics looked of an unusually finer weave and pleating. Even in cool March their wools or linens seemed to be weighted for summer.

They observed, too, how men wore tunics tailored to expose greater areas of body flesh. These were shorter at the thigh and tighter at the hip than would be consider decorous at *Polis*, and showed more of the limbs or chest line. Their hair, too, was trimmed shorter than the tousled mops and long coils worn by *meirakia* young men such as Antinous and Lysias at Bithynia. Their overall presentation seemed aimed to accent their comeliness.

The lads raised an eyebrow at the many men who wore jewelry of varied richness similar to their womenfolk. Rings, bracelets, armbands, earrings, neck chains and decorative collars were common. These were thought decadent at Claudiopolis. It may proclaim the demeanor of a *cinaedus* at Bithynia, one who seeks to attract admirers.

Quite a few such people are visible in Athens. Many younger men even painted underlines of *kohl* around their eyes to enhance their appearance, or powdered their faces to display a fairer complexion. Antinous and Lysias were uncertain of the seemliness of such touches, so Thais did not encourage them.

It became evident many upper-class youths were splashed with expensive perfumes from the East, which too would be unseemly in Bithynia's hinterland. Other young Athenians walked hand-in-hand with glamorously-attired ladies who were evidently not their wives but hired concubines or courtesans. Nicomedia, of course, also displays this custom due to the large numbers of sex workers who service transient sailors from around the Middle Sea.

Some Athenian youths walked similarly with male friends, possibly indicating an amorous liaison or at least an *eromenos/erastes* relationship, but this was so at Bithynia too.

Foreign visitors to Athens register their arrival with their national *proxenos* to record the purpose of their journey for the civil authorities. The current *proxenos* for Bithynia was Tiberius Claudius Atticus Herodes, known to all as Herodes Atticus. Besides being Athens' richest man, he was a major customer of Bithynian produce at Achaea.

However the actual welcoming officer was Herodes Atticus's eldest son, an Athenian whose name was Lucius but who too was known as Herodes Atticus.

Herodes the Younger was a striking looking and well-dressed Athenian in his mid-twenties. The group of three saw how he noted the arriving party with inordinate interest. Lysias told me some time later he sensed Herodes' eyes sizing him up intently, and he wondered at the time at his motive.

At the *proxenos'* office they recognized Senator Arrian with a retinue of clients, stewards, and guards. Arrian strode briskly to them as their details were being recorded by the younger Herodes.

'Welcome to Athens, masters Antinous and Lysias. On behalf of Imperator Caesar Hadrian --- and myself too, of course --- I extend greetings to you. We ourselves have been at Athens for the past week," he said. "The springtime festivities here are very lively.'

The boys bowed respectfully in acknowledgement and saluted. Arrian continued.

'And besides his personal welcome, Caesar has extended an invitation to you. You are to attend Caesar's entourage at the opening ceremony of the Festival of the Great Dionysia tomorrow, the tenth day of the month of *Elaphebolion*. Tomorrow's event honors seven hundred years of Athenian drama.

The day's itinerary includes a ceremonial procession of citizens through the city to the Temple of Dionysus on the slope of the Acropolis. After a rite of sacrifice before the image of the god, a performance of a play from the classic repertoire is to be sung at the nearby Theater of Dionysus. Thousands of the city's citizens will attend.

This will be followed in the evening by a public banquet and masked revel for all Athenians, at Caesar's expense. Each of these events is to include you both,' Arrian said with some pleasure at watching the youths' faces light up at such an attractive invitation.

'It will be our great honor to attend, my lord,' Antinous offered cheerily.

'Good. Then I will take my leave now,' Arrian continued, 'but I also wish you to join me again for private discussion this very afternoon. You are available, yes?'

This extra invitation was extended with a faintly conspiratorial air. It sounded more like a command than a invitation, the boys told me later.

'I have matters to discuss with you of some sensitivity. I bathe daily in Athens at Hadrian's New Baths erected beside the construction site of the Temple of Olympian Zeus,' Arrian said. 'I retire to the Baths each afternoon for cleansing, exercise, and reflection. Occasionally Hadrian and I do so together. It's a necessary luxury in the summer climate here. Join me today at three hours after high sun to clean up after your long journey. Mention my name at the entrance hall and you'll be guided to my private *tepidarium* so we can talk in peace.

Before the lads had time to bow or salute Arrian had swept away followed by his retinue.

'We will attend you there at three, sir!' Antinous called after the disappearing figure.

Thais took razor-sharp shears from the kitchen stores to hack-chop the boys' tousled heads of hair into manes of a more fashionable length. The two wished to have a similar style to the local *ephebes* they had seen in the streets of Athens, yet still retain a length which indicated their *meirakion* young adult status.

Antinous and Lysias saw how the color had returned to Thais's complexion after the sea journey, indicating she was feeling much improved in health. The rolling, swaying, lurching sea journey had taken its toll on the Cyrene's usual affability. Antinous's attentions to her during her five indisposed days had made her sea nausea bearable. But now that she was on steady land again she had returned to her usual good temper.

Once settled into their hired villa in the upper-class ward of Melite close by the Acropolis slope, the two asked Thais to trim their hair prior to the bath-house appointment with Arrian. Thais has a definite gift for anything to do with fashion, so the youngsters felt quite up-to-date and cosmopolitan by the time she had shag-cut their coiling manes into a more-controlled Athenian style. Gone were the rustic locks of provincial youths. Both boys squeaked with delight when they checked their reflection on the stilled surface of the villa's courtyard fish pond.

It was then time to find their way through the city's narrow lanes around the eastern edge of the Acropolis slopes to locate Hadrian's Baths in the new Roman quarter of the city. An opportunity to bathe at a proper bath-house, sweat in a hot room, receive a *strigil*'s oiled cleansing, take a massage, dunk in further pools, and become thoroughly refreshed was indeed a civilized comfort. At the same time the enigma of Arrian's summons might become evident."

Geta rested for a few moments to take a sip of wine. His audience of investigators was growing impatient.

"What is the importance of all this in identifying enemies of Antinous, Dacian?" Clarus interjected. "Do we need to know the *minutiae* of their daily toilet too?"

"Allow me to reveal what I know, gentlemen. It comes from diverse sources of value," Geta explained. "It will interest you, I am sure." He continued his testimony.

"The older man of the three slung another dipper of water across his head and shoulders. Its splashes sprayed across all three figures seated around the marbled well of the bathhouse *sodatorium*.

'Welcome, gentlemen, to your engagement in life,' Arrian declared to his two young companions. He was attired in naught but his single senator's ring on one finger.

Senator Lucius Flavius Arrianus Xenophon, as he is known at Rome, leaned languidly on the water-splashed marbles to relax in the chamber's muggy heat. The gloom of the bath-house cavern was sliced by a thin shaft of sunlight streaking through the simmering haze from a high window's grille. A fug of steam infused with the odors of woody oils and fiery coals perfumed the air. In his private chamber at the best appointed baths in all the East, the Bithynian noble's pores sweated copiously. So too did that of his companions.

Seated on three sides of stepped slabs of porphyry, the naked men exuded rivulets of moisture across their bodies. Both boys acknowledged to themselves how this nobleman is an appealing figure of a fellow, despite his thinning head of hair and deepening facial creases. For a man in his early forties whose career is regarded as being as much a practicing historian, a major trading entrepreneur, and civic councilor, as well as a commander of the military and a senator of Rome, his muscle tone was in fine shape.

Arrian looked over the two naked youths beside him in the manner of an athlete before a wrestling match or perhaps a gladiator confronting an untested combatant.

'You realize, Antinous, your being here is no accident? You have been on a path to this city and this present company for many months before you yourself knew of its possibility.'

Antinous and Lysias listened in attentive silence. They sweated profusely and splashed themselves with ladles of extra water while wondering where this bath-house conversation was likely to lead.

'You, my young friend, have been carefully selected from a variety of candidates to enter the life of our Caesar. Ultimately of course it was he, Caesar, who made the final choice, but there were many forces at work to direct his attentions to someone like you. Hadrian has been studiously assessing people across his Empire, and of course he has surveyed the possibilities at Rome itself.

Your journey to this place and your association with the Imperial Household began several years ago, well before we even knew of your existence. It began with perceptions which friends of Caesar from the Greek East decided may be crucial to the survival of Roman Asia as an entity under Rome's beneficence,' Arrian offered.

'Roman Asia and Greece are the homelands of the peoples we know as Hellenes. Greece is not just a blood line, it is a state of mind shared across the wider Middle Sea by all peoples under the influence of Hellenic culture.

Since his accession nine years ago as *Princeps*, Caesar Hadrian has stabilized the Empire's boundaries, withdrawn from military adventures outside those boundaries, and laid the groundwork for the husbanding of wealth within the Empire. Some of this wealth will pay for the Legions who protect all the peoples of the Empire against invasion by barbarians, the remainder will be invested in Empire infrastructure and services.

Nevertheless, my Bithynian friends, I and many other nobles of Roman Asia are deeply concerned about the future of our eastern provinces. To the north and east of the Black Sea there are vast tribes of nomads of varying races who are shifting westwards from the Caucuses to our very borders.

They are tribes such as the *Sarmatae*, the *Vandali*, the *Alans*, or the *Scythians*, who repeatedly test our defenses and our patience. They may very soon threaten our security. These are not merely groups of herders wandering in search of seasonal pasture or thieving booty, they are migrations of whole races onto the fringe of our world.

The Senate at Rome does not yet fully perceives the extent of this threat. They do not engage in strategies to prepare for an inevitable response. But I have seen the invaders with my own eyes. That is why we are here today, we three.'

The two young men sat motionless, enthralled by this soldier's analysis of threats unknown to their experience. Arrian continued.

'We, the leading citizens of Roman Asia, pursue two things to secure our safety and our future in this dangerous, shifting world,' he propounded. 'We need sturdier defenses across our eastern frontiers to stop the barbarians, and we need sufficient fighters in place to annihilate them if they breach our borders. This will be a huge cost to Rome which our taxes and wealth can barely accommodate.'

Arrian paused to splash another dipper over his frame.

'To achieve these goals we need Caesar's and his Senate's continuing regard for our Hellene culture and our ways. It will require wealth, arms, manpower, and the will.

At this time Rome's surplus wealth is channeled to protect the north of the Empire at Germania. Also, much wealth is frittered away in providing frivolous pleasures to the city of Rome itself with its many unemployed *plebs*. This ratio must shift.

My project on behalf of our homeland, young sirs, is to foster eastern values in the mind of Rome's rulers. This includes using influences such as you, gentlemen, to promote Roman Asia's welfare in an intimately personal way to the highest echelons of the *Imperium*. Hadrian is the uttermost echelon, and he has shown his personal interest in you, Antinous.

Your forthcoming role, Antinous, as *eromenos* to Hadrian means our Caesar can be repeatedly made aware of the necessity for defensive protections at the Eastern frontier. He has the influence and power to persuade his senators, but he himself needs to be regularly persuaded too. This, Antinous, is the role your countrymen now expect of you. You are our frontline defense.

Secondly, the East needs at least two additional Legions to reinforce the existing two Legions based in Cappadocia to protect our borders. This initiative will be a costly investment in coin and manpower at a time when Roman armies no longer siphon wealth from newly conquered enemies to justify its conquests.

For five hundred years Rome has been annexing the land, wealth, and manpower of its neighbors piece-by-piece, but this expansion program is no longer tenable. The cost of the defense and supply-lines exceeds the value of the booty seized. It teaches us how even brute power has its limits.

But where do you, Antinous, fit into these matters, you ask? To be brief, my boy, you are shortly to become Caesar's personal connection to Roman Asia. Your proximity to him will repeatedly remind him of the importance of the culture he already greatly admires. This is your destiny, Antinous, and even yours too Lysias.'

Arrian paused to toss dippers of cooling water across his frame. He continued.

'Your selection, young man, followed wide enquiries among the landed classes to identify a freeborn candidate of a suitable quality, status, and ability for Caesar's interest.

For example you already know of Glaucon the Syri? He was the silver-voiced fellow who sang love songs at the celebration of your hunting kill at Nicomedia last October. Glaucon only lasted a month in Caesar's company despite his porcelain beauty and our every discreet encouragement to appeal to Caesar's tastes. But he was soon returned to his Damascus family crest-fallen and bitter, but also far wealthier than even his wildest dreams could imagine. Gold has its appeal for some, too. Not all contenders prize honor.'

Arrian paused to measure his effect upon his companions. Antinous and Lysias looked to each other questioningly. Arrian seemed satisfied and continued.

'Our conversation here, my friends, is to be confidential between us. It is not seditious or irregular, but it is sensitive and must be respected,' he said softly. 'It was our community's desire to provide great Caesar with an *eromenos* of a superior standard suited to his status. After scouring all the Aegean for a suitably mature *meirakion* and then discreetly wheeling these prospects into Caesar's company, only a single candidate of our collection met with his favor.

Caesar is a fickle aesthete, yet one with an educated eye and very perceptive insight. He knows good horseflesh when he sees it, but he also knows a good heart.

The choice proved to be you, Antinous, after he saw you and Lysias wrestling fiercely at the youth's games of Claudiopolis five months ago, plus subsequent events. Despite a dozen other eligible fellows on display naked in the dust that day, and despite one or two others being feathered later into the boar hunt at Nicomedia, it was you Antinous who eventually became the chosen one,' Arrian divulged with a faint smile. 'The rest you know.'

Antinous at last spoke. He had been digesting this information carefully.

'You say, my lord, that this is my life's destiny. If so, what am I supposed to do about it? I am here in Athens for my final education and continued training in weapons. Letters have passed between my father and various agents of the Imperial Household, yet I have no idea how to go about the project you have outlined?' he said. 'How am I to achieve such a unique goal?'

'Arrangements are already taking place which will take care of this issue,' Arrian replied enigmatically.

'But this does not answer my query, my lord," Antinous interjected. "Under what terms am I to be received by great Caesar? What steps should I take? I'm at a loss to know how to respond or what to do. I am no coquette or teasing courtesan with practiced wiles.'

'Do not worry, lad. As I said, certain matters are being prepared in readiness. Tomorrow you and Lysias should keep your eyes open and stay within Caesar's sight throughout the day's events. Especially, you should watch for anything odd or suspicious which appears in your field of vision,' the noble offered with puzzling vagueness, 'and respond appropriately. There have been rumors circulating, so be prepared for any surprise.'

Antinous and Lysias slopped further dippers of water over their heads. Arrian continued.

'But you should also realize, Antinous, how our Caesar currently has another young fellow gracing his company at Athens. To some degree you have competition.'

Both of the boys sat up briskly amid the lethargic heat, their energy restored.

'Competition? What do you mean by 'competition', sir?' Antinous asked with a hint of alarm. Arrian considered his words carefully.

'Well, my boy, for the past few weeks Caesar has been enjoying the company of his friend at Rome of recent years named Senator Lucius

Ceionius Commodus. This senator is residing with Caesar at Athens not very far from your own villa.'

'Oh,' said Antinous, as he wondered at the import of this. 'Who is this man Commodus? Is he a Roman noble too?'

'Ah yes, he most certainly is. Commodus is descended from an ancient Etruscan family of the senatorial class. He is definitely a *patrician*. They are extremely wealthy and they are of the best blood. As a result Commodus has been raised with not just a silver spoon in his mouth but perhaps an entire golden service. He has very good political prospects. Yet from what I have seen of him he is quite spoiled and temperamental and given to extravagance. However I must admit he is also very good looking.'

'Was he an *eromenos* to Hadrian? I am told on good authority Caesar had not taken an *eromenos* previously.'

'No, Antinous. Hadrian did not display his friend as a formal partner. Commodus has simply hovered discreetly in the background or been out of sight altogether.

Antinous sat in stony silence for a few moments to digest this information. I suspect he began to wonder if Caesar was really a man of his word or not.

'Sir, is there not a law forbidding Romans to accost freeborn maidens or youths?'

'Yes, Antinous,' Arrian conceded, 'the ancient law known as the *lex Scantinia* with its objection to the offence of *stuprum*. It still remains respected among older Romans. However there have been no prosecutions for it for at least a hundred years. What people do between themselves in private, or what a Caesar may deign to venture in his majesty as *Princeps*, is another matter entirely.

People say Commodus might be adopted by Hadrian into his *gens* as his lawful son and prospective successor, just as Julius Caesar did with Gaius Octavius long ago. Octavius eventually assumed the title of Caesar Augustus. Nerva did likewise with Trajan. Yet though Commodus possesses the necessary bloodlines to be eligible, he doesn't possess the military experience or political influence, I'd say. The Legions barely know or respect him. They will count.

Yet we from the East suspect this prospect is being manipulated by forces at Rome who wish the succession to be securely finalized now

Hadrian has entered mid-life and its inevitable health risks. An unresolved succession is a proven recipe for civil war when an emperor dies. A bloodbath can result, with totally unpredictable outcomes.

Also, the succession of Commodus would once again shift priorities and resources away from us in the east into the western sphere. We resist this strongly while the barbarians are at the door.'

'What then is your advice in this matter? I am not experienced in the stratagems of lovers, seducers, or courtesans. I am a plain speaking fellow from the provinces. What is your advice, sir?' Antinous asked somewhat plaintively.

'Love? Lovers!? What has love to do with it? Hadrian only wants to enjoy your pleasant company," Arrian retorted sharply. "Laughter and lust are your functions, my boy, perhaps coupled with a longing for the son he has never bred. Your role is to satisfy the call of Eros. You take his mind off the issues of state. So make the best of it, my boy, for all our sakes.'

Antinous grew impatient with this overly pragmatic philosophy.

'You must think very little of me, sir, if you think I am but a kept boy?" Antinous challenged daringly. "I am not for sale, my lord. I am protective of my honor, my *arete*.'

'Yes, yes, yes, lad, I acknowledge your quality," Arrian responded, realizing he had ruffled the lad's sensitivities. "But you are now entering a realm where everything and everyone are purchasable. Power is a commodity and it is for sale, usually at a high price in coin or blood.'

'But I possess few needs, my lord. I do not seek power or influence. I do not seek great wealth. So is there anything specific you can recommend to me?" Antinous persisted. "I'm not sufficiently experienced in courtly ways to determine a path forward."

Arrian paused to reflect for a moment. Then he looked fixedly at Antinous with a glinting knowingness in his eye. He smiled.

'Yes, there is one important thing. Perhaps it's how you have gotten this far so swiftly. Great Caesar is certainly smitten by your charms, young man. I have witnessed your effect upon his moods. Your physical grace has impacted upon his more earthy appetites, true, as has your sassiness, your daring, and your cool persona. You indeed possess the upper hand in this courtly dance, Antinous. But one thing is worth accenting to you here.

I wish to reveal to you an important matter. Listen carefully because I will tell it to you only once.

You must show your most winning features to him. Yes, display your youth; display your beauty; display your fine young muscles; display your smooth flesh; display your intelligence and most appealing attributes. Display too your impudence, your drive, and daring. But also, ---'

Arrian's eyes started to drift slowly across Antinous's sweatily glistening frame, down its sculpted surfaces, and then low in the direction of his reproductive organs. Arrian was not being provocative, prurient, or suggestive; he was simply scanning the facts of Antinous's physicality. Yet his eyes lingered politely over the young man's adequately proportioned genitalia which now lay wetly shriveled in the *sodatarium* heat. His vision came to rest in a manner which seemed to silently, meaningfully, signal a message.

'--- be audacious, Antinous. Do the unexpected,' he concluded smoothly.

After a few moments Antinous and Lysias both perceived what this unspoken message may have been at precisely the same time," Geta added. "They turned to each other in sudden recognition but also in embarrassment. It was now evident why Arrian had chosen the nudity of a hot room at the Baths for his dissertation and its special clue to Caesar's tastes. He wished to make a particular point without it being too boldly articulated. Arrian continued.

'You possess certain attributes which may appeal to Hadrian, young man. Yes, display a possibility to him Commodus has never offered in the first place,' Arrian alluded obliquely. 'Commodus is renowned for his sexual appetite to the point of being considered an unrestrained *cinaedus* obsessed with sensuality. But I don't think his repertoire with his own gender is reputed to be especially *dominant*, if you catch my meaning? Not at all, in fact. So, Antinous, I suppose it was no accident Great Caesar personally checked your physical attributes at Nicomedia last year.'

Antinous blushed fully crimson despite his existing rosy hue of a hot-room flush. The cat was now out of the bag about who was witness to the event in the amphitheatre at Nicomedia. Lysias too now realized who the other observer had been shifting through the shadows. It had been Arrian.

'Among other things show him a possibility which may have agreed with him when he first observed your qualities, my boy. And do it shamelessly,' Arrian persisted, nodding casually in the direction of Antinous's crutch. 'Others have failed in this role perhaps because Hadrian is Caesar, which can be intimidating, while custom tends to object to the senior partner participating in this way. But custom is blind.

Do you get my drift, lad? But also be flexible, be versatile, be willing to shift according to his changing moods, be open to all possibilities. And yes, be willing to submit too. This is the Bithynian way, my friend.'

'I think I do get your drift,' Antinous murmured distractedly.

'Don't forget Antinous, to be Caesar's *Companion* is to be at the centre of the universe. It is to participate in works of great import. You enter history, young man. You become part of history. It's your life's destiny made concrete,' Arrian concluded. 'You must make of my advice what you will, and act according to your *arête*, your virtue. *Praise be to Caesar!*'

'*To Caesar!*' the boys echoed in unison. Both youngsters were thoughtful for some moments at this newest revelation. Then it was time for a cold plunge bath after stewing so long in the steamy heat.

Arrian led the trio from the private chamber to the vaulted public pools of the Baths. The marbled caverns echoed with two hundred bantering voices amid the splashy hubbub.

The hollow cacophony slowly diminished to furtive murmurs as they arrived. Much whispering tinged with gasps of admiration were accompanied by eager eyes sweeping the arcades as the three took their cooling plunge in the main pool.

This, coupled with the opaque message of the previous conversation, caused Antinous and Lysias to begin to wonder what they had gotten themselves into."

Geta paused momentarily as the team of investigators contemplated the implications of his story. Clarus was disconcerted by its revelations.

"Things soon became more complicated," Geta forwarded. "On the second day of the Great Dionysia, which I attended in my role as Caesar's master of ceremonies, certain developments occurred.

On their arrival at Caesar's villa at high sun, the two Bithynians were made welcome at the courtyard gate by the younger Herodes Atticus.

Herodes Junior had recently been awarded Roman senatorial rank and been appointed *quaestor* at the status level of *inter amicos* – a 'friend of the emperor' – a high honor for a Greek in his mid-twenties. Herodes invited the two youngsters to share in the company of his friends of a similar age awaiting the arrival of Hadrian and the officials of the Dionysia Festival from within the villa.

This mix of Greek and Roman young men seemed an agreeable group to the newcomers, even though they displayed standards of attire, comportment, and ornamentation at a level of wealth far beyond their own. Herodes explained how the entire assembly would soon be joining the public procession currently winding its way along the city's Sacred Way to the Acropolis.

At last clarions sounded and the Imperial party appeared from within the villa. It was led by Hadrian accompanied by notables including Arrian and Athenian officials in ceremonial attire. I too was in this retinue in my usual role as Hadrian's *factotum*.

Later I was told how Antinous and Lysias took special interest in the young patrician following close beside Hadrian. To their eyes he was a delicately chiseled, slender-waisted *ephebe* of pale complexion garbed in a fulsome Roman toga of blindingly white purity. It was striped with the scarlet blazon of a senator.

He wore a meticulously closely-trimmed beard of an unusually slender design. His head was a riot of voluminous curls dusted with sparkling glitter and skewered with elegant needles of silver filigree. He bore a diadem announcing his lofty status as a member of a noble family. His wrists and arms were adorned with bracelets of precious metals while bright jewels were affixed to each earlobe. Both hands displayed many antique rings on each finger and a prominent antique brooch adorned his shoulder. The fellow flourished hand gestures of great fluidity as he talked, accompanied by a jubilant manner with many calculated sardonic smiles and expressive eye gestures. His eyes were finely underlined in *kohl* accents which gave his features a distinctively feline appearance.

Even from their position some distance away in the courtyard the boys could detect the heady scent of an expensive Assyrian fragrance wafting from his direction. His age was somewhere in his twenties yet his bearing had the decidedly stately mode of a far older man. Members of the Roman *patrician* class definitely project an image of class superiority.

'My lord Herodes, please tell me who is that striking figure of a man behind Caesar?' Antinous whispered behind one hand. The Athenian acknowledged his companion's comment on the senator's demeanor as being 'striking'.

'Why, Antinous, it is Senator Commodus. He's a close friend of Caesar,' was the reply in a restrained whisper. 'He arrived from Rome recently and is residing at Caesar's villa.'

I suppose in the eyes of Antinous and Lysias the young senator was a revealing exponent of the current high-fashion at Rome. The senator displayed it with the studied, urbane, supercilious confidence seemingly ingrained in Rome's patrician class.

Hadrian did not wear a toga nor his Imperator's military cuirass, but was dressed in Greek attire. Both his tunic and mantle, however, were of an opulent Tyrian purple trimmed in finely embroidered golden eagles as befits an emperor who is to act as president of The Great Dionysia. He wore no other decorative devices other than a simple wreath of natural grapevines encircling his head. This was a leafy corona heralding spring, symbolic of the cult of Dionysius and the joyful fruits of the vine.

Taking his stand on steps above the courtyard with Arrian and Commodus behind him, Caesar patiently awaited the thirty-odd attendees in the yard to file past and make their proper obeisance. Both Antinous and Lysias followed the others by bending their knee to the yard's gravel while bowing their head in unison and crying *Hail Caesar*!

Hadrian stepped forward and raised the two Bithynians to stand upright before him.

'Rise, young friends, and welcome. It's a pleasure to see you again,' he stated loudly so all could hear, while glancing back at Commodus with a nodded acknowledgement.

'Geta,' he instructed me nearby, 'ensure Antinous and Lysias of Bithynia share our company closely today. Make sure they and Senator Atticus accompany me close through the procession, and remain close throughout the day's festivities. There's much to discuss between us after all this time.'

I beckoned the three to one side so I could assign them a special position in the cortege.

Beyond the villa gateway a stream of Athenian citizens crowded the street accompanying a larger-than-life-sized wooden effigy of the god Dionysus held aloft by sturdy men. They were led by two youths who, traditionally, were ambiguously dressed in women's attire. Arced boughs of vine leaves and springtime plants were being waved in the air while several huge, pronouncedly-erect wooden *phalluses* were trundled by teams of acolytes and choristers. Floral garlands symbolizing the arrival of spring adorned the cavalcade, while drummers and tambourine players beat-up a lively noise above the throng.

Spotless black bulls were led by priests of the cult bearing their sacrificial sledgehammer, knives, blood bowl, and flaying tools. Caesar's party fell in behind the musicians as the entire swarm veered gaily towards the looming crag of the Acropolis a mile distant.

On arrival at the open-air Temple of Dionysus at the base of the steep slope beneath the Acropolis many of the women dispersed leaving the males to witness the ritual slaughter of the bulls with the portion-offerings to the god. The effigy of the deity, whose weathered timbers and faded paints told of having witnessed several hundred offerings of the annual Dionysia, was lifted carefully to the stage of the Theater of Dionysus nearby. The theater is a concave stone slab amphitheater rising up the slope of the hillside with a marbled semicircular stage fronting its base. Dionysus was placed prominently on the stage in view of the sixty ascending rows of stone ledges for seating an audience.

On this day at least seventeen thousand persons, of whom only a fraction were women or older children, were clustered together in its concave arc. Several score of Athens' flamboyant *hetaerae* courtesans in attention-grabbing décolletage, extravagant hairstyles, and exotically inventive face paints, accompanied by their high-paying clients, were attending this first performance day of the year's Dionysia week

The throng of spectators appreciate how this festival is one of the few occasions in the civic life of Athens where citizens, women, freedmen, foreigners, slaves, or even children are permitted to participate in judgment on performances by mass ovation. With many of the festival's dramas possessing discernable parallels to current political life, the applause, jeers, or shrill catcalls could convey popular opinion to the city's rulers with clarity. Century by century, Athens' rulers had wisely listened to the massed ovation of the audience, or to any distinct lack of it.

The row closest to the stage is a line of marble thrones. The central chair is designated to the High Priest of Dionysus at Athens with Hadrian's beside it as the year's President. The remaining thrones seated other priests, the city's Archon, councilors of the city, and senior members of Hadrian's retinue.

Thirteen judges representing each of the city's thirteen *deme* 'tribes' sat at one wing to umpire each new competing play. The judging panel assessed the quality of the drama and the responses of the audience with equal measure.

Arrian too sat close by Hadrian, as did the elder Herodes Atticus. Elegant Commodus was not seated but stood behind Caesar's shoulder in a close place of favor, while others arranged themselves in nearby positions. Horse Guards and Praetorians hovered discreetly at the end of each of the rows rising up the high amphitheatre, while the Athens Militia policed the upper rows.

I guided Antinous and Lysias to sit or stretch on the stones at the feet of the first row near to Caesar, an agreeably casual arrangement for young men held in high regard, fronting Herodes Junior's chair. I myself stood beside Commodus behind Caesar's presidential throne within earshot of the surrounding conversations.

The Bithynians youngsters were fascinated by the sartorial finesse and skittish manner of the young senator whose opalescent skin has rarely seen direct sunlight. His choice of a formal toga at an event where more relaxed dress predominated showed a degree of hubris. Commodus's voguish persona sparkled and tinkled and effused amid the theater's noisy swarm of earthy Greeks, his glittering twitter almost overwhelming Caesar's imperial *gravitas*.

The *patrician*'s sprightly manner was visible to all sixty rows. It was the flashy banter and studied fluttering of a noble Roman dandy.

Perhaps, the two wondered with alarm, these were the Court manners and public style of educated gentlemen-of-quality at Rome? Yet they noticed how despite Caesar appearing to be amused and entertained by the bright young thing's vivacity, he - our most lofty of Romans and ultimate arbiter of public taste - did not emulate the senator's display. Nevertheless Commodus made himself the sparkling center of attention.

Suddenly Antinous had a useful idea. I observed he turned to comment laconically to his friend seated beside him on the paving at the rim of the stage floor.

'Don't you feel it's very hot here, Lys?' I could hear at a distance.

'Hot?' Lysias responded quizzically. 'What do you mean? No, not especially, Ant.'

The spring sunshine of Athens was diffuse that day, but not especially intense now the rainy season had passed. Yet neither Lysias nor I sensed the sun was especially bothersome.

A ceremony of the endowment of weapons and armors to thirteen orphans was underway. The thirteen, each barely into their teen years and slight of build, displayed their upper torsos to the assembled spectators while the donations of armor were being fitted and strapped across their bird-boned frames. This display of bare skin had given Antinous food for thought.

'Yes, Lys, I think it is hot today. I need to cool down a little.'

Antinous began to untie the cloth bows at the arms, shoulders, and midriff of his tunic. The folds of the upper half of his *chiton* dropped away to reveal the full extent of his bare torso lying beneath the diagonal swathe of his *himation* mantle. Antinous's broad shoulders, cut chest line, orbed abdomen, and tanned muscles were exposed to public view. It was a conspicuously buff vision.

In a city once renown for the athleticism of its young men with its long tradition of Olympic competition, plus its naked *palaestrae* training methods and cult of masculinity, Antinous's nonchalant half-disrobing prompted a rustle of muttering across the assembly. A tide of whispers spread. It seemed Athenian youngsters, husbands, fathers, grandfathers, and devoted family men, as well as its more outward-going womenfolk, could still appreciate the contours of an *ephebe* at the peak of nature's perfection.

Lysias immediately understood Antinous's intent.

Using the pretext of the heat of the day he too took his cue to untie his tunic's upper laces. His sturdy anatomy too was now on public display.

Both lads sensed how Caesar's group spied these actions with interest, focusing especially on Antinous. Arrian observably suppressed a wry smile, while Herodes Junior found his eyes settling with enhanced interest upon Lysias.

The elder Herodes leaned to Arrian to comment quietly, while I was close enough to hear when Commodus asked something privately in Hadrian's ear. The senator's giddy manner had ceased its flightiness. Cool sobriety had taken hold.

Reclining side by side on the flagstones to indulge the exhibition of their physiques, Antinous leaned to Lysias to whisper. I can only imagine what he may have asked, but I assume it would be in the order of ---

'I wonder if this is the sort of thing Lord Arrian had in mind for us at the Baths yesterday? It seems to be working, Lys.'

Both youngsters sat in casual indifference to the attention generated among those around them, while people in the rows above craned their necks for a better view.

Antinous indirectly noticed an elderly man dressed in disheveled garb amble in veering paces from a doorway at the back of the theater's stage. He teetered erratically through the lines of orphaned juniors buckling on their oversized armor and weaponry.

The man was a shaggy-haired, wild-eyed fellow with rickety legs and bony flesh. He was loosely garbed in a drab tunic and scrappy broad-brim sunhat tied behind his neck. He was holding a raised object in one hand while waving the other in emphatic gesticulation as he muttered incoherently at his surroundings. He moved unsteadily across the stage area as though he was a comic mime performing a special dance for the ceremony. Yet Antinous hadn't noticed his participation earlier. For that matter, nor had I.

Antinous tugged at Lysias's elbow to draw attention. Amid the prevailing good cheer it hadn't occurred to anyone the fellow might be following a less cheerful agenda. That was until a small, thin object in his raised fist glinted a flash in the sunlight.

Both boys immediately realized the fellow's fist was holding an instrument which, as he drew closer to the assembled row of thrones, took the shape of a small knife protruding from a covering. The man was stumbling forward across the stage intently towards Caesar, whose attention was turned away from the approaching menace.

Instantly without a moment's hesitation the two Bithynians leapt from the stones to fling themselves at the fellow.

Lysias lunged head-first at the man's midriff in a wrestler's flying tackle which pounded the breath out of the old guy. Antinous simultaneously leaped high to snap an expertly maneuvered arm lock on his raised limb. He wrenched the upheld instrument from his grasp. All three toppled to the flagstones in a cloud of dust as several Horse Guards lurched forward with outstretched javelins and drawn swords. A loud collective cry went up across the theatre.

Antinous grappled the man's arm until his grip was released. The dismayed elder cried out and writhed about as Lysias planted one foot firmly on his squirming ribcage. Antinous lifted the offensive object to view.

The old man's hand had been grasping a small rolled parchment enclosing an antique fruit knife. The miniature dagger displayed a dulled point, blunted edges, and a rusty blade. On closer inspection the knife seemed too innocuous a weapon to be capable of any serious wound, except perhaps upon a piece of fruit. It was more likely to inflict nothing other than a nasty bruise on human flesh.

Nevertheless the spluttering fellow with the wild eyes had been fortunate that neither a Horse Guard's *gladius* blade had pierced his throat nor a Praetorian javelin skewer his entrails.

Hadrian, Arrian, Commodus, and myself, accompanied by officials, guards, and the Herodes Atticus pair, circled around the elder. Hadrian looked over the unkempt, writhing fellow whose tongue uttered words of rabid inconsequence while his body struggled beneath Lysias's firm boot. When Antinous displayed the sorry weapon for all to see I retrieved the small scroll from his grasp to unroll and read its contents.

'It appears to be a letter or document from long ago addressed to 'Philip, a hoplite of the Achaea Militia', and carries the name and title of an archon of this city,' I announced.

'Tell me, old man, are you the Philip of this document?' Hadrian demanded, waving the scroll at the struggling fellow.

The man was so visibly shaken he was incapable of a civil response. It dawned on the assembled group the fellow was not simply confused, he was thoroughly disoriented in the manner of a demented geriatric. His eyes displayed little comprehension of his circumstances while his features were visibly gaga. Saliva dribbled from his mouth.

The senior Herodes Atticus, Prefect of the Free Cities, took the scroll to read its contents.

'It seems, Caesar and friends, this fellow was once a soldier of this city. His face is vaguely familiar to me, so I guess he's a military pensioner on the city payroll. He wears no evident nameplate, branding, or the tattoo of a slave, so he's probably a freeborn citizen fallen on hard times.

The paper is in Greek, but appears to be of the time of Caesar Trajan or even earlier? The Archon listed is from very long ago. It commends him for his service to the state as a captain of hoplites. Perhaps he served in past wars or the city militia? Maybe he wished to make a petition to Caesar to improve his pension, or suchlike? If so, he chose the wrong time and way to do it,' Atticus explained.

Hadrian stepped closer to the figure lying beneath Lysias's foot and waved the pressure off him. He looked down upon the startled fellow.

'Old Soldier, what is your meaning here? What are you up to? Did you intend me some injury with your fruit knife? If so, your Last Day would have arrived very swiftly, I assure you,' he called to the stricken ancient who was straining to mouth incoherent words.

The military tribune in command of the Guards made his presence known.

'My lord, if I may, this man should be made an example of,' he stated with his sword point aimed directly at the man's throat. 'A severe public beating or even death itself is necessary to punish him and dissuade others of like mind.'

'No, no, no, no, Tribune. The fellow is plainly mad, demented, or just old,' Hadrian responded. 'He's a tired soldier whose judgment has fled him in his dotage. He's probably done this city great service in his time. But he's also probably received a hard hit on the head that's damaged his reason along the way. Let him be, and let him be unharmed as well,' he soothed. 'Talk with the city's militia to see if the man's family or abode can be traced. If he is alone in life, see to it he receives a useful adjustment to his pension so he can live his final crazed days in comfort,' Hadrian instructed. 'This the second time in a year I've been attacked by a malcontent. Remember that lunatic slave at Tarraco in Iberia last year? Release the fellow and escort him home safely so we may continue with our holy purpose here today.'

The startled graybeard was gathered up by several Praetorians and bundled away.

Hadrian meanwhile, in barely suppressed amusement, looked over the two dusty, knee-and-elbow-scraped combatants with grazed tunics kneeling on the flagstones. Commodus languidly wandered across from the President's throne to join the circle. His presence was heralded by a surge of floral fragrance.

Hadrian scanned the boys as they dusted themselves down.

'Well, my two young friends from the provinces, you performed magnificently on the stage of this theatre today, didn't you?' Hadrian said with a grin. 'I suppose I must be gratified you kept your wits about you? I might have met a fate similar to the old fellow's fruit peels or cheese rinds?'

'It was our duty, sir,' Antinous responded in polite modestly to this whimsy, 'if a bit rough on our new clothes.'

Commodus was visibly put on edge by this exchange. Hadrian continued.

'I think such observant bodyguards deserve to be kept closer about us,' the emperor jollied, 'especially through the performance we are about to witness. I am told the choristers are to sing and dance the ancient drama of *Alcestis* today? I invite both of you eagle-eyed lads to stay by my side through the play to watch against further assailants, and to help me translate its Attic intricacies into my Latin understanding. As students of history you are probably more familiar with Euripides than I, so you can explain his finer points to me.'

Commodus emitted an audible hiss through pursed lips.

He turned smartly on his heel, and strode off brusquely from the stage. He realized Caesar's invitation to Antinous and Lysias had displaced he and I from our privileged places behind the President's throne. He may have interpreted the gesture as implying he should stretch on the dusty tiles at the feet of the first row in his unblemished formal toga. In fairness to his *patrician* status, this is an unlikely expectation of a Roman senator.

No one, including Caesar, tried to stop him departing. Even I resisted leaping to my usual conciliatory gestures, though two of the younger Romans in nearby rows accompanied Commodus in a theatrically dramatic flounce. The senator dispensed with the usual departure etiquette or permission from Caesar.

A Praetorian tribune nearby tensed ready for orders from Hadrian to act on this slur. But no order came. Instead, their departure merely raised a faint smile from Hadrian.

Suddenly drums were beating, cymbals clashing, and pipes and horns shrilled as a priest of Dionysus entered centre stage to proclaim the start of the performance. Seventeen thousand pairs of feet noisily shuffled in their seats while Antinous and Lysias accompanied Caesar to his President's chair and stood behind his shoulder like dutiful sons or honored emissaries. Their close proximity meant Caesar could mutter queries back over his shoulder to one or the other so they could respond in whispers. I too stood close by to overhear as much as was possible.

'Remind me again, Antinous, what are we hearing here today?' Hadrian asked.

'We are to hear ancient *Alcestis* sung, I'm told. It is a tragedy which won its Dionysia trophy for the playwright Euripides in the days during the Great War between Athens and Sparta long ago,' I heard the lad reply. He seemed to know his Greek dramas.

'And what is *Alcestis* all about, remind me of that too,' the emperor enquired.

'As I recall, sir,' Antinous began, 'Euripides was from a family of priests of Apollo similar to my own kinsmen. So the drama is based on the legend of Apollo when he was the lover of the mortal, King Admetus of Thessaly. Apollo rewards the king for his affection by granting him the great boon of freedom from death if he can find someone willing to die in his fated place. After searching widely, the king finds no one is willing to be a substitute for his death. Then his beautiful wife, Queen Alcestis, volunteers to do so.'

'Ah, yes, the drama of the substituted death. Queen Alcestis,' Hadrian recollected. 'And then?'

'Alcestis loves Admetus so much she believes it is her duty to die in place of her husband to permit him Apollo's gift of extended life. That's the basic story, but Euripides cleverly uses the legend to explore sensitive issues between men and women, and between freeborn and slave.

Euripides also discusses the nature of marriage, of marital love, and the generosity of women in the face of their menfolk's privileges and obsessions,' Antinous continued. 'It even asks about the nature of Love itself.'

'That sounds more Roman than Greek,' Hadrian opined. 'As a Hellene you lads probably don't realize how the people of Rome allow more freedom to their womenfolk than you Greeks do. Yet Euripides was already saying these things several hundred years ago! Amazing!'

'From memory, the play opens at the very moment the queen is due to die,' Antinous offered.

'It comes back to me now,' Hadrian muttered as Apollo, an actor wearing a silvered mask portraying the god's eternal youth and handsome features, entered the stage. His silvery costume, draped by his bow and quiver of deadly arrows, stepped solemnly into view in time to music of funereal double-pipes and a deep drum. These throbbed mournfully offstage. He traversed the stage in a unique tripping dance which specially signifies Apollo.

'Where did you learn so much about these things, Antinous, at your age? And from a distant province too!' I overheard Hadrian murmur. 'Aren't horsemanship and weapons enough for young fellows to master?'

Antinous lent forward to whisper his reply over Caesar's shoulder, which I could barely overhear.

'Sir, Lysias and I as acolytes of Apollo and Artemis were taught about the life and affairs of the Healer. Our tutor in literature, a kinsman priest of the cult, taught the young of my clan all manner of matters about the god, his rites, his many lovers of both sexes, his children, including his son Asclepius, the god physician,' Antinous responded. 'He is the sun of our lives and we praise him despite his irascible, mercurial nature.'

Silvery Apollo paused majestically at centre stage as the music subsided to allow the god to chant the opening words of ancient *Alcestis*. Euripides' first lines are well known to audiences across the Greek East.

The pipes and drum's throb trailed away as an expectant hush settled upon the amphitheatre.

All eyes focused on the silver mask of Apollo.

'*House of Admetus!*' the actor's call throatily resounded across the towering steps of spectators. As he continued this initial plea, thousands of additional voices surged to life to accompany him.

'*Here I have suffered bread as common workers must endure .. yes I, a god, Apollo!*' the actor declaimed.

His voice was immediately swamped beneath the engulfing roar of thousands of throats as they too enjoined Apollo's complaint of his servile status at his lover King Admetus' palace. On conclusion of the booming line the mass erupted into uninhibited self-applause. It was an uproar which registered the crowd's collective satisfaction with its own recitation of such a revered line in the presence of Caesar.

I, visibly a Dacian barbarian who had never witnessed *Alcestis* previously, was impressed by this unexpected enthusiasm of the Greeks. Nevertheless I was obliged to lean closer to hear Caesar's asides to his young attendants..

'You say Euripides talks of the role of women?' Hadrian threw over his shoulder as uproar resounded around the amphitheater. 'But what do you two lads know of women, eh? Have you enjoyed a woman yet, you two, or are you abstaining until your betrothal? I am led to believe some Greeks actually do so, though not many I'd wager?'

Antinous and Lysias hesitated, being taken aback by such a forward question about such personal matters.

'I confess I possess only limited experience with women,' Antinous responded, wondering if Hadrian remembered their conversation at the symposium garden at Nicomedia. 'But I am contractually betrothed to a cousin of my family who is still a child at this time,' he added. 'Perhaps we will marry when time matures or the omens are favorable.'

By now *Apollo* was regaling the audience with a mimed outline of the play's plot, accompanied by gentle pipes and a drone. He reported the news of how Queen Alcestis was presently undergoing her death throes to fulfill her promise to Admetus. Another actor wearing the black mask, wings, sword, and costume of *Death* mounted the stage, stepping across its flagstones in a magical, unearthly glide. He provoked the audience to collectively groan in fearfulness.

'I wonder who solicited this particular play for my enjoyment?' Hadrian muttered to himself perhaps too loudly, somewhat distracted by the appearance of the black robed figure. "Was it me, keen to see a famed classic? Could it have been my secretary? The empress's household? I wonder? None of these things happens entirely by accident, I say.'

He then shifted from Common Greek into his own tongue, Latin. This was possibly to test the two boys' comprehension of his exchanges or to assess their skill as students of Latin.

'Tell me, Antinous of Bithynia,' the emperor murmured low in Latin, 'how do you propose to pursue this destiny of yours? What has changed in your ambitions since our nighttime rendezvous some months ago?'

Antinous was silent for a period as he sought to respond in correct Latin to the query. The delay caused Caesar to look back over his shoulder to probe for the missing response.

I, standing some distance away almost out of earshot, was straining to overhear their conversation or was following every lip movement for a clue.

'I am flattered that you should ask, my lord,' Antinous eventually whispered in insecure but competent Latin beneath *Apollo*'s and *Death*'s reverberating orations. 'I believe, sir, a great deal has changed in my life. I think I am more focused on what the gods may have in store for me. There are things I must do in life to fulfill my destiny,' he carefully articulated in better-than-average student's Latin.

'I see,' Hadrian replied with an approving tone to his test, but again in Latin, 'and precisely what might that destiny be, I wonder?'

'This will depend upon the favor of the gods and the grace of my noble lord,' Antinous responded, now reverting back to Greek for ease of expression while adding a dash of diplomacy. He sensed Caesar's openness to informality in the exchange.

'Yet perhaps the most important of them, if I am permitted to be so forward, sir,' he whispered, his voice lowering even further for extra privacy, 'is to communicate a special message to our *Princeps*.'

Both Lysias and I were now alerted to strain to hear his subdued speech.

'*Princeps*? You mean me?' Hadrian confirmed. 'A petition you have, is it lad? I have vassals who attend to petitions, my boy. I do not welcome uninvited petitions.'

'Sir, if I may be so bold, it is a special petition for your ears only,' Antinous dared. 'It is of an intimate nature.'

I could detect Antinous was showing beads of sweat at his brow.

'Intimate? Then tell me, what is this particular petition, our *tiro* bodyguard with eagle eyes?' Caesar asked breezily, if dismissively. I watched Antinous inhale a deep breath to summon his courage. His hand and voice trembled as he spoke very faintly.

'The message is this,' his voice dropped to a husky whisper barely audible beneath the amphitheater's populous hum. He spoke in Latin.

'*Yes indeed Caesar, I am yours.*'

He repeated the statement for clarity in Greek in a croaky voice.

Hadrian's jaw stiffened. His features firmed. His manner resumed its formal Imperial mode of bearing after such an extended period of casual informality. He turned towards the stage and sat impassively in silent absorption through the remaining hour of Euripides' drama. He made no reply.

I suppose we each sensed he was calculating a magisterial response appropriate to an *Imperator's* comportment, or else he had simply dismissed the statement outright. After all, he had been conversing in a highly familiar manner with two foreigner *ephebes* of no social consequence, nil political value, no evident status or superior wealth, and from a backwoods colony at that.

The lads and I noted Caesar's fingers invest intense energy in drumming the hand-rest of the throne. Yet a sense of stillness settled upon him as *Alcestis* progressed.

Antinous exchanged furtive glances with Lysias. He was flushed with embarrassment. It was apparent he wondered if he had overstepped his mark and been presumptuous.

When the final words of *Alcestis* were echoed away its chorus of mimes and the three actors who played the major masked roles presented themselves for judgment to the audience.

Hadrian, in a flourish of his Tyrian purple tunic and mantle, rose to stand before the theater's crowd. He responded to the players with lively applause, which encouraged an even more enthusiastic response from the citizens in the rows towering above.

Amid the cheers and whistles of praise, much of which was directed to the emperor himself as sprigs of vine and new season blooms were tossed to the stage, Hadrian turned towards Arrian, the two Herodes, several Praetorians, nearby officials as well as the two youngsters and myself to call loudly above the acclaim.

"And now, good friends, it's time for feasting and carousing in the famous Athenian way in honor of the god Dionysus!" he cried. "It's time to release pent up emotions and give ourselves up to the sacraments of wine, bread, and meat to enter into communion with the divinity.

My friends, not only must we offer thanks that *Alcestis* is returned alive from Hades into the arms of her kingly husband by the grace of old Euripides, but I too offer thanks for how I am returned to full life this day by the grace of Aphrodite's child, Eros! My long praises and offerings to Eros have been rewarded in this very place today!'

Those of us within earshot initially wondered what event Caesar was referring to? It would hardly be the collaring of the old warrior, we sensed.

Hadrian's eyes swept the nearby rows with a beaming countenance. His informality had revived. His eyes scanned across the lower rows and pointedly settled upon the figure of Antinous standing before him behind the throne.

He took one hand of the young man in a raised grasp to look directly to his eyes. We saw him nod a subtle affirmation which held a telling message to all who saw it, Antinous as well as Lysias and me. We immediately knew its meaning. He uttered a single word which only those nearest could hear. He said it in Latin and repeated it in Greek.

'Accepted.'

Antinous blushed deeply. He had not been too presumptuous after all.

The nearest rows of leading citizens slowly grew to interpret Hadrian's message. Its dawning injected extra energy into the expanding applause. But the applause was no longer simply for the assembled players or Caesar.

Rising to their feet and addressing their ovation towards the young man standing tall before the emperor in his distressed tunic, grazed elbows, and a casually slung cape around his bared torso, their applause swelled.

It was now time for Antinous to smile broadly at the world around him. Lysias too was visibly overtaken by emotion. I think I even detected tears welling in some eyes."

Geta paused in his testimony.

"So, Caesar confirmed his liaison with the Bithynian but also broke with Commodus? Is this your meaning, Dacian?" Suetonius asked plainly.

"Yes."

"Yet I see no real enemy here yet. Unless you say Senator Commodus is an enemy in some way?"

"This will be apparent if you are patient, sirs. May I continue? I must describe the events which occurred at the masked revel later that night?"

"Do so, Dacian, but we don't have all day."

CHAPTER 17

Geta continued as Strabon fluttered his stylus across another tablet.

"The Festival's revel occurred at the Acropolis citadel and its nearby Areopagus ridge at sunset.

I wasn't to share in the boy's company at the time, but I learned of the following events from various sources later. It was a decisive night. And it was a well-lubricated one. Wine flowed readily.

Athena's great metropolis glittered with lamplights as the sun set over the Bay of Salamis. Antinous and Lysias had never before seen a city ornamented with such a profusion of lamps, torches, braziers, lanterns, sanctuary lights, and piazza bonfires. Viewed from Caesar's open-air enclosure along the rocky spine of the Areopagus, the descending rows of roofs and dusty lanes sweeping down both sides of the ridge were a stirring sight for them.

At this first *komos* of the Great Dionysia all the wilder young men of the city with their less-inhibited womenfolk partied amid this fantasy of lights. Serving staff and young slaves dispensed roasted meats, breads, and wine plentifully as a pleasing haze of scorched flesh and burning pine needles drifted across the crowd.

For the Dionysia the city's merrymakers searched out arranged assignations or enticed newfound intimacies from among the surging throng. Facemasks in gaudy designs of Dionysus, Pan, or satyrs, with elaborately painted faces and ingenious hairstyles, blurred the identities of the roisterers. In many cases the elaborate costumes blurred their gender as well. At the annual revel of Dionysus anonymity combined with drunkenness was the approved ceremonial praise for the randy god, coupled with sexual ambiguity.

This opening festival of the new season gives Athenians and foreigners alike the opportunity to rage with Dionysian folly after the torpid months of winter. The city's citizens mix together regardless of status, wealth, or nationality. Social limits are put aside for a night.

Instead, a radical democracy of lust rules the streets. Consequently only very adventurous Athenians attend the public *komos* of the Great Dionysia. For five hundred years its wild, orgiastic frenzy has been legend across the Aegean, and not always approved.

Brazier flames sparked-and-gutted above the steeply ramped Sacred Way leading to the Acropolis precinct. The high fluted pillars supporting the massive pediment of the Parthenon glowed warmly above the firelight into the night sky. Pericles' ancient temple to Athena Parthenos and to the city of Athens itself shone magnificently in the evening's deepening dark.

Of the seventeen thousand spectators at the Theater performance most had retired to their family hearths by nightfall. Those remaining, mainly young unmarried adventurers or *demimonde* wastrels, wandered the *peripatos* road from the Theater to the entrance ramp of the citadel or the Areopagus ridge. There they found opportunities to party and more.

Hadrian, as President of the Dionysia, endowed the night's festivities from his own purse. Yet because he was engaged in the obligations of diplomacy with mature-age city councilors, ambassadors, and other notables, he was separated from his young companions for the evening.

He delegated the younger Herodes Atticus to entertain the two young Bithynians until his imperial duties were completed. This may have suited Herodes well, considering he had had his eye cast over the strapping physique and modest manner of Antinous's schoolchum, Lysias. Herodes, Antinous, and Lysias meandered together among the revelers to enjoy the rowdy display of Athenians letting their hair down.

The two visitors had never before enjoyed so cheerful a public riot of such opulence. Revelers milled around in tipsy chit-chat groups, or prowled shady nooks-and-crannies with salacious intent, while bands of musicians strolled the paths winding between the shrines and chapels straddling the ridge.

Bursts of laughter, shrieks of delight, cries of profanity, and merry banter echoed across the crowd. Flute girls and young dancer boys garbed in spring foliage tripped, pranced, and skylarked between the wanderers to earn an occasional coin for their antics.

Groups of friends who had been cheered by Dionysus's gift to humanity, the season's first pressing of the vine, were forming merry dance circles to sway, leap, and step in mutual unison to the drums, cymbals, and pipes of wandering musicians. Occasional women of carefree manners, or vivacious *hetaerae* in high spirits and spectacularly distinctive attire, along with common sex-workers in shamelessly revealing gauzes to invite custom, dared to join an exuberant men's dance circle and cavort to the lilting rhythms.

Others withdrew into the shadows with newfound companions for sessions of raunchy sport amid gales of laughter or the delectable moans of sensual delight. Flesh met flesh, kisses hungered for new mouths, hands searched over willing limbs, and pleasures were shared.

Antinous, Lysias, and Herodes hunkered together upon a low rocky slab to imbibe in the seductive atmosphere and gaze up to the ramparts of the ancient citadel looming skywards before them. Swigs from a corralled skin of wine and gnaws at legs of game intruded intermittently on their rambling conversation.

The Bithynians' faces were elegantly veiled by silver stripes painted across their eye lines by Thais at their Melite villa when they had retired to replace their torn tunics and freshen up. She had also dusted any exposed skin and limbs with splashes of silver glitter highlighting the animal grace of their physiques, while their shag-cut manes of hair were studded with shreds of glittering silver foil. These glitzy touches transformed each of the boys into an elysian Apollo Incarnate in festive party mode.

Herodes, already a bearded adult with the lean body and bearing of a militia commander, wore a molded leather actor's mask bearing the features of Ares, the god of war who protects young soldiers. It was slanted rakishly across his head. Despite being a senator of Rome he didn't affect a formal toga but wore a simple Greek tunic and polished leather cuirass slung with an embroidered *himation* mantle. His garb was simple if military, but Lysias considered it very striking.

The three took deep draughts from the shared wineskin's nozzle.

'So this is the famous city of Socrates, Sophocles, Plato, Aristotle, and many other thinkers of fame," Antinous mused tipsily to his companions while waving a half-chewed chicken leg at the skyline laid before them. Between downing gulps of wine he added, "This is the birthplace of all our better ideals.'

Herodes smiled knowingly at the young man's rosy view of the city.

'Ah, not only thinkers, Antinous. Don't forget Athens is also a city of punishers-and-straighteners. Remember the severe law-makers Solon, Dracon, Peisistratos, Pericles, and so on," Herodes contributed. "Perhaps they had a greater impact on Athens and the Greeks than the philosophers ever had?'

'But what about of your renowned lovebirds?' Lysias added in a wine-cheery vein. 'Remember Aristogiton and his *eromenos* Harmodius, your famously-smitten tyrant killers? Or Socrates and his young beauty Alcibiades; or Pausanius and Agathon; Cratinus and Aristodemus, and others whose names I forget?'

Antinous had to add his *drachma's* worth.

'Even Great Alexander and his companion Prince Hephaestion were here at one point. Arrian's recent book reminds us so. But only Hades knows how many playwrights, poets, athletes, soldiers, and whoever, found love in this place,' he muttered as yet another swig from the shared bladder dribbled russet drops down his chin.

Herodes took up the theme.

'But don't forget the Romans, you narrow-minded Hellenes. Julius Caesar, Caesar Augustus, Caesar Nero, and many others. Several of the emperors have loved this city, and *found* love too in this city in their time,' the sturdy officer-&-gentleman reminded his companions. His eyes settled lazily upon the darker of the two youths.

'And it seems even today it can be so, as we saw this afternoon,' he added as he drew his gaze back to Antinous. The fair-haired member of the trio blushed briefly.

Herodes continued.

'I'd say this city has a well-deserved reputation as a City of Love.'

Herodes' focus returned to the beefier of the two lads who was casually chewing at a hare's haunch. His gaze lay upon Lysias a few moments too long.

Lysias at last perceived Herodes' attention for what it was, and swiftly averted his eyes from the man's direct view. He was not used to being a centre of attention when in the company of his imposing school pal. Meanwhile Antinous's imagination had taken flight elsewhere.

'Our tutors tell us this legendary fortress before us here, this Acropolis rock, has weathered a thousand years of brute force inflicted by Persians, Spartans, Alexander's Macedonians, other Greeks on the rampage, Athens' own warring factions, and finally Rome as well,' Antinous continued in a surge of Hellenic romanticism. 'The blood spilled on these stones over time would nourish a world conquering army.'

'You Bithynians are obsessed with history, aren't you?' Herodes whimsied. 'Is this all your tutors drum into your heads in the provinces? Do they teach you about the world today? About Rome and its might?

Do they teach you of Rome's architects and builders, of its grand public works, its roads, its aqueducts, its baths? Do they teach you how grain from Africa and Egypt is controlled and warehoused so no one in the Empire starves and the price is stable? Do they teach you how the seas are now clear of pirates? How the law is common everywhere, up to a point? How the currency preserves its value? How we are taxed so the machinery of society is greased for smooth operation? Or is it all Homeric heroism and bone-crushing war for you?'

'We admire Rome and its achievements but we are also taught the meaning of *arete*,' Antinous affirmed while Lysias nodded approvingly in scholarly agreement. 'Yet much of our understanding of Greek *virtue* derives from the debates of the citizens of this very city, we are told.'

'Tell me, Bithynians, does your *arete* include how to love too? Or do your lessons only teach about past events, dead warriors, and dry theories?' Herodes asked with a dose of whimsy. 'Athens is as much about love, passion, and living life, as it is of noble honor.'

'In what way then, Lucius Herodes Atticus, is *love* expressed in Athens?' Lysias waggishly submitted to this authority on all things Athenian. Wine was beginning to shape the conversation.

Herodes sized-up the strapping athlete before him to discern the probable subtext of the question. It was no disinterested enquiry, he guessed. Antinous too perceived in his friend an underlying, if transparent motive. Herodes replied with a teasing smile.

'Athens is a culture of *love*, my well-formed suntanned *kouros* from a far shore. Among our elites,' he explained, 'a citizen's marriage enters him to the private realm of family life beyond the public arena. The special love that grows in a man for his betrothed wife as they produce their children and get to know each other may someday overcome the many years which separates them in age. The home and hearth becomes the secure, sanctified space which blesses a man with many sons who assure a city's honor and survival in war.

At Athens the family hearth is secluded from public view to ensure prudence and fidelity among our womenfolk. A modest, faithful, and demure wife with disciplined daughters are a great boon to a citizen, Athenians believe. Childbearing, spinning, sewing, and the arts of the kitchen are a woman's role. A man may even grow to find his contracted wife becomes his special friend in the course of their conjugal relations. Some even say they love their wives. I've known couples who display this truth openly.

Yet in the public domain of life away from his hearth where a man spends his days in the company of other men, an Athenian seeks the close companionship of like-minded friends to enhance his life. Augmenting the satisfactions of his wife's body, a lusty man may pursue sex and excitement with his slaves, or a hired *hetaera* mistress or two, or sex workers of assorted types. These may satisfy the urges of the groin, if not always the heart. These people will usually be companions of low status, they're not of his class. And they're strictly fleeting relationships by definition, aren't they?

Adultery with another citizen's wife or daughter is forbidden to him here at risk of an avenger's death. Instead, a man of the elites is either likely to take up a female concubine or he might prefer to share the company of a younger man,' Herodes proposed. His eyes drifted meaningfully to Lysias lazing nearby picking the last strands of flesh from a hare's haunch.

'A younger man may find such a relationship instructive. He too might be seeking worthy companionship or introduction into the society of well-born adults?' Herodes continued. 'The two will have similar backgrounds, values, sports interests, military skills, and might even share compatible sexual urges at their respective times of life.'

His eyes remained fixed on Lysias.

'If entered into with mutual respect this companionship is no offence against honor, it is not adultery, it produces no illicit progeny, and carries no issues of property or inheritance. Instead, it consolidates a man's relationships with the wider community. It can provide great satisfaction to both parties, except to those who are utterly immune to its appeal. I am told many are.'

Antinous glanced cautiously across to Lysias to realize his friend's eyes were firmly glued to his hare's chewed bones in resolute avoidance of eye contact. Antinous smiled at Lysias's discomfort at being a target of seduction. Herodes continued.

'*Love*, as you call it, will be expressed between them in carnal ways, very definitely. After all, both will be hot-blooded randy males. It's to be expected. This has long been the custom here at Athens and elsewhere across the Middle Sea. We have a long heritage of philosophy, verse, and art about such love. The recent arise of the ethereal *spiritual* love of the philosophers or ascetics can wait until a later period of life.

When his own contracted wife matures to a betrothal age, the youth will then marry to create his own household and consolidate his fortune. This pattern of events is the consequence of the Athenian view of *love* among the elites,' Herodes concluded as he reached for the goatskin of wine once more.

Lysias had been transfixed by this explanation while he was still contemplating the implications of '*my well-formed suntanned kouros*'.

But Antinous now took the bull by the horns while the 'tanned *kouros*' glued his eyes to the hare's haunch.

'Forgive my impudence, Senator, but do Romans at Rome follow this pattern of masculine relationships too? Or is this strictly a Greek way?' he ventured. 'We are told Romans shun these customs.'

'In the few years I spent at Rome I'd say they follow precisely the same customs,' Herodes replied. 'Some old fogies from earlier times like Cicero, Seneca, or Musonius Rufus were critical of the customs, but do not deny it too is a Roman tradition.

Instead they claim that sex is only justified when it's for making babies. They say the delights of sex are not for our personal pleasure or for improving one's own or another's mind, let alone for nurturing friendships. I do not know from where they derive these objections, but their influence has been strong among the new puritanical cults, if no one else.

Yet it's known neither Cicero nor Seneca practiced what they preached. Moralizers are prone to this hypocrisy. In Athens we advise the young to have as many lovers as they can entice. Success in love is admired and envied. It's a sign of the gods' beneficence or the Fates' fortune. Go for it, we say!, as long as you hurt no one.'

'Does the emperor hold to this philosophy, Herodes?' Antinous asked cautiously.

'Antinous, I am the son of the Prefect of the Free Ports of the Eastern Empire and a senator of Rome. It is not appropriate for me to share private information about the emperor's person with you, it may be interpreted as an indiscretion or even an insult. But I am permitted to reveal how I too was once close to Caesar. I too was very briefly one of the several people who shared Caesar's company and pleasure. But that was some years ago before the *Roman Favorite* came onto the scene. Since those days I sense Caesar has become restrained in his exuberance.'

'Is the *Roman Favorite* the one known as Senator Commodus, sir?' Antinous asked.

'He is. But as you saw today, there appears to be some friction between them.'

'What is his status today in the eyes of Caesar?'

Herodes baulked at the query, but replied nevertheless.

'Privately, I believe someday Commodus will inherit the *Imperium*. He will be the next Caesar,' the Athenian uttered softly with barely suppressed regret. 'There's much argument about this matter in Rome, which it is not politic for us to discuss, Antinous.'

'Does Caesar love Commodus?' Antinous dared extend this line of questioning.

'Love? Hmm, it's not for me to speculate on such things. I'm unsure of the answer anyhow. In fact I sense Caesar has now become a solitary in his role as *Princeps*,' Herodes mused. 'To be emperor isolates a man. A ruler has no true friend, Antinous, he must be wary of all those around him. Intrigue and venality follow Caesar like his shadow.

At an earlier time the youthful Commodus brought sparkle into Caesar's busy life. The fellow can be amusing, witty, and given to wildness. But he's also notorious in his sexual exploits. He rubs them in, before Caesar's own eyes. They once shared these exploits together, I am told, but in the past few years Hadrian has retired from such diversions. He is simply too busy attending to government. You should note the fact of his solitude, Antinous. It might be important for you.'

'How so, my lord?'

'I would not dare to venture opinions on your status in Caesar's eyes,' Herodes said. 'But you have asked, so in honesty I should respond. You bring to Caesar something he sorely misses, my friend. His own youth perhaps. And his lack of a son. Yet as a man, he too needs love. Maybe these are all related phenomena? You, Antinous, express the vigor of youth's latent promise by your very being. Caesar admires vigor, energy, and intelligence.

Hadrian is infinitely sensitive and creative, Antinous. His skills with verse, his knowledge of the sciences, with engineering, with architecture, with inventive approaches to life, are very considerable. He is a great architect, did you know? Better than his own hirelings.

His solutions to the structural problems of the great dome in rebuilding The Pantheon at Rome have amazed his own architects. It is a building of exceptional elegance, equal to our own Parthenon, yet he's modestly assigned its provenance to its original builder, Marcus Agrippa, of a century ago. I think this may be because he suspects Caesar Augustus, his hero and model as *Imperator*, and Marcus Agrippa had been lovers in their youth. His gesture acknowledges that friendship, some say.

Hadrian is constructing a grand palace complex in the cool hills of Tibur beyond Rome. All the most inventive architectural innovations possible are being erected at the site. It will reflect all the styles of architecture depicted across the Empire. It will be the Empire in miniature.

Hadrian knows more about philosophy, mathematics, art, architecture, rhetoric, even the medical sciences and astrology, than do the leading professionals in their respective fields. He argues with them all the time. Of course he is also a formidable strategist, military commander, and leader of men. Yet he possesses a fickle temper. He can be mercurial.

'Nevertheless he is unique, Antinous. His greatness is a wonder. Yet this extraordinary ruler has seen reason to endow you with his favor. This is a rare honor to be treasured, my friend, but also a token in his eyes of your own quality. You should be flattered.'

Herodes paused as the three men observed the cheery mayhem raging drunkenly all about them. Antinous proceeded deeper into his enquiries. Wine had encouraged seriousness not joviality.

'Perhaps you will advise me, Senator? Are younger ones ever permitted the dominant role with a maturer partner in your Athenian custom?' he asked cautiously. His manner was innocently frank; wine was speaking. 'We at Bithynia see no impediment to it, yet Romans do I am told.'

The Achaean noble sucked a deep intake of air.

'It has been known,' he responded ambiguously. 'But usually occurs out of sight in private.'

'Is there dishonor in it,' Antinous probed, 'for either party?' He recalled his father's sober advice of only a month earlier.

'Well, such an imbalanced relationship would draw the attention of others, I'd hazard, if it was visible,' the Athenian replied, 'and it could open the issue of the submissive partner being considered a *cinaedus* or *malthakos* regardless of how noble they may be. Yet what partners enact in their private chamber is their own affair, most would say.'

It was time for Lysias to pose a question.

'You are saying, my lord, that he who willingly accepts the submissive role is called a *cinaedus*, a pervert, or *malthakos*, soft, feminized, weak?'

Herodes was silent for a few moments. He probably realized his response could affect his potential appeal to the Bithynian. He replied carefully.

'Athenians have noted how even though a man may take the submissive role in his sexual exploits, it doesn't mean he is regarded as a *cinaedus*. It's his deference to his partner at that particular moment, that's all. He might respond differently on other occasions. Thoughtless people make too much of these things, especially among those obsessive sectarians deriving from Palaestina.

Besides, sex is reciprocal between people here, just as in Bithynia. A lover should ensure his partner enjoys each occasion of pleasure as much as he himself. It's a two-way thing. And each role has its satisfactions. Only prudes condemn such reciprocity.'

Herodes eyed the blond young man before him with a more intense scrutiny.

'You surely realize too, Antinous, how to be close to Caesar demands a very specific sacrifice?'

'What may that be, sir?'

'To be Caesar's friend, to be Caesar's *eromenos*, Antinous, means to know no other partner,' he said. 'The playfulness of the Athenians or the Bithynians is denied to such a luminary. You will be Caesar's partner exclusively. Rome's emperor does not share his intimates with others.'

Antinous mulled over this thought.

'If it is Great Caesar's choosing, I am entirely at his disposal, sir. I will be proud to walk in the footsteps of such a man.'

Herodes diplomatically shifted the subject. It was Lysias's turn.

'And you, my handsome *kouros*? What are your priorities, I wonder?'

Lysias balked before the question, but decided to be honest with his suitor.

'I am a second son, Herodes, needful to search for my life's opportunities and its destiny. These are my priorities.'

Antinous interrupted the discussion. He sensed his company might not be necessary for a while.

'Friends, I might leave you two to explore these deep things between you while I venture to view the heart of this mighty citadel before us,' he proposed. 'I am eager to visit this center of all things Athenian. It's been in my dreams all my life. Now here I am! Amazing!'

'Let's do it together then, Antinous. Caesar has commanded I entertain you and watch over you until he completes his duties,' Herodes volunteered sociably.

'No, I think you two have much to discuss together privately. You don't need my presence just now. I'll explore the Acropolis for a while and return to you soon. Athena's great temple awaits me. Allow me an hour. I wish to offer prayers to the spirit of this place.'

He gulped down extra swigs from the wine nozzle and wiped dribbles off his chin.

'Antinous, if you must explore, stay within sight of the guards of the City Militia. There are many undesirables and drunken fools about tonight. Some may be predators or robbers,' Herodes warned.

Antinous nodded farewell, wrapped his mantle close against the cool night air, and strode off to the sloping ramp approaching the Acropolis where dozens of revelers milled in noisy, boozy, carefree disarray.

Herodes turned to Lysias and, correctly intuiting the gesture would be welcome, lazily laid one hand on the loincloth-bound mound lying at the Bithynian's crutch. He leaned close to his ear to whisper secret words. Lysias was startled by the intimacy of his gestures, yet remained unresponsive if hopeful.

'Give me advice, *kouros*, on the correct way to seduce a handsome Bithynian *ephebe* so it pleases him greatly?' the Athenian breathed into his ear.

Lysias desperately searched his imagination for an appropriate response which might convey both reticence and encouragement simultaneously.

'Just take him,' he replied eventually. 'But respect his *arete* too. He is no *cinaedus*.'

'Then we should find somewhere secluded to disrobe together, my well-formed *kouros*, despite the chill of the night. It's time for your body's heat to meet mine, Bithynian.'

Lysias flinched at his admirer's forwardness.

'I want to hold you close to excite you,' Herodes teased. "I want you to feel my breath on your neck. I want you to feel my flesh press against yours. I want to lick you clean of your body's sweat and your mind's restraint. I want to open your defenses to my ambush. I want to be savage with you, *kouros*.'

Herodes blew cockily into his ear as he allowed his beard's trim bristles graze Lysias's jaw. His fist lingered thrillingly at the young man's lap pressing audaciously into his groin.

'Allow me to awaken my horny Bithynian's love juices, *kouros*. Let me clasp his body, seize his hips, hold firm his butt, fondle his equipment, stir his vital parts, and feel his bloodstream race. I want to enter his mouth and taste his sweet saliva. I want to hold his hardening manhood in my palm and feel his body melt willingly under my persuasions.

I want my *kouros* to deliver himself up to me entirely. I will *enter* deep into him to penetrate his hidden heart. Does this sound agreeable, my handsome beauty from a distant shore? Is your secret hunger excited at my battle plan?'

Lysias grunted an ambivalent approval while his crutch responded with concrete affirmation. He was exhilarated. Someone was propositioning *him* for once, not his charismatic friend. This was indeed a new experience. His inner spirit soared. He turned with a stupid grin to his libidinous enquirer.

'Sure. Certainly. Yes. I respond. But where?' he mumbled. 'There's no privacy here. Yet we must be here for Antinous when he returns.'

From the corner of his eye Herodes perceived something which caught his immediate attention. Three caped men disguised behind elegant Dionysian masks, one revealing the folds of a toga beneath his cape, had mounted the entrance ramp to the Acropolis citadel. They were following close after Antinous as he approached the precinct's gateway.

Herodes realized the three were moving behind him at a discreet distance, possibly to avoid recognition. He detected one of the men was bearing a short-sword concealed bumpily beneath his cape, a weapon banned at the public revel of Dionysus.

'*Kouros*, perhaps we should find a sheltered place within the Acropolis precinct,' Herodes beckoned. 'There are many hidden cul-de-sacs between the shrines to exploit. I'll show you. Follow me, my dark jewel, you'll soon feel my body's urgency.'

He grasped Lysias vigorously by one arm and slapped him cheerfully across his behind as they hurried towards the citadel.

Antinous looked high into the gloom towards the lofty effigy of the armored female warrior looming before him. Her helmet's crest almost touched the high star-scattered vaulting of the 'chamber of the maiden', the Parthenon. The monument was almost twenty-five feet high.

In the inner *cella* of the pillared hall this towering manifestation of the patron deity of Athens, Athena Parthenos, looked down upon her devotees. She was embellished in flesh of white ivory draped with ankle-length robes of beaten gold. With her upright spear held firm in one hand, her shield at her feet embossed with Greeks fighting forces of Amazons, with a prominent sphinx-head and griffins protruding from her helmet, plus the Gorgon Medusa emblazoned on her breastplate, she impressed upon Athenians how their patron goddess epitomized the eternal fight of civilization against the dark forces of irrationality and chaos.

Basins of flame before the stupendous effigy on this night of the Great Dionysia cast a guttering glow over the treasures arrayed across the marbled floor before her. Gold and silver ritual objects, fine weapons and armors, thrones of ivory and precious stones, all the rich dedications of generations of votaries of her cult sparkled and glimmered among the painted dark blues and gilt bronze of surrounding friezes and metopes.

An ornate security fence protected Athena's treasures from the sacrilege of thievery, while guards of the City Militia hovered motionless with spears to watch over the occasional stumbling partygoers wandering into the *cella* from the roistering outside. But Antinous found himself alone by the ornate fence looking into the shadowy dimness above. An impromptu prayer arose within him.

'Athena Parthenos, virgin half sister to Apollo, my Healer of Heaven and cult champion, receive from me my plea for protection in your domains. I have no worthy offering other than my youth and my honor. Protect me on my journey into the fellowship of the great Caesar of the Romans, Hadrian. *Praise be to Caesar!* Instruct me carefully in your arts of civilization and virtue. Guide my tongue, my hand, and my eye to express your gifts of *arete*. Imbue me with skill, finesse, and subtlety. Guide me in your ancient path of victory against disorder as you have the Greeks of old. Make me a worthy *eromenos* to my destiny's *erastes*, at cost of my body, my heart, or even my life. *Praise, Praise, Praise! Athena Parthenos!*'

Antinous genuflected to one knee in the traditional manner and performed the proper obeisance gestures. He then withdrew to the citadel precinct outside the temple.

To the east of the plateau beyond the Parthenon, beyond an ancient outdoor sacrificial altar and other statues, stood the demure Temple of Rome and Augustus. Its domed modesty was where the cult of the emperor had been increasingly honored since Rome's defeat and impoverishment of Athens after Sulla's conquest two hundred ago. But now under Hadrian Athens was being restored to new glory as the second city of the Empire.

Antinous kept clear of the gaggles of frolicking revelers. Instead, passing an occasional ambiguously-gendered, cross-dress wanton lurking in a pediment's shadows and beckoning with mischievous eyes, or a party-person confirming their Dionysian riotousness by vomiting noisily into a drain's recess, he wandered in delight across the plateau. He played the eternal tourist exploring its monuments, chapels, shrines, altars, and temple facades. He ambled happily to the quiet of the rotunda chapel of the temple of the Imperial cult.

This austere, delicate Temple stood in imposing solitude at the far end of the citadel keep. Life-sized statues of recent emperors stood impassively by the entrance vestibule, while within the small interior chamber a simple stone sacrificial altar scrubbed clean of smoky fats sat beneath the soft glow of suspended votive lamps.

Once inside the Temple, Antinous cast his eyes over the symbols of Rome's heritage proclaimed in bronze and marble for the edification of the city's citizens. Only a small bowl of wispy incense relieved the funereal silence of the chamber with its bronze imperial inhabitants. Antinous contemplated their frozen countenances in thoughtful silence.

A voice intruded.

'You wish to desecrate this holy sanctuary, foreigner?'

The voice intoned its complaint in Latin-inflected Greek.

Antinous spun on his booted heel towards its source. A man in a fulsome cape which covered a Roman toga and who wore an obscuring party mask across his face was confronting him from the shrine's solitary entrance. Two other men in masks stood nearby.

'You show disrespect for your betters, foreigner,' the figure announced menacingly.

'No, you are mistaken, good sir,' Antinous responded. 'I am very respectful of this sanctuary, sir. I admire and celebrate the Caesars, despite being of Greek origin.'

The figure at the doorway moved forward and lifted the mask from his face. Antinous realized immediately it was Lucius Ceionius Commodus, the *Roman Favorite* who had departed the Theater Of Dionysus earlier the same day in a fit of temperamental pique.

'Despite being Greek? You speak with a forked tongue, foreigner. Take him, citizens!'

Without pause the two men leapt forward and grasped Antinous by the arms and head. They held him firmly against the cold stone of the altar.

'So what have we here, then? An alien youth of no consequence, with a face painted like a Kerameikos harlot, loitering-with-intent in Rome's sacred house of remembrance of the Divine Caesars. What are you, boy, a slave whore from the sewers of Kerameikos? Do you seek to ply your gutter trade in this holy place?' the Roman with fine pale skin and glitter-scattered hair demanded. The other two men sniggered from behind their masks.

'No, sir, you know who I am. You surely recognize me? I am a guest of Caesar at the Great Dionysia. I am freeborn Antinous of Bithynia, son of Telemachus of Claudiopolis of the equestrian class,' he called as he writhed beneath the firm grip of the masked men.

Commodus smiled disdainfully at the struggling figure before him. He reached to the side of one of his aide's capes and drew a Roman *gladius* short-sword from its scabbard. Its buffed iron shone beneath the lamps' glow. Its finely ground tip and blade edges gleamed piercingly.

'Foreigners should know their place in the world, whoreboy. They should not step beyond the limits of their class,' Commodus arraigned at his captive. 'They are menials. They are inferiors. They are rural vulgarities intruding into the world of fine manners and well bred values. Their impudence and gall is deserving of correction, foreigner. They enter into realms beyond their understanding and so deserves stern retribution. Their bodies require a visible reminder of their sortie into domains beyond their understanding. Their flesh calls for a permanent memento of their folly.'

Commodus raised the sword and waved its honed blade in too-close proximity to Antinous's frame and face. Antinous tugged his head back abruptly from the hovering razor.

'You are a transparent opportunist who aspires to enter into the society of great Caesar, is that not so? I have heard of you whispered in Court gossip. You're the newest contender for the role of *catamite* to Caesar, true? You're a toyboy, a wastrel offering your body and anus to the passing amusement of the *Princeps*. The presence of such menials in this sacred place is a profanity deserving of immediate penalty,' the *patrician* sneered.

'Turn the harlot around!' Commodus instructed his companions.

Taking Antinous by the scruff of his mane and locking his arms, they forcibly revolved him and pinioned his jaw to the altar's bleached stone. Commodus reached with the sword's tip and delicately lifted the hem of his tunic to expose the young man's securely clothed rump beneath. Antinous struggled fruitlessly under his oppressors' crushing weights.

'It's whispered, hustler, that you've been positioned at Court for Caesar's delectation by covert forces aiming to shift the balance of politics of the *Imperium* in some treasonous faction's favor. They say you're a stratagem or gameplan for deviously cornering Caesar's influence?

Who is your *patron*, whore? Who set you up? Tell me! Do you represent the long arm of Senate discontents reaching far into Asia? Do the Legates at Ephesus or Antioch use you for persuasive ways to shore-up their claim to the succession someday? Or have the tentacles of that monstrous creature at Rome, Praetorian Prefect Turbo, set you up to spy? Perhaps it's merely Vibia Sabina herself has recruited you to punish her husband in some witty, wily feminine way? Which?!"

Commodus was warming to his subject.

'It seems our foreign prostitute deserves his posterior's flesh to be incised with a memento of his intransigence to help loosen his tongue, to take as a keepsake of this night to remember for evermore?'

Commodus waved the iron blade's tip ever closer to the young man's hindquarters.

'Clear the slut's tail!' he commanded one of the masked men, who stripped the cloths from Antinous's hips. His slender pelvis and dimpled butt was exposed to view.

'I have done you no harm, my lord!' Antinous called aloud. 'I am no prostitute or spy. On Apollo's honor I've committed no offence I know of! You assault an innocent freeborn subject, sir!'

'Yet you possess a whore's pretensions! Your true offence is in your very existence,' he continued. 'It's your existence that requires concrete conclusion. You take liberties with the honor and favor of the *Imperium*. You deserve the ultimate penalty. You merit being cast to wild dogs or large cats in the arena. I as a representative of The Senate am empowered to act as magistrate upon such offence, and pass judgment --- '

Commodus idly circumscribed the *gladius* blade in the direction of the lad's exposed rump, aiming erratically as though preparing to strike.

'*Not if you wish to commit violent assault and sacrilege yourself, Commodus!*' a new voice called from the temple entrance. 'Drop that weapon and release the boy! You have no jurisdiction here, Roman senator or not!'

Commodus and the two masked men spun around to see at the door Herodes Atticus, Lysias, and three guardsmen of the City Militia with pikes poised for instant action.

'This is a consecrated temple of the Imperial Cult within the sacred precinct of the Acropolis,' Herodes declared. 'Neither weapons nor sacrilege are permitted in this precinct. This freeborn youth has done you no harm. He has committed no offence. As a commander of the City Militia and a councilor of Achaea, I charge you with public disorder and breaking the peace, Lucius Ceionius Commodus. You have assaulted a special guest of the emperor who is under civic protection. You wield a weapon where weapons are forbidden. You dishonor the memory of the several Caesars about you in this holy place. And you insult the councils, laws, and hospitality of the city of Athens. At least one of these violations will be a capital offence!' Herodes snapped. 'So drop the sword now!'

Commodus responded haughtily in kind.

'I am a citizen and senator of Rome. Do not speak injudiciously in my presence, Greek!' the *patrician* declaimed with lofty derision.

Herodes and his team moved forward with the long *pilum* shafts reaching close to the caped trio.

'You forget I too am a citizen and senator of Rome, Commodus,' Herodes responded calmly, 'endowed personally by Caesar, not acquired by purchase. As a commander of the Athens Militia I posses the jurisdiction to take punitive action wherever necessary.

If you harm Caesar's guest one whit I will fulfill my duty to a matching degree. This sacred place is under the rule of the law of Athens, not travelers from Rome! Release the young man unharmed, discard your weapon, or suffer lethal force. I will spill the blood of any coward who attacks an unarmed man without reason!'

The three militia guardsmen had maneuvered their long blades within reach of the assailants. The trio of Romans wavered.

Commodus signaled to his companions to unhand Antinous. He was about to flamboyantly tumble his blade to the paving stones with smirking bravado when he suddenly spun around. With lightning speed his sword flashed out at Antinous, its blade whispering close by his face. A slim hairline incision two inches in length opened across Antinous's cheek. It welled scarlet.

Lysias raced to his friend's assistance as Antinous lurched away from his persecutors to greater safety, grasping his loincloths about him as he moved.

Herodes grabbed a spear from one of his militia companions to resoundingly whack its metal-studded hardwood shaft across Commodus's back. The impact knocked the *gladius* from his hand and brought him tumbling against the altar block with a sharp cry. He clawed at his spine and fell to the flagstones in an ignominious flurry of toga wools and dust.

Now three glinting spear points were hovering menacingly within inches of the senator's face. The smirking bravado had vanished.

Herodes raised the sword from the flagstones and waved it languidly in the direction of the Roman.

'We are done here, Senator Lucius Ceionius Commodus. You have exhausted your credit in this city,' the Athenian declared as the *patrician* stumbled painfully to his feet.

'You insult Rome, Greek!' Commodus declaimed as he gathered his toga around him. 'You will hear more of this! Make way for your betters, foreigners!' He prepared to flounce out of the shrine.

Herodes stretched his arm in the Senator's path across the door portal. Commodus was halted in mid-flight, the sword's point now waving close to his face, not Antinous's.

Herodes spoke quietly.

'This event tonight will be duly recorded by a magistrate of the City Watch, Senator, and its recording documents witnessed by those present. As a councilor of this city I will ensure the deposition remains secured in perpetuity. I will not take you into custody on this occasion; its embarrassments would disturb the tranquility of Caesar's pleasures at our Dionysia.

But be rest assured, Commodus, the charges will remain alive on file. I doubt you or your pleasant companions will be welcome to Athens at any future time because my father, the Prefect of the Free Ports of the East, will object to such troublemakers receiving passage. We are law abiding in this city. You are not welcome here. I suggest you depart Athens promptly and return to Italy, or else these charges will be enacted upon you within twenty-four hours. They will be to your eternal dishonor in the eyes of all Athenians, especially including Great Caesar.'

Commodus smirked thinly and swept grandly away with a pained stumble as he clutched at his back. He sneered at Antinous as he passed through the door into the night beyond.

Lysias was attending to Antinous's wound while the injured youth fumbled with adjusting his attire. Herodes closely inspected the sliver of red flesh across his cheek.

'The wound is superficial but it needs proper attention, Antinous,' Herodes observed. 'It pains me this should happen to you in such an exalted place. We will withdraw immediately to my villa nearby where my own physician can attend to the lesion. I will send a message to Caesar that you have been indisposed, and where to locate you later if he should desire.'

Antinous took his two friends by the forearms and looked into their eyes.

'Why has this happened, Herodes? What have I done to deserve such an attack? I don't even know this man Commodus!' Antinous implored. Herodes responded immediately.

'Welcome to imperial politics, Antinous of Bithynia. Your journey into its shadows has just begun.'

"So, Geta, you say Senator Commodus is a candidate for being a serious enemy to Antinous? You say he might even be involved in the death of the youth by some nefarious means?"

Clarus as usual was blunt.

Geta looked blankly to the four faces facing him as the river raced in a continuous rush in the background and morning insects buzzed around. The day's warmth expanded rapidly.

"At least, gentlemen, I can identify someone who might have reason to do Antinous harm. Have you achieved such yourselves?" Geta queried. Suetonius ignored the query.

"So, what transpired after the Bithynian had been assaulted?" he asked. "How did Hadrian respond?"

Geta was specific in his recollections.

"I will try to recall the events as I believe they occurred, gentlemen. I myself witnessed much of the action. It was a challenging situation. We who were close to Hadrian protected him from the reality of his former paramour's waspish nature. Antinous too had resolved to avoid blame or retribution, which tells us something about the lad's nature and generosity of spirit."

Geta sipped his wine thoughtfully and returned to his testimony.

'Who did this thing, Antinous?' Caesar asked with concern. 'Did Herodes kill him where he stood?'

Hadrian had lifted the dressing attached to the Bithynian's cheek and peered at the wound beneath.

'No. They were merely drunken ruffians,' Antinous said. 'They were in high-spirits at the festival, I suppose,' he explained.

'How many were they?' Caesar continued.

'There were three of them, my lord, masked for the festival.'

'Where? In my enclosure, or in a public space? Did these assailants offend my hospitality?' the emperor garbed in the Tyrian purple tunic asked threateningly. He was still crowned with a corona of woven grape vines. He fumbled at the *fibula* on his shoulder to release the cloak and drop it to the floor, and tossed the corona like a child's quoit onto a chair's upright.

One of the two Horse Guards accompanying him performed the unmilitary duty of collecting the fallen robe and laid it over a chair while a household servant scurried to offer assistance.

'It was public space. I was scouting the Acropolis plateau by myself. I've never seen such a beautiful space before in my life. It is remarkable, Caesar. I'd been making my obeisance to Athena Parthenos in her *cella* of the Parthenon. I then spied the Temple of Rome and Augustus a little further on. The three attacked me within the Temple's sanctuary,' Antinous explained.

'At a temple to all things Roman, including my own ancestors! So Herodes had been wisely following behind you, had he? I'd obliged him earlier to watch over you two neophytes. The Dionysia has been known to get out of hand in this city. So, did he arrest the hooligans?'

'No, sir.'

'Herodes has the authority of the City Watch at his command, he can prosecute uncivil behavior and inflict immediate punishment by his own judgment,' Caesar continued. 'For their insult to someone under my protection I'll demand the ultimate penalty. But how did the ruffians manage to damage you as they have? Was this an intentional mutilation?'

'My lord, it was foolish of me to wander unaccompanied on such an occasion,' the young man tried to remonstrate. 'I'll know better in future. I'm lucky they didn't do me greater damage, really.'

Antinous had been resting upon a couch after the revel in Herodes' villa's *andron*. Herodes had delivered the two Bithynians to his villa a few blocks from their own house at Melite, and a similar distance from the palatial villa of the Imperial Household of Caesar himself.

Herodes had summoned his family's personal physician, a highly regarded Judaean trained at Pergamum, who had carefully cleansed and anointed Antinous's wound with special unguents, and applied a clean dressing adhered with purified mastic. He said the wound was not deep enough to require stitches, much to everyone's relief. In addition to the risk of corruption, which even simple wounds can induce, stitches would have left a permanent scar across his face.

After ensuring Antinous was comfortable, and after sharing wine, Herodes had asked Antinous if he objected to Lysias staying overnight with him at the villa. Lysias would sleep in the men's quarters with Herodes, and Antinous could bunk down on a couch in the *andron,* the villa's meeting chamber.

Antinous had no problem with the arrangement, especially as Lysias was obviously agog with his unexpected opportunity. Herodes had thought of everything.

'I've sent a messenger to Hadrian's chamberlain and the Dacian, Geta, telling them where you can be found. I mentioned your misadventure, though I haven't mentioned <u>who</u> the offender was. I think tonight you should sleep here and not risk the drunkards or desperates of Athens,' Herodes counseled. 'I'm sure Caesar will send for you when your presence is required. Meanwhile, Lysias and I will retire to our own pleasures, hopefully with his friend's blessing?'

Lysias looked towards Antinous in a faintly pained, querulous way, as eager hounds do when seeking a favor. The carnal intentions of the couple were obvious, yet Lysias seemed compelled to seek some tacit acknowledgement from his friend that this was acceptable behavior. Antinous simply nodded with an amused smile. He thought maybe, at last, Lysias would be properly deflowered or achieve whatever else was his body's desire.

In fact he privately considered his friend's choice of partner to be a highly worthy one. Herodes was older by five or six years, but his behavior was readily approachable by the usual lofty standards of city notables or senators. By the standards of a desirable *erastes*, such an accomplished companion was optimum. The man possessed confidence and charm coupled with a fine physical presence.

After more wine and small talk into the night, the two departed for their sleeping quarters with much tipsy shoulder-hugging and slap-happy body-contact. Herodes certainly had a predilection towards Lysias's butt, Antinous observed. A manservant scurried after them to provide rugs and chamber comforts for a late night sojourn.

Antinous made himself comfortable on a couch and tried to ignore the smarting sting across his left cheek. The villa fell into silence as its lamps burned low. Occasional bursts of laughter and whoops of joy echoed remotely in the night Was it through the thick walls of the men's sleeping quarters, Antinous wondered?

An hour or two later the clatter of horses' hooves on the courtyard paving stones and some gruff talk at the entrance portal was followed by booming knocks at the iron-reinforced, bolted doors. It announced the arrival of Caesar and his attendants. A steward unbarred the doors as Hadrian silenced his Horse Guard companions to late night quiet.

'I shall summon my master, Great Excellency,' the steward of slaves enquired with much nervous bowing. 'He would wish to personally welcome you to his home.'

'No, let him sleep, man. I am informed the Bithynian named Antinous is on these premises?' Hadrian declared.

'Yes he is, my lord. He is within, in the *andron* chamber,' the steward hesitantly indicated. 'He too might be sleeping. Shall I summon him to you, my lord?'

'No.'

The emperor tossed his riding gloves and a voluminous fur mantle over a bust of an antique philosopher as he spied Antinous across the atrium's space standing by a warming brazier at the *andron* doorway. Even in March Athens can be cold at night.

He strode through the foyer followed by his guards and walked up to the young man raised on a step or two above the foyer's mosaic floor. Antinous promptly began the body actions of the obligatory obeisance ritual's genuflections. Hadrian halted the action mid-performance by grasping his arm in one hand.

'Bring wine and cups,' he commanded the steward. 'Four! Ensure it's good wine!'

A slave pattered off into the interior of the villa while the chief steward discreetly stood to one side. The two Horse Guards took their ease some distance away, their helmets under their arms but with their hands at permanent readiness on their sword hilts.

Caesar stepped up into the *andron* for a closer search of the dressing attached to Antinous's cheek. He began his interrogation of the wound's origin and its inflictor.

When the servant returned with the refreshments, Caesar poured four cups and offered one to each Guard.

'Scorilo, Godron, your chores are complete for the night, you are now off-duty. Let us salute the day's achievements, but acknowledge its deficits too,' he declared as he offered the fourth cup to Antinous. All four raised their cups in cheer and drank deep. 'To Dionysus!' the Guards muttered.

'I heard of your injury, lad, so I came as soon as I completed my obligations. Show it to me.'

He gingerly raised and peeped beneath the mastic-held dressing. Antinous suppressed a wince as the emperor's fingers nudged the tender flesh nearby.

'You've been fortunate I think,' Caesar offered from his long experience of inspecting many a wound, from the slightest surface scratch to the most abject butchery. 'It's shallow, an incision not a score, so it will heal quickly if the physician keeps it closed and clean. He knows his trade, that physician of the Herodes family. But the slice will leave a definite scar on your features, Antinous. It's a shame to see such pristine flesh marred by an everyday reality. Is this your first war wound, lad? I'm certain it won't be your last.'

Antinous already knew how Hadrian carried a dozen wounds of varying magnitudes on his frame, including a visible scar across his forehead which was never depicted on the many life-sized statues of him in public squares.

Caesar's proximity to Antinous drew their eyes together. A silent message passed between them. Caesar coughed mildly and drew back. He turned to the two Horse Guards swallowing their wine.

'You are dismissed for the night, men. Scorilo, ensure an exchange of watch covers this villa in the usual way, I'll be staying here overnight,' he instructed. 'On your return to the Household villa inform Geta and the Chamberlain of my intention. Tell Geta to collect me here at first light. No later, Scorilo. It's a busy schedule tomorrow.'

Antinous gulped. This was unexpected. Was he prepared for an overnight assignation? It had been some hours since he last washed and spruced. After an evening's Dionysian partying was he sweet smelling enough for an impromptu encounter? Especially, he contemplated, one likely to negotiate the physical terms of a liaison which could confirm or refute its viability?

He recalled he still owed a bodily debt to Hadrian, and perhaps now was the time that debt would be called in? This was a daunting prospect.

The two guardsmen saluted and withdrew. Herodes' steward became apprehensive.

'My Lord, *you will be sleeping at this house tonight*?!' he asked in escalating panic. 'We are not prepared to a suitable standard for such a great honor! My master will be dismayed, great sir!'

'Yes, I'll be sleeping here. I've slept in far less comfortable places, I assure you. Bring cushions, rugs, and lamps. More wine too. And some fruit.'

'Certainly, Excellency!'

'And then go back to your bed and give us some privacy, fellow.'

After a few moments of frenetic activity delivering the necessities, the steward drew together the four hinged leaves of the cedar shutters of the *andron*.

Hadrian and Antinous were alone at last.

'You told me earlier today you are *now mine*? Explain yourself.'

'It is so, Caesar, if it is your wish,' Antinous replied nervously, bowing his head politely. 'It was as I promised five months ago at Nicomedia. I keep my promises.'

'Yes, you held to your oath, Ant. I am impressed. Take note, I will call you 'Ant' when we are together, as I am told your intimates do,' Caesar proposed. 'Tell me about your relationship with Lysias of Bithynia. Are you lovers? Are you an *erastes* and *eromenos*?'

'No, no, my lord! *By Apollo*, we are good friends, childhood friends. We know each other well and respect each other. We were raised together, and our fathers were friends before us,' Antinous explained.

'Do you sleep together or have sex together?' Caesar asked.

Antinous thought this an odd query well beyond personal familiarity.

'We've slept side-by-side, body-to-body together very often since childhood during sleepovers and on hunts or militia bivouacs, like most boys do. Just as we wrestle body-to-body at the *palaestra*. These things occur between friends. But it's only recently that we've sported together once or twice, and then only to give quick relief to our urges. But in matters of Eros our tastes are dissimilar. To start with, I don't think either of us finds our own generation appealing, as most of our friends do,' Antinous explained.

'Tell me, Ant, what do you mean by *you are mine*? What is it you want? What is your motive in submitting to my gestures at Nicomedia? Were you simply obeying my command? Do I intimidate you? Are you afraid of me as Caesar? Explain yourself. There are those in my retinue who suspect you,' Caesar declared. 'They say I should whip you to reveal your true motives.'

'What do I *want*? If you forgive me sir, I wish to deliver myself entirely into your intimate regard. Do you intimidate me? No, you have shown me a generosity which dispels all such fear. It is as you explained in the moonlight at Nicomedia. I will conform to your will as your *eromenos*, sir, your student of life. I hope to spend my final education in your company and under your *patronage* and tutelage, sir, just as you yourself proposed on that remarkable night.'

Hadrian eyed the sturdy *meirakion* before him with hesitancy. Antinous continued.

'May I speak freely, sir? I've never known a man of such substance before, my lord. Not only as Great Caesar, which is remarkable enough, but as a man who understands the nature of the world and men's ways so completely. I am overjoyed to be shown respect and friendliness by such a noble presence, my lord,' Antinous uttered breathily. 'I am amazed at my good fortune. I am certain I am not worthy of it.'

'But in what way are you *mine*?' Caesar persisted in cool precision.

'What little I am, sir, is entirely yours,' Antinous responded, 'in body, heart, and spirit. I wish to engage fully with your person in all its dimensions, wherever they lead, within my status. My *arete* is yours to mold.

If it's a respectful companion, a page, a squire, or your cupbearer you seek, I am eager to comply. I am yours to forge.

If it's Eros you desire, sir, my being and my body are entirely at your disposal. Your gesture to me of sexual satisfaction at Nicomedia was as a lightning bolt to me that night. I had never been so intoxicated in another's company previously, my lord. I was powerfully turned on by the occasion. Is this a fault or failing?

However, sir, if it's a lover you seek, as you told me under the cloudy stars that night, then you should know how I too am seeking a companion in life. I too crave closeness with someone special in my eyes. It amazes me how the one person in the world whose very presence stirs my emotions so dramatically appears to return a similar favor to me.

I cannot say I know what love is, sir, but I find I am swept with sensations of which I have no previous understanding. I ache with needs I have no control over. Do I speak out of order, sir? Is this childish talk unworthy of an *eromenos*?'

'Indeed, you speak with remarkable lucidity. Your command of ideas is excellent, Ant. But I still wonder at your motives, or those of others behind you.'

Antinous's voice lowered.

'Sir, the day of the Hunt when you knifed the boar which threatened my safety and then patiently unfurled my fingers from the impaled lance, was a day of revelation to me,' Antinous murmured softly. 'No one before in my life has taken the trouble to combat such a threat on my behalf, and then follow with equally gracious attention to my fears and excitement.

You might not believe it to be true, sir, but I ejaculated spontaneously beneath my tunic as you unwound my hands from the lance's shaft. I *came* excitedly without control, my bloodstream was so surging, so enthralled. My tunic was stained, though I managed to hide it from everyone I hope.

Later unexpectedly that same night when again you aroused my horniness beneath the moonlight, I felt myself falling headlong into an abyss of excitement. It was a driven urge I had not experienced previously. Am I being irrational, my lord? Is this foolishness? Does this offend? My body's sensations are seriously in debt to your goodwill and touch.'

Hadrian smiled calmly.

'Did the physician provide you a nostrum to ingest, Ant?' he asked. 'Your tongue is loosened charmingly.'

Antinous shook his head.

'No, my lord, only wine. I always speak from the heart, or else I don't speak at all.'

Hadrian was moved to act. There had been enough talk.

'I am told, Ant, how it is traditional for an *erastes* to confirm his homage to an *eromenos* by gifting a token of his intentions? A weapon or other small gesture is the custom I'm told.'

'You have already supplied fine gifts in the form of treasures and our Latin tutor, Thais of Cyrene,' Antinous reminded his company. 'These have been extremely adequate tokens, sir, without par.'

'That's so, Ant. However I'm reliably informed it's also the custom to offer a catch of game, such as a hare or wild fowl, as proof of an *erastes'* skills as a provider. It's usually something edible or life sustaining, a leftover from ancient trials of proof. Is this true?'

'So I've been told too,' Antinous responded, wondering where this quirky conversation might be leading as no crowing cock or wild game was in sight.

Hadrian took a small cloth purse from his belt. He stripped off the leather tie and emptied its contents into his hand. A single object fell onto his palm.

It was an elegantly carved intaglio signet ring of deep blue *lapis lazuli* in a setting of silver. Delicately engraved into the vivid azure stone was a cockerel, a farmyard rooster with a high cock's comb. Yet this bird was depicted with a human body and legs represented by two twisting snakes. It had words inscribed around it in an archaic script.

'I have been carrying this jewel for two years now. It was found for me in my domains at Antioch where the most precious magical amulets and talismans circulate from across the East and Egypt. This ancient find is a rare blue stone named *lapis lazuli* carried from a distant land named Bactria. It has been carved on both sides with special charms and blessed by Magi of the East at rituals invoking exotic gods. It is supercharged with magical spells for the wearer's protection and eternal life.

I acquired this ring with its mysterious cockerel to offer at the appropriate occasion as my *erastes'* token to my chosen companion, in place of a living cockerel. Unlike a live fowl, this ring offers unique protection against illness, misadventure, and even death, it is claimed. This surely is the most one human can offer to another -- health, safety, and eternity? My chosen companion is to wear it always.'

Hadrian took Antinous's left hand and pressed the slender band onto his index finger.

Antinous held the delicate treasure before his eyes to inspect its beautiful color and its strange markings. It was certainly an object of distinction to his perception, but it was also a token of extraordinary significance.

'How does the cockerel provide these boons, my lord?' he asked. 'What is the magic?'

Hadrian again took the young man's hand and raised the ring to their eye level.

'This cockerel is the symbol of the god *Abrasax* from the East. His origin lies in ancient Babylon,' Hadrian explained. 'The cockerel is a creature which hails the advent of the day, at sunrise. He represents Phoebus, The Radiant One, just as Apollo too is described as Phoebus, shining like the sun. He is the deity of light set in a world of darkness. Beneath the cockerel's head is a man's body encased in a sturdy breastplate as protection against evil, while in one hand he clasps a whip to protect wisdom against ignorance, and in the other a shield to project his omnipotent power.

His legs of snakes tell us of Eternity, the faculty to shed their skins to renew their being.

In the Greek science of *geometria*, the method of calculating the numerical value of the letters of the alphabet making up a word, his name *Abrasax* achieves the number 365. This indicates his enclosure in the annual solar cycle. You can see the inscription *AEON* indicating his 365 *eons* emanating from his function as First Cause, one for each day of the year.

I am told this makes *Abrasax* the Pantheus, the total god of all manifestations, the One God. Other secret signs are carved on the reverse to enhance its power. The full complement of its mystical characters are said to provide protection and eternal life to the wearer.

It is this unique treasure I give to you, Antinous of Bithynia, to wear as a gesture from your *erastes* in place of an edible cockerel. I give you eternal life.'

Antinous was immediately swept deeper into his abyss of intense longing. He beheld the compact blue ring upon his finger and marveled at its provenance and purported wonders. This was truly a divine science, he thought.

'Who was, or were, the previous owners of this marvel, my lord?' he asked.

'I don't know, Ant, but I am told that Alexander the Great, our mutual hero, once wore this magical gem,' Caesar replied.

'But Alexander is dead, my lord. And at a very early age too. It didn't work for him, did it?'

'Ah, but yes it did, Ant. Death he brought upon himself, either by drink or disease, though some claim he was poisoned. Yet you must concede how Alexander became divine in our eyes and his fame lives eternally,' the emperor rationalized with a grin. 'The ring's magic may work in ways which are a mystery and an enigma to we mortals. Who knows? Egypt and Babylon possess secrets we are yet to understand. I hope you will acknowledge the nature of the gift, *son of Apollo*, and my good intentions in bestowing it. It is my special mark upon you.'

'I am humbled, my lord, by your gesture,' Antinous offered quite sincerely.

'Yes, we must discuss that too. In truth, Ant, you need not be so humble in my presence. You are not my slave, servant, or staff member, Antinous. You possess no military rank to submit to.

You are a freeborn independent entity with your own mind, body, and virtue. You are Greek, Ant. I do not own you, despite appearances. Independent thinking is one of your race's attractions. So you and I must now find a less formal way to respond to each other or else our time together will be wasted in interminable deference to my eminence.

So you need not call me 'Caesar' or 'My Lord,' all the time,' Hadrian instructed with brisk clarity. 'And nor need you bow and scrape at every exchange. The entire world says 'Caesar'-this and 'Caesar'-that to me, which is proper and correct before me as *Imperator* or *Princeps*. But when you and I are alone together, or we are with our very closest intimates, we must relate less formally. I need to relax sometimes, too.

You are entitled to use the name 'Hadrian' to me, and desist from too much kowtowing. Respect, yes, always Ant, I am a man. But excessive etiquette, no. Our time is too precious.

The *nomen* Hadrian is acceptable between us. It's less distancing than unending honorifics. My days are made up of interminable accolades and fawning petitions. I tire of it sometimes. So I expect my closest intimates to have a more relaxed manner in my presence. That is, unless I command otherwise.'

Antinous attempted an understanding, but with some uncertainty.

'We must get to know each other, Ant. I am no ogre. I am not a tyrant. I am *Princeps* to the world, yes, but I am also a fellow man. I am not dead, burned, and deified among my predecessors quite yet, though my day will come.

Nevertheless, there still remain definite rules between us,' Hadrian elaborated. 'Put simply, in our personal space we are entitled to relate in a personal, familiar way. I am a man like any other, even as your *erastes*. Yet in my official capacity as *Caesar* we must conform to due protocol. It boils down to being personal when in our own company but suitably formal in public. In one I am your personal friend '*Hadrian*', in the other I am '*Lord*,'" he said. "These are the consequences of my station. Understand?'

'Yes sir,' Antinous responded cautiously. 'I think I do.'

'No, it's *Hadrian*, Ant. The titles of sir, sire, My Lord, Caesar, or other terms of honor are to be reserved for your duty role. I tire of everyone bobbing up and down, kissing my hem, saluting, or falling to their knee at every opportunity.'

'Duty role? I beg your meaning … Hadrian?'

'You and your friend Lysias will be entered into my Household as *Companions of the Hunt*. You will be attached to the schedule of the Master of the Hunt, Salvius Julianus. You know him from Nicomedia. He will act as your supervisor of duty assignments and so on, especially for my recreation. It gives you proper duties in my retinue which you will enjoy, and attaches you both to the Chamberlain's schedule of finances.

You and your young friend will be awarded an endowment suited to your needs. The stipend assigns funds, services, protection, and accommodations in my travels for you and your attendants to a suitable standard. This includes your Latin tutor from Cyrenaica and stewards. Meanwhile, as a Companion of the Hunt, you'll find the Hunt Master Julianus will teach you a great deal about hunting, including of larger beasts, as I will myself. This is your duty role.'

'I see, Hadrian.'

'Your primary duty is to enjoy the supervision of the hunt under Julianus. This will keep you both out of mischief. You'll find your duties give you access to good horses, horsemanship training, weapons and security training, and the company of selected sons of notables from around the Empire.

You and your staff will join me when I tour to visit the Legions. You will accompany me when I attend public audiences and Court celebrations. You will sleep with me when occasions permit, though you will be assigned your own apartments as well. My Household, my *contubernium, are* a lively crowd, if given to too much gossip, frivolity, love affairs, and wine, but you will probably enjoy their company. Any other questions?'

'Not that I can think of at this time, Hadrian.'

'Fine. Then pour some wine for us both and take your clothes off. I want to see your shape again after all these months. Your physical line pleases me. Then you can undress me too.'

Antinous hesitated before responding. His brain raced. After several moments' pause he made his advance.

'The wine is already poured, Hadrian. The servant filled the cups before he left. Help yourself. But I wish to view you unclothed too, and all of you this time. If I'm not to mimic a servant or even a slave, why don't we undress each other? I'll undress you; you undress me. Then we'll both witness the other's physical shape.'

Hadrian was taken aback for an instant, but smiled at the ploy.

Antinous gamely reached for his *erastes'* hand and drew it to the swelling package rising at his crutch. Caesar's unresisting hand was obliging, even willing.

The *meirakion*'s audacity immobilized him momentarily. That is, until he was tugged firmly at his shoulder to press his bearded jaw down towards Antinous's groin. There was only an amused resistance by the master of the Empire.

'I said I am yours, Hadrian. All this is yours too, with more to follow,' Antinous whispered breathily close to his ear.

He felt the clothbound flesh of the young man's firming member press provocatively against his face and jaw. He too sensed his blood race to his genitals despite Antinous's challenge to his Roman machismo.

By inciting *irrumene*, where the mouth engages in a supposedly impure act which impugns the masculinity of a *vir* by its receptive nature, Antinous was being incendiary. Hadrian amusedly declined this invitation to fellate his partner, but possibly as a secondary afterthought.

Then a rush to strip tunics and undercloths away from bared flesh, limbs, and organs was unleashed. Revealed entirely in their bare humanity, the pair now stood eyeing each other's sinewy condition beneath the flickering lamplight.

One was of a sleek, rangy muscularity, the other of powerful weathered toughness. One possessed the finely-honed contours of a practiced athlete; the other showed the well-knit tissues of a seasoned fighter, hunter, and working soldier. Erections announced their mutual admiration.

Antinous took a fresh initiative. Impulse drove his heart. He moved close to Hadrian's side where hip touched hip and flesh touched flesh. He drew the emperor's arm around his waist, and tilted back to invite a face-to-face response. Hadrian took the invitation and grasped his jaw in one hardened palm to hungrily devour the Bithynian's mouth, lips, tongue, and saliva. Antinous happily assented to the aggressive urgency.

He felt himself yielding to the grasping hands and arms, the tightly pressing torso, the intimately provocative pelvic thrust, and the fierce probing by a searching tongue. He then responded to these gestures equally fervently.

In a flurry of discarded clothes, linens, leathers, buckles, and boots the two collapsed in an intertwined coupling to the stony *tesserae* of the mosaic floor. Their limbs interlocked in alternating strategies of domination, submission, and rude intimacy above the floor's mosaic design of Greek hoplites at battle with scantily-clad Amazons.

Antinous was now enveloped in an increasing wildness. His bodily resistance to his grappling combatant was waning. This was no concession of defeat; it was his recognition of the exhilaration of close proximity to someone thrilling. He vividly imagined he was melting inexorably into the other's flesh as they bound tightly together. He was besieged by the rough caresses and wet urgency of Hadrian's mouth, felt the brush of trim bristles graze his jaw, and inhaled the salty aroma of a day's sweat. Yet he gave as well as he received.

While wrapped together in abject intimacy he discerned the rigid shaft at his partner's groin searching the nooks-and-crannies of his limbs to locate a susceptible portal into his interior being. Its determination in sliding ever closer to its intended target was tenacious. He felt his pursuer's lust press relentlessly forward towards its goal.

The driven urgency was so unashamedly flattering, his resistance willfully relaxed to open his defenses to the incursion. It was a gift to his companion's previous generosities with a dash of prurient curiousity.

Hadrian's resolve pressed his arms and limbs apart to hold him firm to the mosaic tiles. The militant strategist maneuvered a forward assault at the intended target. The younger man threw caution to the winds as he opened his heart and body to the incursion. What the heck, he thought.

A myriad mixed feelings, thoughts, needs, fears, and bodily sensations swept Antinous as he realized his body was happily succumbing to a very intimate corporeal invasion. His partner held him firm by a feigned wrestler's hold whose determined power maneuvered him to utter vulnerability. Yet it was a consensual vulnerability which happily savored its own helplessness.

Hadrian spat several times onto his palm and applied the lubricious balm to his member. Antinous emitted a surprised gasp as the penetrating organ found its target and eased into its intended berth. Yet the zealous invasion was a careful, benevolent assault.

Antinous was overcome with contradictory feelings of victory and submission, joy and discomfort, honor and shame, as Hadrian engulfed him in a carnal embrace. He also realized he had succumbed to the driven power of another man's lust, while equally recognizing he was strangely untroubled by it.

After tense moments of wary expectation the Bithynian gradually perceived a spreading sensation of elation coupled with inner serenity suffusing his organism. An entirely unfamiliar feeling of bodily wholeness was aroused and acknowledged by his perception. He had to concede he felt pretty good.

Antinous hadn't experienced such a novel sensation since the time several years earlier when he first stumbled upon the cascading sensuality of self-induced orgasm. But no brief, excited spasms at the hand of his more lurid fantasies bore comparison with this new experience. Its glow pervaded his entire being, head to foot, as he subsided into a mysterious rapture emanating from the dark inner world at his body's center. It thrilled his mind, it enlivened his muscles, and it pleasured his organs. It induced whimpering, toe-curling contentment.

The feeling automatically cemented a convergence with his all-engulfing companion. Their face-to-face, eye-to-eye proximity invoked an enclosing cocoon of radical intimacy. While Hadrian's rhythmic bodily action undulated above him, Antinous's natural inner solitude acknowledged how he was now accompanied in his sense-of-exile by a like-minded fellow explorer.

Hadrian's searching eyes hovered above him to monitor the minutiae of his sensory responses. The younger man's entire organism radiated waves of exquisite delight from his inner core. Hadrian sported patiently, teasingly, adventurously, with these sensations to fine-tune their playfulness.

He manipulated himself this way and that, slowly entering and withdrawing in leisurely alternation, slowly pressing ever deeper or holding still in steadfast confirmation. He toyed deliberately with the febrile responses of tissue, muscles, nerve end, interior node, and the conscious psyche too, to exact maximized gratification. Both parties smiled knowingly to each other's responses.

Hadrian lifted the young man's frame high for greater penetrative power, or doubled him over to bring himself into closer eye-to-eye intimacy, all the while playing his physicality with inventive pleasurings. Antinous was consumed by an animal relish which compelled him to emit plaintive squeaks of sublime delight. His habitual, protective, impassive guard was being demolished as a newfound openness to personal connection was rebuilt on its foundations.

In the process he began to appreciate facets of his father's revelations of a few months earlier. This intense closeness to a person for whom he held such high regard created an unanticipated concord within him. Hadrian was engaged upon an active, radical intimacy far more deeply *personal* than anything Antinous had ever practiced upon himself. Now two decades of emotional curbing, restraint, discretion, and conscious personal distance were being crumbled away in a rush of acute physical sensation. Antinous felt Hadrian and he had melded into a single human organism.

Is this, he wondered, what Achilles and Patrocles, or Alexander and Hephaestion, had experienced? Is this what they call love?

His friendly tormentor's rhythmic pacing increased in tempo and ferocity. The pulsing rise and fall of the interlocked bodies grew in ardor and heat. Beady sweats on glistening surfaces shone wetly beneath the chamber's flickering lamps. Muscles distended, limbs became malleable, bodies entwined aggressively. Antinous heard himself sigh his companion's name again and again. His companion reciprocated.

Eventually and inevitably, the torrid fervor burst in a shower of exclamations, gasps, shudders, and cries of delighted anguish. The two collapsed across the mosaic tiles in a pile of exhausted energies and spent body moistures.

Antinous felt becalmed in a manner unlike any previous occasion of his life. His abyss of solitude had dissolved into memory.

Minutes passed in silence before one retrieved a wine cup to share between them. They sipped alternating draughts.

'You learn quickly, Ant,' Hadrian rasped breathily.

Antinous raised himself on one elbow to eye his sweaty, naked companion lying outstretched beside him. He smiled his most ingratiating, calculating, charmer's smile. It was loaded with intent.

'Yes, I do Hadrian. But it's your turn now,' he murmured softly.

The maturer man baulked. He looked to his companion questioningly.

'A ride there for a ride back,' was the immediate response.

'Are you sure you have a sufficient lion-heart to do it? And so soon, Ant?'

'Yes I do, Hadrian. Turn over.'

Hadrian's lazy smile widened into a knowing, if faintly insecure grin.

'You do learn quickly,' he said.

Antinous good-humouredly grasped his companion's pelvis at the hips and mock-pressed him to roll over onto his belly. It was time for the assailant's driven fury to be turned back onto itself."

Geta fell silent once more to sip his wine. His eyes returned to Surisca more often than seemed necessary, Suetonius sensed, as he conveyed his testimony to the group of listeners in the morning sunlight. He began his account again.

"You may wonder how I know all these intimate details, gentlemen – and Lady Surisca. I learned most of them from Herodes' steward who kept watch outside the shuttered *andron* so Caesar's needs would be immediately provided if demanded. He kept an eye on things through a join in the shutter leaves, but has kept his tongue to himself ever since, except with me. I learned of the others from Antinous himself over wine in later conversations.

But I was now to personally witness the next development in this occasion. Should I continue with my tale, gentlemen?"

"Do so, Geta."

"The clatter of horse hooves on flagstones followed by muffled whispers at the house portal told the two dozing bodies dawn had arrived. As first light peeped through the *andron* window Antinous awoke to hear Herodes' villa's great door being unbolted to allow entry to arrivals.

Military-booted footsteps approached the *andron* across the atrium's tiles towards the chamber's shutters. A soft knock upon its cedars announced callers were waiting.

'Come!' Hadrian called.

Servants pressed the panels apart to reveal two Horse Guards and myself standing to attention outside. Scorilo, Godron, and I absorbed the scene before us with keen interest.

A potent charge of the musky scents of body sweat, wine dregs, stale incense, and the miasma of hard sex exuded from the space. Sex has its own special sweet aura, and it steeped the *andron* like a charged storm cloud.

Cushions and blankets lay across an impromptu bed arrangement with other pillows scattered across the floor. Assorted tunics, cloaks, belts, and boots were littered elsewhere, while crumpled toweling with dank stains were flung carelessly over chair backs. A small urn holding a deeply-scored emollient had rolled to one side across the floor.

Hadrian sat upright at the edge of the double-couch arrangement bare to our view but holding a corner of a rug across his privates. He scratched his head and rubbed early morning eyes.

Antinous lay lengthwise along the couch behind Caesar propped lazily on one elbow to casually eye the intruders. His sun-bleached mane was in wild disarray. Only a small cotton compress attached to his left cheek covered his buck-naked frame. My eyes were drawn to the pale-straw lightness of his underarm fluff and pubic hair. A hickey adorned his frontal upper throat.

The guards and I instantly recognized the vestiges of the energetic activities which had been enacted in that place. The tell-tale debris of the night's couplings was self-explanatory.

'Caesar, it is dawn. I am instructed to attend you,' I announced, my eyes scanning the room, its detritus, and its implications before settling upon the finely drawn figure of the naked *ephebe* lying behind the emperor. His free hand idled lazily at Caesar's crutch.

'And good morning to you too, Antinous of Bithynia,' I added diplomatically.

He responded with a languorous nod, his jaw resting on his clenched fist and no attempt to cover his nudity.

Palaestra nudity is a given in the life of young men of the elite classes in Greece. Nakedness possesses shame only in the eyes of our older Romans, some colder clime barbarians, and certain weird religious eccentrics. But in Athens it is a commonplace.

'I hope you slept well, my lords, after the night's festivities?' I offered very politely. Antinous probably realized I had elevated him into the ranks of a lord. I guess he wondered whether 'festivities' referred to the Dionysia revel or the bedchamber antics?

I was to learn much later how the night's engagement had been a revelatory experience for Antinous. The intensity of their mutual passion and the fierce aggression it incited had astonished both parties. I gather neither was especially vexed by this fact though.

'Call the servants, Geta, I must dress,' Hadrian commanded. 'I'll wash at the Household.'

I clapped my hands and two of Herodes' servants came scuttling to the chamber. They immediately set about retrieving the emperor's clothes and re-dressing him.

'I bring news, Caesar.' I took my opportunity as Hadrian was being clothed. 'Senator Lucius Ceionius Commodus and his companions departed the Household villa before dawn to reach Piraeus and sail on the earliest tide to Corinth.'

I sensed both Antinous and Hadrian prick up their ears.

'Commodus's steward said his party must return immediately to Rome from Corinth,' I added, 'because he had received news his mother had taken ill, so they left early to hire passage.'

'Has he left a note?' Hadrian asked.

'Not that I'm aware of, Caesar. He was eager to depart at some speed.'

Hadrian was silent as the servants arranged his dress to a suitable degree of comportment. Meanwhile Antinous contemplated the effectiveness of Herodes' handling of Commodus.

But not at that time knowing these details, I took an initiative.

'Will Caesar wish to pursue his friend by sea or overland? The Praetorian horse network could speedily deliver Caesar to Corinth, before his vessel arrived or at least before he could negotiate a further passage to Italy?'

Hadrian was silent again as his laced boots were drawn on. When he turned his back while being buckled I noticed two distinct bruises at the back of his neck above his right shoulder. They were already pale purple and told of an infliction of passion on the emperor's flesh.

I think my eyes and eyebrows fluttered slightly at the sight of the love bites when I calculated the direction of their reception. They would have been applied from directly behind. This possessed a significance about the nature of the act underway during their imposition. My eyes may have widened in astonishment at this realization, I guess.

Antinous detected my fluster from his recumbent position on the bed. Our gazes crossed fleetingly, but I flicked away in embarrassment. Antinous was smiling to himself. It was an enigmatic smile suggesting triumph. It communicated notions I had not anticipated about Caesar, nor for that matter about Antinous.

'No, Geta, I won't follow Commodus,' Hadrian resolved. 'I've tired of the young man's impetuosity. Perhaps it's time he returned to Rome. We'll see him later in the year.

In the meantime, Geta, I've told Antinous how he and his companions will enter the Imperial *contubernium*, our living arrangements for the Household. Both they and their attendants will accompany us on our forthcoming tour of Achaea. We will be visiting historical sites, making awards, visiting troops, hunting a little, and so on across the Peloponnese this summer before we sail to Italy.

Antinous is likely to sleep in my chamber regularly, but he and his household are to have their own independent apartments wherever we travel. Is that clear?'

'It is indeed, Caesar!' I declared.

My wide-eyed gaze returned to Antinous. I suppose it conveyed an unspoken message akin to awe at the lad's extraordinary accomplishment. He responded with a serene, knowing grin. He exuded the cool confidence of an arena's victor, and he let me know it. Decurion Scorilo of the Horse Guard too would have comprehended the circumstances from his own perspectives.

Antinous's arrival in Caesar's sphere now cemented many of the questions of what my own role was to be in Caesar's life. I had spent my lifetime under Hadrian's aegis, so perhaps it was time my own ambitions should at last find a satisfactory resolution too?

'Leave us for a moment,' Hadrian commanded, as he shooed the servants and the guards beyond the *andron*'s closing doors. Only I stayed in attendance.

Hadrian kneeled over the twin couches to lift Antinous's chin within close reach by a single fingertip. Their eyes were only an inch or two apart. He smiled at the sleepy Bithynian.

'We enjoyed ourselves through the night, didn't we Ant?' the emperor charmed as he leaned closer. Noting Antinous's gesture of one hand modestly cupping his genitals, I perceived he had sensed his bloodstream stir to life once again.

'We did, Hadrian,' was his reply, unexpectedly using the special *nomen* in my presence. This was new from his lips and told me something they each perceived about their relationship.

'We'll do those things again tonight, my strong-willed Lion-heart.'

'Yes, we will Hadrian. And much more too I expect."

"Lion-heart? So what are we to read into this account, Dacian?" Clarus demanded.

"You must use your imaginations, gentlemen," Geta responded, still with his eyes firmly settled upon the Syrian courtesan.

"All I see is an opportunist using his wiles upon our *Princeps*?" Clarus opined. "Yet Caesar takes what he wants from the engagement."

Suetonius took the reins of the interview to shift the perspective away from matters which troubled Clarus.

"A further question, Dacian, tell us here honestly, plainly, between us only, are you suggesting there are things about Hadrian's relationship with Antinous we should know? Are there facets of their five years together which could compel recent events, in your view? We must know all. Think hard about it, Dacian."

"I don't know what you mean, Special Inspector? I've told you all I know," the Dacian uttered believably. "It's enough, I'd say."

"Then, Dacian, tell us where were you yourself on the night of Antinous's death?"

Geta smiled thinly.

"My lords, I was engaged in providing services to Caesar in the company of *the Western Favorite* throughout the entire evening, and slept in close proximity to Caesar's chamber after," the courtier replied.

"All night and morning? With witnesses?" Suetonius demanded.

"All night and morning. With witnesses. I must leave you now."

Suetonius and Clarus looked to each other in silent foreboding after he departed.

Surisca spoke up in a quiet voice. "Masters, may I offer some words?"

"Only if you have something worthy to contribute, woman," Clarus huffed. Suetonius nodded approval to the veiled figure seated some distance behind him.

"Masters, Geta the Dacian spoke of Pachrates. I too have witnessed this priest perform his magical arts."

All eyes around the bench beneath the morning sunlight turned towards her.

"I too have seen this famous magician transform living animals into other beasts, and restore life to the recently killed," she said. "The famous Priest Pachrates has performed this magic in public on many occasions.

I have been contracted to dance and play the flute at temple celebrations for the faithful in the city of Memphis downstream from this place, so I was among those who were backstage at his performances in his temple courtyard. His devotees watched from one side of the platform while I and others engaged in the day's celebrations awaited behind the platform.

His people try to keep it secret, but the animals he transforms are simply substituted by an ingenious mechanism which his assistant priests manipulate while his audience is distracted by shifting curtains, cymbal crescendos, and flashing lights. His is a clever magic which substitutes one thing for another out-of-sight while people are distracted by activity.

I have also seen him behead a living creature on his stage and apparently return the creature to life. I saw him kill a mangy dog, scavenger vermin whose death no one complains, and then with a flourish of curtains and magical words with beating drums, it was replaced with a live dog of similar age, coloring, and markings. To the innocent eye it seems he has revived the dead and replaced the severed head. His audience did not see the headless carcass being thrown to one side and replaced with a living dog whose matched color patches were painted on.

I submit that the fellow beheaded before Caesar's and Antinous's eyes may have been the condemned brother or even an identical twin of a similar looking fellow.

Pachrates' priests probably purchased the two condemned men from the authorities of the arena at Cyrene or Leptis Magna. All his sorcery is trickery. There is no wonder to it once you know its secrets, but he is clever in performing it."

Surisca demurely sat back in her chair.

"But Caesar and Antinous were moved by his display?" Clarus complained. "Caesar is no fool! He can't be deceived about such things!"

Surisca drew her head scarf across her face to reply.

"If the spectator is in an accommodating mood and wishes to see magic, inexplicable magic will be seen. Such illusions can be persuasive to those who don't know the guile of Egyptian sorcerers who play on human needs."

"It's true many at Court are enticed by feats of magic and magical charms," Suetonius soothed. "Remember, both the astrologer Aristobulus and the Governor's mistress, Anna Perenna, do a fine trade in providing charms, potions, and spells to the Household. Hadrian too is known to respect these arts."

It was Clarus's time to speak directly to Surisca to raise an undiplomatic matter.

"Syrian, did I perceive you and the Dacian are known to each other?" the magistrate asked.

Surisca looked across to Suetonius for permission to speak. The biographer nodded, just as keen to hear her response as Clarus.

"I confess we do, master. But briefly," the Syri disclosed apprehensively. "Your Dacian courtier was a client some months ago at Palaestina. I was contracted to the newly built spa at Shuni, outside Caesarea in Judea, where the wealthy retire for their pleasures. I and many other girls were hired as dancers and entertainers to engage in water frolics and sex games among the thermal spring pools of Shuni.

The Imperial Household travelling from Antioch to Egypt through Palaestina resided for some weeks at Caesarea, as you know, so the Dacian came to Shuni for rest-and-recreation. He engaged my services for a whole week. Geta and I enjoyed our time together in playfulness."

Suetonius looked at Surisca with some dismay. He wondered whether he had any right to feel cuckolded by this revelation.

"And that's it? Nothing more? A business relationship?" Clarus added imperiously.

"My lord, this is my profession. I receive many clients. If not, I and my assistants would soon starve. But it's true I found your Dacian colleague to be very appealing company at Shuni," Surisca offered wistfully.

"Did you fall in love with Geta, young lady?" Suetonius searched a little too keenly.

Surisca looked to her questioner with a quizzical expression.

"I'm not sure what *love* is, master. But if it's to feel needed and secure in the company of another person then, yes, I did find the Dacian appealing," the young Syri reminisced. "Besides, he is very handsome in my eyes. And he makes love well."

"Love? Needed? What's this nonsense we're talking of?" Clarus protested. "We have serious matters of life and death to contemplate, Special Inspector Suetonius Tranquillus."

"Friends, morning is advancing and Lysias hasn't returned to us as he promised," Suetonius resolved bitterly. "He's now overdue by an hour. I had faith he would appear of his own volition at the appointed time. I am disappointed in him and his so-called *arete*. Unless misadventure has befallen the lad, a warrant will instruct the Guard to search for him and apprehend him. Meanwhile the slave Thais of Cyrene too will be sought on our behalf.

However, if our interview subjects will not come to us then we will go to them. Clarus, Strabon, guards, Surisca, follow me! First on our list will be Caesar's advocates of wonders!"

"Advocates of wonders?!" Clarus exclaimed uncertainly. "Who are they?!"

CHAPTER 18

Aristobulus of Antioch and Phlegon of Tralles weren't prepared for the visitors. The Court Astrologer and the Teller of Tales fluttered chaotically in their chamber checking their wardrobe, decors, lip paints, and face powders in the bumpy reflections of bronze mirrors. They were finalizing their effect on their likely clientele for the day's public exposure. Artful appearance is as important as actual efficacy in their respective sciences.

The portly, ruddy faced, wine-veined astrologer was still engaged with his early morning toilet as his slave trimmed, oiled, and combed his silvery beard.

Meanwhile the gaunt, bony features of the recorder of wonders, Phlegon, were being splashed with river water to revive his energies after an excess of the delicious local date wine during the previous day's rites grieving the death of Osiris. The death, too, of the Bithynian youth was deserving of recognition and appropriate mourning.

"It's been a miracle, in the eyes of the natives," Aristobulus explained to Suetonius's first questions. "They now expect their problems with the Nile flood to be resolved in next year's deluge. They're convinced the death of a Roman noble has been Caesar's gift to them, the gracious gesture of a Pharaoh to his subjects in times of difficulty."

"The fact that our Great Pharaoh is himself exceedingly distressed by the incident evades them, I suppose?" Suetonius commented. "So, Imperial Astrologer, are any more unexpected deaths being told in the stars?"

"Today is the second day of the month of Hathur to the locals, Suetonius Tranquillus, or the fourth day to the Kalends of November to we of Rome," he proposed sagely, "and the day's omens are quite auspicious. Tomorrow's will be even more so. Osiris will resurrect at dawn with the sun, so The Isia will then extend to a weeklong celebration. For many in this strange land it's the year's major festival."

Aristobulus, a native of Antioch at Syria in his fifties, was renown for his command of Chaldean astrology and divination.

Phlegon was a native of Tralles, a small city inland from Ephesus at the coast of Caria in Roman Asia. His scholarly specialty was as a collector of marvelous tales and fabulous wonders for both Hadrian's amusement and Rome's avid book collectors. Phlegon's enthusiasm for recording reports about hermaphrodites, unusual births, monsters, giant skeleton bones, ghostly revenants, or mythical creatures, enlivened the Court's days.

"Before you depart on your day's pleasures, good worthies," Suetonius interjected, "we have some questions to ask you about the deceased, the Bithynian youth Antinous. He was well known to you, I believe? Clarus and I have been commissioned by the emperor to explore the circumstances of the boy's life and death. We possess the powers of a magisterial enquiry. I am appointed *Special Inspector*."

The two Greeks sobered swiftly in response to this announcement. The use of torture upon non-citizen foreigners was a given in a magistrate's armory of investigative aids. Neither man of science is a citizen of Rome.

"We're entirely at your service, gentlemen," they sang in unison.

"Tell us, Aristobulus, what you know of Antinous and his activities," Suetonius queried. "To begin your legal deposition, first tell us who you are, state your profession, and where you were on the night of his death? Further, what is your view of this misadventure?" Suetonius queried.

The astrologer shuffled uncomfortably for a few moments before rising to the occasion to declaim theatrically in Greek-inflected Latin.

"I, *Special* Inspector, am Aristobulus of Antioch, astrologer to Great Caesar. I am a *magus, theurge,* and *hierophant* of the ancient priestly dynasty of Emesa. The blood of Babylon flows in my veins. As an exponent of the Chaldean Oracles and a student of Marcus Manilius, I practice the sciences of the stars, mathematics, dream interpretation, occult ritual, and divination.

My recall of the youth Antinous is his birth to have been on a late date in the coming month of November. The actual time of birth was unknown to the lad. He told me so on those occasions when he consulted with me on astrological matters, which were increasingly often in recent times.

He told me his mother died shortly after his birth, so his precise hour of birth was uncertain to him. It seemed even the year of his birth is uncertain. He said his family's nurse had told him he was born on the twenty-seventh day of the month of Cybele of the Bithynian calendar. This corresponds to our November. At least this would be a reasonable start to charting his destiny.

However, *Special Inspector,* to cast the chart of someone so favored by Caesar's is to calculate in proximity to Caesar's own stars. This is forbidden and a dire offence. I did not dare calibrate a horoscope for the boy, so his recent fate was entirely beyond my predictive skill."

Suetonius thought to himself here was yet another of those serendipitous fortuities in the professional life of a fortune-teller, a fortuity by omission in this instance.

"Where were you on the night of his death?"

"As you well know, Suetonius Tranquillus, I travelled with you much of yesterday across the river at Hermopolis with our academic colleagues. I then lunched and bathed with you at the local Baths in the early afternoon," the Antiochan explained. "It was I who informed Tribune Macedo of the security service of your whereabouts at *The Street of Pleasures* in the late afternoon. This was when Caesar summoned your urgent attendance."

"Where were you the previous evening, the night of the Favorite's death, Aristobulus of Antioch?" the Special Inspector repeated.

"Once again, Suetonius Tranquillus, I was with you and our Alexandrian companions at a drinking party aboard your *felucca* moored off Hermopolis. As you may recall, we shared considerable quantities of Chios dark sweet wine and much local beer," the astrologer imparted.

"What do you know about Antinous which might contribute to our understanding of the young man's death? I am led to believe you shared his company often?"

"Hmm, this is a difficult matter," Aristobulus offered as he stroked his splayed beard thoughtfully. "There was much about the boy which invites consideration, I'd say."

"What do you mean?"

"Well, he certainly did have odd interests for someone so young."

"In what way?"

"I quite clearly recall my first impressions," he responded. "Two years ago when the Household returned again to Athens while touring the Empire, several of us joined Caesar in taking initiation into the Mysteries at Eleusis. The Bithynian was among us. We, along with three thousand others, did so to bask in Caesar's company at the rites.

I accompanied Antinous with Caesar from the first day of the initiates' procession to Eleusis. We are not allowed to tell you about the final rituals of the sixth night at the *Telesterion* of Eleusis. That's a sacred secret. But I can certainly tell you about the effects the event had upon Antinous.

Prior to the final rite the initiates drink a sacred brew, the famed potion called *kykeon*. I don't know what's in the brew, or whether it affects some people differently to others, but Antinous was deeply intoxicated by the stuff. Too deeply, I thought.

It tasted to me merely like a bitter medicine, but it seemed to affect others differently. I even wondered if the particular draught Antinous consumed had been cunningly poisoned in some way, its effects being so profound on him. Gossip said his intimacy with Caesar had made powerful enemies at Court by his very presence, so anything is possible."

"What precise effect did the potion have on the lad?"

"Well, to my eye as a *magus* experienced in observing all manner of oracles, mediums, and mystics at work, the boy had been thoroughly beguiled by the *kykeon*.

I have witnessed enchanted sibyls inhaling the fumes of burnt leaves or grasses to achieve their insight, or ingesting sacred medicaments extracted from toads or mushrooms, or engaging in prayerful rituals to achieve a deep trance, but I sensed Antinous had been propelled into a thoroughly bewitched state of mind by the brew. I think Caesar, Lysias, and Geta too were concerned at his condition because, to me, he didn't look too happy about his situation."

"How did the potion affect you?" Clarus interjected.

"Well nothing happened to me really," the astrologer explained, "I was slightly distracted by the draught, but not to a degree I couldn't manage. Perhaps the boy wasn't familiar with intoxication? Yet he is known to enjoy his wine."

"Isn't the *kykeon* poured from a communal bowl? Doesn't everyone receive the same potion? And wouldn't Caesar's Praetorians have watched what Hadrian and his companions were receiving from the priests?" Clarus explored.

Septicius, being a former Prefect of Praetorians, intimately knew the precautions the security corps took in monitoring comestibles and drink for Hadrian.

"Well, yes. We all took the *kykeon* from the communal cauldron in the individual cups provided to us. Yet only Antinous was affected in this way, no one else I observed. Perhaps the lad's cup was contaminated with some malignancy or laced with some secret poison? That is, unless Hadrian had been the intended target and the boy had received Caesar's mug in error?"

"And then?" Suetonius queried further.

"The final rites proceeded as they were supposed. I thought someone might be wise enough to whisk Antinous away for his own safety, but both Caesar and his school pal ensured the fellow was comfortable during the final hours of the overnight ritual. Actually, it was afterwards that things grew worrying," the astrologer recalled.

"In what way?"

"Well, in the following days I heard how Antinous had taken to his bed. Apparently he was having visions and suffering attacks by mystical *daemons*, or such things. He was quite distressed for several days."

"You mean he'd gone mad?" Clarus stated in his usual unsubtle manner.

"I don't know if it was the madness of insanity or the madness of divine revelation," the Syri offered, "but I was eventually summoned by Caesar's physicians to offer my opinion."

"And, your opinion was?" Suetonius asked.

"Well, I think the *kykeon* had either poisoned him or thrust him into a strange, dark place," Aristobulus said, "I'm not sure which."

"But he recovered?"

"Yes, he recovered. Yet along the way he asked his physicians and myself some very strange questions, very strange indeed."

"What sort of questions?"

"Well, he revealed to us he'd travelled to the Land Of The Dead, and returned again. He asked if this was usual at the Mysteries of Demeter at Eleusis," the astrologer said.

The interrogating team showed distinct interest in this meandering testimony.

"The Land of the Dead?" Suetonius reiterated.

"Yes. And he was serious. He was convinced. He said he had taken flight *'to the place where the sun never shines'*. It is the home of the dead, he claimed. He said he glimpsed the endless oceans which surround the Underworld and the four rivers of woe. He viewed its ruler, Hades of the unspeakable name, brother of Zeus.

He comprehended how the manner of one's death and the proper rituals affect one's fate in the next world, and realized the dire necessity of a coin in the mouth for Charon's guidance, and that sort of thing. He said he saw the face of Thanatos himself, the god of death, and yet returned to the light of Life.

I have only heard great priests and priestesses of secret cults make this claim. Even I as a *magus* cannot make such a claim," the Antiochan declared with unexpected modesty.

"Anything more?" Suetonius enquired.

"It was enough at that time. To go to The Land of the Dead and return to life is the dominion of an Orpheus and his Eurydice, or an Odysseus, or Hercules retrieving Alcestis. It was a form of rebirth, like Demeter's daughter Persephone from Hades' dominion. A resurrection."

"A resurrection? What happened next?" the Special Inspector asked.

"After a few days he returned to normalcy. His physicians and I advised he sacrifice to his chosen deity, pour offerings, and offer thanks for his safe return. He did so," Aristobulus concluded, "but he was a changed fellow."

"Changed? How so?"

"Well, the experience aged him several years. It was written in his features. He was no longer simply a handsome young man in his prime, he had suddenly assumed maturity's demeanor," the astrologer explained.

Phlegon's interrupted.

"In more ways than one, gentlemen. I saw his personality change considerably. Whatever it was he 'saw' or experienced under the *kykeon* had made a deep impression," the Carian scarecrow said. "He *saw* something that disturbed him greatly. He was no longer a callow youngster given to pleasures. Despite his youthful age he had matured overnight. This was different to Initiation into the cult of Demeter at Eleusis, this was a shift of personality."

"How did Caesar react to his Favorite facing such a mystical experience?" the biographer asked. It was now Phlegon's opportunity to reminiscence.

"Great Caesar was very attentive to his Favorite's needs. Despite his schedule of duties he led Antinous and the Companions of the Hunt on a restorative tour of historical sites across Achaea. This provided the youngster fresh air, exercise, and new stimuli to encourage healing. They travelled to places beyond Athens where *erastoi* and *eromenoi* had been highly regarded in ages past, or where the custom was still alive.

At Thespiae, only two days journey from Athens, they commemorated the success of Caesar's dedication to Eros of his kill of a wild bear years earlier. Hadrian had made an offering of the bear's spoils to seek the god's benevolence by endowing him with a worthy *eromenos*. He now celebrated how Antinous was that god's gracious gesture. Such sentimentality is comforting in a ruler, don't you think?"

"What else?" Suetonius asked.

"They also visited ancient Mantinea, the city state from where Antinous's forebears had migrated to Bithynia," Phlegon enthused. "Mantinea had been the site of great battles among the Greeks in antique times. At the final battle fought between the Thebans led by their general Epaminondas against the Spartans, Epaminondas won the battle but died soon after of his wounds.

He was the leader of The Sacred Band of Thebes, the army of pairs of warrior-lovers renown across the Greek world. At his death at Mantinea the great commander was buried by the side of his *eromenos* lover, who'd also been killed in the conflict. Hadrian and Antinous honored the couple's grave with offerings and ceremonies of great poignancy."

"But why do you tell us this?" Clarus interjected. "In what way do they affect the Bithynian youth's drowning?"

It was Aristobulus's turn. Now he was introspective

"Some in the Household have perceived a pattern in these events. It had not passed without note how the boy was consumed with matters of death and dying, and of issues of return from the Land of the Dead. Yes, he was young and impressionable, yet the young rarely express such morbid thoughts due to being convinced of being invulnerable," the *magus* replied.

"And there's more," Phlegon added. "I myself have witnessed his increasing obsessions. There is the matter at Alexandria."

"What is the matter at Alexandria?" Suetonius asked, becoming somewhat distracted.

"Well, my friends, as you know, Alexandria is a hotbed of competing ethnic rivalries, obscure philosophies, new religious ideas, and mysteries galore. One can easily have one's head turned in a place like Alexandria. The atmosphere is conducive to eccentric beliefs and avant-garde practices," the Syri murmured, "especially if a young companion discovers his halcyon days as Caesar's Favorite are numbered."

"Numbered? How so, Astrologer?" Suetonius sought.

"Well, as we all know, a month ago the *Western Favorite* joined the touring retinue at Alexandria. He'd been summoned from Rome by someone, possibly Caesar himself, possibly not; who knows?

Lucius Ceionius Commodus and several of his fashionable friends turned up by sea from Italy a week or so after Caesar had arrived at Alexandria. It instantly put Antinous on notice about the state of his relationship with Caesar."

"There's still nothing to relate to a drowning, is there? Unless you're suggesting the boy was so upset he committed suicide?" Suetonius probed.

"No. But there's much else. You are aware of Caesar's cough, of course?" Aristobulus asked cautiously.

"Careful, Astrologer," Clarus interjected, "you enter sensitive territory."

"Honorable Senator, I defer to your noble station and your wisdom, but you asked the truth of us under threat of legal imposition. Caesar's cough is not a matter which passes by uncommented at Court," the Syri muttered low. "There are those whose future hangs upon such a cough, not least of whom are we ourselves. It's a matter of concern to all. If Caesar became, say, *indisposed* or fared even worse, then the careers and livelihoods of a large number of people will be suspended until political stability is re-established.

But more importantly, Senator and Special Inspector, are you aware of the cough evinced by Lucius Commodus as well?"

"Commodus too?! The successor designate?"

"Yes, gentlemen."

Suetonius, Clarus, Strabon, and even Surisca were stirred at this revelation.

"The *Western Favorite*, Caesar's likely successor, also displays an infirmity which is *not-to-be-discussed?*" Suetonius confirmed.

Aristobulus nodded sagely.

"It is so. Commodus now possesses a hack which, to my ear, sounds extremely similar to the same dry rasp Hadrian was emitting some years ago. I hesitate to suggest they're a related phenomenon," Aristobulus proposed. "Besides, I'm convinced the Bithynian youth knows these things too; he's closer to their source than we are, and he's smart."

The chamber hung heavy with consideration.

"Yet you have not told us how you think these things can lead to a drowning?" Suetonius reminded his company. Phlegon took up the theme.

"On arriving at Alexandria the travelling Court was consumed by its respective obsessions. The bordellos of the Rhakotis and Canopus pleasure quarters received a huge influx of randy clients, while the various exponents of the city's competing ideologies received invitations to dinners.

Hadrian and Antinous were no different. Caesar's passion for foreseeing the future and understanding Fate had him summons experts in Egyptian astrology or had him attending the Serapeum with its priestly adepts of Serapis.

Serapis, this patron god of Alexandria, is extraordinary in that he knits the contending races and gods of Egypt together into a single veneration. Hadrian admires this cohesive facet of Serapis. Our times call for cohesion and unity yet our many diversities pull us apart. The eccentricities of religion are fatal without tolerance, so Hadrian is consumed with his search for an answer which unifies.

Meanwhile Antinous was exploring questions of life after death. I should know, I accompanied him on his excursions into that city's labyrinth of magicians, mystics, and wonder workers."

"The drowning, the drowning, Phlegon," Suetonius reminded the flighty Asian.

"Well, on one occasion we were visited by a man known as Marcion of Sinope in the Christian sector of the city. This Greek is a leading philosopher of one particular school of the Christian superstition," Phlegon offered with a curl of the lip. "This superstition is everywhere these days. Many people regard it as sorcery, sinister and seditious, and deserving of being curbed. They're magicians who pursue eternal life, people say. They worship an executed felon who resurrected from death, they claim. They drink blood at rituals. That's sorcery plain and simple!

But like the Judaeans, they're a volatile lot. They argue against each other fiercely as competing sectarians often do. They have many differing sects and leaders, and don't agree with each other.

This fellow Marcion had assembled a group of fellow fanatics to meet with Antinous. Antinous possesses no legal power yet his closeness to Caesar exerts its own charisma. They were eager for an opportunity to display their allegiance to Rome and have Antinous make a good report to his imperial companion. Leaders of the sectarians were among the group, though I sensed that they differed vehemently on issues of their cult.

The most vocal one, Marcion of Sinope, practices the ascetic, austere teachings of a Christian mystic named Paulus of Tarsas executed in Nero's time. Another, Basilides, is an Egyptian Greek who's expert in the many competing texts of the Christians. Then there was an articulate young fellow named Valentinus, also an Egyptian, who proclaims a complicated philosophy of a *gnostikos* mystic. His is a fantastical panorama of angelic Archons and a Creator Demiurge among levels of being in the heavens, and so on interminably.

There are many similarities to Judaean teachings, except the *Chrestus* cults are open to we Romans. They don't demand painful circumcision of the penis or quaint rules of diet and habit as the Judaeans do, but they do demand asceticism. Antinous was eager to hear their views on the afterlife, which they offer plentifully. I suspect their perspectives colored the boy's attitude to life, and perhaps even to drowning."

"In what way, Carian?" Suetonius asked, showing increasing interest.

"The Christians offer a teaching that's all sweetness and light. They paint quite an appealing picture of their odd beliefs," Phlegon expounded. "They claim to show a path from the miseries of life and from sin, which is a type of intense self-punishing guilt about infractions of their ascetical code. But you have to die first to benefit, it seems. However the End of Time is approaching soon anyway. So unlike we Romans, it's not about how to adjust to living life in this world, it's about the promise of an After-Life-To-Come. It's very focused on death and being resurrected someday by their god.

Antinous was given a copy of their most important scripture *The Teachings of the Twelve Apostles*, known to Greeks as *The Didache*. It offers a hundred maxims on how you should live your life, which to them means how to prepare for death. It aims to avoid sin, yet they detect sin and fornication absolutely everywhere. They're obsessed!

Their special *Savior* was a man called *Iesous*, some sort of Judaean rabbi and wonder-worker crucified as a rebel at Jerusalem a century ago before we destroyed their capital. They claim this sorcerer was their God enveloped in the rabbi's flesh, somehow.

But the important bit for Antinous was the superstition's emphasis on an afterlife. Like the followers of Zoroaster and Egypt's Osiris, they promise their worshippers a resurrection after death followed by some sort of eternal existence. The rest of us are doomed to eternal suffering. It's a compelling philosophy which Antinous took to heart."

"Do you think he believed this pernicious superstition?"

"Well, there's a downside to their teachings which I doubt Antinous could uphold. Their moral code is extreme. They have a low opinion of wealth, of trading, they abjure lending at interest, or being rich, as his family are.

Their executed *Savior* proclaimed an eccentric sort of freedom similar to the austerities of the followers of Diogenes who reject family, career, fame, the *Imperium*, and so on.

All their sects forbid 'fornication', which they say is an offence against their *Father's* laws. Their teachers say we Romans are all harlots and live whore's lives. They particularly condemn relations between unmarried people, adultery, divorce, and same-sex relationships. It's very other-worldly and austere. I'd say a young hot-blood like Antinous with fire in his loins would find such demands difficult in the extreme. Rome will never endorse such asceticism."

"But do you have more to offer about the Favorite's death? Do you know what happened on the night before last?" Suetonius probed. "When did you last see or speak with the youth?"

"No one seems to know how he died, gentlemen, but there's already much talk around the encampment of its aftermath," Aristobulus offered.

"Aftermath? Saying what?" Clarus demanded. Aristobulus was hesitant.

"Well, it's said there have been shadowy men with knives searching the tents for people close to Antinous. The lad's school chum Lysias and the freedwoman Thais have disappeared, they say," the astrologer murmured. "No one knows where. A steward of their household was murdered overnight, but it's not been made public yet. It's hard to keep secrets here, though many try. Shrouded men have also been seen in the nearby village searching for someone else, but I have no idea who.

Other gossip says Caesar has gone into secret conference with the governor of Egypt, Flavius Titianus, and his most senior officers, on high matters of state. This is unusual considering Hadrian's delicate frame of mind only an evening ago, wouldn't you say? Something important is going on, and perhaps we shouldn't enquire too closely."

"Yet I have been precisely instructed by Caesar to explore closely," Suetonius stated.

The two courtiers fumbled for fresh tittle-tattle.

"There was another occasion which I think possesses interest. It occurred in Memphis only recently on our journey here," Phlegon offered wistfully. "We're supposed to keep it secret or confidential, but it's something you should add to your understanding, I think."

"Yes, what?"

"It's not very pretty, but it was certainly a wonder to behold. Hadrian and the Favorite have been impressed by the arts of the wizard Pachrates of Memphis, who holds to the Old Religion of this strange land.

After witnessing several sessions of his magic, healing, and trickery, we had been told he can bring a man back to life in certain circumstances, just as the ancient wonder-workers were reputed to do," the Carian recorder of marvels murmured in hushed tones. "So while the rest of the entourage were climbing the Pyramids or carving their names on the Sphinx and enjoying themselves, we were invited to attend a private ceremony at the huge Temple of Amun complex in the heart of the city of Memphis.

Unlike their small Temple here at Besa, the Memphis temple is a gigantic edifice. Caesar, Antinous, and a small party including the women Julia Balbilla with the priestess Anna Perenna, who both possess interest in things of mystery, with a detachment of Guards, attended a special demonstration of the priest's skills. It was a wonder to behold!

On a high scaffold platform dressed with layers of curtains in the courtyard, the priest Pachrates and his acolytes performed elegant liturgies and rites with much incense, burnt offerings, prayers, drumming, and chanting. It was all very impressive, if somewhat percussive, with flashes of igneous powders and clouds of colored smoke.

The attendants brought a nondescript fellow in ragged attire onto the stage who appeared to be entranced or drugged into abstraction. One of the temple guards read a pronouncement in Greek to we observers which said the fellow was a condemned criminal who had been made available by the authorities for this occasion.

The fellow seemed utterly untroubled by his involvement in the event, even when priestly attendants held him to his knees and forced his head to the sands on the scaffold floor. Another priest of beefy proportions wielding a razor-edged scimitar entered the stage while Pachrates made strange mystical gestures and chants of great profundity above the fellow. Pachrates waved to the sword-bearer and the priest flashed the scimitar to cleave the head from the victim in a single slice.

There was much blood flow and writhing amid shouts and cries of magical formulae. Cymbals crashed, drums beat, sistra rattled, and voices chorused noisily as the curtains of the stage were thrust together by the attendants. Pachrates stepped forward between the clouds of smoke to continue proclaiming his Egyptian incantations. Then after a few seconds when the drums and cymbals ceased their racket and Pachrates waved his priest's staff, the curtains were again dramatically drawn apart to reveal the beheaded fellow standing healthily upright and serenely intact. He was facing us with his eyes wide in surprise, almost as surprised as we the viewers.

Though his own gore was copiously evident on the sands beneath him, his body had been restored into a single piece and his tunic was miraculously clean of stains. He had tears in eyes, tears of joy I'm sure. Pachrates waved his priest's staff over the fellow and splashed holy waters to sanctify him in the elaborate Egyptian style.

Caesar, Antinous, Julia Balbilla, members of the Guard, but not the lady Anna Perenna I noticed, broke out into cheers of applause. Anna Perenna simply settled her eyes upon the Favorite to observe his reactions to the magic.

Pachrates was modest in accepting praise for this marvel. But he was visibly exhausted by his endeavors, as we could readily appreciate."

Suetonius turned to Clarus and Surisca in silent communication and raised one hairy eyebrow. All three plus Strabon remained meaningfully mute, while Surisca lowered her eyes demurely.

Phlegon and Aristobulus were mystified by this silent response.

"Assuredly, what I say is true," the astrologer declared.

CHAPTER 19

Senator Septicius Clarus, being self-evidently a member of the elite of Rome as proclaimed by his purple striped toga and elegantly dismissive manner, brushed aside the hesitant watch-guard and a vacillating steward with an imperious flick of the wrist. He led Suetonius, Strabon, and Surisca through the silken drapes of Arrian's capacious apartments situated away from the river's mosquitoes.

No amount of pleading, groveling, or bowing performed by Arrian's steward would dissuade Clarus from his unannounced sortie into the Bithynian noble's tented precincts.

After passing noisily through several well-appointed chambers loudly calling *Senator Flavius Arrianus!*, the group burst into an inner apartment to witness the man himself, freshly leapt from his bed and garbed in a minimal sleeping tunic. He was hurriedly unsheathing a *gladius* short-sword from its scabbard in prompt response to the onslaught of the invaders.

As Clarus and Suetonius lunged through its entrance drapes the two inadvertently perceived a fully shrouded figure disappearing equally as speedily beyond drapes at the far side of the chamber. The heady bouquet of a rich perfume charged the air.

"What is this, fools?! You enter unannounced! Explain yourselves!" Arrian called sharply, his sword at the ready but with his hair akimbo and his grooming astray. His steward stumbled forward between the intruders in fearful apprehension.

"Forgive me, master, they forced their way in!" he proclaimed, afraid of retribution for his failed resistance. "They would not await your consent."

Arrian, recognizing his intruders were not bent on injury, tossed the blade onto the rumpled bed and gathered himself to be presentable in their presence.

"You catch me unawares, gentlemen. I have no recall of any appointment expecting your company? You almost even caught me *in flagrante delicto*, as you saw," Arrian joked politely, quietly seething with suppressed rage.

"If I had known you were to visit, I would have prepared myself suitably," Arrian offered with the barest degree of politesse. "But you must be wary of barging into private quarters unannounced, my friends. I'm told there are shady figures moving around the camp, and some people might react aggressively or even fatally to an uninvited incursion. Is it true there was a murder here last night by men unknown? Were you the culprits, perhaps?"

Clarus responded to the comments, now aware of the embarrassment his zeal had incurred.

"You must forgive us, colleague, we had not expected to intrude into your private affairs. We are simply eager to solicit your considered opinions and advice," the ageing senator tried to soothe a ruffled ego. "Suetonius Tranquillus and I seek your wise counsel on the Antinous incident. Of a murder last night, though, we know nothing of substance."

"Let's not be detained here, friends, let's retire into the cool air of my garden court," Arrian offered, perhaps to remove his intruders from his boudoir, "where my staff can provide refreshments as we talk."

Signaling to his steward for the appropriate services, Arrian led the group into an outdoor terrace. It was a charming area graced with planters and pots of well-watered greenery. Valuable ivory-inlaid ebony chairs edged with gilt trim and supporting comfortable cushions in Asian ethnic weaves were interspersed by individual trestle campaign tables. With the sun's direct rays screened by a thin overhead canopy, the diffused light bounced softly off white marble tiles and scattered Ionian rugs. Busts of notable philosophers and the likes of Alexander the Great fringed the gardened area.

Mugs with jugs of wine and water appeared promptly, accompanied by nutty nibbles, honey cakes, and dried fruits.

"I'd heard from Caesar's own lips how you are instructed to enquire into the death of his Antinous, his Favorite. Well, what have you come up with?" Arrian asked with interest, either genuine or feigned. "What have you discovered thus far about the poor lad? You've almost consumed a day of your two day's allowance, haven't you?"

"That's why we're here," Suetonius replied. "We have no time to lose."

"Senator," Clarus appealed to his fellow member of The Senate, "we're in something of a bind. So far we've learned very little we didn't know already."

"Anything I can throw light upon?" the Bithynian noble responded.

"Well, hopefully," Clarus responded. "Are there matters you feel we, as investigators, should know about Antinous which might relate to his cause of death?"

Clarus nodded towards Suetonius and Strabon, who promptly started recording the proceedings on his wax pads. "Or are there matters you advise we explore?"

"Before we begin," Suetonius interrupted, "we should identity your person in our record. Perhaps, Senator, you will describe to us in your own words your personal details for our scribe to notate?"

Arrian looked askance at the portly senator and former Prefect of Praetorians who would know all that needed to be known about a fellow courtier, but took the hint and responded with legalistic deliberation.

"These are the duties of my secretary, gentlemen. But I will speak in his stead. As you well know, in the West my Latin designation is Lucius Flavius Arrianus Xenophon. I was born in the fifth year of Caesar Domitian's rule at Nicomedia to a noble Bithynian family. I was awarded Roman citizenship in the seventh year of Caesar Hadrian's rule at the age of thirty-eight, and appointed senator. I am the first Greek of Bithynian origin to be Consul at Rome.

I am currently researching the administrative procedures involved in governance of the province of Cappadocia at Roman Asia, where I am soon to be nominated its Prefect Governor. I need not add I am also a biographer of the military strategies of *Basileous Alexandros*; an adherent and compiler of the aphorisms of the philosophy of Epictetus of Nicopolis; and so on. But you already know these things."

The quality of his career and works silenced his auditors.

"You knew Antinous of Bithynia well, Senator?" Suetonius eventually asked.

"Of course. I know his family at Claudiopolis intimately, and was very fond of the lad. He showed great promise, I assure you. I would have offered the boy a role in my administration at Cappadocia had he lived. His father and elder brother are trading partners with my stewards," the senator outlined. "I've been an informal *patron* to the lad for the past five years. In fact, I am directly responsible for his entering into the company of Caesar. It was I who arranged the original introductions five years ago."

"What is your opinion of the manner of the young man's death, senator? Do you have information of its nature and likely causes?" Clarus queried. "Is there something you feel we should know?"

"No, Septicius Clarus and *Special Inspector* Suetonius. I am entirely without understanding of the manner or reason for his death. It's said he drowned in this mighty river we can hear behind us. Many do, you know," Arrian offered. "I am not aware of any malice of substance against the lad, and nor am I aware of any motive on his behalf to commit such an act."

Both Suetonius and Clarus could see they weren't getting very far with Arrian. Suetonius had an idea.

"My lord, yesterday when inspecting Antinous's apartments we came across a notepad with a message of some interest. It is written in archaic Greek, ancient Attic, and we'd appreciate if you, as a great scholar of Hellene antiquity, would check our translation into today's Greek. Our antique Greek is rusty," Suetonius uttered. He snapped his fingers impatiently while Strabon searched his basket for the tablets. The wooden blocks tied in cloth were lying at the bottom of his jumbled pile in the basket. He opened the wood-covered wax pages and offered the block to the senator.

Arrian peered at the inscription engraved in the wax.

"Yes, it's Attic, or an attempt at Attic. It's poetic after a fashion. Though why anyone other than someone like myself would wish to write in a five-hundred year old language is beyond comprehension. I do so under a scholar's duress; it's expected of me. This inscription is ---"

He ceased explaining as his eyes widened in astonishment.

"Where did you acquire this?" he asked sharply.

"It was lying on the floor of Antinous's apartment complex in this very city of tents yesterday evening," Suetonius stated plainly. "We retrieved it before someone else whisked it away. Do you agree it appears to be a boyish ditty written by Antinous or his chum Lysias? Do you recognize the hand-writing? And how do you translate its rhyme?"

"Yes, I recognize the hand-writing. Yes, indeed," the nobleman muttered as he regained his comportment. "A rough translation of the Attic might go something like this :

WHEN THE KING OF THE
LIONHEARTED
TOYS WITH HIS MAN CUB NO MORE,
IT'S TIME FOR THE LACKEY
TO RESTORE HIS OWN PRIDE.

It is written by someone with only rudimentary antique Greek, an amateur."

"You mean like Antinous or Lysias?" Clarus asked.

"No," Arrian replied, "they would do better than this. Probably someone for whom Greek is not their first language."

"Then you mean, perhaps, Thais the language tutor?" Suetonius explored.

"No," responded Arrian softly. "She is no *man cub lackey.*"

"Then you mean ---?" Suetonius trailed away, his wispy eyebrows rising in recognition of one particular possibility.

A heavy silence descended. It made Clarus distinctly uncomfortable.

Arrian suddenly whisked a napkin from his tunic belt. With a single swift movement he wiped across the surface of the wax. Suetonius and Strabon protested loudly. The stylus impression of the quatrain on the wax was smeared beyond recovery.

"I don't think you need retain this tablet, gentlemen. It's not within your commission," the senator blithely concluded.

"King of the Lionhearted? Man cub? Lackey?" Suetonius vented in provocative recollection. "What did the writer mean?"

"I think you should desist from speculation on that matter, Special Inspector," Arrian advised. "Devote yourself to more concrete issues. Such as *'where was Antinous on the night of his death'*, or *'what company did he keep on that day?'* You might be on safer ground on that path, gentlemen."

"In that case, my lord: Where do you think Antinous may have been on the night of his death, and do you know what company he kept?" Suetonius responded.

"Of the first I have no idea. The last I saw of the boy was through the early afternoon of the day before, but very briefly," Arrian confided. "He was on an odd mission. He came to these tents to retrieve his secured coins and treasures from my steward for some purpose.

My household provides safekeeping services to many people, including Antinous and Lysias. He secures his wealth in my steward's care because this encampment is an open invitation to thievery of one sort or another. I offer complete security to my *clients*, with full guarantee of capital and proper records. He retrieved a sum of cash and jewels and papers, my steward told me."

"To what degree, my lord," Suetonius enquired.

"My steward said he withdrew virtually his entire wealth in gold coins plus several select jewels and property deeds. It was a considerable treasure," Arrian stated.

"The value?" Suetonius queried furthered.

"If I recall correctly, fifty gold *aurei* and a similar amount of silver, plus elegant baubles worth a tidy sum. It was probably his entire liquid wealth, though he's also acquired two good properties at Nicomedia and Athens. Being Caesar's companion provides many opportunities for investment advice. I estimate his withdrawal was worth several hundred thousand *sesterces*, minimum, including the properties," Arrian concluded.

Surisca emitted a soft but audibly impressed gasp. Arrian ignored her, as Arrian did all women.

"How did he explain his withdrawal?" Clarus interjected.

"He didn't. He made no prior mention to me of the action, so my notary ensured a properly signed and witnessed record with identity seals of the transaction was registered.

Antinous took this sizeable purse away with him to attend to his business privately. I can only imagine his withdrawal was to buy some larger purchase, pay a debt in gambling, or provide gifting to some person unknown," Arrian offered. "However, upon learning of his death the following day, I too am keen to search for the reason for his drowning and the whereabouts of this treasure. I owe it to his family. I'm sure the second point will provide the answer to the first. Remember, Suetonius, the ancient jurist Cassius's great query: *Cui bono*, who benefits?"

"*Cui Bono?* It was Cicero's adage as well. This mystery deepens, Senator," Suetonius muttered. "Where is his treasure? Perhaps the treasure will lead us to a resolution of the death?"

"I don't believe he's gambled the treasure, he was not a gambler. And I don't think any fool would be unwise enough to extort money from Caesar's *Favorite*. Their wealth would be short lived."

"Then where is it?" Clarus repeated. "We have another unknown to add to our mystery."

Arrian reminisced a little.

"Antinous seemed a lusty enough fellow to my eye, healthily bent upon the earthier pleasures of life as well as giving satisfaction to his chosen partner. And you must understand, gentleman, the boy was neither a *cinaedus* nor a eunuch either, I can assure you. He enjoyed his pleasures."

"Were his habits *conventional*, would you say, Senator?" Suetonius pursued.

"Do you mean, was he sexually conventional? Was he a *vir*? I think I can vouch for his disposition, gentlemen. I have reason to know something of his tastes from observation."

"So, perhaps Antinous was the *King of the Lionhearted*?" Suetonius interjected dryly.

"Perhaps, Suetonius, perhaps. Yet I am content with the *Lionheart* who currently wears the imperial purple. There are very many of us, gentlemen, who'd be pleased to see Hadrian extend his rule and his life into the distant future," Arrian declared. "The Empire has rarely seen such a period of serenity."

"But what could Antinous do about it?" Clarus queried. "He was a mere toyboy, a source of pleasures."

Arrian frowned.

"Prior to the drowning the lad's role as Hadrian's *eromenos* had expired. It was over. And it must be seen to have ceased, by all. This is a public necessity for Caesar's sake to avoid the accusation of being a *cinaedus,* despite the residual affection the emperor has for the lad. He has brought great joy to Hadrian over the past five years, and I suppose this was reciprocal. But the days of his public display as consort are over.

So what does a young man who's been the recipient of such favor do with his life?

At Alexandria when the *Western Favorite* made his appearance from Rome, I suggested to Antinous I would enjoy him entering my own staff at Cappadocia. He was smart, capable, well educated, had good contacts, and was experienced in Court procedure. He read and wrote well in the two major languages, with a smattering of others. He'd seen a great deal of the Empire and its peoples, he knew what life is like for them.

He also knew too how to handle himself in elite society with aplomb. He even treated slaves and women respectfully. He was admired by the Court and by the military.

Yet his response to my offer was evasive. In fact he started talking of *finding his true destiny*, of *emulating Alexander*, of living according to *Achilles' short but glorious existence. I* began to wonder what nonsense had gotten into the lad."

"Had his head been turned by the new cults among us? Had Antinous fallen under the *Chrestus* spell?" Clarus queried.

"I doubt it, Clarus," Arrian calmed his senatorial colleague, "but his sudden separation from Hadrian may have triggered a personal crisis."

"Has there been some devious conspiracy to ensure the *Favorite* is 'retired' from Caesar's company for State reasons?" Suetonius queried provocatively. Arrian stiffened at the suggestion through clear cool eyes.

"My good man, Hadrian's choice of a successor is his own business. But it's fair to say there are many forces at work to steer him in preferred directions. A great deal is at stake. At this point in time Hadrian is all we have standing between a carefully chosen successor or the chaos of civil war when he dies. Rome has been down that bloody path before."

"Would the supporters of Senator Commodus, the *Western Favorite,* go to any lengths to entrench their candidate, Senator," Suetonius asked audaciously, "including eliminate the so-called *Eastern Favorite* from Caesar's companionship?"

"All things are possible, Special Inspector, all things," Arrian offered quietly. "But Commodus may have his own issues to contend with."

"Well, what do you make of that?"

Clarus, Suetonius, Strabon, and Surisca had retired to a viewing platform on a hillock above the river. Below them the broad expanse of molten waters flowed to the north and far away Memphis, with the metropolis of Alexandria even farther.

The four looked out over the streaming waters dotted with fishermen's coracles, light-loader boats, the local ferry *feluccas*, and small houseboats hired from towns and ports along the Nile's length to accommodate the tour's privileged travelers.

The high hulk of *The Dionysus*, Caesar's specially-crafted fabrication of two laced river biremes to provide a platform for a structure above, was moored offshore in deeper water. It provided apartments and entertainment space for the empress, Vibia Sabina's, retinue and her daily feasting soirees.

Anchored beyond *The Dionysus* to the north lay the Prefect Governor, Flavius Titianus's, river barque *The Alexandros*. Its elegant gilded timbers and ornately carved décors provided Titianus and his companion, Anna Perenna, suitably exalted accommodations but in an appropriately scaled down way. Despite its antique age *The Alexandros*, like *The Dionysus*, provided evidence of Rome's triumphant grandeur to awe Egypt's peasantry.

Roped to moorings alongside the larger craft were the runabout vessels of the tour, single-sail gondolas maintained by several Imperial agencies. Two had sails emblazoned with the scarlet eagle and wreath of the Imperial Household.

Another displayed the blood-red double-scorpion insignia of the Praetorian Guard.

A fourth displayed the Prefect Governor's cartouche of a golden Ptolemaic eight-pointed starburst, an insignia inherited from Cleopatra's Ptolemy forebears.

"Senator Arrian seemed ambivalent about Antinous's passing," Clarus offered. "I couldn't detect whether he was saddened or simply disinterested in the boy's death? Yet I'm told he was fond of the fellow."

"He told us enough, I think," Suetonius resolved. "But what did you think of the shrouded figure fleeing ahead of us when we arrived? And who was it, I wonder?"

"The woman with the pronounced perfume?" asked Clarus. "Who was she, do you think? A secret affair of the senator's? Someone's wife? Arrian does not travel with a wife."

"Who indeed?" Suetonius added, looking to Surisca. Surisca smiled enigmatically.

"May I speak?" she asked politely. Suetonius looked to Clarus, who nodded grudging approval.

"The perfume is known to me," she said, "it was a blend of oils of lavender and wild marjoram. This tells us something, my lords."

"You recognized the perfume, my dear? What does it tell us?" Suetonius charmed.

"It tells us the wearer was from Rome, my lords. I know the perfume well, as you might imagine. It is new, is highly prized, and very expensive. I've used it myself when I'm fortunate enough to be given a small gift of it by a wealthy admirer," Surisca revealed.

"Why does it tell us the wearer was Roman, Surisca?".

"Lavender blooms are only harvested near Massilia on the coast of Gaul, while the perfume's heads of wild marjoram are from Florentia north of Rome. Nowhere in the East produces these blooms in sufficient quantity to make perfume," Surisca explained, "it requires very great quantities of blooms. These two blooms are impregnated in oil, and then blended and have their scents fixed by a secret process. This is known only to an apothecary who owns a shop in the emporium arcade of Trajan's New Forum at Rome.

Trajan's arcade houses the Empire's leading dealers in fashion silks, jewels, and perfumes. This particular blend of scents is the apothecary's rarest product. Only the wealthiest, most fashionable people wear it."

"So, Surisca my dear, this woman was from Rome?" Suetonius enquired in a manner suggesting he already knew her likely response.

"I am not familiar with the Roman women at this encampment, master. But I do not need to because I am sure this was not a woman."

"Not a woman!?" Clarus lurched.

"No, my lords, the figure was the outline of a man," she clarified, "he was wearing a toga beneath the cape, and these days men of fashion wear strong perfumes too."

"*By Zeus*, who do we know at this godforsaken desert outpost who acquires products from Rome's leading emporia and wears a perfume which impacts the nostrils of those on the other side of a room?" Clarus asked rhetorically.

"Senator Lucius Ceionius Commodus!" several voices intoned together.

"So what was Commodus doing in Arrian's private chambers?" Suetonius added.

"Well, they weren't playing knucklebones," Clarus said. "Are Commodus and Arrian *intimate*? Did Arrian's boudoir debris tell us as much? But I thought Commodus was strictly Caesar's intimate friend? And a long term one at that. Perhaps that's why Arrian and Commodus weren't keen to be discovered together? Hadrian would be offended."

"Are we putting too grand an interpretation upon our intrusion?" Suetonius offered. "They may have been simply talking politics, trade, or of Caesar's mourning?"

"Or does Commodus aspire to fill Antinous's boots again?"

"My friend Septicius," Suetonius corrected him, "Commodus is now in his late-twenties. He is married at Rome to an equally noble *patrician* family with Imperial bloodlines. I am told his wife Avidia is currently pregnant with his child.".

"Yet what do we know about Commodus?" Clarus asked.

"Well, gossip tells he was Hadrian's lover at one time. Today he is a good looking fellow in his way. But in his late teens he was truly an elegant beauty, if somewhat feminine in his manner," Suetonius recalled from his days as Hadrian's secretary.

"He's also notorious for his sybaritic ways and love of luxury. I've heard he prefers to sleep amidst flower petals and Persian fragrances. It's said he holds extravagant dinner parties with inventive, if somewhat eccentric, dishes. He has a serving staff of very young boys with Cupid's wings attached to their shoulders to amuse his guests. He's irrepressible, if perhaps also irresponsible. His wife Avidia already complains about his sleeping around, which he justifies with his joke *Pray allow me my indulgence with others because 'wife' is a term of respect, my dear, not of pleasure.* Overall, he is a mixed bag of values."

"And this is the man Caesar wishes the Senate and the Legions to accept as his successor!" Clarus exclaimed.

"Strabon, I hope you recorded that quatrain which Arrian erased from your tablet," Suetonius interjected. "Please read it back to us again."

The scribe speedily rummaged through his wax tablets to retrieve the notepad recorded. He read aloud from his coded inscription.

"I've notated Arrian's reading of the translation as being –

> When the king of the lionhearted
> Toys with his man cub no more
> It is time for this lackey
> To return to .. no .. To restore
> his own pride."

"Fine, Strabon," Suetonius confirmed. "Tell me, gentlemen, who is *the king of the lionhearted* and who is the *man cub* or *lackey*? Identify who is doing the *toying*, and who is being *toyed with*? Who is this person who needs their pride restored? What hunter's game is being played here, my friends, and who precisely are the hunter and the hunted?"

CHAPTER 20

A tall slender woman swathed in fine silks with her shawl draped elegantly across her high-plaited hair to shade her against the midday sun trod gracefully in kidskin sandals from the riverside access jetty. She stepped with a securely confident gait up the sloping embankment path towards the waiting group of four.

She was accompanied a few paces behind by an officer of Caesar's Horse Guard acting as her protector in public places, with a slave holding a parasol high. All three had journeyed in an Imperial gondola from *The Dionysus* moored offshore nearby.

"Welcome, Lady Julia Balbilla of Commagene," Clarus intoned on her arrival. "You evidently received our message from Secretary Vestinus?"

The 30-ish year-old, fine-complexioned woman stepped beneath the shade of the lookout's enveloping sun umbrella and dipped a restrained curtsy. She drew back the veil from her face onto her shoulders to reveal unadorned features, clear skin, bright eyes, a piled hairstyle in the conservative aristocratic Roman matron's manner, and a confident but supremely polite manner.

"Greetings, Senator Gaius Septicius Clarus of Rome," she purred softly in purest Palatine Latin. "Gentlemen, in what way may I be of value to you, seeing you've requested my company?"

"My lady," Suetonius opened the interview, "we have been commissioned by Great Caesar to explore the circumstances of the death of his *Companion of the Hunt*, Antinous of Bithynia. We are instructed to determine the manner of the lad's death and by what path he came to it. We are hoping you can throw some light on the matter."

"Do you mean Caesar's *Companion of the Hunt*, Suetonius Tranquillus, or do you mean Caesar's *eromenos*? Or perhaps you really mean Caesar's *catamite*? Which definition suits you, Tranquillus?"

The elegant figure challenged the Special Inspector with a faintly deprecating, amused smile. Suetonius and Clarus choked.

"Caesar's *eromenos*, perhaps, my lady," Suetonius responded diplomatically.

"You need not be too polite in my company, gentlemen. I am not a delicate flower, easily crumpled. My Lady the *Augustus* and I have no illusions about Antinous and his allure to our imperial master. I'm told the fellow possessed definite enticements to very many at Court, though such attractions pass me by I'm afraid.

Yet we both certainly agree Antinous was a charming young man. Vibia Sabina and I enjoyed his conversation on many occasions, so we were very saddened to hear of his fate. He deserved better, we feel, despite being a foreigner diversion of no real consequence.

But I can see, Suetonius Tranquillus, you're still up to your old tricks. The past decade hasn't taught you much, has it, since your debacle with My Lady at Rome?"

"I don't know what you mean, madam," Suetonius lied as a bright flush swamped his features. Surisca took an enhanced interest in this dialog while Clarus shuffled his laced boots uncomfortably beneath his toga.

"All the ladies of court, Suetonius, were aware of your chauvinism, and probably still are. Even your wife or concubine, or whatever she was at the time, poor thing. *She was your second partner, wasn't she?* Did she leave you, like the first one?

But it was only when you decided to put your lechery to the test with Caesar's wife that the sky fell in, taking our good friend Septicius Clarus with you," the gentlewoman with the purebred accent and an almost imperceptible smile lobbed devastatingly.

Suetonius smarted.

"The entire Court knows how Caesar doesn't share his wife's bed, he far prefers the company of virile males," Balbilla continued unabated. "Perhaps the twelve year age difference when the *Augusta* was married to Hadrian impeded their marital relationship? We note, however, how a thirty year differential between the emperor and his *eromenos* doesn't induce similar consequences.

Yet this doesn't mean, Suetonius Tranquillus that menials therefore have license to be familiar with the *Augusta*. The empress wasn't then, and isn't now, in urgent need of a mercy fuck."

Gulping, Clarus interrupted this unexpected, escalating exchange. It was getting out of hand.

"Be that as it may, Julia Balbilla, we're here to explore other matters today. The death of Antinous, in fact.

We wish to take your legal statement of what you might know about the boy's death. We've reason to believe the lad engaged in sexual activities through the day he died, though we don't know where or with whom," Clarus explained. "We're trying to clarify the picture of how his death occurred and who might know something about it."

"Well, I can assure you, gentlemen, I have never been a recipient of the young man's attentions. Half the Court aspired to his charms, but I was not one of them," Balbilla teased. "Why don't you ask Caesar himself? Surely he knows what his young friend gets up to in his free time? Besides, hadn't he been preparing for it for weeks?"

Julia Balbilla's four auditors were smitten silent for several moments. Clarus dared revive the dialog.

"Madam, both the *Princeps* and likewise the *Augusta* are forbidden to us for interview. You know, *above our station*, and all that," Clarus explained. "So instead, we wish to take a deposition from you on these matters. We're obliged to report with our summary to Caesar before dawn tomorrow under pain of penalty."

"Why dawn tomorrow? Why specifically that date, the third day of The Isia? Is it to do with the summons everyone has received about tomorrow's dawn ceremony?" Balbilla queried.

"We do not know, m'lady. This was Caesar's instruction. I am sure he will have his motives," Suetonius reassured. "Shall we begin? Please state your names and titles, and then we'll follow questioning from there."

The lady smirked calmly at Suetonius in the standard-issue *patrician* dismissive mode.

"Who and what I am you know better than I do myself, Tranquillus," she announced. "Your books prove it so. Proclaim my pedigree to your satisfaction, and I'll respond to your questions if they suit my temper."

"Oh," Suetonius responded, somewhat fazed. "Scribe, record me now. This is an interview with Julia Balbilla Philopappus, the daughter of Antiochus Epiphanes, Prince of Commagene, and grand-daughter of Antiochus IV, King of Commagene. This was the same Antiochus who was once friend to Caesars Gaius Caligula and Claudius. On her mother's side she is a grand-daughter to Tiberius Claudius Balbillus 'The Wise' of Rome, advisor to Caesar Nero on matters astrological and spiritual.

From recall, m'lady was born at Rome in the third year of Caesar Trajan. At twenty-nine years of age she travels as a gentlewoman-companion under the protection of the empress, Julia Vibia Sabina *Augusta*. Mistress Balbilla is renowned among her peers as a poet and a master of classical languages, as well as a consultant on mystical issues."

"*Consultant on mystical issues?*" Clarus asked querulously. "Please explain to us this role, m'lady."

Balbilla sighed impatiently.

"*By Isis*, gentlemen, you already know more about my heritage than I understand myself, and you both know it! Tranquillus, you report in your scandalous diatribe *The Lives of the Caesars* details of my family's history which have sorely injured my reputation," the frank-and-forthright lady expounded censoriously. "You know precisely what I mean in this!"

"M'lady ---," the biographer stammered in escalating agitation. Balbilla was persistent in her withering regard of her present company.

"Don't be so obdurate, Suetonius Tranquillus. Your account of my grandfather's service to Caesar Nero in your scandal-sheets has implied many things about my heritage which people find distasteful."

"Such as, m'lady?" Suetonius uttered timorously.

"You will recall, Tranquillus, how you accused my grandfather, the astrologer Balbillus at Nero's Court, of colluding with that foolish emperor in some of his more cruel crimes?" she rebuked. "Your book on Nero's reign-of-terror reports how Balbillus acted cravenly in telling that erratic ruler how, when the omen of a comet appeared in the night sky over Rome, its warning of the death of great rulers such as Caesar could be diverted by the *substituted death* of lesser distinguished men.

Nero, you report, fearful for his own life because of my grandfather's prediction, viciously turned upon all the eminent men of the time. Nero invented the Piso and the Vinicius Conspiracies to justify killing all so-called conspirators, their wives, and even their children and slaves. But it was really done to confiscate their properties and wealth into his own profligate coffers.

Your book suggests my ancestor Balbillus was party to this grievous mischief. We of the line of Balbillus now carry this slander forever."

"But, my lady, these things are true. Your ancestor is recorded acting in this way. It's in the archives stored at the Palatine," the biographer pleaded. "He did indeed advise Nero in this manner, and the human cost to those brave critics of Nero's larceny was harrowing. Much blood flowed."

"Yet my grandfather too was a victim of Nero's malevolence, Tranquillus!"

Suetonius sparked up at this exchange. One feature became prominent.

"You remind me, my lady, how your ancestor advised Caesar that a *substituted death* could defer his mortality?" he reiterated.

"Yes, Tranquillus," she responded, irritated. "My pedigree is now burdened with this defamation for evermore."

"--- of how a *substituted death* could defer or deflect Nero's own fatality?" Suetonius repeated.

Balbilla nodded querulously at this repetition.

Suetonius, Clarus, Surisca, and Strabon looked towards each other. There was something of pertinence in Julia Balbilla's words, they each realized.

Suetonius shifted his line of questioning.

"Tell me, Julia Balbilla of Commagene, with whom have you discussed in recent times either my book on the *Life of Nero* or, more likely, the actions of your ancestor Balbillus in recommending the strategy of a *substituted victim*?" the biographer prodded. All eyes turned to the Commagene.

"Of a substituted victim? Oh, I recall it passed through a dinner-party conversation at the old Antirrhodos Palace of Cleopatra's at Alexandria some weeks ago.

I was telling the guests how I had visited The Soma with Hadrian and Antinous a few days earlier. We were a small party including the Governor and the priestess Anna Perenna, to view the ancient sarcophagus of Alexander the Great on display at The Soma. Caesar had ordered its lid to be removed so we could have a better inspection of the embalmed body within.

I suppose, considering Alexander *Divus* had been lying in his tomb for four hundred years, he was in fairly good shape. His flesh has darkened with age to a waxy dark gray, and he didn't look quite human to me. In fact I wondered if it was the real Alexander at all, these Egyptians can be so tricky in these things, can't they?

Governor Titianus told us how a century ago the accursed Caesar Caligula had stolen Alexander's breastplate and cloak from the sarcophagus because of their presumed magical properties. In the previous generation Caesar Augustus had accidentally knocked a piece off Alexander's nose, proving how even a *Divus*, the *godlike*, are corruptible like the rest of us.

Yet in the course of this recent visit both Hadrian and the lad were entranced by Alexander's survival after so long a time. We each asked if we too would still be enticing visitors in four hundred years time? Without that corpse as its core symbol, Alexandria would have come to nothing as a city.

While dining at Antirrhodos, this theme led to the fashionable subject of surviving death. It seems to be everywhere these days. Antinous was particularly fascinated. Not satisfied with the tale of Osiris being killed and re-assembled by Isis, or the story of Bacchus surviving death to be resurrected, and so on among others, Antinous regaled us with even newer tales.

The fellow was struck by the story put about by certain people at Alexandria. He seemed especially interested in fanciful tales of surviving death told by the followers of *Chrestus*, who are everywhere across the Empire these days.

Well, in the course of all this heady discussion Antinous and the woman Perenna began talking together to one side. I didn't catch the drift of it, but I think Titianus's consort impressed the lad with her reputation as a mystic-priestess and dream-reader of her antique Roman lineage.

At the dinner I reminded the Governor's consort of her earlier Soma visit, but she had the gall to claim she had no recollection of it at all. It irked her to remember it, it seems. I have no idea why she was so obstreperous about something so readily recalled by everyone else."

Julia Balbilla sat back to relax beneath the riverside lookout's shady parasol. The blinding white haze of an Egyptian noon seared one's sight.

"In what context did your ancestor's advice to Nero arise?" Clarus reminded the gentlewoman.

"*Of a substituted* death?" she reflected. "After discussing all these fashionable resurrection cults at dinner, I responded how the *Anna Perenna* form of resurrecting the dead seems far more plausible than the Eastern ones. At least you get to see the living result."

"What way is that?" the biographer queried.

"Well, each high priestess of the ancient cult of Anna Perenna, who is known as *the grandmother of time*, assumes the title and name of her predecessor, also named *Anna Perenna*. After all, 'Anna Perenna' means something like *the perennial year*, it's not a family name, is it? It's a priestess's rank, not a bloodline," she stated. "When the high priestess of the cult dies she *resurrects* as a new priestess, her former assistant priestess, who is now endowed with the same name. The *Grandmother of Time* becomes eternal, generation by generation, onwards into eternity. That's what I'm told. It's a very clever ruse."

"What happens to her original family name before being named *Anna Perenna* ?" Clarus enquired. "Does she deny her heredity and her family *gens*?"

"It's subsumed behind her cult one," Balbilla replied. "It's relinquished for the remainder of their lives. This particular priestess at Alexandria travels under the Prefect Governor's protection as his consort while Titianus's legal wife stews in Rome with his four children. Perenna even has a detachment of Praetorians to protect her.

But in discussing such 'resurrection', she grew irritable with me. This lady is quite strong willed. It was she who loudly reminded me of my grandfather's faux pas under Nero. She had read your book, Tranquillus, and knew the details."

"I see. You said earlier how Caesar *had been preparing for Antinous's death for weeks*. What did you mean by that?"

"I didn't say preparing for Antinous's death, but I did say he'd been preparing for *something* for weeks. Surely, gentlemen, you've been aware of the unusual activities going on around this Encampment?" Balbilla asked. "We at *The Dionysus* have been very aware of these activities ever since we moored here a week ago.

Governor Titianus and his architects have been busy surveying and measuring the landscape for many weeks now. Macedo's Praetorians have been running messages up and down the river at haste speed. Vestinus's couriers have been trotting to and fro with more-than-usual Empire correspondence, and teams of engineers, tradesmen, and builders have been assembled at a special camp just outside the nearby village. Something big is going on."

"What do you think Caesar has been preparing?" Suetonius furthered.

"I don't wish to spread gossip, but some around the Court report how Caesar was hugely impressed by that magician-priest Pachrates' killing of a condemned man, who was then magically *resurrected*. It gave him the idea of extending the same principle to this year's Isia," Balbilla revealed. Her voice had lowered to a confidential hush. "It's said how, because the annual Nile deluge has been so paltry for the second year in a row, he would sacrifice a condemned criminal into its waters to fulfill the people's expectation.

This appears to be the traditional solution to low flooding. The sacrificed man assuages the gods somehow; he is magically *resurrected* in their view to become Osiris Reborn on the third day of The Isia. This act guarantees next year's flood will be normal. Well, that's what they claim. It's all very convoluted, but these superstitious people have faith in it."

"My lady, seeing we're talking plainly, allow me to question you plainly," Suetonius roused himself. "Where do you think Antinous spent the day or night of his death?"

"Gentlemen, you appear to know as much as I do, and that's absolutely nothing. But if you want my advice, considering the preparations underway nearby, I'd suggest you talk with Governor Titianus. He knows everything worth knowing in this land.

Besides, Tranquillus, both the *Augusta* and I suspect the young man's death is too convenient by half. We'd say there's more to it than meets the eye."

CHAPTER 21

"Reporting as instructed, sir!"

Urbicus saluted the group of four. His Alexandrian Praetorian troop was approaching the riverside jetty giving access to *The Alexandros*. Suetonius, Clarus, Surisca, and Strabon were proceeding along the same pier.

"You requested my report by the highest sun, sir," he announced with a fumbling stammer. He seemed ill-prepared to meet the four.

"Greetings Centurion!" Clarus responded crisply. "Make your report."

"*Hail Caesar!* I and my men have searched for the river craft painted blue bearing the Eye of Horus and without sail markings, just as the fishermen who discovered the deceased described to us yesterday.

We have located such a vessel secured in slips by the river at an inlet close by the Temple of Amun near the Imperial Encampment. I am told on authority it is the only such boat on the river here. The temple is less than a *stadion* north of our protected stockade, surrounded by palm trees. You'd never know it was there it's so well concealed."

"Have you been able to establish whether this vessel was sailing the river at dawn on the day of Antinous's death, and who its sailor or sailors may have been?" Suetonius queried.

"This was difficult, sirs, as our enquiry would have raised suspicion among the chief priests of the temple. But yes, we apprehended a worker-priest attached to the temple who was performing manual work in the vicinity of the docked vessel. We persuaded the man to join our company so we could question him in private," the officer announced in crisply-articulated soldier-speak.

"Question him? You mean you abducted the fellow, put him to the sword, pressured him, and probably threatened him to some degree?" Suetonius asked genially, if apprehensively.

"Indeed this might be so, Special Inspector," the Praetorian confirmed with no hint of irony. "The fellow resisted and claimed he knew of no such voyage. But he was eventually amenable to persuasion and revealed what we wished to know."

"Amenable? So what was revealed?" Suetonius queried. He was alarmed at the Guard's impetuosity in dealing with a workman, priest, or slave under some other institution's protection.

"He told us the master of the Temple, a priest of Amun named *Panchrates* or *Pachrates of Memphis*, had been sailing the river at the appointed time in this vessel accompanied by an acolyte," Urbicus concluded. The Praetorian officer fell silent, displaying visible satisfaction.

"Pachrates?!" both Clarus and Suetonius exclaimed. "But why? What was he doing on the river at that time, Centurion?"

"Well," the Praetorian offered as an information coup-de-grace, "the slave told us he'd heard gossip how *Panchrates* had ritually sacrificed the youth Antinous in a magical rite to invoke health, and was delivering the corpse upstream to be discovered in the river at dawn. Perhaps this is why the youth's left wrist had been slashed when he was found by the fishermen, and why he was attired in his formal parade armors."

The group of four was astonished. At last a breakthrough!.

"But why would the priest Pachrates slay the Bithynian? What profit is there in this to an Egyptian priest? Especially a Bithynian who was Caesar's Favorite?" Clarus demanded. He was entering his legalist's temper of *cui bono?*

Urbicus replied carefully.

"The temple slave did not know these things, my lords, he was a lowly laborer, but he'd heard it said it was to allay *Pharaoh*'s concerns about correcting the low flooding of the Nile," the Praetorian stated. "It was a public gesture for this year's Festival of Isis."

"Where is this slave informant now, Urbicus?" Suetonius demanded. "We must keep him isolated and protected until we can authenticate this story. These are sensitive claims you make, and this workman is our only witness to such charges."

"This is not possible, sir," Urbicus offered with a lowered voice. "The slave expired under our exactions. We may have overdone the persuasion a little, sir. He bled liberally under the duress. So we tossed his carcass into the river to appear to be a drowning accident too. It seems Osiris will have two claimants to resurrection this Isia." Urbicus was engaging in droll Praetorian wit.

"Separately, Special Inspector," he continued, "we've been searching for your interviewees Lysias of Bithynia and the freedwoman Thais of Cyrene. They too have gone missing, despite your demands they attend your interview today. We searched for them last night at their tents. They could not be found anywhere.

However, we did find the mutilated corpse of their senior steward, a Judaean freedman from Bithynia. He'd been decapitated in a similar manner to the fisherman from Besa. But we couldn't locate either the offenders or the two young people in the vicinity."

It was Suetonius's turn to feel discomfort at these revelations.

"You didn't mention this incident earlier this morning when you delivered the head of the fisherman Ani to our breakfast table?" he enquired. "Nor mention another decapitation. Had you forgotten such a grisly discovery?"

Urbicus shuffled momentarily with unease but did not lose his verbal stride.

"No, my lord, I had not forgotten. It was simply that the fisherman Ani's murder and return of his head to his family, as well as the search for the river craft, had a higher priority in your instruction. Were we being negligent, sir?" the officer offered with an air of impervious innocence.

Suetonius was now beginning to feel even greater discomfort. Looking to Clarus for confirmation, the biographer was coming to appreciate how the death of the Bithynian youth seemed to provoke increasingly violent, yet inexplicable, responses from unknown forces.

He recollected the lad's drowning had induced two beheadings, one death by over-zealous torture, three disappearances, plus a glut of conspiracy theories to complicate the basic search for a motive. As the hours towards the appointment with Hadrian raced by, the number of issues multiplied, not declined. A further query arose in his mind.

"Tell me Centurion, how did you manage to find us here at *The Alexandros* jetty?"

Urbicus expressed surprise at the question. He hesitated before responding.

"Why, my lord," he uttered with obvious sincerity, "we had been searching for your party in the vicinity of Senator Arrian's chambers to make our report, but then spied you and your colleagues at this river landing from a distance. It was accidental. But having reported, we request we receive your further instructions."

The guardsman from Alexandria was collectedly cool in his response. Suetonius wondered if he was perhaps too cool, and his eyes turned to Surisca for a shared opinion. Clarus interrupted.

"Yes, Praetorian," Clarus declaimed, "this is our instruction. We must urgently locate the two friends of Antinous, Lysias and the girl Thais, before anyone else apprehends them and does them harm. Continue your search for the couple. Assign further troops to the search if necessary through Tribune Macedo. Do whatever is necessary to secure their safety! Certainly let there be no *accidents* with the couple, we don't wish to lose further sources of testimony."

"It will be done, sir," Urbicus confirmed. He snapped to attention as his troop swept their helmets to their heads in unison, saluted in military style, and marched off.

"Strabon, did you record the past few minute's conversation?" Suetonius enquired.

"Indeed I have, Special Inspector," the scribe responded.

"Good. Keep those tablets close in a safe place. Something is amiss here, gentlemen," Suetonius confided insecurely, "and I'm not at all sure what it is. Any thoughts, anybody?"

He cast his eyes over his trio of companions. Surisca cautiously raised a finger.

"Speak, my dear," the biographer prompted. Surisca spoke hesitantly.

"Master, forgive my impertinence, but when the centurion and his soldiers were approaching I had the definite feeling it was not My Masters they were coming to visit. To my eye, it was this jetty to the barque they were approaching," she offered, "not the enjoyment of your company."

"To this jetty?" Clarus enquired with a hint of exasperation. "Meaning what especially, woman?"

"I sensed, sir, they were at this wharf to travel to where you yourselves are travelling, not to report to your lordships, as they claim. They were on their way to that mighty vessel offshore."

"I felt the same, my lords," Strabon added to Surisca's comments. "I sensed they were surprised to come across us at this place. The centurion had not really expected to meet us here."

"You mean they were on their way to visit the Prefect Governor aboard *The Alexandros*, not talk with us as they claimed?" Clarus rationalized.

"Except, my good Clarus," Suetonius intruded, "the centurion pointedly told us it was our company he was seeking, not the governor's. We have another contradiction to contend with. Yet instead of such mere speculation, my friends, let's pay the good governor a visit ourselves to find out."

The main deck of *The Alexandros* was an open area shaded under a filmy canopy emblazoned with the Alexandrine starburst. It provided space for entertainments, feasts, ceremonies, or juridical occasions.

The barque's decoration was an elaborate fantasy of carved timbers inset with honey-hued porthole windows of thin alabaster. A riot of sculpted figures depicting the victories of Alexander over his enemies graced its exterior. Similar to its larger companion *The Dionysus*, the governor's barque was a visible demonstration of the opulence and power of Rome to her provincial Egyptian subjects.

The Prefect Governor was seated upon his chair-of-state on a rostrum under the midday glare diffused by the canopy. Flavius Titianus was attended by several staff, guards, a scribe at a lectern desk, and young pages. They were engaged in business when Titianus spied his visitors awaiting his attention. He rose from his seat and dismissed all his attendants except one.

"Come forward, gentlemen!" he called aloud to his visitors. "Make yourself known!"

Suetonius, Clarus, Strabon, and a hesitant Surisca approached the throne. Suetonius coaxed the Syri to follow close behind him despite her non-status as a non-person.

"Greetings, Prefect Governor," Clarus responded. "We salute you. *Hail Caesar!*"

"Senator Clarus and Suetonius Tranquillus, *all hail!*" was the reply.

Titianus was in his early forties, short of stature, thickset, and of sturdy farmer stock in the classic Roman soldierly way. He exuded the prim but efficient air of a practical man who gets things done. Titianus had the emperor's complete confidence in his management of the Empire's most important province, Egypt. The African colonies are Rome's bread basket.

Titianus has the obligation of ensuring an inexhaustible supply of grain to Rome. He must also secure from pirates the Red Sea trade with Nabataea, Arabia Felix, India and the farther mysterious Orient. A further priority is to encourage the capture of wild animals from beyond the distant lands of Kush and Punt in the African hinterland for the Empire's blood-sports arenas. Overall, Hadrian's governor had forbidding responsibilities. Not least among these were the strict control of the various ethnic, class, and religious rivalries which repeatedly threatened to explode across his jurisdiction and jeopardize these chores.

"What brings you to my office, gentlemen? And without an appointment," Titianus asked in the abrupt manner of a military man. He gathered his toga's folds and re-seated himself upon his throne of office, waving to his visitors to take their seat in the elegant chairs arranged before him.

Clarus rose to address the governor.

"Prefect Governor, we come on Caesar's instruction. We have been commissioned by Caesar to investigate the recent death of the Companion of the Hunt, Antinous of Bithynia," Clarus announced grandly while holding the slender ivory-spined scroll high as his authority. "We are charged to complete our investigation by dawn tomorrow and report our findings to Caesar. We are here to enquire your views of the boy's death and seek any relevant information you or your officers may possess about the manner of his death."

Titianus sat immobile for a few moments contemplating this presentation. He stared at Clarus with an unwaveringly searching eye.

"Well, you'd better get underway, hadn't you? Tomorrow's dawn is about eighteen hours away. Ask of me what you will, gentlemen. I will respond appropriately," he stated flatly.

"We're to take notation of your views and testimony, my lord. Our scribe is to record our interviews for Caesar's information, and so requires a preceding statement of your titles and honors, Prefect Governor."

Titianus rested back in his high chair as a tired, impatient expression cast across his features. It was evident the governor was not especially interested in this intrusion upon his day's chores, and the sooner it was over the better. He began sharply.

"I do not announce my titles to my inferiors, Senator Septicius Clarus, I have a secretary for that purpose. He'll give you the details. Let's get on with it."

Titianus waved to the secretary to perform. The Greek took the hint and proclaimed loudly to Strabon..

"Scribe, take note. This is the testimony of His Excellency Titus Flavius Titianus, Caesar's appointed Prefect Governor of the Imperial province of Upper and Lower Egypt. His Excellency has served Great Caesar in Roman Asia, Gaul, and Rome itself since the time of his succession. He is married to a wife resident at Rome, and has four children by her."

Titianus waved impatiently to his secretary to cease and leave-out out the long list of titles and honors which usually followed. He waited impatiently for an interview question.

"What is your understanding of the nature of the death of the youth Antinous?" Suetonius asked.

Titianus shifted peevishly on his throne.

"Special Inspector, all I can surmise is that the lad fell overboard after a drunken revel, or suchlike. I have no idea what may have transpired with the fellow," he offered brusquely.

"Do you possess any knowledge about the young man's movements on the day of his death, the first day of the Festival of Isis, or what company he may have kept?"

"No, I do not.".

"We have received the impression he may have had at least one sexual assignation on the day of his death with a person or persons unknown. Are you aware of his activities on that day which may interest us, or know of such persons?" the biographer queried.

"Gentlemen, I am the governor of this province. I do not bother myself with the sexual exploits or peccadilloes of my subjects, let alone passing tourists to this land. These are not affairs of substance to me. Let's move on," Titianus concluded dismissively.

Suetonius was not deterred.

"We have been told, my lord, how you and your companion, the lady Anna Perenna, had shared some time with the Bithynian in recent times?" the Special Inspector continued. "Perhaps you possess observations of the character of the deceased which might reflect upon our investigations and provide insight into his death?"

Titianus responded warily.

"Firstly, my involvement with Caesar's Favorite has been transient and nominal; I do not share the society of Companions of the Hunt or Caesar's intimates unless the Imperial couple is attending or there's a State significance.

Secondly, the Lady Anna Perenna is no business of your enquiry, gentlemen. This woman is my *client* and my companion who is under my protection, that's all. She possesses no value to your endeavors. May we please wind up this fishing expedition for scandals, I have other business to attend."

Suetonius decided he needed a change of tack to engage the governor's greater interest and explore certain areas of enquiry.

"My lord, is it possible that Antinous of Bithynia shared private time with your ward and companion?" Suetonius asked with just the barest hint of provocation.

Clarus looked to his Special Inspector in cool dismay; he could not recall such a possibility being aired in any testimony provided thus far. Titianus was startled by the question. It had an unsubtle implication.

"Special Inspector Gaius Suetonius Tranquillus, the affairs of those under the protection of my household are no concern to you. My good lady, the priestess Anna Perenna, is within the oversight of myself and my staff at all times," he stated with clear precision. "My ward and companion has met the youth Antinous on only a handful of occasions, each occasion being in my own company or in the company of those I appoint to protect her.

I assure you, the lady has had little opportunity to enjoy the pleasant society of young men like Antinous in private, if this is your suggestion. I suggest you reconsider your line of questioning."

"Who do you appoint to protect the lady, my lord Governor?" Suetonius probed further.

"This too is no matter of yours, Tranquillus. I appoint reliable officers of my Guard to such duties. In fact, the Lady Perenna has a permanent bodyguard corps assigned to her protection under a senior officer of indisputable regard," the governor proclaimed.

"Who is this officer, my lord Governor?" the Special Inspector queried.

"Why, the officer in charge of her security corps is an Alexandrian centurion I hold in high esteem who shows great promise for the future. He is an achievement-oriented leader of men, an unusual quality in recruits from the African colonies, and he takes initiative well," Titianus explained.

"What is his name?" Suetonius searched further.

"Centurion Quintus Urbicus of Numidia. He's been with my Alexandrian Praetorians for two years now," the governor stated.

The team of four emitted a faint sigh of recognition.

"Are you aware, my lord Governor, that Centurion Quintus Urbicus has been assigned to support our investigations into the death of Antinous?" Clarus interjected.

"No, I am not, Senator. But such things are possible for a short period without my direct attention. My staff is very efficient. When was he assigned?" Titianus queried.

"I would have thought you might be across such an assignment?" Suetonius commented. "He was assigned yesterday on Tribune Macedo's orders. Are you also aware that Quintus Urbicus was one of those nearby to haul the Bithynian's body from the river's water when two Egyptian fishermen discovered the drowned youth at dawn yesterday?"

"No, of that too I am not aware. Yet such coincidences do happen, gentlemen. Someone had to find the body eventually. Urbicus's assignment to you will be quite legitimate. He's an effective officer, and his command of the local customs and tongues is probably useful to you, yes?" Titianus rationalized.

"Indeed. Prior to his assignment to us yesterday, what would Centurion Urbicus and his troops have been doing in the vicinity of the drowned youth by the riverside at earliest dawn?" the Special Inspector raised speculatively. At last Titianus appeared to be showing greater interest in the group's enquiries.

"I have absolutely no idea, Suetonius. You should be asking Urbicus, not me. The previous night I attended a formal banquet at Hadrian's apartments celebrating The Isia. Caesar has reason to honor the festival this year. There were many at the banquet, including new guests to Caesar's tour, but it didn't include the youth Antinous as I recall," the governor reminisced. "Hadrian's candidate for possible adoption as his son, Senator Lucius Ceionius Commodus, was the guest of honor. It seems the adoption will be proceeding sometime soon, despite great resistance to it in some quarters. It puts Lucius on the path to nailing the succession, they say, should Caesar pass away suddenly, perish the thought.

Also, I'm told there's bad blood between him and Antinous, so perhaps the Bithynian lad diplomatically stayed away? But by dawn I was still fast asleep on my banquet couch. Too much roast pork and Falernian, I'd say, plus other amusements."

"Did the Lady Anna Perenna celebrate with you too?" Suetonius probed.

"No, it was a men-only affair of course," Titianus explained. "Besides My Lady has her own rites to address. The three days of the death and resurrection of Osiris are sacred to her cult too. The influence of Isis is ubiquitous across the Empire these days. The two cults are very similar, I'm told.

My companion, the priestess, has enclosed herself for the first three days of The Isia. I doubt I shall see her until the official mourning period is over and the feasting begins."

"My lord, what did you mean *Caesar has reason to honor the occasion?*" the biographer continued his queries.

Titianus moved forward in his throne as though to share a confidence. He spoke low.

"I suppose, gentlemen, you are sufficiently senior to receive the following news, if you promise me absolute confidentiality. Caesar and I have spent months preparing our announcement of the foundation of a new metropolis in Middle Egypt. It's been a secret, if such elaborate plans can ever be kept secret.

At last I've persuaded Hadrian how central Egypt needs an influx of Roman and Greek settlers to act as a barrier against future incursions by rebels, invaders, or a local uprising. The old cities of Memphis, Hermopolis, and Thebes are stocked mainly with indigenous Egyptians because the previous Ptolemy regime allowed the Hellene population to be nominal outside Alexandria.

But these Egyptians are not a fighting people, as we rudely learned fifteen years ago when the Jewish community rose across Africa against Trajan under their pretender-*messiah* king, Lucuas. These rebels destroyed many of our temples and killed huge numbers until Turbo finally put them down.

So now we need sturdy, discharged legionnaires to colonize the area and repopulate it with families of new blood. Roman and Greek blood, that is, in a new city. They are to be a buffer here so insurrection will not succeed again. We will allocate substantial gifts of land, seed, and money at this place to make it happen, despite so many others across the Empire making claims to Rome's priorities.

The new city will require a huge investment of manpower and moneys. Caesar will persuade the Senate to appropriate the necessary wealth and arms, and Rome's leading financiers will support its construction. But at the end of the day it will require the new settlers to be cohesively unified for the plan to provide its defensive bulwark. Cohesion is essential."

"What will the city be called?" Clarus asked.

"In Caesar's honor and to encourage cohesion, I have recommended *Hadrianopolis*," the governor declared. "This might be why Caesar is so engrossed. It will carry his name into history."

Suetonius was prompted to remember a detail which troubled him the previous evening at the priest Kenamun's riverside embalming pavilion.

"My lord, last night we met a citizen of Greek blood from the Fayum Oasis who is a painter of portraits for funerals. He is a sculptor too. His name is Cronon, and he told us he'd been invited to this encampment many weeks ago," Suetonius posed, "well prior to the Bithynian's drowning. Would such a tradesman be summoned to attend your announcement?"

"Indeed," the governor affirmed, "my staff has assembled many, many artisans for Caesar's announcement, to discuss the planning of the new city. They've been sheltered at a camp site outside the nearby village and told not to talk of it."

"Then it's plausible after all that Cronon could have been invited to this camp by the Priest of Amun, Pachrates from Memphis, well prior to The Isia and Antinous's death?"

"Yes, that's possible," the Governor acknowledged.

Suetonius and Clarus now had reason to accept Kenamun's protestations on the previous evening. Titianus continued.

"But the priest Pachrates is an ambitious fellow, my friends. His like are very cunning. And he's found favor in Hadrian's eyes.

Pachrates understands the peculiarities of the Roman, Greek, and the Egyptian views of life, and so offers advice on how to implement our plans among each community. I'm told the dead youth was especially impressed by Pachrates' magical arts," Titianus confirmed. "So the wizard's input and contacts have been welcomed by Caesar. But for my money that priest is too clever by half. He's not a man to trust."

"We've been told Pachrates is known to commit murder for his magic," Suetonius proposed daringly.

The Governor fell silent for some moments. He drew himself back into his chair.

"He's been authorized by my office on rare occasions to utilize condemned criminals destined for a fate in the arena in his magical performances. But I'm not aware of any claim of the murder of innocents. The man is devious, but so are most in the East. It's in the air here," Titianus offered.

"Was Antinous out of favor with Caesar, my lord?" Suetonius asked, shifting tack. Titianus was cautious for a few moments. The four sensed the question had entered sensitive territory.

"There appears to have been some form of fallout some weeks ago at Alexandria when the *Western Favorite* joined the tour. As you know, Commodus was popular with Caesar some years ago. But I've not discerned a dispute between Hadrian and Antinous about the matter. Yet the lad had his own issues to contend with," the governor submitted.

"What are those, my lord Governor?"

"Well, to start with, after five years attachment to Hadrian he's now no longer a *meirakion* young man anymore. He's too old now for a role as Caesar's consort. It's too open to scandal, even here in the East where such things are widely tolerated," the governor speculated. "Note I separate the man Hadrian from the role of Caesar. The man is entitled; an emperor is not.

I was with them both at the time when Caesar expressed this view pointedly to the lad. It was at The Soma in Alexandria only a month or so ago."

"What was this occasion, my lord?" Suetonius enquired as all ears pricked up.

"Hadrian and several of his retinue, including Antinous, visited The Soma on two or three occasions. The Soma, Alexander the Great's tomb, is a pivotal institution at Alexandria. It's the city's *raison d'etre*, from a spiritual point of view. Not only do tourists from across the Empire visit and pay homage to the ancient hero, his tomb unifies the contending communities of the city into a single ethos, otherwise they'd be at each other's throats interminably.

All great cities have a key icon giving them their meaning; like a tomb or temple or hard-fought citadel. It's no accident the regime of the Ptolemies guaranteed the security of The Soma for over three hundred years," Titianus expounded. "Well, a member of Hadrian's retinue suggested the mausoleum and Alexander be moved to the new city. The notion was to provide a logical focus for creating the new *Hadrianopolis*, correlating the heroic virtues of Caesar and Alexander under one rubric.

It's a good idea, though I'd never allow Alexander's corpse to leave Alexandria. Yet it would encourage tourism to the new city and attract immigrants drawn to the Roman way of life. *Hadrianopolis* will need such a draw-card in this godforsaken place, otherwise it will become another dead city lost beneath Egyptian sands. There are dozens already."

"But how did this effect Hadrian's attitude to Antinous?" the biographer asked.

"Well, Hadrian is an avid admirer of Alexander, as too is Antinous. We agreed Egypt needs the sort of public spectacles the Ptolemy Greeks once provided to give the various communities a sense of being unified. You know, grand public gardens, magnificent temples, spectacular tombs, rites like *The Ptolemaia* festival, plus the hippodrome's races and games, and so on. At Alexandria all these attractions were held together by that single cadaver whose shadow we discern through the alabaster of his sarcophagus," the Prefect explained. "Otherwise it becomes Roman against Greek, Greek against Jew, Jew against Christian, free against slave, rich against poor, and all of them against the Egyptian natives.

Instead, Antinous inventively suggested how a *Caesareum* honoring the Caesars at the new city of *Hadrianopolis*, not Alexander's coveted body, would better fulfill the role. But he added it be accompanied by generous Imperial bequests, games, statues, commemorative coins, and cultic events, all with their emphasis on Hadrian as Caesar as the focus.

Hadrian was encouraged by the idea, it took his fancy, and the group applauded the lad's enthusiasms. But then Caesar shifted the conversation into a darker terrain. He took this cheerful opportunity to tell the young man loudly before us how their continuing relationship must cease. He put it very plainly to him. He said how a Caesar who befits the values of a Caesareum at Hadrianopolis must display public probity in all things, including his consorts.

He explained how worshipers at a Caesareum must know their Caesar is worthy of their adoration. Such a Caesar must relinquish any relationship with a partner who is no longer beardless. He terminated the relationship then and there before our eyes. Antinous was stunned by the announcement and quite visibly distressed."

Titianus paused to recollect the day. The four listened patiently.

"I'm sure the lad wasn't concerned about his future prospects because I've reason to know how he'd accumulated wealth far beyond a youth's needs, and was considered a prime candidate for posts in the cavalry or administration corps," the Governor expanded. "No, his concern seemed otherwise. Some have insinuated to me Hadrian had become uncomfortable about aspects of their relationship, though no one tells me what they are. Even my spies and paid informers don't know.

Meanwhile, it was evident Antinous was slipping into a state of disquiet. I didn't know the lad especially well, but I could see he was troubled by his predicament."

"What do you think that predicament was, my lord?" Suetonius asked. Titianus thoughtfully considered his response for a moment.

"Well one explanation, the simplest explanation I'd say, is Antinous was in love with Hadrian and reluctant to let go," he stated flatly. "It's that simple. He didn't wish to be parted from his lover. People can be like that, you know."

"Love?!" Clarus interjected, beginning to hear the language of a *cinaedus*. "Love! A young man barely beyond an *ephebe*'s age loves a man now in his fifties? That is bizarre, Prefect Governor. What is such a pitiable love?"

"Yes, my good senator, Love. That sad, tragic affliction of Aphrodite or her son Eros. It happens to many of us, you know? It's unpredictable," the Governor confirmed. "Haven't you felt Aphrodite's call at some time in your life, Septicius Clarus, '*the stream of longing*' with someone, somewhere, somehow?"

Clarus sat in resolute silence.

"Another interpretation even more controversial. It is our Caesar is in love with the lad," the Governor continued, "and Antinous was conscious of this reality and the necessary impending conclusion. This too offers an explanation, though I wouldn't promote it too loudly if I was you. And you might leave that comment out of your transcript, scribe."

The Governor smiled thinly at his guests.

"My assessment of Antinous was that he too had become aware of this conundrum and was drawn to seeking a resolution on behalf of his *erastes*, Hadrian," he continued. "Despite his widely-perceived role as merely a pretty face in a well-hung body, Antinous struck me as having greater depth. 'It's what you *do* in life which matters, not merely how you *look*', I heard him say onetime. That's not bad.

His search for a resolution to his *erastes'* dilemma was his ambitious, youthful, hero's quest. Perhaps he saw himself following in the footsteps of a Ulysses or Jason or Achilles, or even Alexander? But I doubt he found his resolutions before events overtook him, whatever they were."

"Is it possible, my lord Governor, you would have informer's reports of the young Bithynian's exploits outside his relationship with Caesar? Surely your contacts at Court have followed the lad's activities and made his alliances known to you?" Suetonius enquired.

"Believe it or not, gentlemen, I have multiple reports and colorful tidbits about everyone attending Caesar, including yourselves may I say, but nil regarding Antinous. The young man's faithfulness to Caesar seems exemplary. I cannot recall a single informer's report or piece of choice gossip pertaining to the man which suggests otherwise," Titianus replied. "Only my *ward*, the Lady Anna Perenna, seemed to find the fellow of some concern."

"Why so, Governor?"

"My companion possesses many unusual gifts, gentlemen," he responded. "She sees and knows things others cannot discern. Or so she tells me. As the high priestess of her cult at Alexandria she engages in all manner of arcane activities and provides esoteric advice to members of the Court."

"How so? In what way?"

"Well, I don't subscribe to some of her claims myself," the Governor explained, "my relationship with my lady is based on other needs, I assure you. Yet she provides charms and talismans to assist in the love lives of our courtiers; she prepares love-potions, philters, tinctures in oil, and occult tisanes. She creates figurines for *daemonic* invocation to dispel undesirable influences; she can calculate the power of words through the science of *geometria*; and she's expert in addressing women's matters of a private nature. At least so I'm told by her herself.

In her calling as the *Grandmother of Time* it's said she's skilled in interpreting the will of the gods through the divination of entrails in the Etruscan manner. She interprets dreams, and most arcane of all, she is said to engage through trance as a medium of clairvoyance. At least so I am told. My companion is a woman of unusual capacities, gentlemen. Naturally, she is also a lively bed companion."

"Prefect Governor, perhaps your good lady friend will share her clairvoyance skills in telling us what may have happened to the dead youth?" the biographer enquired sweetly.

The governor cast a steely look over the biographer.

"Don't be fast with me, Special Inspector. I don't necessarily support each of my companion's claims to *mystagogy*. But if you wish to explore her faculties for yourself, then you should approach her personally.

Anna Perenna is an independent woman who possesses her own wealth and is not subject to my will."

Titianus fell moodily, angrily silent. Clarus took the opportunity to enquire about the night of the boy's death.

"Lord Prefect Governor, you said you slept the night in question at Caesar's marquee after the banquet. Did you share company in this?" he asked in his usual unsubtle manner.

"My good Senator Septicius Clarus, don't you trust the Governor of Egypt? Several of those at the celebration were sufficiently persuaded after the banquet to remain at our couches, excess wine or not," Titianus regaled. "Mine was the wine plus an Iberian serving-lass named Sotira. Others made other choices."

"Who else remained accompanied in this manner, or departed accompanied?" Suetonius pressed the questioning further.

"Why, I wasn't especially observant of what others were up to, Tranquillus. But that up-and-coming Tribune Macedo seemed to have his hooks into a pert young girl, a local of Egyptian descent I think, while the former Master of the Hunt Salvius Julianus, who is now an important legal advisor to Caesar, was accompanied by his usual equerry friend."

"What of Caesar himself and the guest-of-honor Commodus?" Clarus explored.

"Caesar retired alone, as has been his usual habit since this tour began. Commodus and he do not share a bed these days, to the knowledge of my agents," the spymaster knower-of-all confided. "Commodus retired late about the same time as Caesar's friend Arrian. Put whatever spin you wish upon that, my friends. But I had my Sotira to amuse me, so I was comfortable where I was."

"And where was Antinous, do you suppose?" Suetonius asked.

"Perhaps he was down in his cups drowning his misfortunes, if you forgive the bad pun," the stocky Roman contributed. "The last I saw of him was some days earlier when he was consulting with my companion, Anna Perenna, on matters of *advice for the lovelorn*. At least that's what I assume they were discussing.

Perhaps my lady was invoking some potion or magician's effigy with special powers for him to attract Caesar's attentions again? You'll have to ask her yourself, my friends. She knew the lad far better than I. She can be found on this very vessel at the stern cabin.

Go knock at her door, gentlemen. I must now bid you farewell."

CHAPTER 22

After a long pause a husky female voice responded from behind the locked portal.

"Tell them to be gone, girl! I'm engaged in sacred rites," the voice firmly instructed her servant from within the cabin.

Clarus would have none of this.

"Lady Anna Perenna of Alexandria, your visitors attend you on command of Great Caesar!" he bellowed. "We are on Imperial business and demand your immediate presence! We possess Imperial authority and the right to enforce it!"

Again a few moments elapsed before the group of four and the serving girl heard the bolts and braces of the cabin door being shunted open. The gilded carvings of the portal widened marginally to reveal a shadowy interior whose darkness at midday was illumed with a few lamps or tapers.

A billow of air steeped in expensive Arabian frankincense wafted through the portal from within the gloom. Fine streams of daylight pierced the vessel's timbers as suspended dust particles shimmered sinuously through the pall.

"Enter!" the woman's voice commanded gruffly. The serving girl pushed the door wider to permit entry to the visitors.

When the four came to rest a few steps within the cabin's gloom their eyes settled on the solitary figure standing aloof before them. Amid the velvety glow of oil-lamps and an amber radiance emitted by thin alabaster portholes diffusing the afternoon's external blaze, the Special Inspector's group found itself in the presence of a tall, slender, dark skinned, dark haired female of a strikingly grave countenance.

Her ebony black pupils pierced the gloom from behind a face lacquered in an opaque mask of white pastes in the fashionable Palatine style. Her lips were painted with cosmetic oil the color of drab clotted blood. Carefully applied outlines in *kohl* eyeliner highlighted her eyes in the manner worn by the upper-classes at Egypt, with scarlet dots and edgings to augment the impact elaborately.

Suetonius perceived on closer scrutiny how the generous coat of face paint was also a camouflage aiming to conceal significant skin lacerations or the eruptions of a defunct pox beneath the ashen patina.

Poxes are egalitarian in their impact on both the *plebs* and the elites of the Empire, at least among those who had survived their vicissitudes in youth, Suetonius recalled. Poxes and leprosies were a cautionary sight, possibly intimating a risk of the presence of some vile contagion.

Anna Perenna's hair was carefully wound and woven into a high mound of elaborate whorls giving the woman an even greater sense of height, while her plain silken tunic was cross-tied and belted with silk cords announcing her to be of Latin rather than of Greek or Egyptian provenance. She wore little jewelry other than delicate shoulder-length drop earrings of a primitive design with fine iron rings on three fingers of her left hand.

Something about the woman's appearance was familiar to the biographer, though he couldn't put his finger on the precise recall. She spoke educated Latin in a studied manner which communicated strong resolution of purpose.

"You are here upon imperial business, you say?" she asked without any hint of apprehension.

"Indeed, madam," Clarus responded, once again waving his scroll of authority.

"Perform your duty then," she announced in a manner suggesting an instruction rather than her own compliance.

She turned to perform a ritual wafting of her hands across a set of miniature *lares* figurines arranged in a sand tray between ornate lamps and incense burners as she murmured a liturgical formula in some indecipherable language. She then took her seat on a high matron's chair facing the visitors where she primly awaited their obedience.

The group of four scanned the contents of this aft-cabin at the stern of *The Alexandros* as river waters audibly slapped against the timbers of the brace of *biremes* lashed underneath. Open chests on the cabin floor revealed stacked arrays of small bottles, jars, and flasks containing fluids, powders, herbs, or morsels of organic materials.

A work table was laden with writing instruments, a mortar and pestle, mixing bowls, and a frosty glass beaker on a tripod with a heating lamp beneath. A nest of aged scrolls stood to one side while around the walls hung fronds of dried flora, wild grasses, and unknown organic debris.

Finely worked instruments of bronze including knives, spoons, serrated saws, probes, and surgical paraphernalia were suspended along the hull in racks. Crumbling remnants of a mummified cat, an ibis, an infant crocodile and, Suetonius suspected, a desiccated human fetus were slung on hooks across a corner stall, while knitted drapes veiled sections of the compartment from view.

High on a crossbeam one solitary lamp sat before a shrine's niche to cast its sacramental glow across the nebulous features of a miniature figurine in human form. The effigy was looped with a thong securing a gilded locket or coin purse around its shoulders. The figurine rested against a terracotta *amphora* used for storing middling measures of oil or wine. The amphora appeared to have leaked a thin drip of its contents down the timber bulwark.

Each of the intruders suspected how without the generous effusion of aromatic incense and perfume the cabin would probably reek of musty decay, or worse.

"What is your purpose, gentlemen?" the Alexandrian priestess enquired

"Madam, we are here under Caesar's instruction to enquire into your knowledge of the details of the death of Caesar's *Companion of the Hunt*, Antinous of Bithynia. We seek all information possible about the young man's death and his whereabouts the night before last. We are obliged to record our interview for the legal register, if you please. So you will respond to our individual questions," Clarus intoned crisply

"I see," the woman said with complete composure. "This is an interrogation? I doubt I can be of much assistance to you but, well then, take your dictation."

"For our record, name who you are and under whose household do you receive protection or patronage? State your origins, age, and personal details."

"Me? I see. Well sirs, I am known as Anna Perenna, the priestess of the cult of Anna Perenna at Alexandria. I am a freeborn Roman citizen and have been trained in our arts since childhood at our ancient foundation at Rome.

I was assigned to Egypt three years ago as the cult's representative under the protection of the Prefect Governor, Flavius Titianus. I live as a member the governor's *clientela*, but am sustained by an endowment independently afforded by my foundation at Rome. I also receive fees and gifts as a priestess to adherents of my cult. My age? I am told I was born in the first year of Caesar Trajan, which makes me thirty-two years of age. I do not know which month, but I celebrate my birth on Anna Perenna's traditional date."

Suetonius thought that an odd uncertainty in someone of the *patrician* class, but many people are uncertain of their exact age regardless of class.

"So you are a citizen of Rome, madam?" Suetonius enquired out of heightened curiosity, recognizing how interrogation-by-torture would not be a legal option.

"We priestesses of one of the most ancient consecrated orders of Roman tradition are citizens by definition," she replied confidently. "But we're a permissive cult unlike, say, the Vestals who are committed to absolute chastity on pain of death. For many centuries we've been known for our merry ways and we live to our liking.

We especially serve women with the medicaments, herbs, and practices necessary for controlling fertility. We also provide all manner of charms and potions to assist in love making or romance and dealing in matters of sex, childbearing, or attracting a partner. The services of Anna Perenna are highly sought after."

"I'm sure you are, madam. You are aware of the young man Antinous's death, my lady?" Clarus asked plainly.

Perenna considered her response thoughtfully.

"Why, gentlemen, should I know anything about the young man's death?"

"It is known to us, madam, how you have shared the company and conversation of the youth on occasions over recent times," Suetonius proposed. "We seek your views on the matter."

"So? I share the company of many members of the Court, gentlemen. I offer advice on matters of a personal nature to quite a few of the Household. This has included the youth Antinous in recent times. It is my duty and my vocation as a priestess of my cult. It also enhances my income."

"I return to our original question, madam. What is your knowledge of the death of the Bithynian? Please remember, madam, we are recording your words in due legal process," Suetonius stated purposefully as Strabon's stylus fluttered over a wax tablet.

"Nothing, gentlemen. I know absolutely nothing of the Bithynian's death," she declared conclusively, "though I was saddened to hear of it. I've included the shade of the dead lad in my daily prayers and offerings. I will pray for him through the nine days of his shade's progress through the Underworld to assist in his resolve."

"*His resolve*, did you say Madam?" Suetonius queried.

Perenna baulked for a moment before such an ignorant query.

"The newly-deceased need all the prayers that may be offering, gentlemen," she confirmed. "His journey through the Underworld deserves our support, don't you think?"

"In your past conversations with him did you detect any issues which could lead to such an unexpected outcome? We are led to believe he discussed matters with you on occasion, possibly of a personal nature?" the biographer asked.

"I do not share the confidences of my clients with others, gentlemen, as you would expect. But the fellow is dead and it's true he was unhappy about many things, to my view. As many at Court were aware, his relationship with Great Caesar had expired. Yes, he did seek advice from me on certain matters, and I offered my assistance as best I could."

"What was the advice he sought and the manner of your assistance?" Clarus forwarded.

"Some things remain confidential, gentlemen. Yet I suggested to Antinous I would prepare a suitable potion and advise him of an appropriate ritual which might fulfill his needs. This appeared to address his motives," she offered quietly. "He was a willing supplicant."

"Was your potion for Antinous, or for Caesar, priestess?" Suetonius asked with just the barest hint of skepticism. "And did your rituals achieve their desired effects?".

The eyes of the woman with the painted, scarred features flashed intently from behind their ashen pallor for a moment, but then resumed their unwavering gaze.

"The potion was only for the youth. I would not dare prescribe an elixir for Great Caesar unless requested personally by our *Princeps* or his physicians."

"What were the lad's motives precisely then, madam?" Suetonius continued. Perenna hesitated.

"The Bithynian wished a magical substitution, a special mystical substitution. My potion and ritual was created to give Antinous solace in this matter. The ritual was to affect a transfer of energies, once a traditional specialty of my cult. Whether it has achieved its goals is yet to be seen, my lords," the priestess uttered, somewhat ambiguously.

"*Yet to be seen?*" Clarus barked. "The boy is dead, madam! What is there to see?"

"So you have told me, gentlemen," she replied simply.

"Do you expect the lad to revive from his fate, Priestess?!" Clarus continued.

"People reach from beyond the grave in differing ways, gentlemen," Perenna replied enigmatically. "I am not denying or confirming such possibilities."

She uttered this with the confidence of either the true believer or an utter confabulator.

Suetonius decided to take a different path.

"My lady, we are told you possess remarkable skills. It's said you commune with the dead. Is this true?" the Special Inspector asked. The priestess shifted bolt upright.

"Where did you learn this notion?" she asked.

"From several sources, madam," Suetonius replied, "including the Prefect Governor."

"I am the priestess of my tradition at Alexandria, sir. From our inception at Rome in the time of the Etrurian kings we have engaged in wonders. Originally we were simple celebrants of the seasons and the annual harvest at Rome, but over the ages we've become mistresses of Cyclical Time itself. This, as well too as fertility, childbirth, or spiritual healing," the calm figure before the group expounded without diffidence.

"From time to time as the *Grandmother of Time* we are called upon to make contact with the deceased. We look deeply into Time and search out the shades of the dead. In this art we explore ways to heal the living or put the dead to rest. Or, we utilize Time itself to exchange a devotee's fate with another's to affect enhanced life. We attend the infirm and the hale alike. There is much in our tradition which challenges the notions of the mundane world, yet we bring comfort or reassurance to our devotees."

"Are you able to make contact with our deceased, Antinous, to enquire his view of his passing from his own lips, woman?" Clarus interposed provocatively.

"Not at this time, my lord," was the shrewd reply. "His shade is on its long journey to its final rest. Even nine days barely begins the adventure."

"Then can you *look into Time*, madam, and see what occurred to the boy two days ago?" Suetonius added even more provocatively.

"Not without his shade's cooperation," was the plausible if eluding reply. Suetonius had again heard a fortunate omission from a professed seer.

"Yet you believe he will reach from the grave, milady?"

"Possibly, when he is ready. I will await the signals," she offered generously.

The group of four looked upon the haughty figure with wavering confidence.

"Where were you, madam, on the day of the boy's death?" Suetonius proceeded.

"I have barely departed the precincts of *The Alexandros* since the barque's assembly here on the day of our arrival last week. There is nothing in this remote place to interest me."

"Do you realize, madam, how many of the natives of this part of Egypt are claiming the death of Antinous will induce a miracle?" Suetonius stated. "They say he's a sacrifice to their gods, and that the river flowing beneath us here will flood to its desired height next season because of his death?"

"I too have heard that said," she responded.

"Some say the priests of Amun may have engineered this event? Do you believe these Egyptian wizards are capable of such a crime?" Clarus probed. "In fact, we've been told the priest known as Pachrates of Memphis may have had a role in such a conspiracy."

Perenna remained seated in a pensive mood for some moments.

"I am not aware of such a conspiracy, sirs," she replied, "and I do not know the gifts of this priest Pachrates. But I've come to learn how in this odd land conspiracy abounds and deceit is commonplace. It is true the priests of the Old Religion here are eager to regain their influence with *Pharaoh* and have their temple lands restored to them. I'm sure they'll stop at nothing to achieve their goals."

"But would killing Great Caesar's consort be a suitable gesture? Surely this would seem a risky enterprise likely to deeply offend their *Pharaoh*, not appease him?" Suetonius asked.

"Only, gentlemen, if the crime was ascribed to them," the woman with the white painted features assured. "Perhaps the perpetrators, if this indeed is what has occurred, have performed some masterly magic in covering their tracks?"

"What advantage would provoke them to such daring?" Clarus interjected. "*Cui bono*, who benefits?"

Perenna smiled limply.

"Perhaps the drowning sacrifice of such a lofty yet disposable member of the Court would give Great Caesar reason to declare this place the appropriate site for *Hadrianopolis*, his new city in Middle Egypt? I am sure you have heard of this project?" Perenna proposed. "Such a sacrifice sanctifies this place in the eyes of the natives, which gives it enhanced value." She continued in a conspiratorial vein.

"And if *Hadrianopolis* was established here at the east bank opposite the stamping ground of Amun's opponent sects at Hermopolis, then the priests of Amun here would greatly benefit from Caesar's new city.

Pachrates has been at Caesar's side on the planning of the project for months. He may have recommended the efficacy of such an sacrifice?"

"Do you suggest Hadrian was party to a conspiracy to kill the Bithynian?! Do you accuse Caesar of murder?!" Clarus uttered with a rising flush.

"Indeed no. Great Caesar need have no knowledge of such a plot," she offered calmly.

Both Suetonius and Clarus sensed this unconventional woman was toying with them.

"Once again, where were you at the time of the boy's death?" Clarus demanded.

"As I have said, gentlemen, on the night of the young man's death I was secure in my chamber here at *The Alexandros* performing preliminary rites for the Festival of Isis. Isis is celebrated at Rome too. Isis has become a feature of our cult as much as it has with all women of the Empire," she replied. "We too honor Isis and the resurrection of Osiris. Our rites are lengthy."

"Do you have witnesses to this, my lady?" Suetonius enquired. "We've been told your protector, the Prefect Governor, was enjoying his pleasures elsewhere that night."

Anna Perenna thoughtfully considered her response.

"Indeed, gentlemen, I possess witnesses. My assigned bodyguard was on my watch at *The Alexandros* throughout the night," she offered.

"And those officers were ...?" Clarus asked.

"The captain of my guard can vouchsafe for me, gentlemen. He is known to you. The Alexandrian Praetorian, Centurion Quintus Urbicus of Numidia," she responded. "I am told he and his patrol have since been allocated to your service?"

"They have indeed, madam," Clarus confirmed.

"Then you will know he is a witness of the highest credibility."

Suetonius offered a new thought.

"Madam, you say Antinous was a *lofty yet disposable member of the Court*. In what way was the young man *disposable*?" the Special Inspector asked.

"Why, as charming as the lad may have been, his usefulness to Caesar had expired. He knew this himself, too. He was no longer

Caesar's closest intimate. At least, this is what he told me," Perenna confided. "It was one of the issues for him seeking my services."

"He told you this? What other issues were there?" Suetonius queried.

"Well, his future was one. There was his other relationship. And Caesar's health too. There were several things of great concern to him," she revealed.

The group of four were startled.

"*His other relationship?!* We are under the impression the boy was utterly faithful to his long-term *erastes?*"

"Gentlemen, since Caesar put the fellow aside at Alexandria many weeks ago the lad has found solace in another's bosom. Surely you appreciate he was attractive to many at Court? There is no shortage of suitors," she responded breezily.

"Who? Who?" Clarus demanded.

"I'm afraid he didn't reveal a name to me, sirs," she said. "But I can imagine it would be easily expected of so appealing a fellow."

"What too do you mean by *Caesar's health?*" Suetonius queried.

"There are many at Court who express concern about Hadrian's coughing bouts. They are no longer a mere nuisance to him. They are known to draw blood from his chest," Perenna stated confidently. "His young consort was troubled by this circumstance and hoped someone such as I would have a herb or decoction to treat such ailments. But this is a physician's art, not a priestess of Anna Perenna. We concentrate on fertility, romance, beauty, and divination, not sickness."

"Tell me, madam, you use your name objectively in the third person? Why is this so?" Suetonius queried.

The tall woman faced him blankly for a few moments. She cleared her throat before responding while Suetonius looked intently at the brightly colored gem upon a finger of her right hand. He felt the gemstone reminded him of something or someone. It was familiar.

"The name Anna Perenna, good sirs, is as much a title as a personal name. All senior priestesses of the cult of Anna Perenna are named *Anna Perenna. I* am Anna Perenna at Alexandria. My teacher and leader at Rome is Anna Perenna at Rome. Two others are elsewhere in the Empire," the pockmarked matron clarified pertly. "But each of us is guided by the invocation *'for leave to live in and through the year to our liking'*. It is our motto."

She returned to silence.

"Then you have a previous name and family after all? Before you became Anna Perenna, that is?"

"No that I recall, sir. Since childhood I have always been *Anna* to my priestly community at Rome. I have been raised to receive and enact the hallowed duties of an *Anna Perenna*," she explained. "The priestesses adopt orphans and out-of-wedlock infants of good family to train them in this manner, unless they prove unsuitable to the task. I was eminently suitable."

"Then you cannot throw any light at all on the death of the Bithynian, madam?" Suetonius now finalized his line of questioning.

"Not I, Inspector. Perhaps the wizard Pachrates can cast such light as you may require," she offered. A sense of remoteness appeared in her eyes. She continued.

"I am told we have been instructed by Caesar to attend the reception platform before his chambers an hour ahead of dawn on tomorrow's Third Day?

The third day of The Isia begins the days of celebration, the day when Osiris is restored to life in Isis's arms after his journey in the Underworld. Seth and evil are defeated. Life is restored to this land and its *Pharaoh*. It is an *apotheosis*. Caesar is assembling his key advisors and colleagues for this dawn's arrival."

"Life is restored to its Pharaoh, did you say?" Suetonius queried.

"This is what these people believe in this land," Perenna claimed.

"We too are obliged to attend the dawn assembly," Clarus interjected, "so we'd better get a move on with our interviews. Time is passing."

Suetonius was reluctant to depart. He was not entirely satisfied with the woman's testimony. He also wondered where he had previously seen a striking ring similar to the one on the priestess's hand.

CHAPTER 23

"Well what do we make of her?" Suetonius asked the others. "She's a very cool lady, despite the afflictions beneath the pastes and the *kohl*?"

The biographer scanned his three companions for a response. They had alighted from a gondola ferrying their return to shore from *The Alexandros*.

The runabout to the Governor's barque was an elegant vessel whose single sail was emblazoned with the Governor's symbol of an Alexandrine eight-pointed golden star upon a field of sky blue. A wharf patrol in similar colors carefully recorded the group of four's return from *The Alexandros*. Their return was inscribed in the patrol's papyrus list of movements to-and-fro from the riverside jetty. Suetonius noted this clerical diligence, but had other things on his mind.

"Surisca, my dear, from a woman's perspective do you have an opinion of this *Grandmother of Time*?"

The Syri entertainer held her own counsel momentarily.

"Well, what did you think?" he pressured again. "Don't be shy, my dear, we've come to value your views."

"This lady is a dissembler, Master. She is lying to you, I'd say," Surisca quietly offered.

"Lying? A liar? In what way, Surisca? What makes you think so?"

"It's my intuition, Master. A woman senses these things. She often knows when another woman is hiding a truth," was the young woman's reply. "There's something amiss with the Lady Priestess in my view, my lords."

Clarus and Suetonius paused in suspended agreement to the statement. Strabon now interrupted.

"I agree, gentlemen. I don't know why I believe so, but as I notated her words I sensed she was holding something back. It was in the tone in her voice. It was a feigned confidence. I have listened intently to many voices in my time and can often detect fraud."

"What sort of thing, I wonder?" Suetonius asked. "We can't judge a woman merely on the tone of her voice."

Surisca again raised her hand to speak.

"Were you aware of the blood, Masters?" she asked.

"*Blood?* Blood!? What blood?" Clarus yelped.

"If I'm not mistaken, my lords, there were droplets of blood or something similar oozing from the *amphora* up on the wall niche. They were leaking through a fine crack in the clay lip and dripping down the timbers behind. Perhaps it was some other dark fluid such as wine or *garam* sauce?" she proposed.

"Did anyone else notice a fluid?" Suetonius asked. "I certainly didn't, though I did notice a thin dark line running down the hull. You sense it was blood, was it? My eyes aren't what they once were."

"But what would a respectable Roman priestess companion of the Prefect Governor be doing with a jug of blood in her workshop?" Clarus asked. "Is the juice of life a component of her priestly *pharmacopeia*, or does she store the gore of her daily divination victims for sanctification? Theurgists are known to harvest and hoard many odd materials. But stored blood goes off very speedily. It gels and rots. It smells very badly very quickly, like an arena's sands or a charnel house. It's not a pleasing odor, I assure you."

"But not if it was relatively fresh," Suetonius said. "Yet the jar seemed to be enshrined in some way? It was being *venerated* by the Governor's consort. It was being *adored* with a votive lamp and a talisman or two."

"What did you make of her facial lesions?" Clarus asked his companions. "Surisca?" he invited again.

Clarus was warming to the courtesan's opinions.

"The lesions? Are they a pox? A canker? Leprosy?" Clarus added. "Or some nightmare Egyptian affliction not worth contemplating?"

"I have never seen such abrasions before, my lord," Surisca said, "except, perhaps, her abrasions are similar to the scars left by surgeons who try to scrape away a freed slave's branding or owner's tattoo."

"Scrape away?" Clarus repeated.

"And what to make of the three rings? Or the beautiful stone on her right hand?" the Special Investigator put forward. "Three fine iron rings on consecutive fingers. Iron, not silver or gold. Is this a local Egyptian fashion, young lady?"

"I do not know of such a fashion, Master," Surisca replied, "neither here in Egypt nor elsewhere in the East. Perhaps fine ladies wear such things at Rome, or they are tokens of her sacred vocation."

Suetonius became darkly serious.

"The Lady Anna Perenna made two comments of interest to me. One was her observation about the deceased youth's *resolve*. What could she mean by his *resolve*, I wonder? Resolve to do what? And separately, she spoke of *the night of his death*. She, without any advice from us, had concluded his death had occurred *at night*, not some other time of day. Is this a justifiable query?"

"She explained his *resolve* by suggesting the Bithynian was on a mission to regain his *erastes'* favor in some way," Clarus explained. "Yet I too sensed she was talking of some other purpose in the lad's intentions. What could that be?"

"And her certitude of the *night of his death*?" Suetonius reminded.

"Well the options are only two aren't they, daytime or night?" Clarus said.

"Further, she said the effects of Antinous's death are yet to be seen. She implied the matter is not closed. What did she mean by this?" the Special Inspector advanced. "She also claimed Antinous had a new companion since his dismissal as Caesar's *eromenos*. Yet who would dare be so unwise as to supplant Great Caesar so soon in this way?"

"No one else has mentioned this fact," Clarus indicated. "Is she confabulating? Would the boy pursue a new conquest so soon after five years of fidelity to his *erastes*? By the useful principle of *cui bono?*, what benefit has this woman to gain from the young Favorite's death, I wonder?"

The biographer's eye was caught by the keeper of the jetty records at his duties. The officer was seated on a high stool at a lectern on the wharf protected by a trio of Alexandrian guardsmen. Suetonius beckoned the others to follow him to the clerk's desk.

"My good fellow," Suetonius sweetly addressed the officer, "you maintain a daily record of the comings and goings to *The Alexandros* on behalf of your master, the Prefect Governor, do you not?"

The Special Inspector *equestrian* adjusted the folds of his purple-striped toga with a generous flourish as he spoke, drawing attention to his status in the pecking order of Rome. The clerk was already cognizant of his status and rose abruptly from his seat to attention before his social superior.

"Yes, indeed we do, sir. We maintain daily records on behalf of His Excellency," the trooper announced helpfully in the strongly Greek-inflected Latin of Alexandrians. "We register each of those who pass to and fro to the Governor's barque through the day."

"Each day, every day?" Suetonius probed.

"Yes, my lord, from midnight to midnight in three changes of watch," the clerk explained.

"Do you still possess your records for the past few days, officer?" Suetonius continued in his best legalist voice.

"Indeed, sir, we retain three days at a time. After three days we dispatch the pages to the Governor's staff for safe-keeping."

"Do you still possess the traffic records for the day and night before last?" Suetonius enquired further.

"Yes, my lord, I do. This is the third day of the cycle."

"What is your name and rank, Officer? And may I inspect your register?" the Special Inspector intoned as Strabon meaningfully waved the ivory scroll of commission with its imposing purple Imperial *bulla* tag in the direction of the clerk.

"Certainly, sir. Of course, sir. I am Danaos, a *Tessararius* clerk to the Alexandrine Fleet."

"*Tessararius* Danaos, were you the officer recording this jetty's traffic to *The Alexandros* on the day or night before last?"

"Only for my eight hour watch, sir. I supervised the evening watch two days ago, not the morning or afternoon watch," the clerk-of-records explained.

Suetonius cast his eyes across the two sheets of coming-and-goings registered for the day. Running his finger down the list of names and titles his finger stopped abruptly at a single name. Further down the list he noted the same name twice more. He showed the sheet to Strabon as Clarus moved closer to observe.

Surisca, though not having reading skills, could nevertheless identify personal names on a page. She too glanced over the pages as Suetonius turned away from the officer's hearing.

"Here, it's *Centurion Quintus Urbicus*, our Praetorian. According to these sheets he arrived twice but departed only once on that day. His final arrival was quite late," Suetonius whispered. "The priestess Perenna's story of her bodyguard being witness to her presence that night is confirmed here."

He turned to the clerk.

"May I see the register for yesterday, the day after these pages, *Tessararius* Danaos."

The Alexandrian provided the further papers. Suetonius again ran his finger down the lists and came to a stop-place.

"*Cent Quintus Urbicus*. One arrival and then one departure, both in the middle of the day. It seems our centurion friend arrived at the Governor's vessel on the day before last, but there is no record of his departure prior to his further arrival the next day," he said. "This can't be feasible, can it?"

Suetonius turned to the clerk.

"Officer Danaos, is your register of people travelling to and from *The Alexandros* always accurate? Is it possible you miss some arrivals or departures?" the biographer asked.

"Indeed not, my lord! Our careers as guards to the Governor would be immediately struck out, and we'd receive a thorough beating for our negligence," the clerk protested. Clarus intervened.

"Test the sheets' veracity with another name. Try for *Flavius Titianus*. The Governor told us he slept at Hadrian's dining marquee on the night of the celebration of The Isia with his paramour lass from

Iberia, so surely his departure and return would be noted accordingly?" the senator suggested.

Strabon ran his finger down the first page of the first day once again as Surisca followed his finger closely.

"Here it is. *'Excellency Prefect Gov departs with entourage of three.'* They're each listed by name. It is indicated at four hours after high sun. But there's no record of his return to his vessel later that day, nor of his retinue's return, until mid-morning the following day," Strabon announced. "This register agrees with the Governor's own words."

Surisca, who had been looking across Strabon's shoulder at the first day's pages, pointed hesitantly to a name late in the list. Strabon looked more closely at the penmanship. He turned to the Alexandrian clerk. His eyes were alight.

"Officer Danaos, can you read this name to us please," the scribe enquired as he pointed to a name low down the list. The clerk checked the written entry and spoke aloud.

"Yes sir, it is the name of *Lysias of Bithynia*. Six hours after midday, around sunset. His travel authority was a personal invitation from Lady Anna Perenna. It was sighted by the watch officer and duly recorded," the clerk announced.

"*Lysias?*" Clarus exclaimed. "What's this about? What was Lysias doing here?"

"So, what time did he depart then?" Suetonius asked.

Strabon and Surisca trailed down the sheet, across to the second sheet, and then to the following day's page without success.

"There is no record of his departure," Strabon announced. Suetonius turned to the clerk.

"Tell me, fellow, how do you explain that you have two visitors in the sheets of the day before yesterday marked as arrivals to be ferried to *The Alexandros*, but no record of their return journey from the vessel?" the Special Inspector demanded. "Yet one of these two, Centurion Urbicus of the Alexandrian Praetorians, arrives again the following day without his prior departure from *The Alexandros* recorded?"

The officer stammered a mumbled reply.

"My lords, I don't know," he wavered. "The Watch has not troubled to compare the sheets. It seems the clerk at that Watch has been negligent. I am at a loss! It is not my fault! He will be punished for it, I'll see to that!"

The officer was visibly shaken by the error and in fear of his superiors.

"Yet you were supervising one of these watches on both these two days?" Clarus intoned, the senatorial stripe running down his toga assuming a menacing magnitude in the clerk's vision.

Suetonius interrupted with a more helpful question.

"Were you also the officer who recorded the arrival of Lysias of Bithynia two evenings ago?"

"Yes, my lord, I was."

"Do you recall the occasion?"

"Indeed, my lord. Lysias of Bithynia is a fine young noble, well dressed, well built, and bearing fine weapons. I was impressed by his magnificence."

"Was he in company?"

The clerk looked to his sheets to check.

"He was not personally accompanied, but he arrived at the same time as other officers of the Guards. All three were ferried to *The Alexandros* together."

"And they were?"

"You have already noted Centurion Quintus Urbicus. The other was an officer of Caesar's Horse Guard accompanying the centurion. They visit *The Alexandros* regularly."

"Their arrival was recorded, but you have no record of their departure. Is it possible your visitors to the Governor's barque can depart by some other means? By other river craft, another route, or some other means?" the Special Inspector asked.

"We retain a complete record, sir, of those who attend the Governor's barque in any manner," the clerk stammered. "Even the late night watch passes such comings and goings to the daytime shift for our records. We aim to protect His Excellency from stowaways who could well be assassins, brigands, thieves, or even seekers of favors."

"What about in the dark of night? Could a visitor to *The Alexandros* slip away overboard without your clerk or guardsmen seeing it?"

The Alexandrian was stricken mute for a moment.

"I suppose such a thing is possible, sir. But the river is not safe to travel after dark even if the moon is high," he offered. "The currents are dangerous. People drown."

Suetonius resolved to make a deal with the officer.

"*Tessararius* Danaos, we will remain silent about your offence with these records if you give us with these pages. We will confiscate the pages for our own legal purposes. Be satisfied we are being gentle and won't press charges," Suetonius declared imperiously.

"Thank you, thank you, thank you, my lords," the clerk bowed profusely as he handed over the six pages of the register. Suetonius rolled the papyri carefully and handed them to Strabon.

"Keep these in a safe place. I will have to search my mind for what their omissions mean to our investigation," he muttered. "Meanwhile, what was Lysias doing at *The Alexandros* with that mystic priestess? He did not mention this matter at his interview. Have we stumbled upon a romantic tryst or is Lysias, too, a seeker of the lady's panaceas?"

A new voice intruded into the conversation. It called from the jetty's end.

"As you say, gentlemen, just *where is* the Bithynian youth Lysias?" It was a deeply modulated, educated voice. The four turned to look towards its source.

Standing in tall silhouette against the glare of the midday sun at the far end of the wharf was Caesar's onetime Master of the Hunt, Salvius Julianus. Aged about thirty and garbed in a summer-weight *chiton* suited to the Egyptian climate topped by a broad-brim sunhat, Julianus's tall, gangly silhouette made a striking outline against the blaze. Marcus, a young equerry, stood nearby.

"Did I hear the name of Lysias of Bithynia being bandied about?" the silhouette called back.

"By Jupiter! It's the *Quaestor*, Salvius Julianus. Welcome to our company, senator!" Clarus called aloud gleefully. "We are due to visit your person shortly."

"In fact, Septicius Clarus," Julianus said, "Secretary Vestinus told me I was due to visit you an hour ago at your chambers. I did so and waited, eventually to be told your team had ventured elsewhere. One of the staff reported you were interviewing the Prefect Governor at *The Alexandros*. So I've wandered here to locate you."

Julianus spoke in the clipped Latin of the legal world. Both his roles as Hadrian's leader of the hunt and as the educated investigator of the arcane complexities of Roman Law demanded skill in prosecuting a chase. Yet unlike those of Hadrian's retinue who travelled everywhere in the company a flock of clients, stewards, and assorted hangers-on, Julianus was accompanied only by his solitary equerry.

Both were armed as a precaution, however, except when in the presence of Caesar. The imperial encampment was relatively secure against undesirables, nevertheless only slaves moved around without protection. At a time when unknown intruders had been circulating within the camp and causing affray, Julianus walked unafraid.

"The afternoon heat is debilitating. You must be thirsty and hungry?" he commiserated. "I suggest we retire to my apartments at the Companion's stables. They're just at the top of the rise nearby. It will be cooler and private, if you don't mind the smell of horseflesh. Besides I have something very special to show you," the affable Roman suggested. "In fact, two somethings."

"Two somethings? What would they be, Senator?" Suetonius asked.

"You'll see soon. They will be useful to you."

CHAPTER 24

At first it sounded like a flight of birds fluttering high in the incandescent sky of a blazing African afternoon. But it was not birds fluttering. It was the first indication of an impending assault.

Julianus and Clarus were sufficiently experienced in war to immediately recognize the fluttering for what it was. It was neither birds in flight nor benign. They immediately peered skywards. A shimmering shower of arrows was flowingly rising, curving, and turning to descend. It was arcing earthwards towards the group.

"We're under attack!" Julianus cried. "Get to cover immediately!"

Suetonius, Clarus, Strabon, and Surisca found themselves in an entirely unexpected theater of danger. An attack? On them?! By who? Why?

With a series of whispering *zippps*, a shower of thin-shafted arrows feathered the baked earth around the group. One shaft transfixed Strabon's basket of wax tablets and papyrus rolls. Strabon groaned a scholar's grimace as he tugged the offending dart from his precious kit and cast it aside.

Suddenly Julianus's equerry emitted a sharp cry as another arrow struck his open-laced boot.

A second wave of arrows rose similarly leisurely into the sky from behind a nearby marquee as the group of six scrambled clumsily up an earthen grade to the safety of the Companions' compound. The first shower may have been the archer's range markers, the second a more accurate positioning of the deadly shafts.

"Get to the horse yard!" Julianus shouted as he leaped to his equerry's assistance. The missile had pierced the side of the young man's foot but not pinioned it to the earth. The pain was not yet sufficient to disable him, but Julianus grasped him around the torso and heaved the two of them up the slope. They toppled into and under the cover of the horse compound's palm-strewn trellis vaulting.

Suetonius had the presence of mind to scurry to Surisca's defense, though the nimble eighteen year-old made a speedier advance to refuge than her chivalrous sixty year-old defender.

The group tumbled under the cover of the palm fronds in a flurry of toga wools, linens, and Damascene silk. A dozen stable-hands ran to their attention. The compound's trellis cover offered dappled shade to forty horses with their attendant grooms.

"Get Marcus to safety," Julianus commanded, "and call Damon the Horse Doctor!"

Two of the younger grooms supported Marcus into the interior of the compound as a large Cretan in his island's distinctive garb ambled to the group. Julianus shouted orders to the others and then the Cretan.

"We're being attacked! Arm yourselves, and protect the horses! Follow procedures and stand your stations! Send someone to make contact with the nearest Watch to report the attack and call for urgent aid. Tell him to watch his movements; the assailants are unknown. But no stranger is permitted in this shelter or near the horses! And protect our visitors, too!"

Julianus turned to the Cretan. "Marcus has taken an arrow in his foot. Attend to the wound and assess its risks, Damon. The arrow might have been dipped in soil or shit to encourage infection."

Damon, a burly horse surgeon-cum-slaughterman, looked to the young man's foot. Pain was rapidly settling into the wound and was evident in Marcus's whitening lips.

"Bring boiled drinking water, clear vinegar, and fresh oil from the kitchen," the vet instructed a nearby groom. "Clean cloths, too!" He looked to Marcus. "Be calm, lad. We'll snip off the barb and withdraw the shaft, clean. It's through flesh, not vein or bone. The Fates have been kind to you. We'll give it a good cleanse then bind it tight. Later I'll apply a healing salve. You'll be limping for weeks though."

Suetonius, Julianus, and the others peered from beneath the trellis towards the source of the attack. From its higher ground the compound provided a clear view of the surrounding lanes, tents, and booths towards the river. But no sign of activity was evident in the soporific sun-drenched stillness of the afternoon's *siesta* time.

The attackers, who had loosed their arrows from behind the cover of a marquee's wall, had withdrawn back into the camp out of view. Whoever they were, they were nowhere evident.

"Are you alright, my dear?" the biographer asked his young Syri ward. She nodded her affirmation, if somewhat shaken by the experience.

"What was that all about?" Clarus demanded rhetorically. "Who was targeting us? And why?"

"Somebody doesn't like us, I think," Suetonius offered weakly.

He saw the nipped head of the arrow from Marcus's foot drop to the beaten earth under Damon's crisp shear with a flensing knife. Suetonius picked it up and surveyed it.

"It's not Roman, it's not a Legion arrow-head. The shape and style are wrong. Is it Scythian, Alexandrian, Egyptian, or Nubian?" the Special Inspector asked of all around him.

Only Damon responded.

"That's Europa barbarian, I'd say," the horse doctor offered. "It's German or maybe Gaulish. Yet it could be a re-used sharp from almost anywhere in the Empire. They're too precious to use only once."

"Who has archers in the camp other than the Legion? The Scythians? The Praetorians? The Alexandrian mercenaries?" Suetonius enquired of the group. "Are any among them German?"

"The Horse Guards are mainly from Germania," Clarus reminded the group. "Caesar holds the Germans high in his estimation for their warrior skills and reliability. As his personal bodyguard they are steadfastly loyal and fierce fighters to boot. But they're also very *German*." Clarus, being a former Prefect of the Praetorian Guard a decade earlier, knew these things.

"*Very German?* Meaning?" enquired Julianus.

"They have a fixed mindset. They're stolid, they're not imaginative. One could say they're obsessive. Once they get their teeth into a matter they cling on like hyenas bringing down victims in the arena," Clarus opined.

"But who were these archers trying to kill? Me? You, Clarus? Julianus?" Suetonius asked in a hurt voice.

"Perhaps each of us, my friends," Julianus offered.

"Each? Why so?" Clarus queried with barely suppressed alarm.

"Well, I imagine each of us here could possess something or some knowledge which others would like to see eradicated?" the jurist speculated.

"Eradicated? You mean something someone wants silenced?" Clarus asked.

"Certainly. I'm sure each of us here, possibly even your scribe and female attendant too, is party to information someone at Court wants erased," Julianus calmly proposed.

"They want it so badly they're willing to kill for it?" Clarus queried with unfettered dismay.

"Think about it, gentlemen," Julianus continued. "What have you learned in the past day which someone might wish you not to know? Have you uncovered something about Antinous's death that sniffs of foul play? Have you reason to suspect someone, somewhere, or some faction of a mischief?"

"I think to date we've uncovered about half a dozen possibilities, each of them contradictory to the others," Suetonius contributed. "But his death may also have been a simple accident. Until we find out how he spent his final day before his drowning, and with who he kept it, we're at a loss."

"And your two day time limit expires tomorrow at dawn I'm told?"

"It does. This is why we wish to interview you promptly on what you may know of the lad's ways or movements," the biographer intimated. "You have shared his company over several years. You must surely have an opinion on the boy's fate, or know his mind, or know of his private companions and other relationships?"

"Well, as I said earlier, I have something to show you. Two somethings, actually," the former Master of the Hunt clarified.

"Two of what, *Quaestor*?"

A clatter at the rear gateway to the horse compound diverted attention from the conversation. An equerry of the Companions approached the group circled around Marcus. He was followed by an officer of the Horse Guards with six troops of the Watch, all with swords drawn. Clarus moved to greet them.

"Decurion Scorilo! Welcome!" he called at the sight of the leading officer.

Scorilo was a mature hulk of a man dressed in the soft woolen tunic and russet mantle of the Germans of the Horse Guard. He bore the double-handed *falx* sword beloved of the northern barbarians. His hair was bound in the parted plaits of his race with an accompanying sheep-fat glistened moustache above a bushy beard. His ruddy skin displayed the faded remnants of old tribal tattoos typical of his race. These told of his skills in combat and hinted at his fierce possibilities.

Scorilo approached with a steady, confidant gait. He was followed by others of similar breeding and similar self-assurance. They scanned the lanes beyond the horse compound for signs of the attacking intruders or signs of movement. There were none.

"We were beset by archers who took cover behind the marquee below," Clarus pointed. "We didn't see them, they used the marquee as a blind, but one of their arrows struck a young equerry of the Companions." He waved to Marcus as Damon was winding a tight bandage cloth around the foot wound.

Scorilo saluted perfunctorily. "Was anyone else injured?!" he asked. The decurion was wielding his *falx* scimitar in threatening readiness. A strike from such a weapon would cleave a man in two or bring down a galloping horse in a legless collapse. Clarus shook his head.

"No, but if we hadn't been so close to these stables and their cover it might have been a different story," he offered. "We've no idea who they were or why they attacked. I'm told unidentified renegades have infiltrated the camp ---"

Scorilo sharply gave an order to his troop.

"Check the marquee, inside and out. See who's around. Kill opposition only if necessary, but keep at least one alive to interrogate," he ordered in thickly accented Latin. Four of his men scurried off towards the offending tent complex with their short-swords and bill-hooked blades glinting menacingly.

Suetonius looked the decurion up and down. Scorilo had been the officer who greeted him at Hadrian's tents the day before. Like so many older-generation professional soldiers from the northern climes, his face tattoos denoting tribal fealties, successes in war, or aristocratic status, were a grim sight calculated to strike fear into any adversary.

"We have one of their arrows here," Clarus offered, taking the shaft which Damon had extracted from Marcus. Clarus passed the missile to Scorilo.

"Nubian," the decurion stated with unreserved certainty. "Or Egyptian. Crudely made. Primitive. Inferior bronze, feathered with water fowl quill, so it's local. Probably drifts far from its target. Useless thing."

"We thought it might be from *Europa*?" Julianus hesitantly suggested. "It seemed well enough made to my eye."

The decurion was dismissive with a shake of his shaggy head.

"I'll try to find matches with any of our allies' weapons," Scorilo growled. "We'll also check the *bona fides* of Nubians or their captains servicing the camp. A household steward was murdered last eve defending his masters from attack. These attackers too were reported to be of Nubian stock."

"Was it the steward of the household of Antinous of Bithynia?" Julianus asked. Scorilo nodded a gruff affirmation.

"But who told you the attackers were Nubian?"

"It was reported to us by a serving slave, the same one who found the steward's body," the German said.

Julianus seemed diffident about this response Suetonius thought.

"The Bithynian *favorite* is dead, and his two closest companions too have disappeared," Scorilo continued. "We are commanded to locate the *ephebe* Lysias and the woman Thais of Cyrene by order of Praetorian Tribune Lucius Macedo."

"Have you considered they may have departed the camp and found voyage on a Nile boat to Memphis or Thebes, Decurion Scorilo?" Julianus enquired with no little impatience.

Scorilo's face darkened. His eyes darted backwards and forwards between Clarus and the *quaestor* in a manner Suetonius could not interpret.

"My lords, this camp has been sealed against entry and exit," the decurion rumbled in his Germanic accent. "All boundaries are secured. This has been so for twenty-four hours, some hours before the last sighting of the pair. I believe they still remain within the camp, probably hiding in fear of their lives."

"I see," Julianus concluded the conversation ambiguously. "Thank you Decurion Scorilo for coming to our aid. It seems it has not been necessary, the attackers have fled. However I hope you will assign extra Watch around this complex to protect Caesar's horses and grooms against further assault. As a *quaestor* I can provide you with the necessary document in my own hand and seal."

"No need, Lord *Quaestor*. I will have the necessary troops assigned immediately."

Suetonius was moved to interrupt because his memory had suddenly clinched a query.

"Decurion Scorilo, I am Suetonius Tranquillus, Caesar's *Special Inspector* of the circumstances surrounding the death of the youth Antinous. I have a question to ask you," the biographer raised.

"At your service."

"Tell me, Decurion, do you or your colleagues know anything about the young man's drowning? Is there gossip among the Guard about what befell the emperor's companion? Do any of you know something about this tragedy?" Suetonius asked formally with a quiet nod aside to his scribe.

Strabon's move with stylus on a tablet caused Scorilo to hesitate at this double surprise. He realized he was subject of a formal interrogation with an equally formal written recording.

"Why, Special Inspector, I was on Guard duty the day and night of Antinous's death. I was a captain of the Watch attending to security for the protection of Caesar. I was assigned to a banquet at the Imperial Household. It was a celebration of the arrival of Senator Lucius Commodus at the encampment," the German stated.

"You attended all evening and night?" Suetonius queried further as Strabon scribbled.

"From before sunset until very late, to just before dawn, sir," Scorilo assured the group. He was apprehensive at the surprise questioning.

"You are certain of that, Decurion Scorilo?" Suetonius labored the point.

"Yes, Special Inspector. It was my roster duty for the day."

"Thank you, Decurion. Before you depart please tell us for the record your status, origin, age, and other identifying information," the biographer outlined as Strabon's stylus continued. Scorilo gathered himself for his response. This was unexpected.

"My lords, I am Scorilo of the *Bastarnae Celts*," he began in the guttural tones of a former German tribesman. "I do not know my age or place of birth. I am a decurion in the service of Great Caesar's special Horse Guard. I have been an officer of the Guard for ten years. Before being pressed to enter Caesar's service I fought under Caesar's command as an auxiliary to the Legions at Pannonia and Moesia in the wars against the *Sarmatii* and *Roxolani*. Caesar admired my fighting skills and recommended me for duty in his special Guard. That's all I have to offer, my lords."

"It is enough, Decurion Scorilo. But your tattoos, do they have meaning?" Suetonius probed further. "Explain them."

The Horse Guard was thoughtful for a moment.

"Special Inspector," he replied, "I received my tattoos early in my life. They are mementos of warfare between The Bastarnae and other tribes in my youth. They tell of victories I achieved against my enemies. We of The Bastarnae treasure our tattoos and the heroism they proclaim. They tell the quality of a man."

"Very good, Decurion. You may depart," Suetonius concluded.

Scorilo snapped to attention, saluted, and departed as his men rejoined him from their fruitless search. Suetonius turned to Julianus and Clarus.

"Who are The Bastarnae?" he asked. "Septicius Clarus, you served in those wars, you know these things. Besides, you know something of Scorilo?"

"Scorilo was already known to me at the time of Trajan's campaign twenty-five years ago. He was very young," the senator responded. "*The Bastarnae* are one of the dozens of Germanic and Dacian tribes who are scattered all over Europa beyond the defensive *limes*. Scorilo was such a one, and a good fighter too. They are tenacious, the Germans, they don't let go."

Suetonius turned to Julianus.

"Did this officer share in the celebration for Commodus you attended, as he said? Was he a guest or a member of the Guard?"

"I have no recollection of him there at all," the former Master of the Hunt confided. "Perhaps I had too much wine to notice? I didn't note who the guards were. They're often invisible to me. Marcus might remember? He was there too."

All eyes turned to the wounded equerry.

"I have no memory either. My recall is that Praetorians were the watch for that occasion, not Germans."

"Damon, you said you think the arrow head is German?" the jurist and *quaestor* queried. "Scorilo believes it to be Nubian. Do you agree now?"

The horse doctor scratched his head in uncertainty.

"Well, a man of the Guard must surely know weapons better than a humble friend of horseflesh," Damon offered. "But the arrow head which pierced Marcus's foot was too well shaped and cast to be of Nubian origin, and it's quality bronze."

"Scorilo further says the intruders who killed the steward last night at Antinous's apartments were Nubians too," Suetonius added.

Julianus interjected with an offer.

"Well let's find out, gentlemen. I have someone who can advise us on this very matter. We'll retire to my private courtyard to hear. Come this way ---"

CHAPTER 25

Beyond Salvius Julianus's tent chambers beside the horse pavilion lay a gardened terrace open to the late afternoon sky and its rising breeze. The space was furnished with several dining couches, chairs, and low tables accompanied by boxes of Egyptian greenery and busts on pedestals of well-regarded legalists of Rome.

"You have until an hour before the next dawn to resolve your enquiries, gentlemen. That's about fourteen hour's time. Ask of me what you will, and then I will show you something which will be of great value to your investigation," the jurist stated. The investigation team immediately showed increased interest.

"Well, we'll begin by taking your testimony, lord *Quaestor*," Suetonius asked formally while waving the scroll of authority to view, "with your cooperation. Strabon will record your words so we have a transcript of all interviews in accordance with Caesar's commission."

"A formal deposition, with my identity noted? I see. Well to save us time, gentlemen, I am Lucius Publius Salvius Julianus Aemilianus, Senator at Rome, lawyer by profession. I was born at Hadrumetum in the second year of Caesar Trajan, so I am thirty years of age. I studied law of the Sabidian School at Rome under Javolenus Priscus.

I have been appointed *quaestor* by Caesar Hadrian to review the Praetor's Edicts of Roman Law. I am traveling in Egypt within Caesar's

Household in anticipation of advising the *Princeps* on judicial matters relating to the establishment of new settlements in this province. I have a wife at Rome and two children, both girls. What else do you wish to know?"

Strabon's stylus was in full flutter.

"What is your understanding of the death of the Imperial Favorite, Antinous of Bithynia?"

Julianus paused thoughtfully before responding.

"I am deeply saddened by his passing. He was a worthy Companion of the Hunt, and he brought light to all who shared his company. He possessed admirable Hellene aspirations, yet to be fully realized. They are now no more. The young man will be sorely missed, at least among his many friends at Court," the *quaestor* confided.

"Do you believe he also had enemies?"

"Not many, I'd say, not many. But whether they had anything to do with the drowning is beyond me," Julianus clarified. "I don't intend to denounce any individual without clear evidence. Besides, *cui bono?* Who benefits? If I was to delate anyone at all it would possibly be the young Bithynian himself."

"Antinous himself!" Clarus gasped. "How so, Julianus?"

"Well, there were facets of the young man's character which may well have led him in unhappy directions," the jurist offered. "His sense of honor, his virtue, his noble principles, his Greek *arête*, could well have led him to risks others might think twice about."

"Do you have an example?"

"Yes. Antinous possessed a refined sense of obligation. Perhaps it's a Greek thing," the huntsman supposed. "A favor performed for him obliged he return the favor in kind. Now we know the ethic of mutual obligation is an admirable lubricant to interaction among equals, yet in exchanges between unequals it may become onerous to those who are lesser equipped.

Antinous, to his credit, aimed always to respond to favors with parity. He was in no man's debt. Nevertheless, the lad was not Great Caesar and didn't possess the powers or resources to respond to his *erastes'* gestures in like or kind.

If Hadrian offered his Favorite some gesture of regard, it was not always easy for the younger man to match a return gesture, despite his eagerness to do so. Perhaps Caesar felt the gestures of the boudoir, or even simple companionship, were sufficient recompense? However there was one particular occasion where a reciprocal gesture would have been problematic for the Bithynian."

"And what was that?" Suetonius asked.

"It was the recent lion hunt in the western desert beyond Alexandria. It occurred almost two months ago.

The previous week Hadrian had announced to his inner circle while visiting Alexander's tomb in the centre of that city how the time had arrived for Caesar and Antinous to relinquish their respective roles as *erastes* and *eromenos*. Antinous must surely have known the relationship was overdue for dissolution, public decency demanded it. For the thing to have continued would have had people talking. Yet Antinous was obviously thunderstruck by the announcement.

Then a week later a team of the Companions including Antinous, Lysias, and myself were summoned by Caesar to join him in hunting a feral lion, a giant man-eater, which had been terrorizing villages and farmers on the desert road beyond Siwa Oasis. It had killed several farm workers and quite a few animals. It had shut down travel on the road.

The beast was old and dying, but Hadrian wished to show the fickle citizens of Alexandria how his sheer presence provided security in the Roman way against nature's wildness. Because of its age the brute was to be killed, not captured for arena games.

Well, to cut a long story short, Caesar himself courageously spearheaded the attack at its lair, but his first strike seemed to miss its mark.

I assure you, Hadrian rarely misses a kill. Very, very rarely indeed, gentlemen. To my eye, Hadrian intentionally missed the strike so that the second in line, our brave young *ephebe*, could make his play.

An enraged old lion is not an easy target, and to miss a strike can be fatal. The lion had sufficient energy to anticipate its next attacker, Antinous. It brought down the lad's charger. The horse fell on top of its rider to hurt and imperil Antious piniored underneath. If Hadrian hadn't circled swiftly for a third strike, which was his intended strategy I suspect, I think neither Antinous nor his horse would have survived.

The lion was destroyed by Caesar's decisive javelin strike. But for some moments our hearts were in our mouths," Julianus recollected.

"How does this meet your comment about *reciprocal gesture*?" Clarus asked.

"Well, having earlier informed the Bithynian how their relationship must expire, and having so obviously saved the boy and his horse from the lion, Antinous was then caught in his obligation conundrum. To be saved from death by Great Caesar is no small matter. Such a debt is enormous.

Despite the sporty bonhomie of the hunt, Hadrian is no ordinary man, even to his chosen Favorite. And Caesar made sure Antinous knew it that night around the desert campfires shared by the hunt team. I perceived a degree of reluctance in Hadrian's manner about the dissolution of the relationship, as though he was of two minds about it.

I suspect this situation put thoughts in the young man's mind, if I'm not mistaken, thoughts which may have led to his demise," the *quaestor* concluded

"Is that all? This seems an unlikely motive for a drowning, my lord, if you forgive my skepticism," Clarus offered with his usual lack of subtlety.

"There's more, of course. But your scribe must cease recording for the moment," Julianus intimated. Clarus was about to object to this request when Suetonius waved to Strabon to lay down his stylus. Clarus desisted.

"What more, Senator?" the biographer enquired.

"The matter of the cough. Caesar's cough. It does not dispel. It grows. There are some who are concerned about Caesar's health," Julianus confided. "This is neither sedition nor treason; it's a justifiable concern about Hadrian the man, our friend, not Caesar the *Princeps*. His intimates worry a great deal about this, Antinous most of all I suspect."

"So what can a dismissed *eromenos* do about this? He is no physician, dream-reader, exorcist, or magician," Suetonius queried.

"No, but his interest in magicians, spells, and the more arcane healing arts seem high in his mind these days. I've been witness to many conversations about the skills of those mad Egyptian *theurgists* who claim to perform healing magic," the *quaestor* commented. "Mind you, Antinous and his Bithynian race seem to be disposed to such things by their passion for their deity Apollo, Healer of Heaven, and his son Asclepius, god of healing. It's in their bloodstream."

"So you believe Antinous has given himself up to some sort of sorcery?" Clarus asked.

"No, senator, not sorcery, but some way to help restore his *erastes'* health and longevity. Precisely what or how, I'm not sure," Julianus resolved, "it's pure supposition. I wish he had talked about it."

"Perhaps you talk too loosely, Salvius Julianus?" Clarus interjected, but Julianus was on a roll.

"Then, gentlemen, there is the matter of Caesar's bedroom tastes. But I won't pursue that line of enquiry too far. That knowledge dies with the boy," the *quaestor* offered evasively.

"Enough!" Clarus demanded. "This is sedition! Their bedroom activities are their own affair. You are too forthright in your speculations, Senator *Quaestor*! I do not believe our Caesar has engaged in treachery with his Favorite."

"Then it seems we indeed agree, gentlemen?" the legalist countered. "My point is that I too believe none of these things. Instead, I look at the *humanity* of the relationship and see an attraction between the man and the emperor which sketches a different scenario entirely."

"How has this influenced Antinous's death? That's why we're here today, senator," Suetonius reminded his colleague. Julianus leant forward closer to his inquisitors.

"I have enjoyed many conversations and much wine with the charming youth around campfires when on Caesar's hunts, and he's no fool I assure you. So to my eye there have been several intersecting lines of thought affecting Antinous's actions. Firstly, he has spent five years centered in a political climate where direct imperial action is seen to change the world around him. He sees how considered action can achieve intended results.

Secondly, he is driven to enact our philosopher Epictetus's dictum of *it's up to him!* No one will do our life's work for us. We have to do it ourselves. These notions have shaped his worldview."

"Meaning?" Clarus asked.

"I believe Antinous has taken it upon himself to take direct action in history, and to fulfill his goals on his own initiative, not via his *erastes'* endowment," the *quaestor* proposed conclusively. "I sense Antinous may have constructed his own death to achieve some eternal benefit for his companion, his *Princeps*. His motive is his likely to be his affection for our *Princeps*."

Suetonius, Clarus, Strabon, and Surisca looked to each other momentarily.

"What could that benefit be?" both Suetonius and Clarus asked together.

"Perhaps I can introduce you to someone who may know," Julianus offered.

"Pray do," Suetonius instructed in increasing wonder.

Julianus put aside his nibbled dates and goblet of wine, rose from his couch, and strode to one of the curtained portals of the marquee to the garden terrace. He carefully drew aside the beaded drape veiling an inner vestibule beyond. Basked in the soft glow of the interior chamber, a slender female figure stood demurely waiting.

"Thais of Cyrene, freedwoman of the household of Antinous of Bithynia, please join me and the gentlemen here," Julianus requested.

CHAPTER 26

"Who am I, you ask, kind sirs? I am Thais of Cyrene, a freedwoman whose manumission is registered at Rome. I am no longer a slave," the pert young woman with the brightly intelligent eyes announced in crisp Palatine Latin.

"My master Antinous declared my freedom by *vindicta* two years ago in a public court at Rome. It was notarized under the auspices of the *quaestor*, Salvius Julianus. So for the past two years I have been a freedwoman in the *clientela* of Antinous of Bithynia."

Her shining white eyes were saddened by tears. "I travel with the Imperial Household under his and Caesar's protection."

"Tell us of your fealty prior to manumission," the Special Inspector requested.

"Good sir, I am the only daughter of Lais of Canopus, born at Cyrene in Cyrenaica in the thirteenth year of Caesar Trajan. My mother and I were both registered in the quinquennial census at Cyrenaica as the property of the Proconsul Legate of the senatorial province of Cyrenaica-Crete. I was born as property of the Legate's household at Cyrene. I am twenty years of age and my mother is deceased."

Suetonius and Clarus were astonished at the young girl's sudden appearance at the Companions' compound, while Julianus enjoyed their visible surprise. Suetonius continued questioning.

"Tell us, Thais of Cyrene. You are saying to us your mother Lais was of the slave class?"

"Indeed I do, sir. Prior to my birth my mother had been a dancer at the Canopus entertainment district on the coast of the Delta beyond Alexandria. She was acquired by the Proconsul Legate at Cyrene as a concubine during a recreational visit to Canopus. She travelled to join his household at Cyrene on the Legate's return. I was born only months later," she added breezily. "My mother Lais was perceived to be a great beauty. Her purchase from her masters was at great price."

Suetonius glanced across to Surisca, who was near the same age and had experienced a similar style of life, but who kept her eyes lowered during the young girl's testimony.

"Um, ah .." Suetonius burbled with a self-conscious degree of prurience, "did you too follow in your mother's profession as an entertainer, my dear?"

"No, sir, no. I was secluded in the traditional way to protect my virginity for marriage. I was raised in the Legate's household as a daughter of the family and educated accordingly. The Legate's wife, my Roman mistress, had borne four children to her husband of which only one son had survived childhood. He was named Aulus. I think I may have been welcomed as a daughter to the family in the light of their other losses.

Also, though my birth-mother taught me dancing and musical skills, I was specially trained in the administration of a noble household by my owner's wife. I was taught to read and write in Latin, common Greek, and Aramaic under tutors in the company of the Legate's son Aulus. Aulus was two years older than I, but it transpired I was a better student than the Legate's son."

"What happened then?" Suetonius enquired, entranced by this history.

"I remained in service with the Legate's wife at Cyrene until my fourteenth year, when she resolved I should find a master or mistress elsewhere. My mother Lais had died of a canker of the bosom in my tenth year despite the very best medical attention from the Legate's personal physician. This left me as an orphan who remained the property of the Legate.

My mistress, through her husband, arranged for my transfer to the slave emporium at Delos Island in the Aegean where the better class of bonded people are traded. My price was to be subsidized to ensure I located a superior quality of master or mistress, and not a dealer in virgins or entertainers," she revealed with some pride.

"You were still a virgin you say?" Suetonius enquired, perhaps with a little too much interest.

"Indeed, sir," Thais declared. "Perhaps this was an issue, I suspect, because my mistress was concerned either her husband the Legate, or more likely her son Aulus, had become too fond of me."

Thais's responses were without any evident conceit.

"In truth, sirs, Aulus and I had become very close at the time. Very close. He was a very beautiful young man of great quality," she murmured wistfully.

"Why didn't the Legate simply give you to Aulus as his body servant and companion?" Clarus proposed. "He was entitled to do so."

"There were impediments to such an arrangement," Thais offered hesitantly. "One was Aulus wished me to be married to him. His mother, my mistress, would not permit this."

"Then we must assume from what you say, Thais of Cyrene, that the Proconsul Legate of the province would have been your father and his son Aulus was likely to be your half-brother?" Suetonius put to her plainly. "Inter-marriage between such closely related may not be wise."

"Why didn't the Legate -- if I'm not mistaken it was Calpurnius Flaccus, the senator and son of the renown rhetorician, yes?," Clarus interjected speculatively, "simply give you your freedom, as is his right as your owner?"

Thais was thoughtful for a moment without commenting upon the Flaccus speculation.

"I think the household was concerned I would then have no protector, no *paterfamilias*, if I was freed, being utterly orphaned," she responded. "Yet they did not wish me married either, despite already being a year or two beyond the accepted age for betrothal."

"So instead they resolved to send you away to a household of quality?" Suetonius contributed. "I imagine your Aulus was distressed? Even heartbroken?"

Thais appeared distracted for a few moments before moving on without responding to the question.

"At Delos I was acquired by an agent of the Imperial Household due to my education and language skills," the dainty young lady continued solemnly. "Then on Great Caesar's instruction the Household steward supplied me to Antinous as his teacher of conversational Latin and instructor in *Palatine* comportment. This was over four years ago at Nicomedia during Caesar's tour of the provinces."

"I see, you were to be his *sleep-in language teacher?*" Clarus implied teasingly. Clarus was not one to miss a wry, if vulgar, observation.

"But what now that this patron, Antinous, too has died?" Clarus searched.

"Antinous has made suitable provision for this," Julianus offered enigmatically.

Suetonius looked to Thais to see how she responded to these queries, only to perceive tears had formed almost imperceptibly at the corners of her eyes. Slowly, gradually, her eyes were welling. The group was silenced by this visible human sentiment. Surisca drew to Thais's side and gently took her hands in her own. Thais did not resist.

"Suitable provision? What sort of provision?" Suetonius continued.

"My *patron* and good friend Antinous has endowed me with sufficient resources to be independent of his patronage," the Cyrene offered as she wiped her eyes. She fell silent.

Julianus spoke up to confirm this enigmatic statement.

"On the day before his death Antinous furnished Thais with sufficient gold coins, precious objects, and the ownership deed to a residence at Athens to support her in her future life. This endowment was of considerable substance, and very adequate to her needs. Her trove is secured against theft or misadventure under my personal seal, and duly recorded by documents drawn by Antinous on the day," the *quaestor* stated. "But we had no idea at the time that Antinous would be dead within that very same day."

"So in the months before the Bithynian's death," Clarus legalistically clarified, "he gave this woman, Thais, her freedom by manumission, and followed this with a large endowment to ensure her financial independence? And he finalized these legalities the very day prior to his own death?"

"Indeed," Julianus agreed.

"What's going on here? I find this very suspicious, or at least unlikely?" Clarus labored the obvious. "Surely we see *cui bono* in operation here! Who has benefited from Antinous's death? We begin to see, perhaps."

Suetonius interrupted him.

"Senator, remember Arrian's report to us of the boy's withdrawal of his personal wealth from safekeeping. Recall too the report of the lad's reputed liaison in an earlier interview...," Suetonius murmured, casting a raised eyebrow at the young Cyrene.

"Reputed liaison?" the senator responded. "Oh. I see. Tell us Thais of Cyrene, is it true you have been an intimate companion of the deceased, Antinous of Bithynia?" Clarus asked forthrightly. "In fact you have been his secret paramour?"

Everyone's eyes turned to Thais.

"Intimate companion? Paramour?" she uttered with some dismay. "Fine sirs, despite my own feelings about my wonderful master, and despite the many occasions when such sentiments could easily have arisen, not once in five years did Antinous impose upon my person in an intimate or amorous manner.

While all those around us at Court shared affairs of the heart and licentious behavior, Antinous and I remained entirely chaste. He was devoted solely to his *erastes*. It was their compact. Even in the two years since my manumission, we have maintained sober relations. That is, well, until very recently," she said, her voice trailing away to a whisper.

"Until recently?"

"Yes. In fact until only weeks ago at Alexandria." The Cyrene was almost inaudible.

"Explain, please."

"Sirs, Antinous of Bithynia was Caesar's *Favorite*. For five years Antinous was an *eromenos* to Caesar's *erastes*. Antinous fulfilled this role according to the accepted custom still celebrated in the East by many men of the nobility. He sought no other companionship, even though many offered their enticements to him. Many, I assure you," Thais recounted. " I and his friend Lysias are witness to this fact."

"*By Jupiter*, what is it the others wanted from this youth?" Clarus asked disingenuously. "Are well-formed features so utterly tantalizing?"

"Antinous indeed possessed rare gifts, sir," Thais responded, "I believe it was his *arete*, my lords, his manly pursuit of excellence. His beauty of character was tantalizing. Women who view creatures endowed by Aphrodite as generously as Antinous has been well appreciate the bodily symmetries informed with such blessings. It tells of an inner enchantment, a boon of the gods, and so women seek to know and absorb this *arete's* spirit into their flesh. It is to hold his *arete* captive within their being -- even to make babies to preserve this rare *arete* into continuing eternity? Women are deeply stimulated by such gifts.

Men are more contradictory. Their urge pursues the recovery of their passing youth so as to bathe in an undying source within their innermost being. It's an ageing man's envy of a younger man's still-dormant, but unlimited, life opportunities. Men envy this stage of life and wish to share it again and again.

The outstretched arm of eternally beautiful Apollo saluting the cyclical day reminds mortal men of the swift transience of youth and its once-in-a-lifetime allure. Youth's visible *arete* casts a spell on them. They recognize its primal force and fleeting beauty. They wish to relive it, possess it, and consume it, to once again participate in its aura both spiritually and bodily.

Some men yearn to engulf such a blossoming lifeforce and absorb it into their own being. Yes, good sirs, to many of us Antinous was indeed utterly tantalizing."

Thais fell silent with lowered eyes. The group contemplated her words.

"So what happened three weeks ago that changed things?" Suetonius asked.

"Sirs, in being close to my master for five years I had grown very fond of him," Thais continued. "I have reason to believe my master had grown fond of me too. We shared much time together in talk and play. We were friends.

At first I wondered if, in making his choice between differing types of love, my master had taken the path of many men of the elites to channel his emotions towards other men, not to womenfolk. Many men around us do so. His commitment to his *erastes* agreed with this preference.

So it came as a surprise when Antinous announced at our apartments in one of those crumbling Ptolemy palaces at Alexandria how Caesar had terminated his role as his *erastes*. The time had arrived, that very day, he told us.

This meant Antinous was now free to make new choices, new experiences, if he wished. That is, if these things are a matter of choice rather than of inner nature."

"And did he?" Suetonius queried.

"Antinous was devastated by Caesar's announcement. He hadn't prepared himself for it, though he knew it was long overdue. Besides, he felt he was in Great Caesar's debt for many things. He felt obliged to make recompense."

"How did this affect your relationship with the young man?"

"In the days following Caesar's declaration, Antinous resolved to offer his first beard's trims to Zeus. His beard and his side-burns had recently grown sufficiently to be evident, despite being fair hued.

Antinous asked me to razor his hair and his sideburns for a formal burnt offering. We were silent together while I applied the knife to his thick mane so it retained its lushness. Antinous possesses beautiful thick locks. He is a golden blond all over.

While I was razoring his hair we both gradually perceived our close proximity. We were within inches of each other while I cut. Our flesh grazed from time to time. Neither of us withdrew from the other's touch. I could smell the perfume of sweet olive oil on his skin lingering after bathing. I sensed his flesh waken in interest. One thing led to another. We both realized our fondness for each other and Aphrodite smiled graciously upon us," Thais offered quietly.

"Aphrodite?" Suetonius asked, perhaps unnecessarily.

"Antinous took me," she said simply. "He is impulsive. He's young. He was lusty with me in a man's way. I felt no regret. I acceded willingly, eagerly. Our bodies held each other close. We stayed together that night. We made love several times. That's all."

Thais slipped into silence again as her voice faded.

Julianus picked up the thread.

"Please note gentlemen, Thais and Antinous did not become intimate in this way until some weeks after Hadrian had dissolved the mentoring relationship," the jurist confirmed definitively.

"Was this the only occasion of this intimacy?" Clarus probed further. Thais responded in a low voice.

"No. We have slept together several nights since that time," she said simply. "And my monthly cycle is now overdue by more than a week. Antinous knows this."

The men looked questioningly at each other while Surisca caressed Thais's hand. It was Clarus who asked the obvious.

"Does this mean …?" he blurted. Surisca replied in Thais's place.

"Not necessarily, but perhaps. Only time will tell. Mistress Thais might have to wait until her next cycle to confirm the possibility, or if other signs appear. That is if she wishes to retain a child to term," the Syri explained.

"I do, I do, I do!" Thais declared brightly. "Especially now he is no more!"

Suetonius turned to Julianus.

"Had Antinous given <u>all</u> his wealth to his young friend?" he asked.

"My understanding of the youth's accounts," Julianus responded, "which were stewarded by Arrian's custodian, a reputable man of discreet tongue, is that Antinous has apportioned about half his personal wealth to this young lady."

"And the remainder?" Suetonius probed.

"I will introduce you to someone shortly who can throw light on those details," was the evasive response.

"If the dead youth was giving away all his wealth," Clarus challenged, "surely this means a great deal about his vision of his future?"

Thais returned to the conversation.

"On the day Antinous provided the treasures and documents to me, I asked him *'If you give me so much of your wealth, you must be going away?'* He replied with the words *'Only a short while, not long. But I'm not sure when I'll return.'*"

"Not long? Not sure?" Suetonius asked. "What ever could he mean by that? Have we stumbled upon some secret adventure of the youth's that misfired? The boy was certainly known as a risk taker."

Julianus nodded agreement.

"I asked even further, sirs," Thais continued, "and he gave an answer I still do not understand. He whispered while we shared the comfort of my own bed on the very morning of his last day *'I must perform one last service for my Eromenos, Hadrian!'* He then added *'After four years of service, I must make one final gesture -- the Lion must protect its Cub.'*

Thais looked to the group with a perplexed expression. Strabon immediately ceased inscribing. His ears perceived sedition.

"You must mean *Erastes*, don't you, young lady? Not *Eromenos*, yes?" Clarus hastened to correct.

Thais shook her head slowly. "No, I don't. He said *Eromenos*."

Julianus stroked his chin thoughtfully as Clarus coughed nervously.

"What lion? What cub? We're back there again," Suetonius tried to clarify, knowing full well the terms were already known to his colleagues. "What did he mean, do you think?"

"That's all I know. These were among his last words to me that morning before we parted. As he left me he said he had other important business to complete."

"Did he say where he was going or what he was doing or who he was to be meeting?" Suetonius queried.

"No sir, he did not."

"A question of a personal nature, Mistress Thais," Clarus intruded. "Did you in the course of your intimacies have reason to kiss your young friend's neck, possibly with some passion? You know, sufficient to leave skin markings? Love bites?"

Thais blushed at the question's audacity but considered it thoughtfully. She replied in a frail voice.

"It could be said so, sir. Yes we were passionate together on several occasions through our final night. I recall very many moments when I caressed him all over."

"And precisely where would you say you placed your caresses?" Suetonius asked with forensic coolness. Thais blushed even more deeply.

"Everywhere sir, everywhere. But I find his neck and throat to be an especially desirable place to kiss," she whispered.

"Could you say where specifically upon the neck or throat?"

"Where specifically? Well, sir, I am not as tall as Antinous. In his arms I recall I find his throat near the bridge of his chest to be closer than, say, his jawline or lips, unless he bends towards me. Is this what you mean?"

"I see. And did Antinous have any wound evident anywhere on his person on the day?" Suetonius continued. "A fresh wound in his flesh? A severe cut?"

"A wound? Not that I recall, sir. The old scar on his cheek is the only wound I have been aware of, but that was long healed, though he had many light abrasions around his trunk from scratches inflicted during a lion hunt some weeks ago," she replied.

"But nothing on his arms or wrist, you would say?" the biographer probed.

"No sir."

It was Clarus's turn to interrogate.

"Where were you on the night the young man drowned, Mistress Thais of Cyrene? And do you have a witness?" the senator searched. Thais was flummoxed by such a question.

"I naturally awaited my beloved's return in my own chamber, sirs," she responded. "My witnesses would have been his household's servants or Simon, the senior steward of Lysias's household, a Jewish freedman of good repute. Lysias too joined us later. But Simon was murdered last night near our tents, before our very eyes! He, Lysias, and I were attacked at our tents by cloaked ruffians. We don't know who they were or what they wanted. But they seemed intent on killing us nonetheless.

They cruelly killed Simon, a kindly man of honor, who was bravely defending us by covering our escape as we fled the attack. We were unarmed and could not help him.

Yet these villains seemed to get past both the Praetorian and Horse Guard protections and the passwords of the camp! It's for this reason I have taken refuge here with Senator Salvius Julianus. He is known to me as a friend of Antinous."

Suetonius perceived this line of questioning was achieving little.

"Then what do you think might have happened to Antinous, Mistress Thais, on the night of his death?" Suetonius asked, returning to the heart of the issue. "Was he too a victim of ruffians or robbers?"

"I had hoped, sir, you might tell me," Thais replied as the glint of moisture returned to her eyes.

"Strabon, locate the paper records of the personnel traffic at the wharf to *The Alexandros* we stored earlier. Mistress Thais might advise us on a matter."

The scribe immediately began rifling through his basket with its wax tablets, scrolls of transcriptions, and paper sheets.

"Tell me," Suetonius continued, "do you know where Lysias was on the evening of Antinous's disappearance? Does Lysias share such details with you?"

"Yes sir, he does. He was at our chambers throughout the evening. I believe he had spent some hours earlier that afternoon in the company of my beloved. We talked together in the evening after Antinous had departed to his unhappy destiny. We both shared how we were perplexed by my beloved's actions, and by his secrecy about his intentions that day."

"Gentlemen, I believe we have a great contradiction here! Strabon, what do the wharf records say about Lysias two days ago?" the biographer called to his scribe. Strabon scanned the papyrus sheets collected from the wharf clerk

"Sir, the documents record Lysias arrived at *The Alexandros* in the early evening of that day, complete with a formal invitation for him from the Governor's consort Anna Perenna. But there is no record that he departed the vessel later that day or night or at any time the following day."

"You say there's a record of Lysias arriving, but no record of Lysias departing, on the very night Antinous died?"

"Not on these sheets, Inspector," Strabon confirmed. "Oh, however there's something here you might care to note, sir." Strabon offered one of the sheets to Suetonius and pointed at a particular place, his eyes showing studious concern.

"*Great Zeus!*" the biographer exclaimed. "Why didn't we note that before? That puts a different light on something we heard earlier!"

Strabon nodded acknowledgement, withdrew the sheet, and rolled it carefully for his basket.

"What was there, Tranquillus?" Clarus enquired.

"Nothing, Clarus, nothing. Just an oddity of perception we had missed, that's all," Suetonius replied dismissively.

Clarus turned to the young lady interviewee. He was puffing scarlet with a victory.

"How do you explain, Thais of Cyrene," the burly magistrate asked gruffly, "that according to the record of the Watch at the river jetty to the governor's barque, your friend Lysias of Bithynia was not with you that evening, as you claim, but enjoying his pleasures aboard the barque in the company of the priestess Anna Perenna? Why should you aim to provide a covering alibi for him? Is there some conspiracy between you and Lysias?"

Thais stared at the mature-aged, portly Roman senator in visible dismay.

"That's simply not possible, sir!" she responded with some alarm. "Lysias was in my company throughout the evening and night of Antinous's disappearance, and again yesterday from just after dawn when the shocking news of the death was revealed. Like me, he was stricken by the news."

"Then how do we account for Lysias going aboard *The Alexandros* the previous eve, according to this record, but never departing?"

A heavy silence hung in the air. It was broken by an unexpected voice from one side of the patio.

"That, Special Inspector, is because he didn't go aboard *The Alexandros*," the muffled voice interjected from a near proximity. "He's never ever been onboard the Governor's barque, ever, in his life," the same voice proclaimed from beyond a marquee's flap. The group turned towards the source of the vocal protest.

Salvius Julianus strode to the tent portal and again lifted its flap to expose the shadowy vestibule beyond.

"I told you I have something else to show you, my friends."

Once again he drew a bead curtain aside to reveal a figure standing in the dimness of the vestibule chamber beyond.

"Lysias of Bithynia, please join us," the Roman jurist called.

CHAPTER 27

"Explain yourself, Lysias of Bithynia! We are Caesar's investigators into the death of your companion Antinous!" Suetonius demanded sharply. He aimed to impress Clarus with his determination.

"You dare to put yourselves above the law! You, Lysias, only yesterday swore under oath you would attend our interview today. You did not! Your claim to *arete*, to honor, is the worthless promise of a dissembler and hypocrite!"

"You also offend against the *Imperium*!" Clarus added menacingly.

"Gentlemen, gentlemen, gentlemen," Salvius Julianus interceded, "perhaps he had good reasons which we should hear first?"

"Noble sirs," Lysias stammered, "Thais and I were attacked late last night at our chambers. Ruffians with drawn swords fell upon us. Our worthy steward, my freedman Simon, was brutally killed before our very eyes. I grabbed Thais by the arm and dragged her to safety while the wounded Simon fought to hold off the attackers. I had no weapon to defend us other than a small dagger, so Simon was cut down without honor.

I fled with Thais by an evasive route to come here to the Companions' enclosure for sanctuary; otherwise we too would have been killed. I'm sure we were the intended targets"

"Nevertheless, why didn't you attend this morning's interview?!" Clarus demanded.

"Perhaps more importantly, Septicius," Suetonius interjected, "<u>who</u> is making attacks against members of this investigation, and why? And where are this camp's military protectors? Where are the Guard or even men of the Legion? Where are they when you need them? They seem to be everywhere when you don't need them."

Clarus shifted tack in his examination.

"Explain why Nubians are pursuing you, Lysias of Bithynia? What do you know or possess to sufficiently incite Nubians to kill you? And whose Nubians are they, anyway?"

Lysias was dismayed.

"Nubians? What Nubians? I don't know what you mean!"

"We've had it on good authority you said you were attacked by Nubians," Clarus responded, keeping Scorilo's earlier words in mind.

"No, my lord, this is not so. Though the troublemakers were disguised behind mantles and cowls, the skin of their arms was not the darkness of Nubians nor Egyptians, and their weapons were either Roman, Greek, or of the northern barbarians," Lysias announced. "Even their open-lace boots were military issue, not peasant work, I saw clearly."

Suetonius, Clarus, and Julianus looked towards each other questioningly.

"Renegade troops? Bandits? Undercover operatives?" Clarus asked rhetorically.

"And finally, Lysias," Suetonius probed further, "how do you explain your journey to *The Alexandros* on the evening prior to Antinous's death? You are recorded in the vessel's traffic sheets as having boarded the vessel in the company of a Guardsman late in the evening of the day of Antinous's death? You did not mentioned this to us earlier!"

Suetonius halted momentarily when Strabon coughed politely and pointed to the furled sheet in his tablets and scrolls basket. Suetonius continued.

"And perhaps accompanied by another senior officer too? Yet there is no record of your return from the vessel that night or the following day, which we assess may have been the time of your friend's death?"

Clarus glanced quizzically at the biographer at mention of the further officer while Lysias expressed utter dismay if not actual offence.

"I have no idea what you are talking about. I've never been aboard either *The Alexandros* or *The Dionysus* in my life. My status doesn't entitle me. I've never been invited, by anyone, either. I was nowhere in the vicinity of the two Imperial barques on the day or night of my companion's death, so how can you believe otherwise?"

"Can you prove this? This paper record is our irrevocable proof. It says you provided a written invitation from the lady Anna Perenna as your pass authority. What can it mean? Are you involved in a secret dalliance with the Governor's consort?" Suetonius demanded. "The clerk described your youthful qualities and presence very adequately."

Lysias appeared visibly confounded by the queries.

"Sirs, I have had no reason to go anywhere near the two barques, and I have never ever conversed with the Governor's consort, ever!"

Two servants of the Companions appeared at the terrace entrance carrying lamps and tapers for the coming evening's illumination. Dusk was now falling and it was time to provide light in anticipation of a swift Egyptian sunset. Julianus nodded to his staff to place the lamps and depart for privacy's sake.

"Bithynian, if I recall correctly, you told this investigation yesterday how Antinous was faithful to the emperor and didn't sleep around with those who solicited his favors? I recall you said the youth *only slept with his lover.*

Yet we now hear your companion has been intimate with a manumitted slave, the Cyrene female Thais, and has been so for some time. She might even be pregnant from his attentions."

Clarus was not known for subtlety in dealing with intimate details.

Thais cringed. Lysias heaved a despondent sigh.

"My lord, yes, you repeat my words correctly. I said *he only slept with those who love him,*" the strapping young man confirmed. "But Great Caesar relinquished his role as *erastes* to Antinous many weeks ago at Alexandria. This was weeks before our flotilla sailed the Delta canals into Egypt's interior. Since that time Antinous has again *only slept with those who love him*, but now it is no longer Caesar. Nevertheless, it seems on the day before his death my long-time friend made a point of *special sharing* with each of those who loved him, even some who did not expect the honor - --"

"*Special sharing? Each?* What do you mean by *each*? Your meaning, Bithynian, is he had <u>sex</u> with those who loved him?" Suetonius repeated. "After all it's *sex* we're talking about, isn't it?"

Surisca made a discreet gesture to the biographer and leaned forward to whisper some words. Surisca reminded the Special Investigator of a matter from their earlier observations. Suetonius reacted with new interest. Yes, there had been two sets of lesions at Antinous's neck and throat, not just one, he belatedly recalled.

"Tell us, Lysias, why do you word your statement so generically?" he asked. "You say he, Antinous, only had sex *with those who love him*? Are you saying there is more than one supplicant to his affections?"

Lysias paused before replying. He was discomforted by the question. His voice was strained.

"On the night and day preceding the night of his death Antinous indeed slept with and made love to one who loves him, and who I believe he too loved. This was his freedwoman Thais. However, it is also true how later in the afternoon of the same day preceding his death he shared his *arete* and his body with another, too, who loves him."

"And who would this further paramour be?" Suetonius asked in exasperation. "The *Augusta* herself?"

"No, of course not, my lords," he murmured softly, "but it was who you have probably contemplated it may have been all along."

The group was frozen in anticipation.

"It was I myself."

They stood silently for some moments.

"Are you saying," Clarus offered frankly after a pause; "you and Caesar's *eromenos* have been lovers all along? So you've been lying to us, yes? Some form of *laesa majestas* offence is committed here, if not capital perjury!"

"No, sir, I assure you Antinous was indeed faithful to Caesar! Antinous and I were not partners, regular or occasional -- not since our adolescence long ago, anyway. But it seems in Antinous's final twenty-four hours he chose to favor both Thais and I. He did so with each separately and at that time unknown to each other," Lysias revealed. "However, neither of us knew of this, nor that this was to be his final day. He left hints to that possibility without us being wise enough to realize it."

"Hints? What hints?"

"At the time I wondered at his urgency," Lysias continued. "His desire to favor me after so many years seemed precipitous, especially as at that time no such thought had entered my mind.

But he seduced me, purposely, unquestioningly, intentionally, and very successfully. It was untypical of him, it was unexpected and unexplained, but I cannot honestly say it was unwelcome. He fulfilled a lingering desire I had harbored since our *Polis* days, but had never experienced so completely previously. I had forgotten how devoted I was to him.

Yet in a moment of deep closeness between us, at a moment of powerful impact, he took pains to beg of me that would I look after Thais on his behalf. He sought I should protect her and her progeny should anything untoward befall him. He didn't explain what he meant, despite my protestation, but he implied I should make Thais my wife if he met with misfortune. He extracted my holy oath by Zeus, Apollo, Artemis, and Aphrodite that I would fulfill his plea. He was adamant.

In the intense passion of the occasion I willingly swore to do as he asked. And I certainly will, if Thais agrees," Lysias explained while Thais kept her eyes lowered. "Yet at that time I had no idea what was to occur through the following hours."

Suetonius probed further.

"Did you, Lysias of Bithynia, during moments of your ardor, also inflict lesions upon his features?"

"Lesions?!"

"Love bites, hickeys, bruises from kisses?"

"Um, yes, I guess so."

"And what of a wound to his wrist? His left wrist. Did you inflict such a wound?"

"What wound? There was no wound." Lysias was quite certain.

Clarus broke the stillness.

"What is it," Clarus asked vaguely rhetorically, "this dead young man possessed which inspires such ardor among admirers?" The pause survived only briefly.

"As I said earlier, sir, it is beauty, my lord," Thais volunteered. "A beauty of character, a beauty of spirit, a beauty of humanity. Beauty, too, of form and shape, but this was not the primary beauty. It would pass soon into time. Antinous was a beguiling personality whose openness communicated sincerity, security, and wholeheartedness. His spirit was alive to life and love!"

She fell silent after her outburst, embarrassed by her own emotion. Lysias was moved enough to take up her theme.

"Truly, sirs, he possessed such a personable appeal. This charisma was coupled with an extraordinary magnificence of body, and visage as a living creature. Antinous was Apollo Incarnate, he was Apollo alive in this world, here, now, with us to see and touch today. He was not distant, out of reach, silent.

Old philosophers tell we Greeks how human beauty is a reflection of the divine among us. Yet unlike remote Apollo or the fearful deities of the Levant, Antinous possessed an emotional warmth no god displays to devotees. For Antinous, *love* must be tangible and active. In him, it was, generously."

The group was silenced by these quaint sentiments. Clarus emitted a nervous burst of laughter.

"You are talking of a mere *Favorite*, a decorative appendage to the Caesar of all the Romans," Clarus provoked. "A ruler's toy or plaything, his catamite, a mere bugger-boy. Something to screw at night."

Lysias suppressed his rising anger.

"Sirs, I see in Antinous what I myself would like to be, but am not. Antinous accepted to be Hadrian's *eromenos* not in childlike subservience or in willing submission to a power fuck, but because of his respect and affection for the man Hadrian. Does age really matter if you love someone? Yes, it's true his relationship with Caesar placed him at the heart of the universe, at the heart of our times. But it survived because the man Hadrian had matching needs and character.

Yes, by becoming companion to Caesar he entered into his own legend, his own Homeric saga. He could echo Odysseus, Hector, Achilles, and Alexander rolled into one, but alive now, today, in our times, not just in dusty scrolls. Antinous brought delight into the hearts of all who knew him."

"This is nonsense," Clarus probed sarcastically. "What has he done with his life? What has he achieved? He was a Homeric hero who enacted no heroism."

"You may think so, sir. Yet he existed alive before our eyes to show us how what matters in life is not who or what one loves, it is the very fact of being able to love, the act of loving and being loved. Sex is a stepping stone to that realization. This revelation is enough for those who were captivated by him. I happily was such a one, and I believe too Great Caesar is."

"Do you, Greek, love him too?"

"Yes, sir, I do."

"Tell me, Lysias of Bithynia, is there anyone centered in your life other than Thais, or do you impose on your slaves or engage in other diversions for bodily satisfaction?" the biographer continued.

"No, Gaius Suetonius Tranquillus, there are neither slaves nor 'diversions' in my life," Lysias replied. "I offer my four-year relationship as *eromenos* to my *erastes* Lucius Vibullius Tiberius Claudius Herodes Atticus of Athens as evidence of my honorable morals. Our lengthy liaison was concluded only last year at Rome.

I ceased being his *eromenos* just prior to Herodes' announcement of his marriage to Annia Regilla of the Annii, a worthy and noble *patrician* family of Rome," Lysias regaled his inquisitors.

"I see you are indeed a man of passion? You agree then, Bithynian, you may have inflicted lesions of passion upon your school chum's neck on the day of his death?" Suetonius probed unhesitatingly. "At the front?"

Lysias blushed beneath his soldierly, suntanned features. "It's possible. Very possible."

"Well that satisfies that issue," Clarus muttered to his colleagues with a nod to Surisca for her earlier perceptiveness, "we've accounted for two sets on the cadaver's neck at last."

"Why do you suppose Antinous would grace both you and the Cyrene with his *favors*, as you call it, on the day of his drowning?" Suetonius searched. "Did he know he was about to die?"

"I do not know," Lysias replied. "But in looking back at his urgency as well as the promise he extracted from me, he must have had some premonition of his fate.

Whatever it was, I wish he had shared his fears with those who love him, and not face it alone, whatever it may have been."

"*Foreknowledge* tells us it was no accident," Suetonius declared. "I don't accept he had foreknowledge from soothsayers or diviners. Foreknowledge means either he was an intentional suicide or had reason to expect to be killed. So who are those who wished Antinous to be dead? Or did Antinous wish himself to be dead? This is the basic question of our enquiry now. Also, who benefits from it?"

Salvius Julianus interjected.

"To that you then have to add why unknown renegades would seek the death of his associates afterwards, including even those engaged upon his death's investigation. This apparently includes even me. Overall, there are hidden forces at work in each supposition. *Hidden forces* suggests to me miscreants at work, not suicide. "

"Which indicates it was murder," Suetonius added. "At least that much seems unarguable. Yet what is the motive? And who is the perpetrator?"

Salvius Julianus spoke.

"Do realize you have less than nine hours until your appointment with Caesar?"

"It's true," Clarus agreed, "our time allowance is passing swiftly. And we're no closer to a solution to our investigation than we were a day ago."

"Yet, friends," Suetonius murmured, "I see an outline appearing in the midst of the murk. I don't know its importance or accuracy, but several notions are taking shape in my mind.

Perhaps next on our list of interviewees should be that Egyptian priest whose name recurs so interminably in our enquiries?"

"Pachrates of Memphis?" Clarus trumpeted. "Let's pay him a visit, despite the late hour!"

"Let's do so," the biographer declared. "But first, Julianus, I have a very big favor to ask of you. In case we are delayed by our interviews before tomorrow's dawn, I wish to seek your assistance in a legal acquisition on our behalf with your *lictors*. This is my request. Keep it concealed, it's important. So I'll tell you, just between us, in a moment.

I also ask your *Companions* and grooms to secure the safety of Lysias and Thais until dawn and escort them to Caesar's ceremony. I want them to meet no further harm."

"It will be done, Tranquillus, it will be done."

"Good then, here's my chore for you ---"

Clarus, Surisca, and the others watched as the Special Inspector drew Julianus to one side to murmur privately into his ear.

CHAPTER 28

"Fine gentlemen of Rome, this is an unexpected and welcome visitation!" the exceedingly polite Egyptian priest declared while his features expressed contradictory sentiments. His feigned conviviality was confirmed by his loose night tunic, smudged *kohl* around his eyes, and crumpled appearance indicating he had been disturbed in his sleep.

"On behalf of the high priest of Amun, Pachrates of Memphis, I apologize for our inability to offer you proper neighborliness at this late hour," Kenamun said. His manner was not inviting.

"Why so, Priest? We are here on Caesar's business," Clarus demanded.

"My lord Senator, Priest Pachrates resides tonight at the Temple of Amun beyond this camp. He and his acolytes are preparing for the ceremonies ordained by Great Caesar at dawn today. Only I and a visiting elder of our cult, with our attendants, remain here at our tents within the Imperial camp."

Kenamun, the priestly mortician embalmer, regaled his visitors with low bows and elaborate eastern genuflections while a temple guard hovered nearby marshalling an assegai spear held ready for action.

"Dawn today? Is it already approaching the new day?" Suetonius asked.

"Yes, Senator. Dawn is in five hours," the priest responded.

"We are here, Egyptian, to enquire further into the death of the young Favorite whose remains you have been preparing for Caesar's rites. We have new questions to ask you. It is official State business," Clarus added as Strabon waved the scroll of authority again. Surisca stood quietly in the background observing the priest's manner.

"These tents are closed, Senator. We completed our duties long ago, and our holy figurine of the deity is resting in his shrine. We dare not disturb Amun's sleep, Senator. It is a great sacrilege," Kenamun offered as a reason to terminate the visit.

"Enough Egyptian! Fulfill the law of hospitality and bring us refreshments. We haven't eaten or taken drink in hours, and we won't disturb your god, I promise you," the senator snapped.

Kenamun took the hint and waved smartly at a servant priest to attend to the matters.

"That's for four of us including the woman, Egyptian!" Clarus shouted after the disappearing servant in case.

"We've come to ask questions of your master Pachrates. But if he's elsewhere, then you will have to suffice," Suetonius explained.

"I cannot speak for my master Pachrates, sirs. I can only speak for myself, and I am not worthy of your attention," Kenamun responded, genuflecting in humility.

"You will have to do, priest, and we will be speedy. But we'll record your words, priest, for our documents. You are to reply to our questions with precision. Do you understand? This is legal testimony, and we possess the force of law."

"Why me?" the priest protested in increasing alarm.

"We are still pursuing information about the fate of your client, the cadaver of Antinous of Bithynia, just as we were at the embalming pavilion with you yesterday. But we have new questions now."

"I know no more than you've already heard," the priest whined.

"Begin, scribe," Suetonius instructed Strabon. "Priest, state your name, title, and duties. We will record your words."

Kenamun responded grudgingly.

"Me? My name? *By Amun*, I am Kenamun, a senior priest of the cult of Amun, the Old Religion of this land. I serve at Memphis at the great temple of Amun. I am a specialist in the arts of preparing the dead for their journey to The Land of the Dead. My master is Priest Pachrates of Memphis."

"Where were you on the day and the night of Antinous's death?"

"If you mean the night before the discovery of his body, I was at the Temple's enclosure outside this camp preparing rites for The Festival of Isis. The Isia is an important celebration in the liturgical year of our cult."

"You have witnesses?"

"An entire congregation of priests, including Priest Pachrates himself. You are free to ask."

Suetonius decided to take a risk and confront Kenamun with a provocation.

"We have been told by witnesses you may be the priest who sailed your temple's *felucca* vessel on the River Nile on the day of the discovery of the youth's body? Was it you? And why were you upon the River so early? Explain yourself, Egyptian."

"Our *felucca*? What *felucca*? We do not possess a working riverboat at this time, sirs."

"Your boat with the Eye of Horus at the prow in your temple colors? We have been told it lies moored at an inlet close by your temple?"

"My lords, the *felucca* you speak of is not in sailing condition. It is our only riverboat. It was damaged a month ago in a collision with another vessel. It lies docked in a slipway awaiting repairs by a boat-builder. To travel the river we must hire other vessels or the services of local fishermen for our river transport."

Suetonius and Clarus were disconcerted by this claim as servants arrived with simple foods and drink.

"We have been told by one of your own workmen that this is so. He told our investigators a great deal about your master Pachrates. In fact, he is the very workman who recently disappeared from your confraternity. We're must warn you, he's dead. He lost his life during an excess of questioning, so we've been told," Clarus explained. "We will pay blood money to your Temple, as is the custom here."

The priest was visibly surprised.

"Workman? What workman? We have lost no workman. We head count our confraternity at each sunset ceremony, and there is no one missing. Are you sure you speak of us, my lords, and not some other fellowship?"

"You say you possess a single boat which cannot sail, and you have lost no workman since yesterday?" Suetonius searched.

"That is so," Kenamun said, evidently mystified by the queries.

Suetonius and Clarus were similarly puzzled. Centurion Urbicus's reports conveyed a reliable sense of authority..

"Who has given you this information? It is mistaken," Kenamun added.

Suetonius moved right on.

"Well then, instead, explain to us what you know about the Bithynian's death or have heard as gossip?"

"I know nothing other than what has been displayed by his corpse, which I have prepared for exhibition, as you know."

"So, does his corpse tell you anything we should know?"

"I am a mortician. I have seen many corpses in my time. I notice things. But I do not necessarily understand what it is that I have observed."

"What have you observed in regard to Antinous?"

"Well, for one, the youth is said to have died by drowning. His lungs had been drained clear of river water, which is to be expected of his finders. But it does not explain why his veins contained almost no blood. They too seemed similarly drained."

The group of four were wide eyed in interest.

"In my view, the youth died of severe bleeding some time well before he drowned. The lad had a deep incision in his left wrist, cut in a way to promote bleeding. We packed it with wax to hide from view when his body is displayed, as you yourselves detected. Unless he slashed his own wrist while in the river, I cannot see how after being bled into unconsciousness he could find his way to the river's banks unaided?"

"Why couldn't he have slashed his wrist before falling into the river?" Clarus asked. "As a suicide might."

"Well," Kenamun proposed, "I am told he was left-handed. Surely such a suicide would slash his right wrist, not his left? But even so, the blood loss would have been very great."

"Are you aware, priest, that there have been rumors circulating that your master Pachrates is involved in a conspiracy to sacrifice the youth to the river? To impress Caesar. And if so, you too are implicated," the Special Inspector charged threateningly.

Kenamun now grew frightened.

"That is not possible, sirs! Neither my master nor I would engage in such a crime. Where did you get such an idea? Such a crime would undo all the work we of the Old Religion have labored upon to establish Caesar's confidence in us. The risk and its price would be far too high! We would not dare such a felony."

"This story was given to us by …," Suetonius paused momentarily. He realized Urbicus was the source of this claim too, as the investigators glanced questioningly among themselves.

"Besides, my lords," Kenamun continued, "my master had already refused the youth such a project of his own making. Pachrates did so in the presence of Great Caesar."

"What, *by Zeus*, do you mean by that?!" Clarus exclaimed.

"The Bithynian, Antinous, approached my master and myself in the presence of Caesar and others while the Household was passing through Memphis some weeks ago. The youth proposed he offer himself as a sacrifice to the river to alleviate this summer's low flood ahead of next year's inundation. He said he owed it to Caesar in obligation."

"He owed it in obligation? And so ..?" Suetonius asked.

"He suggested the great priest Pachrates could then *recall him from death*, just as he had retrieved other creatures from death in his magic displays."

The group looked to each other knowingly. Such magic was not credible in their eyes.

"What response did this generous offer receive?" Suetonius asked.

"My master was amazed, of course. Alarmed even. His magic is great, but recovery from death can only be achieved on rare occasions of the stars' configurations. Unless it's with small animals or other vermin, that is. Antinous and Caesar had witnessed such a unique demonstration with a criminal who was beheaded."

The group of four silently held their own counsel.

"Pachrates said No! to Antinous. But it was Caesar who was adamant. He refused the young man his wish outright.

He said the boy had no obligation to pursue such a course of action, despite his noble intentions. He angrily forbade it. Very angrily.

Besides, Pachrates and I impressed upon the youth how someone drowns in the Nile every day. One of these daily accidents would be a sufficient sacrificial victim to the river's temper."

"Did this persuade the lad?"

"No, I don't think so. He also talked of *exchanging boons*. This is something to do with two people exchanging their life span in some magical way. It is a Greek or Roman or Chaldean magic I do not know."

"Who else attended this occasion at Memphis?" Clarus asked.

"Besides my master Pachrates, I recall Caesar and the young man, Governor Titianus, Senator Arrian, Senator Commodus, Secretary Vestinus, and their respective attendants and guards. The meeting was held to discuss the foundation of Caesar's new city of Hadrianopolis."

"Who were the attendants you mention?" Suetonius probed further.

"Why, if I recall correctly, other than slaves and servants, the Governor's lady companion Anna Perenna, with Tribune Macedo of Caesar's Praetorians, his Alexandrian officer Quintus Urbicus, and officers of the Horse Guard."

"Do you know the names of any of the Horse Guard?"

"Only the one with the face tattoos, Decurion Scorilo. He was in charge of Caesar's protection that day."

"These people were all party to this conversation?"

"Yes, they were in the chamber at the time, they witnessed the discussion."

"One question, priest. Do you recall what Antinous was wearing that particular day?" the biographer asked.

"How was he dressed? Oh, it were his usual sporty Greek attire, short Greek tunic, mantle, headband. That's all. The Bithynian did not dress to be noticed."

"Anything else? Adornments, buckles, bracelets, earrings?"

"No, he always dressed simply. He was wearing his finger ring, of course, the deep blue one with the mystic symbols. *Abrasax*, isn't it? Dark *lapis lazuli* from Bactria. I am told it's a special gift from Caesar found at Antioch. We of Egypt are wary of *Abrasax*."

"Why so, priest?"

"It's Chaldean magic. It's very potent. It possesses mysteries we do not understand. We are fearful of it. Only great beings can harness its powers. I would not dare wear such a talisman. It's said it destroys those who are inferior. It has a mind of its own, a cruel mind."

"You mentioned Anna Perenna. What do you know of this lady, priest?"

Kenamun hesitated briefly. A cloud passed across his features.

"Just between us, priest," Suetonius reassured the mortician, "just between us."

Kenamun prevaricated, but loosened up.

"This woman, gentlemen, is the Governor's Favorite. We must be careful in talking of the Governor's consort. When Caesar returns to Rome, it is Titianus who will rule here as *Pharaoh*. His consort will possess subtle influence. She will have great importance in our lives."

"Who is this woman? Where is she from? What are her merits?" the Special Inspector asked. "We have learned very little about her."

"Our contacts in Alexandria as well as Rome and Antioch, have tried to seek out her details. She arrived in Alexandria from Rome at the same time as the Governor about four years ago. We thought she was his wife, but she is not. She doesn't look Roman, yet she is the representative of one of Rome's most ancient cults. It is a tradition very popular with women among Romans and Greeks, like Isis."

"She doesn't look Roman, you say?"

"To my eye she looks to be of a barbarian race. But that cannot be. Her cult is Roman by definition."

"Anything more?"

"She is reputed to engage in arcane rituals. Some at Alexandria say she sacrifices to alien gods. There are stories, unpleasant stories."

Kenamun fell meaningfully silent.

"Yes. Go on. What stories?"

"There are whispers. At the Governor's Rhakotis Palace children are known to disappear. Very young children. Boys only. Bones and flesh debris have been found in palace drains. Palace slaves say they have been obliged to clean rooms sprayed with gore. There are grisly tales. But perhaps these are slanders by inferiors about their Roman mistress."

"I see, I think. Anything else?"

"She is reputed to possess a lively sexual appetite. She is thought to be a female *cinaedus*. She charms many men. She has her way with them.

She is the Governor's consort, but she has lovers elsewhere. One or two have disappeared, I've heard it said."

"What else?"

"Anna Perenna is not her real name."

"What is her real name?"

"We don't know. When Pachrates journeyed to Rome last year he sought to find out. All he could discover was she was a chosen adoptee of her cult, no more. Perhaps they do not know her real origins themselves, the source has been lost."

"Do you think she had some influence over Antinous?" Suetonius posed.

"Yes. Perhaps. They have been seen talking together."

"So, do you think you know what happened to the boy?"

"I only know facets of his mind. The youth was set upon a mission. I overheard his urge often in Household conversations. But I do not know what the mission may have been.

At one time he asked certain services of us, services we will not – or cannot – provide, and Caesar refused to us anyway. How these services connected to his mission is unknown to me. But, my lords and lady," Kenamun offered thoughtfully, giving Surisca's presence an unexpected acknowledgement, "I can recommend to you a special method of enquiry into Caesar's companion's fate."

The group of four stirred to life again. It was very late, and their attention was drooping. Kenamun continued.

"We have residing with us here the famous Priest Si-Amun of the Temple of Zeus Ammon at Siwa Oasis. Si-Amun is this generation's Oracle of Siwa. Si-Amun is a master medium. He has travelled the long journey from Siwa to pay his respects to Caesar and participate in Hadrian's announcement today."

"Today? It's here already?" Suetonius asked without expecting an answer.

"A medium? An oracle? A seer?" Clarus queried.

"Yes indeed. Si-Amun knows nothing of your companion Antinous yet I am sure his gift as an Oracle will tell you much you do not yet know."

"What do we do? Ask him questions? Beg his advice? What form does this Oracle take?"

"You ask a few simple, direct questions. Si-Amun will respond in the language of the Oracle, which is the language of the *Amazigh* peoples of Libya. They often have blue eyes with fair hair, their origin is unknown. I will translate his words into Greek for you. His responses are for you to interpret according to your understanding. Afterwards you pay the Oracle whatever sum you feel he deserves for his insights."

"Let's do it now," Suetonius said.

The venerable ancient had been woken from his sleep. His bleary eyes, crumpled linens, and tattered ethnic knits hung from his bony frame in untidy drapes. His shaven head had a week's growth of blotchy grey fuzz while a straggly single lock of hair bundled to one side of his cranium tied with a ribbon signified his racial origin.

The *Amazigh* priest put on his weathered headdress of ostrich feathers with curled ram's horns at each temple, and snapped beaten metal bracelets to his arms with decorative chains hung around his neck. They were inscribed in all manner of arcane symbols.

The priest was no youngster. In fact his age, like that of Pachrates, was indiscernible. His skin had tanned under the Siwa desert sun to a leathern dun, with deep corrugations creasing into craggy facial flesh. He had the weathered appearance of a sun-dried, dusty Siwa date of considerable age.

He observed his late night clients with an unblinking, intense gaze.

Both Suetonius and Clarus were immediately struck by the penetrating blue-gray of his eyes squinting from within his bronzed crevasses. The squint's focus probed deep into their eyes. His gaze penetrated behind their corneas, behind their deeper vision, and searched into some distant part of their being hidden at their core. The gaze was disturbing.

Kenamun spoke to the priest in an unfamiliar tongue. Surisca feigned disinterest in the dialogue as occasional familiar words and phrases stumbled through her comprehension. She listened as carefully as she could.

Kenamun spoke in a hushed, reverential whisper. A solitary oil lamp cast flickering light across the old man's features.

"The Great Oracle, Si-Amun of the *Ammoneion* of Siwa, will prepare for his special vocation," Kenamun announced. "Si-Amun will consume the special sacrament of his gift. It is a substance found only among the desert stones of Siwa."

The ancient of days produced a small receptacle filled with several unprepossessing lumps of a substance with the appearance of crumbled rock or wood ashes. He took silver tweezers and placed a few small lumps onto a metal ornamental tray. One of Kenamun's servants held a lighted taper beneath the tray to heat its thin base.

After some moments wisps of white fume rose from the tray. Si-Amun did precisely as Suetonius had done only two days earlier at *The House of the Blue Lotuses*. He fanned the fumes into his face and nostrils with both hands while muttering a low chant in his foreign tongue. Minutes of chanting in the stillness passed.

Si-Amun was suddenly galvanized. He sat bolt upright on his stool. He fumbled to unpin a *fibula* to permit a beaded veil to fall from his headdress across his face, masking his features from sight. His voice assumed an energized clarity of tone. His antique age seemed to dissolve as he fell into a thoughtful silence awaiting Kenamun's questioning words.

"You may begin," the priest mortician nodded. "Ask, but be respectful."

Clarus was moved to ask the opening question.

"Oracle of Siwa, who speaks to us here tonight?" he asked magisterially as Strabon's stylus prepared to flutter over fresh wax.

There was a lengthy pause before Si-Amun spoke. He repeatedly shook his ostrich feather headdress, which gave a rustling sound akin to a feathery *systrum,* while he rattled a real *systrum* in one hand. The voice was no longer the sharp clear vocal character of the ordinary priest, it had a rumbling depth of throatiness as though calling from the bottom of a deep well. His *Amazigh* words were haltingly translated by the mortician.

"*I am Amun, the hidden god. Amun is Ra. Amun is Ptah. Zeus Ammon is Amun. Jupiter is Amun. Serapis is Amun. I am Osiris who Seth destroyed but Isis restored. I am who I am.*"

Suetonius was startled by this heady declaration, yet adventurously posed the next question.

"Great Ammon of the Oracle of Siwa please tell, why did Antinous of Bithynia die?"

Again a long pause as the ostrich feathers shimmered, flurried, and trilled while the *systrum* rattled. Kenamun slowly translated the stumbled response.

"The son of Apollo ascended to the sun. The sun burnt the youth. The wild forces of Eros overcame the civil power of Aphrodite. A hidden secret unleashed the chaos of Eros so stalking wolves could devour their prey."

The group looked among each other, mystified.

"If that is 'why', Si-Amun, then *how* did Antinous die?" Suetonius asked, faintly unsettled by talk of wolves devouring their prey.

Another long pause prevailed as feathers and *systrum* rustled, shimmered, and rattled.

"The son of Apollo bled into Darkness. The stalking wolves sipped his blood."

"Are you saying Antinous was murdered, Great Oracle?"

Again a pause of rustles and rattles.

"The son of Apollo made an offering at the altar of his brother Asclepius. He offered his only true spoils to the altar, his life. Stalking wolves devoured the spoils with relish."

"Asclepius?" Clarus exclaimed. "Why Asclepius, Apollo's son and the god of healing? Are you certain?"

Suetonius dismissed the query; he felt he was close to some answers.

"Who is the murderer, Great Oracle? Who killed Antinous?" Suetonius called aloud with quavering emotion. All held their breath after a long period of rustling passed and then ceased.

"A wolf's sword exacts its revenge. A she wolf's delusion drinks its fill. But the path to the sacrificial altar was smoothed by a king's secret."

"Wolves. She wolves. A king's secret. Where are we in all this?" Clarus groaned plaintively.

Si-Amun's voice responded immediately in crisp Common Greek.

"On a journey of justice for the king. Identify the She Wolf. Apprehend the wolves. Send them to the Underworld of the alien god."

"Who is their god?" Clarus asked, realizing to identify the deity might identify the malefactors.

Si-Amun expelled a loud cry of pained anguish. His body trembled violently. His voice quavered with emotion.

"The Baal of the East who came to the West. The Drinker of Blood. The Wolf Deity."

The group looked to each other, utterly perplexed.

"How will we punish the murderer or murderers, Great Oracle of Amun?"

Pause.

"*Fire purifies,*" came the simple response. *"Fire purifies!"*

"What of Antinous? Will Antinous return from Hades?" Suetonius dared to propose, atypically, illogically, unexpectedly. Is resurrection on the agenda? The pause was brief, the voice clear.

"*The son of Apollo rises with the new dawn, when the king's heart bursts with anguish. Self-knowledge renews his soul.*"

The rustle of feathers and systrum ceased. Everyone in the chamber was silent.

Si-Amun slowly toppled from his stool to the pavilion floor. His feathered headdress fell from his face revealing his shaven scalp and features streamed with beads of sweat. His mouth was drooling spittle while his hands quivered finely by his side.

"Is your Oracle alright?" Suetonius asked Kenamun as Surisca tried to help raise the ageing man from the beaten earth floor. He was reviving from his drug trance.

"He puts his all into it," was Kenamun's simple answer. Suetonius delivered a small gold coin from his purse into Si-Amun's sweaty palm.

"Well, what do we make of that?" Clarus asked when the four had departed the Egyptian pavilions. "It was quite a show. Did you get a full record, Strabon?"

The scribe nodded.

"What do you think he was telling us?" Suetonius queried. "Was it all nonsense, or was there some truth to it? Surisca, what do you think, you know the ways of these people?"

"I know very little of the *Amazigh* tongue of the desert barbarians," she responded, "but I've picked up some words and phrases from clients of the Libyan Desert. Their unusual language and bloodline are found in many places across the African provinces."

"And, so?" Suetonius queried.

"I don't think the priest Kenamun was translating the Oracle's words at all. I think he was imposing his own views upon the Oracle's pronouncements."

"You mean he deceived us?"

"No, not at all," Surisca explained. "I think he was giving us his inside knowledge of what may have occurred, but disguised as the Oracle's insights. In fact, perhaps he was giving us a view he would be afraid to communicate directly. Perhaps he knows more than he tells? Or else he aims to deflect our investigation away from Pachrates towards other suspects."

"How so?"

"The oracle talked of stalking wolves and a she wolf. What or who are these wolves? Where are they?" she queried. "Is this a deception, or is it code for some group among your travelers?"

"Kenamun told us earlier he wondered at the absence of blood in Antinous's veins. He said the fellow did not die by drowning, he died of blood loss despite being found beneath the Nile. Yet the Oracle's words spoke of a she wolf drinking his blood? Of a wolf's sword exacting revenge? Where is this bizarre wolf pack? There are no wolves in Egypt," Clarus was evidently as perturbed as anyone.

"He tells us to identify the She Wolf. A female. How do we identify this beast?" Suetonius asked rhetorically. "We have to ask those who mixed with the youth. We have to ask Lysias, Julianus, Geta, Arrian. Is Thais the She Wolf? Is that possible? But Thais is no wolf creature, I am sure!"

Surisca submitted some thoughts.

"The women in the dead youth's circle appear to be few in number. There is Thais, yes, but there is also the woman Balbilla .. there is the empress, the *Augusta* ... there is the priestess Anna Perenna. Is there anyone else? Is one of these the She Wolf? If so, which?"

A few moments elapsed. They then responded in unison with a single name.

"Anna Perenna."

CHAPTER 29

"Welcome back, even if so late at night," Secretary Vestinus offered politely through sleepish eyes. "You realize it is now two hours before dawn?!"

"It's two hours before dawn and *we've* not been to bed!" Clarus snapped.

"The entire Household will soon start to come to life to meet Caesar's summons," Vestinus said. "He's called everyone of quality to assemble an hour before dawn. No excuses."

A muted *cornu* sounded as troops calling the hour echoed from watch to watch.

"We need to see Geta the Dacian. We have something important to discuss with the fellow. Can you have someone summon him here?" Clarus enquired.

"Better. I'll do it myself. While you wait you should freshen up and take some nourishment. You will need to, good people, because Caesar's project today could be a lengthy one," the dour *Ab Epistulis* advised. He clapped hands for service.

Slaves escorted the three males to a washhouse to attend to their toilet, while Surisca was led by a serving girl to a separate women's chamber to spruce.

Suetonius and Surisca were the first to return to Vestinus's courtyard. They now exuded fragrant oils announcing refreshed cleanliness. They were greeted by a table spread with edibles beneath the dancing light of flaming torches burning into the night sky.

"Surisca, my dear, it seems how for the third occasion on two days and nights I am not to partake of your charms and arts, whether I like it or not?" the Special Inspector lamented. "Another night has passed and I am no closer to the promise of your sensuality than anytime earlier."

Surisca affected a demure manner with her face downcast in shame.

"Master, it has not been my purpose to deny you your purchased pleasures. Have I been remiss in this? Should I return your fee to you? You have been so patient."

"No, no, my dear. It's just the way things have turned out. And I assure you, you have more than earned your fee with your perceptions about aspects of our enquiry. Perhaps with interest!"

"You flatter me, master," she offered modestly.

"When this imbroglio has passed, Surisca my dear, and hopefully before Caesar demands my head be removed, I hope to reward you in a more worthwhile way for your endeavors with us here. I wish to assist you to pursue your chosen future for your contribution to our searches. Tell me, my dear, what is your greatest desire for the future?"

The Syrian *hetaera* was smitten silent for a few moments. No one had ever before asked her such a generous-minded question. No one was interested. Except perhaps one single person, she recalled. She stumbled her honest reply.

"I think, master, I wish to leave my trade before I am too old to attract custom or am afflicted with a deadly pox. I hope to devote myself instead to creating beauty aids and perfumes for market. I already know the crafts of their manufacture; but I need the capital to buy the necessary tools and time to create sufficient stock and to rent a suitable trading shop. I have monies stored away securely, but it is only half the sum I am likely to require. You see, I have thought through this matter well during many long nights satisfying a client's pleasures."

Clarus and Strabon returned to the courtyard.

"What about marriage? A husband? A family?" Suetonius continued. "Does this appeal to you?"

Surisca grew clouded in her response.

"Very few men seek the companionship of women of my profession, my lord. My trade breaks trust. Though there are those who wish to live off the earnings of such as I. But here in the East a woman loses her wealth when she falls under a husband's *aegis*. I have worked far too hard and long for my wealth to be so easily acquired by another. I've heard it said women at Rome possess greater freedom of property ownership in retaining their wealth in marriage? Is this so, master?"

Clarus intruded on this pragmatic conversation.

"Where are we with our investigation?" he demanded. "What have we learned? In an hour we join Caesar's assembly, and we're likely to have few opportunities to interview others after his ceremony. So we're back to: *Why did Antinous die?* And: *was it an accident, suicide, or murder?*"

"Well, what do you think yourself, Septicius?" Suetonius asked.

"I don't really know. It's very complicated and I sense we're missing something essential. Two days and nights is insufficient time."

"But, *cui bono?* Who benefits from the death?" Suetonius probed.

"Other than a mysterious pack of 'stalking wolves', it seems no one except the Bithynian himself benefits. Perhaps he's died in an act of sacrifice," Clarus proposed.

"Or possibly Caesar via an agent, if he's party to sacrifice and sorcery?" Surisca murmured carefully. Clarus was disturbed by such talk.

A figure appeared at the courtyard accompanied by Secretary Vestinus. It was Geta. He had overheard the final comment.

"You hold Caesar to be under suspicion, colleagues? But you forget too many others. The empress Vibia Sabina, for example? She would do anything to upset our Caesar on principle," Geta proposed. "Perhaps she hired renegade Nubian freebooters to create mischief with her husband's loved one? Or the security chief Tribune Macedo on behalf of Senate forces in Rome, such as his master Turbo, the Praetorian Prefect? Or a faction of the Senate, or an ambitious Legion commander or two?

Or even me? After all, I'm the closest to both our Caesar and the dead lad. Perhaps I have some hidden advantage to gain?"

Geta's and Surisca's eyes locked momentarily. A message of welcome flashed silently between them. Suetonius felt immediately cuckolded once again, but continued nevertheless.

"But do you have a motive, Dacian?" Suetonius smoothed. "In what way could you possibly benefit from the death of the Bithynian?"

"Enough!" Clarus demanded. "Our time is running out. You called for Geta. He stands before you, Suetonius. Make your enquiries."

The biographer gathered his wits about him.

"You know all those of the Household well, Geta. You know their personalities and habits. We have received a puzzling message whose coded terms we cannot interpret. We wish you to hear the message and for you to offer your view on who it best describes in the Household or its hangers-on."

The Special Inspector turned to Strabon.

"Read the Oracle's message. Read his words. Let Geta decide who it identifies or what the message is being communicated."

The scribe delved into his collection of wax notebooks and drew the recent block from his basket. He scanned his scratchings on the wax and began declaiming its notation out loud.

"*The son of Apollo ascended to the sun. The sun incinerated the youth. The wild forces of Eros overcame the measured power of Aphrodite. A hidden secret unleashed the chaos of Eros so stalking wolves could devour their prey.*"

Geta suddenly sat bolt upright. "Stalking wolves?" he exclaimed. Strabon continued.

"*The son of Apollo bled into Darkness. Stalking wolves sipped his blood. The son of Apollo made an offering at the altar of his brother Asclepius. He offered his only true spoils to the altar, his life. Wolves devoured the spoils with relish. A wolf's sword exacts its revenge. A she-wolf's delusion drinks it fill. But the path to the sacrificial altar was smoothed by a king's secret.*"

"A wolf's sword?! Revenge?! A she-wolf drinks blood?! A king's secret?" Geta exclaimed with increasing panic.

"*On a journey of justice, identify the She Wolf. Apprehend the wolves. Send them to the Underworld of an alien god.*"

"The Underworld! An alien god?!" Geta was rising slowly from his seat, alarmed.

"*The Baal of the East who came to the West. The Drinker of Blood. The Wolf Deity ...*"

Strabon's reading was drowned by Geta's cry of "The Drinker of Blood!" but he continued nevertheless. Geta groaned a mighty howl as he staggered to his feet. The group was rigid in bewilderment at his action. Surisca drew to his side to steady the man's faltering steps. Strabon continued.

"Fire purifies. The son of Apollo rises with the dawn, when the king's heart bursts with anguish."

Strabon put down the wax tablet as all eyes settled on the Dacian who was standing supported on the Syri's arm. He was seriously distressed.

"The Baal of the East! Where did you hear these words?! Who spoke them to you?!" he demanded.

"Quiet, Geta. Settle down. Take it easy," Suetonius soothed. "We're here to ask you what you know of this strange message. We want you to tell us the meaning of these words or the persons they may be referring to. We're at a loss to shed light on the thing.

Who are the wolves? Who is the She Wolf? Why is the god of healing, Asclepius, in this? Who is drinking blood? What blood? Why? We believe it all has something to do with the death of Antinous."

Geta fell into a chair nearby and held his head in his hands. Surisca discreetly tried to comfort him. He muttered to himself in a foreign tongue, possibly the language of The Getae people. He turned to Suetonius to offer answers.

"Your message is from a dire enemy of Zalmoxis. Zalmoxis is *the Baal of the East who came to the West.* Zalmoxis is my holy forebear of many generations ago. I am said to have the blood of Zalmoxis streaming my veins. The faded tattooed circles upon my face are the insignia of this heritage.

The god Zalmoxis lives in his Underworld of the dead. He awaits his Dacian devotees in his Underworld. They join him in the infinite Night of Zalmoxis and his eternal shaman's dance. In life Zalmoxis is worshipped with blood, the fluid of life. Like a forest's stalking wolf we Dacians sacrifice chickens, sheep, steers, and horses for Zalmoxis to savor their fresh blood. The Getae drain an animal's life-blood in ritual adoration and drink it as strengthening food.

In war it is the blood of the enemy that's sipped. The blood of captives is drained from their living bodies and venerated and consumed directly by the devotees, or indirectly by Zalmoxis via the putrefaction process. Such blood gives the Getae the wild strengths of a wolf. The Getae are Wolf Warriors. Like wolves, we suckle on blood."

"So, who is the wolf and She-wolf of the message? Are you the wolf whose sword has exacted revenge?" Suetonius ventured daringly.

"No, Suetonius, I am no Wolf Warrior. I do not drink blood. I am no stalking wolf.

Long ago I may have fancied I would revenge my dead father's memory. I swore an oath to my father before he killed himself how I would revenge his death by killing the loved one of the king responsible. At that time it was Caesar Trajan. I was a child. I knew nothing of the world, of life and death, war, or revenge, let alone happiness and love.

But since those days I have seen ways to live other than the *Way of the Wolf Warriors* and death-hungry Zalmoxis. The cruel law of wolves, blood feuds, blood revenge, savage living, and eager death, have been overtaken by the Roman way of living peacefully with others to enhance *this* life, not idolize death and the afterlife. At Rome even condemned criminals are given an opportunity as gladiators for extended life, for a while.

Under Hadrian, Rome's way of using man's ingenuity to grow harvests, press oil and wine, build fine edifices, have cleansing drains and sweet drinking water, public facilities to stay clean of body, to enjoy sociable company at the Forum or at the Baths or in happy festivals, becomes our priority. Under Hadrian even war is constrained by sealed borders with barbarian invaders, and by sensible laws within those borders. This allows energy to be invested in peace and productivity. My childhood oath to revenge the disorders of my heritage has faded beneath the attraction of gentler goals and happier ways."

"Then who are the wolf and the She Wolf? Who still drinks blood? Who still exacts revenge? Who killed Antinous *like a stalking wolf?*" the Special Inspector asked.

"I don't know, Gaius Suetonius Tranquillus," Geta responded. "Yet these people, whoever they are, are still among us somewhere. If we mistakenly seize the wrong contenders then we will have revealed our suspicions. This will unwittingly place Caesar's life at risk from the real offenders. We must not do that. I have too much respect for our Caesar and will protect him to the end. Long may he live!

Instead, we must set a trap so the stalking wolves reveal their crimes from their own mouths. They must confess their conspiracies aloud for all to hear before witnesses. Otherwise they will await another opportunity to stalk and kill.

In saying this to you, my final purification occurs and my child's oath of revenge is finally erased. The burden of a lifetime is discarded. I am free of Zalmoxis at last!"

Geta's hand reached up to another hand lying across his shoulder. He grasped Surisca's knuckles and held them firm. The cuckold in Suetonius felt his stomach churn.

"Are Lysias and Thais protected safe within the Imperial Household, Dacian?" Suetonius queried. "We understand ruffians were seeking to kill them?"

"Yes. Quaestor Julianus is protecting them at the Companion's stables. They will rejoin your group at the assembly before dawn."

"When do you think Caesar will demand our report on Antinous's death?" Clarus enquired. "He told us it is to be by dawn today, no later."

"I have no idea, Senator. He hasn't mentioned your investigation. Dawn is to be the Bithynian's memorial, plus the inauguration of the new city of *Hadrianopolis*. But everyone who's anyone is summoned to attend. It is likely to include the *stalking wolves*."

"But Geta, how will we determine who are these wolves and the She Wolf?" Suetonius asked helplessly.

"Use your wits, Special Inspector. Caesar relies on your intuition and perceptiveness," he said. "We must identify and destroy the stalking wolves. We must uncover what actually happened to the young Bithynian."

CHAPTER 30

Brazier cauldrons raised high on iron tripods cast shimmering flames into the night sky. They flickered and flared above the wide expanse of the Imperial Household's reception platform. Pre-dawn mists clung close to the earth snaking in thin, meandering drifts.

A dais draped in scarlet cloth was surmounted with the emperor's personal standard while gilded stools and chairs awaited the arrival of their Imperial occupants. Rows of Horse Guards and Praetorians in polished uniforms glinted beneath the flickering light.

Ghostly shapes swathed in black wools or silk shawls emerged from the darkness of the surrounding lanes and alleys preceded by lantern-bearers. The figures streamed in mourning's deep solemnity to their appointed stations around the platform. Few spoke except for an exchange of murmurs accompanied by a restrained nod here and there.

To one side stood a high palanquin with stalwart Egyptian bearers at respectful attention. The waspish Pachrates and his thickset associate Kenamun were arrayed in majestic leopard-skin mantles above their starched linens, and adorned with bracelets, chains, and jeweled ornaments. They brandished ornate scepters of office while methodically flicking insect whisks of bleached horsetails as they stood before the bier. A brace of Nubian temple guards stood watch nearby with glistening, long-bladed assegais shining beneath the brazier light.

The four-posted palanquin supported a sumptuous bed of white blooms exuding a potent scent. The pale figure of Antinous lay along the bier atop his white cloak, his arms crossed to each shoulder in the Egyptian style, in seeming relaxed repose.

He was dressed in his silvery parade-ground hunting uniform of leathers inlayed in white enameled decors. His white-crested *Companions'* helmet in the Attic style and silver cavalry mask won as a trophy at the Trojan Games of Athens, were stowed to one side. His *gladius* sword and dagger lay belted at his right hip as befits someone disposed to left-handed action. A finely-worked silver filigree corona wreathed blond coarse-chopped locks.

Suetonius noted there was no jewel on his hand, especially not the vivid *lapis lazuli Abrasax* ring gifted by Hadrian.

Only the unhealthy pallor of skin's complexion suggested Antinous was other than taking his ease. His powdery hue confirmed it was certain to be eternal. Six Egyptian canopic jars, three along each side sealed with sculpted stoppers in the shape of the goddess Isis, attended him in his eternal slumber.

Suetonius, Clarus, Strabon, and Surisca approached from Vestinus's chambers led by *Companions'* grooms holding torches high. Thais and Lysias followed close behind. Lysias was holding Thais's hand.

Both gasped at their first sight of the palanquin and its occupant.

Thais distractedly continued walking towards the funerary carriage but Lysias drew her back by one elbow and a gentle squeeze. Suetonius detected tears welling at the rim of her eyes, and perhaps Lysias's too. Neither had seen their friend since the memorable day prior to his death. The spectacle of his eternal repose unsettled them.

The *Augusta,* Vibia Sabina, with several female courtiers accompanied by Julia Balbilla and a brace of Horse Guards, approached from a laneway leading from *The Dionysus* moored offshore. The band of women moved collectively as a cabal of somber, shrouded black veils.

Sabina took her seat in a high-backed matron's chair on the dais with Balbilla standing a pace off nearby. Both demurely retained their head cover in such a public place.

Suetonius cast his eyes around this taciturn, brooding ensemble. He made mental notes of several of the attendees in the light of the recent testimonies. Here, he contemplated, were the governing elite of Rome with their assorted hangers-on, all arrayed in rank order in an improbable silence in the desert's deep dark several hundred miles distant from any real centre of civilization.

Governor Flavius Titianus and his consort Anna Perenna stood to one side on the official dais accompanied by a cohort of Alexandrian Praetorians. The consort's ashen face-paint and bleached powders with striking *kohl* outlines and scarlet highlights pierced the night's gloom. Centurion Quintus Urbicus, stood ahead of his troop to one side of the consort, his fish-scale armor, crested helmet, and weapons glinting beneath the flames.

Arrian, Vestinus, Alcibiades, Phlegon, Favorinus, the astrologer Aristobulus, and even the ever-elegant Lucius Commodus risen untypically early, arced around the other side. Each was garbed in the black cloth of formal Roman mourning. Fellow-travelers from the Senate, advisors, Legion commanders, administrators, and accompanying academics, poets, architects, writers, or artists were arranged in a scaled priority around the platform.

Tribune Macedo of the Praetorians and Decurion Scorilo of the Horse Guard stood ahead of a detachment of their respective corps. Scorilo's face markings, though similar to others of his Guard, now had a disturbing effect upon the biographer. Suetonius's recollection sifted through the manifold impressions of the interviews of the past forty-eight hours, and such facial inks now communicated ambivalence.

He also noted how Scorilo's right arm, which crossed his body to permit his weapon hand to lie in readiness upon his sword hilt at his left, disclosed an unexpected object of interest. The jewel upon the *Bastarnae Celt*'s right index finger attracted the Special Inspector's eye immediately.

"Surisca, my dear," he whispered, "carefully look to Decurion Scorilo's right hand and describe the jewel you see. My eyes can't quite perceive its details. Be discreet. Describe it to me."

Surisca provided an informed description of the ornament. Suetonius emitted a soft "Aha, I see!" Its implication had relevance, he realized. Useful connections were falling into place speedily in his mind now, though their full implications were uncertain.

Salvius Julianus was accompanied by four *lictors* bearing their *fasces* symbol of justice, Rome's punishment axe embedded in a ring of thrashing rods. He arrived with four *Companions'* grooms bearing torches.

They were late, and so hurried from the direction of the river. Julianus was nursing a bulky globular shape in his arm's crook beneath his cape.

He nodded a gesture of affirmation towards Suetonius as he approached. Suetonius responded with a smile of appreciation. The *quaestor's* efforts were gratefully received, especially as he had also brought with him a uniformed officer of the Alexandrian auxiliaries. This was the jetty clerk who monitored activity at the approaches to *The Alexandros*.

The fellow was obviously unnerved to be in the midst of such exalted company until his eyes settled and fixed upon the supine figure on the bier. Then they were wide in dismay.

When a time-caller announced the final hour to dawn of this third day of The Isia, the Imperial marquee's curtained enclosure hoist open and Hadrian's retinue stepped forward in single file from within.

Hadrian was wearing the robes of his office as *Pontifex Maximus*, the supreme high priest of the Romans. The voluminous white toga with its frontal and rear scarlet flashes and its priestly *pallium* draped dramatically around, all edged in gilt eagles, glistened beneath the torchlight. He tossed back his head cowl to reveal a slender wreath of leaves of gold surmounting his head.

Suetonius drew his eyes back to Scorilo. The object of interest adorning the decurion's right hand was no longer evident. It had been removed sometime during Hadrian's arrival and probably stored in the leather pouch at his belt. Suetonius made a mental note of this odd event.

In his thoughts he canvassed a number of speculations deriving from these newer perceptions. Patterns of possibility now appeared which dispelled some of the murk surrounding his investigation. Yet a definitive vision of why and how Antinous died still eluded him.

Hadrian stood beside Sabina's chair in silence. He did not look well. He was gray with mourning, and his eyes had lost their usual spark. At a weary wave, he signaled to Geta the Dacian to step forward to proclaim an announcement. Geta raised his hands to the night to make a public announcement into the skies.

"People of Rome, senators, *equites*, officers of the military, staff, and friends of the Household on this dawn of the third day of the Festival of Isis, greetings on behalf of the *Princeps* and *Pontifex Maximus!*" Geta declaimed loudly. "We are here to honor the life and death of Antinous of Bithynia!"

The assembly shuffled momentarily in uncertainty at this declaration about a foreigner of no substance or status. Geta continued.

"The Household will progress behind Caesar to the Temple of Amun beyond this enclave. The mortal remains of Antinous of Bithynia will precede the procession, led by the High Priest, Pachrates of Memphis. All in attendance, proceed!"

Pachrates struck his scepter to the earth with three rousing blows. His pall-bearers heaved their palanquin high onto their shoulders ready for procession. With a swinging rhythmic gait led by the two hierarchs, the bier carriers stepped forward in unison. In a stately march accompanied by priestly voices intoning a somber liturgical chant, they ushered the cavalcade through the lanes of the Encampment. The mass of courtiers began to surge into a processional formation behind them.

The funereal throb of tambours with the scintillant rattle of *sistra* pulsed each phrase of the priests' chant. Caesar's party followed behind the bier as the entire assembly channeled into a streaming cortege. It filed methodically through the lanes of the camp towards the hulking, fluted, lotus columns of the Temple of Amun brooding beyond the encampment amid the palm trees. The temple too was bathed by its own braziers of firelight.

This squat, fat-pillared Temple wore its hoary antiquity without shame. It was a stained pile of eroded stones, faded paints, and surfaces covered with massed carvings of hieroglyphs. It spoke of an edifice which had been weathering tiredly at this site for untold generations.

As Caesar's cortege progressed towards the temple compound, great gates swung open to reveal a further line of priests streaming from its interior yard bearing night lamps high.

They too were draped in veils of mourning promenading beneath guttering braziers. A deeply booming gong repeatedly sounded a throaty resonance from some place deep within the bowels of the structure as the cavalcade came to rest before its columned porch.

Priests surrounded the palanquin to bear Antinous into the interior of the shrine. The entire procession followed behind as the priests maintained their sonorous chant and rhythmic march.

The interiors of these Egyptian temples can be scary by night, Suetonius mused to himself. Their halls and chambers are spectral with shadowy spaces sporadically illumed by torches or tripods. Lurking demons, ghouls, or specters must assuredly be their hidden inhabitants, he wondered?

Upon entering this cavernous structure the cortege's nostrils were assaulted by an intense charge of cloying incense. Indecipherable inscriptions danced across the pillars in the shifting light, while the upper reaches fading into shadow were stained by centuries of incense and torchlight smoke, suggesting the sheer burden of time itself.

The procession trailed in repeated zigzag directions along pillared corridors and down sloping ramps until they reached a final goal. The narrow corridors of honeyed stone eventually opened into a capacious sacramental chamber. This voluminous expanse was sealed on three sides by lofty cedar doors secured between columns rising into the heights above.

Three towering statues in the Greco-Roman realistic sculptural style, not the stolid style of Egypt, stood looming upon pedestals in the central well of the chamber. Suetonius felt decidedly uncomfortable beneath their stony gazes.

One statue was of the Holy Mother Isis herself, swaddled in her mantle holding a *systrum* aloft and carrying an urn symbolically containing pieces of her dismembered husband Osiris.

A second statue was of Osiris in the guise of Serapis, the most revered deity of the former Ptolemaic dynasty of Egypt. It was beloved of the Alexandrians of the Greek quarter.

The third was of Amun, the chief divinity of the old Egyptian pantheon, but here in the guise of Ammon, a Greek adaptation of Amun into *Zeus Ammon*, the highest god.

Between these three icons, Suetonius estimated, the entire mythology of Egypt's archaic religion was encompassed and dressed with an acceptably Roman face. Their divinity was expressed in human figuration, not the fantastic menagerie of grotesque animals Egyptians revere. Had these priests, he wondered, decided it was time to update their imagery for wider consumption? He sensed there was more to this occasion than met the eye.

A fourth pediment lay bare, its platform naked of any deity. Suetonius wondered at its implication.

The priests lowered the bier to the flagstones beside a low podium paved in glazed faience tiles. Antinous's pallid, unearthly hue now became the focus of the shrine. Torch light was reflected off polished mirrors to stream a shower of beams onto the bier, highlighting its occupant.

As the assembly silently filed into the chapel and arranged itself around the tiled podium, the two senior priests Pachrates and Kenamun intoned melodious incantations and wafted incense censers towards the bier. Meanwhile Horse Guards and Praetorians took defensive positions around the chamber as the assembly rambled to a halt.

Two grandiose thrones of ivory and precious stones worthy of Pharaohs were standing to one side. They were accorded to the Imperial couple as Pachrates performed fluid oriental genuflections of obeisance. Hadrian and Sabina took their seats while Geta, Arrian, Macedo, Commodus, Balbilla, and other notables arranged themselves close by.

A gigantic platter of beaten gold embossed with arcane symbols was carried by two priests and placed onto the faience-tiled podium. Suetonius did not think he had ever before witnessed so large a single object in pure mellow gold even among the lavish trove abducted from the Temple at Jerusalem generations ago and still displayed at Rome. The sheer weight of the platter required two men to carry it to the platform. This gleaming treasure must have been worth a nation's ransom.

A hush fell across the throng as it awaited the *Pontifex Maximus* to make his presence and purposes known. The corpse of the Bithynian youth lay in calm ceremonial repose.

The Special Inspector was impressed how, in such a parched climate, the cadaver appeared to retain its normal shape, textures, and color. Neither bloating, mottling, nor corruption was discernable, and only the pungent odor of blue lotuses and wafting incense exuded across the space. Mortician Kenamun was certainly a master of his craft.

Pachrates, ever the showman, took his staff of office and brandished it majestically before the bier. He wafted the wand across Antinous while chanting mysterious formulae towards Ammon as he tossed handfuls of grasses of wheat and barley into the air. His gestures implied some ancient holy harvest rite of truly awesome sanctity, which none of those attending either understood or heeded.

Two of his assistants removed from the bier two of the clay canopic jars which lay alongside the body. Unplugging the stopper of the first, one assistant carefully poured the contents into a shallow indent at the rim of the golden platter. A visceral internal organ the size of a pomegranate, glistening with emollient, plopped into the platter with an audible slurp.

On unplugging the larger jar and tipping its contents onto the basin proper, a bundle of well-oiled variegated tissues slid and tumbled into the centre of the dish with an unctuous slush. Everyone in the chamber immediately realized their origin. The first was a human heart and its connective veins; the second was the intestinal complex of gut, stomach, and associated tubes.

Caesar sunk back heavily into his ivory throne, his discomfort palpable.

Pachrates assumed an air of great solemnity and waved his staff over the viscera with profound *gravitas*. He uttered loud incantations in the old liturgical language in a harshly guttural voice. Handfuls of igneous powder were tossed into braziers, making flashes of flame and fume spurt into the chamber's gloom. The bursts projected multiform shadows in a neurotic dance upon the surrounding pillars. Their reeks sank into nostrils and invaded the bloodstream.

When he had performed this spirited display the priest peered closely at the glistening innards lying on the platter to give the tissues a studious inspection with the tip of an ivory pointer. Prodding carefully at the entrails, he nodded appreciative mutterings to himself and shared approving glances and mutterings with Kenamun. The assembled priests voiced choral responses confirming his wise discernments in their native language.

Suddenly with a gasp and an exclaimed "Yes, *by Amun!*" he sighted something significant among the fleshy debris. It demanded closer inspection.

Calling on Kenamun to respectfully hold a section of delicate gut to a lamp between his fingers, Pachrates peered closely at a bump in the connective tube of an organ. He reached to the innards and rolled the bump delicately between his venerable priestly digits.

"Yes!" he cried in his heavy-accented Latin, "A miracle, my lord! Great Caesar of the Romans, please allow me permission to incise your companion's remains to retrieve a special boon of the god Osiris himself."

Hadrian grudgingly nodded to Macedo to inspect the priest's claim. Macedo, not usually squeamish about matters involving corpses, moved to see what Pachrates was talking about. He gingerly fingered the intestine at the place the priest was holding, and turned to Hadrian with some apprehension.

"Caesar, there appears to be a scarlet jewel within the entrails," he announced. Do you wish me to retrieve it?"

"The gut is sealed by Nature's hand, so it can't have been inserted into the tissue," Pachrates declared.

Hadrian again tiredly nodded. Macedo took his hip dagger and carefully incised the diaphanous tissue. Something small and hard popped out into his hand. A priest came forward with a small bowl of perfumed water and a towel to rinse the object, which was then passed carefully to Pachrates. Pachrates held the object high between finger and thumb to the light of the nearest torch to inspect its features closely.

He turned to Hadrian and uttered an impressive exclamation in his inscrutable language while holding the object high to display to the assembled notables.

"Great Caesar, your humble servant of Amun, Pachrates, Sage of Heliopolis, offers proof to vindicate the death of the youth Antinous. In divining the auspices of the entrails of the young man I see no messages of despair or disease or death. No, not at all. I see no imperfection, no dire omens, no divine warning. I see nothing but health and wholesomeness, healing, and future hope!"

Pachrates paused to assess the effect of his pronouncements upon the assembly. Their eager eyes and engrossed attention were very winning.

"Yet further Caesar, on inspecting these entrails more intimately I discover this miraculous trophy. Concealed within the entrails at a place no mortician can reach, inches beneath the heart of the boy, lies a blood-hued gem generated spontaneously within the organs of the youth. Behold! I raise it high!

It is a likeness of the god Osiris himself fashioned as a blood jewel. It is just as our ancients prophesy of a Nile sacrificial drowning! The youth's own bloodstream has transfigured into an icon of the god Osiris himself! Within the very organs of the drowned victim is the visible sign that the youth metamorphed into the god Osiris, the Dionysus of Egypt, the dying and reborn god of the seasons! It is a holy, sacred *apotheosis*!"

Pachrates was warming to his role. His voice rose higher in increasingly joy.

"Through the death of the mortal Antinous our god Osiris resurrects again on the third day! Osiris is reborn in Antinous! Antinous is reborn as Osiris! Antinous is sanctified as *Divus*! *Divine*-like! The youthful vitality of Antinous transmutes into the lifeforce of *Pharaoh*! Praise to the life-giving boon of Antinous-Osiris of Egypt!"

Pachrates voice soared in rising emotion, encouraging the assembly to heightened enthusiasm.

Suetonius immediately recalled the phrase *"an exchange of boons"* from somewhere among the recorded testimonies. It suggested Pharaoh/Caesar had now acquired the vitality of the twenty-three year old Bithynian by some sort of magical exchange. Was Urbicus correct in his claim about Pachrates after all?, Suetonius pondered, or was Balbilla following somehow in her grandfather's steps on behalf of the *Augusta*?.

Pachrates proudly strode to Hadrian and placed the small scarlet figurine into the open palm of his hand. Hadrian cast his eyes over it with delicacy and distinct reserve. He seemed uncertain of the object. Pachrates continued his performance.

"My Lord Caesar, wear this mystical amulet deriving from the very bloodstream of Antinous of Bithynia. Adorn yourself for evermore with this jewel," the hierarch declaimed for all to hear. "This miraculously-generated icon transfers the health and years of the dead youth to you, our *Princeps*, the *Pharaoh* of our world. It expresses the Hidden God, Amun-Re's, beneficence to our generation! We all rejoice in Antinous, Osiris Reborn!"

Pachrates, Kenamun, and the assembled priests bowed low in a choreographed flourish towards the emperor.

The biographer and Surisca exchanged questioning glances.

Hadrian's demeanor transformed. His brow darkened. His skin perceptibly grayed. Signs of excruciating pain glinted from his eyes. His lips blanched into an aggrieved thinning. A stoop descended upon him whose very burden aged him a decade in seconds. His cough revived in his craw.

He raised himself shakily from the throne to glance dartingly from the blood-red jewel in his palm, to the cadaver serene upon the bier, to the glistening viscera lying larded on the golden platter. Several hundred pair of eyes watched his every motion.

Those observing this escalating transformation stiffened in uncertainty at the emperor's looming disposition. The priests intuitively stepped back a pace as they braced in anticipation of something ominous. None had previously witnessed such a rancor fall across their emperor's features. Hadrian was on the verge of eruption. Its sight numbed marrows, chilled blood, and weighed tongues.

With a wounded howl fit to harrow Hades himself, Hadrian leaned at the side of the throne to forcefully discharge his entire stomach's contents onto the flagstones nearby. He vomited a voluminous projectile spray across the slabs, splattering the sandals and boots of both Governor Titianus and Geta standing to the side of the throne, as well as Macedo and a guardsman nearby.

The putrid discharge displayed streaks of black blood and emitted a malodorous stench into the sanctuary.

A deep groan surged across the assembly.

Geta leaped to Caesar's aid to hold his elbow to offer support. The *Augusta,* remained upright in her seat, immobile, entranced. The entire entourage remained stiffly rooted to their places. No soldiers moved, no pages approached, no priests knelt.

Suetonius glanced around the faces before him. All were grave, except one. Decurion Scorilo, standing at the head of his detachment of Horse Guards, his eyes firmly planted on his commander in chief, the emperor, was assimilating every tremor of Caesar's distress. He was subtly alight with an expression akin to a smile. Suetonius determined it was the token of some inexplicable victory.

Meanwhile, on looking to Governor Titianus, his consort Anna Perenna, and Centurion Urbicus nearby, he could see each was severely restraining their emotions. *The Augusta* was formally, immutably composed, while Balbilla was visibly discomforted.

Arrian was troubled. Vestinus was agitated. Macedo displayed increasing alarm. Commodus exuded confident apprehension, distracted by checking his vestments and hair for stains or spots.

Hadrian braced himself on the throne's armrest to cast his eyes at the two hierarchs before him. After a short, choked coughing bout and clearing his throat, he gathered his composure sufficiently as his voice weakly rasped into the cavernous gloom. His gaze had settled wistfully on the figure upon the bier. But his words were not what the gathering could have anticipated.

"Little soul, roamer and charmer,
My body's comrade and its sometime guest,
What dominion now must be your goal,
Pale and stiff and naked?
Unable now, like us, to jest."

The assembly stood rock still in oppressive silence. Many wondered whose soul Caesar reflected upon. His own or that of the figure on the bier? And what did '*sometime guest*' convey?

Then Hadrian's voice resumed its usual commanding resonance. It grew in power as he spoke.

"Priests of Isis, Serapis, and Amun, place a worthy gold coin on the Bithynian's tongue for his journey's fee with Charon to the Land Of The Dead.

Say holy rites over Antinous to prepare him for his journey. Impress a death mask from his features to retain for our fond memory.

Take his earthly remains and perform your most effective arts upon him to embalm him for posterity. Spare no cost to preserve his tissues with loving respect. I will send the Dacian, Geta, to you shortly with special instructions for ceremonies to honor the youth's life."

The assembly relaxed from its dread.

"It will be done, Great Caesar," Pachrates affirmed as he waved hurriedly to temple attendants to cleanse the mess on the flagstones. Attendants in workman's leathers scurried in the background with sponges, water, and generous splashes of perfume.

The emperor returned to his formal manner.

"But we are not finished here yet, Egyptian *magi*. Stay! It is time for my Special Inspector to make his report to the Household in our presence," Hadrian announced.

Alarm! Panic! Suetonius clenched his fists while Clarus drew breath and bit a lip. They were both unprepared for such a duty. They assumed the report would be delivered later in the privacy of Hadrian's chambers. Suetonius realized his hundred thousand *sesterces* and the security of his head on his shoulders could be at risk.

But as he contemplated this less-than-desirable fate his attention was drawn by Strabon's tap at the elbow. The scribe pointed to the group of temple workers cleaning the temple floor before them. Among the gathering he spied a particularly unexpected face.

Suetonius peered toward the man. For a brief moment he couldn't place precisely where he had seen the fellow previously. It then struck him.

It was Hetu the fisherman who had discovered Antinous's body beneath the river's waters two dawns earlier with his cousin Ani. Hetu had not been killed by Ani's murderers after all!

Hetu and Suetonius's eyes met in fleeting recognition while the Egyptian was addressing to his tasks, but the fisherman flicked away in fear.

Suetonius immediately realized his fund of fragments from the two days of testimony possessed some slim unifying threads. The puzzle's solution was gradually taking shape. Or was it? How were these threads to be woven together in a meaningful way, he asked himself? What did they tell?

Yet were the stalking wolves themselves now being stalked, he wondered?

CHAPTER 31

Suetonius stood before the assembly to deliver his report. Clarus, Strabon, and Surisca stood a pace behind him, each wondering what their Special Inspector could possibly assert under the circumstances.

"Great Caesar, you have instructed Senator Claudius Septicius Clarus and I, Gaius Suetonius Tranquillus, to examine the circumstances of the death of your Companion of the Hunt, Antinous of Bithynia.

You commanded us to investigate the manner of his death and the reason for his death. The enquiry was to be completed within the space of two days and two nights," Suetonius declaimed magisterially in his least-quavering barrister's vocal technique. It had worked well enough decades ago at the Bar of Rome but was a little rusty, he thought.

"No excuses, Special Inspector. Get on with it," Hadrian huffed.

The emperor slumped deep into his throne as the workers bustled silently around him eliminating the odious effluvium of his discharge. Suetonius braced himself as Clarus stood firm nearby concealing sweating palms.

"Firstly, my Lord, a chain of violent events begins when Antinous is found lying beneath a moored fishermen's coracle at the river's edge at first light two dawns ago. That day was the morning of the first day of The Festival of Isis.

Two netters of fish and birds, Ani and Hetu of the village of Besa nearby, drag the body of the youth from the river and raise the alarm. Antinous was beneath the river's waters attired in his ceremonial parade uniform as a Hunt Companion, still wearing the helmet and cavalry mask of a formal imperial parade. It is the regalia of a special ceremony, not of a casual night's pleasures or some sporty lad's horseplay.

Ani and Hetu call for help. Fortuitously, a troop of three members of Governor Flavius Titianus's Praetorian Guard from Alexandria happen to be nearby under the command of Centurion Quintus Urbicus of Numidia. Urbicus and his troops try to revive Antinous, but to no avail. They aim to clear his lungs of water and search his body for signs of the cause of death.

Other than light bruises, the only visible wound is a deep incision in the lad's left wrist. The guardsmen do not report the wound, leaving this revelation to an official magistrate's enquiry or inspection by a physician.

Later when checking the young man's attire it is noted how two of the lad's personal possessions are missing -- his youth's *bulla* locket, the golden necklet containing some favored scripture or charm, and his ring depicting the deity *Abrasax,* known to be a gift received from you, Caesar, as a protective talisman.

Ani and Hetu later report to us how the only vessel sailing on the river at such early light was a single craft identified by them as bearing the insignia of the priests of the very Temple of Amun we currently inhabit. Their recorded testimony says it is possible those sailing this vessel had deposited the youth at the river's edge and hurriedly departed the vicinity."

Suetonius paused to let the information sink in to his audience, and give him time to assess his next stage of description.

On hearing about the Temple vessel the security chief Tribune Lucius Macedo made a discreet gesture to one of his officers. Guardsmen closest to the priests Pachrates and Kenamun quietly shifted into a formation of nearer proximity to the pair, much to their immediate alarm. Suetonius continued his presentation.

"One of these two fishermen, Ani, is murdered later that same night by masked assailants of unknown origin. Fortunately, we had inscribed a record of the fishermen's testimony. The following morning Ani's decapitated head is exhibited to us by Centurion Urbicus as evidence of the murder. Urbicus had been assigned to us as an investigative operative. Hetu, the other fisherman, is reported chased by the same masked assailants to a fate unknown at this particular time. I will return to Hetu later.

Lysias of Bithynia, Antinous's close friend, and Thais of Cyrene, the youth's language tutor, are attacked at their tents in the Imperial Encampment that same night, also by masked assailants. Simon, a steward of Lysias's household, is murdered and decapitated defending the couple. They flee by devious routes to take secret refuge at the compound of the Companions of the Hunt. *Quaestor* Salvius Julianus, the former Master of the Hunt, offers his protection to the two at the Companions' stables.

At early afternoon the following day – this was yesterday - our party of three citizens of Rome – *Quaestor* Julianus, Senator Clarus, and myself of the *equites* class – accompanied by three worthy staff, are attacked by concealed archers while we were travelling from a riverside jetty to the Hunt compound. Julianus's equerry is wounded in the foot, but all six survive the attack unharmed.

Since that time your investigators suspect their lives are at risk, having been set upon by unknown forces bent on committing harm for unknown reasons of purposes.

So Great Caesar, to tally up, in the space of only two days within the confines of the protected enclave of the Imperial Household your assigned investigators are confronted by the inexplicable drowning of an innocent youth, Antinous; two or possibly three assassinations by decapitation; a murderous attack by unknown archers in which an equerry is wounded; and a general climate of insecurity and uncertainty within the enclosure.

This is a high casualty rate for such a secure facility in the space of two nights -- four unexplained deaths and a life-threatening injury, along with general mayhem and havoc. It is my belief, sir, these events are closely linked."

"Linked by who or to what?" Hadrian murmured tiredly. His features displayed a distinct lack of enthusiasm for Suetonius's presentation.

"I must raise the renown principle of *cui bono?*, sir. Who benefits? It seems a member or members of our court may have good reason to see these offences come to pass. I include the death of the young man Antinous as the primary offence. There appears to be some person or persons among us who possess the resources, the authority, or the determination to prosecute such violence in our midst, Caesar."

Hadrian shifted uneasily in his seat.

"Explain, Inspector! Why do you believe the youth was subject to violence? Importantly too, who can be shown to benefit from Antinous's death?"

"Possibly several people my lord, either directly or by purposeful influence."

"Get to the core of the matter, Special Inspector. Time is passing. Dawn is almost upon us," Hadrian declared impatiently.

"I will be brief, Caesar. Let us first explore our present company at Court to see what motives may exist among us. We will begin with the outer ring, those who are not official members of your Household, the priests of Amun before us. Pachrates the *Sage of Heliopolis*, and Kenamun the Embalmer, should tell us what they know of the youth's death," Suetonius offered. He gestured to Kenamun nearby as he spoke.

"Kenamun, as the presiding mortician, has an intimate knowledge of the state of Antinous in death, my lord. We should listen to what he has to say on the manner of Antinous's death."

Kenamun glanced nervously at the surrounding assembly of notables and the somber emperor before him. Suetonius nodded to him encouragingly and opened his questioning.

"Priest Kenamun, what can you tell us of the manner of the young man's death?"

Kenamun gulped nervously. His response tumbled out.

"Special Inspector, it is my belief Antinous of Bithynia did not die by drowning. I believe he died instead of a loss of blood which occurred before he entered the holy river's waters. Possibly well before."

A rustle of whispers swept the assembly. Hadrian shifted uncomfortably on his throne. Kenamun continued.

"In preparing the noble youth's cadaver for public display it was evident how very little blood had remained in his veins in the usual way of the deceased. When blood ceases its flow at death a residual quantity lingers in the veins. It coagulates in the veins as mucus which speedily putrefies.

In the case of Antinous, there was very little blood gelled in his veins. Very little indeed. I would hazard a guess he had been thoroughly drained of almost all blood while his life-force still animated his tissues. The faint blood which remained suggested he had died by massive bleeding at least an hour or more before his discovery at the river. This is my opinion.

Also, Antinous possessed a deep incision on his left wrist. It was an incision as a surgeon might perform, not an accidental tear. This tells me he had intentionally cut and bled himself. Alternatively, he had been purposefully cut by another as a slaughtered beast is bled of its impure blood."

The assembly emitted another rush of murmurs. Kenamun continued.

"Further, great sirs, though he was discovered under the river's waters, water damage to his skin and organs was minor. Prey-seeking river vermin are far more aggressive to a corpse over time than was evident on this youth. I believe he had been in the water less than even a single hour prior to his detection.

Considering the incision at his wrist, unless he razored his wrist just moments before he entered the water, he would have been unconscious from blood loss long before he entered the river. It takes time for a living creature to be drained entirely of its blood, as we see at a slaughter man's killing trough."

Suetonius decided to probe this notion closer.

"Priest Kenamun, couldn't he have cut his wrist by accident at the river's edge and then fallen in after fainting? Or cut and thrown himself in as a willing suicide?"

"This is possible, but I doubt it. Far more blood would have gelled in his veins than was apparent when we prepared his body. I sense the incision was made sometime well before him entering the river. This could mean it was inflicted elsewhere than at the river.

I am told too Antinous was left-handed in his activities, yet this incision was in his left not his right wrist. This is unusual. It is irregular.

I believe therefore his arm was lanced in the company of another person or persons to promote bleeding. And then, when his life's humors had been diminished by his own failing spirit, further manipulation may have been applied externally to complete the job. This is just as a butcher does with a beast to drain it of polluting blood. Perhaps only then was his body placed in the river."

The assembly grew agitated and edgy.

"How would someone slit a healthy young person's wrist while they were fully capable of resisting such an attack, unless they were party to their own death? Antinous was no helpless weakling," Suetonius asked rhetorically.

"I don't know," Kenamun offered. "Perhaps he was restrained and it was forced upon him? Perhaps he was given a blow to be unconscious? Or perhaps he was eager to be incised?"

"But why would someone wish to bleed a victim so thoroughly?"

"It is seen by some to be a less painful way to die than other methods. I understand slit veins are a noble tradition among Romans pursuing a pain-free death? But in truth I do not know, Special Inspector."

Suetonius turned to the craggy high priest standing nervously in anticipation beside the mortician.

"Pachrates, high priest and *magus* of Amun, is it true you promised the youth you had the skill to revive him from death if he aspired to sacrifice himself on the occasion of The Isia? We have been told you have exhibited such skills."

The self-professed wizard uncharacteristically trembled.

"*By Sacred Amun!*, what can you mean?! My magic does not dare indulge in such blasphemies against Fate."

"Yet you are known to resurrect from death small animals and the occasional condemned criminal with your arts? It has been testified so by witnesses. You do it in public before us."

The priest was quick to respond.

"This is a lesser, minor, inferior Egyptian magic, Inspector, suited only to meager creatures like dogs, criminals, and other vermin. I do not perform magic with the bloodstream and honor of nobles of the *Imperium!*

Besides, Inspector, my humble arts are only effective at times of an extraordinary alignment of the stars, configurations which occur only once or twice a lifetime," the sorcerer explained unpersuasively.

"Yet, priest of Amun, we have been told the youth Antinous prevailed upon you to perform such magic? We have a witness to your conversation in our written testimony. The youth had seen your magic in action, and requested your special powers be used for his own purpose? This was in the company of Caesar too, we have been told?"

Clarus was becoming tense at the direction the deposition was taking. It veered too close to Caesar's person.

"But I refused him! I said No!" the *magus* objected. "And then Great Pharaoh intervened to refuse both of us to even discuss the matter! Caesar had spoken! The matter was final!"

Suetonius zeroed in for his coup-de-grace, he thought.

"Nevertheless, Priest, you had sufficiently remarkable prescience to summon priests at Memphis and Thebes to this place, including the very faraway Oracle from Siwa," Suetonius charged, "plus an entire embalming team including Cronon, a Greek painter of funerary portraits from Fayum. They were obliged to travel long distances to this place in anticipation of the youth's death?"

Suetonius felt pleased with himself in this proposition. The assembly rustled with murmurings.

Pachrates rose to the fullest height of his diminutive race, his eyes ablaze.

"You take liberties with our sacred mission, Inspector! This is not so, I tell you!"

Suetonius had struck an open nerve.

Hadrian interrupted this exchange wearily. With a dismissive wave of one hand, he spoke.

"Suetonius Tranquillus, you should be told how the priests and personnel you list were summoned here on my command two months ago. These people are engaged with the planning of our new city of *Hadrianopolis*. You will hear more about this project shortly.

Pachrates is an honored advisor to us for this purpose. His understanding of the local customs is comprehensive, so he advises us how the various communities of Romans, Greeks, and Egyptians can live in harmony at *Hadrianopolis* someday. There was no conspiracy in his summons to his artisan compatriots, Inspector. It was on my own authority he did so. Leave it alone, Tranquillus."

Caesar had spoken. Pachrates resumed his usual confident manner.

"I welcome your words, my lord, however there is more to explore," Suetonius continued bravely, if doggedly. His leap of intuition had failed; he moved on.

"We think we know those around us, but we don't really know them at all. There are several undercurrents flowing among us here, tides which might carry us in unwanted directions. Antinous may have been swept along by more than the Holy River's currents."

"Be plain, Inspector. No riddles," Hadrian sniped. His appearance was growing haggard.

Suetonius stepped out in a dangerous direction.

"Take the women among us, for example, Caesar. Julia Balbilla, princess of Commagene and gentlewoman companion to our Great *Augusta*, your wife, has been outraged by the recorded revelation how her astrologer grandfather in the time of Nero advised his emperor to kill his own counselors.

Her notorious ancestor, Balbillus the Wise, interpreted a comet in the sky to foretell that Nero would die. Rich with the mystical lore of the Orient, Balbillus advised Nero to nominate substitute deaths instead. He put it into Nero's head he should kill the eminent men-of-state of his era to deflect the omen's risk. So the notorious Piso and Vinicius Conspiracies against Nero were invented to fulfill this goal.

It was a most successful strategy, it seemed. Many innocents died cruelly and their families and slaves with them. Their rich properties were confiscated by Nero into his own coffers. It was a winning play for both Nero and Balbillus."

"What has this to do with the death of Antinous?" Hadrian snapped.

"On occasions as you know, Caesar, your Bithynian companion was a guest in the *Augusta*'s household. He and Julia Balbilla, as well as the empress with her retinue, shared playful conversation over wine and snacks. It doesn't strike me as too far-fetched to predict the granddaughter of Balbilla the Wise could suggest to an impressionable youth how a substitute death was a feasible project for the lad. After all, we already know the youth was intent on some form of recompense, some form of self-sacrifice. Balbilla suggested; Antinous considered; Antinous died. The youth fulfilled his purpose."

Suetonius was going out far on a shaky limb, causing Clarus to perspire even further.

Julia Balbilla and others of the *Augusta*'s attendants seethed beneath their elegant silks.

"Recompense, you say? Substitute? What on earth could inspire such a distasteful proposal, Inspector," Hadrian protested.

"My lord Caesar, your Court is not insensitive to the *frisson* which prevails between the respective Imperial households. Perhaps the irregular death of the young man could be construed as a slight upon your own integrity? Perhaps Antinous was goaded to commit an act of self-sacrifice, an act which would inevitably cast a shadow across your own virtue. Such a shadow may have political consequences, or at least be the result of revenge?"

Balbilla was aghast. She was about to vehemently remonstrate against the accusation when the *Augusta* spoke for the first time. Vibia Sabina's voice and forceful manner resonated around the chamber. Her speech possessed a timbre more redolent of a military commander than a demure wife.

"Hold your tongue, Tranquillus, or I'll find a way for you to lose it!" she boomed. "Once again you commit *laesa majestas* in my presence. You are insufferable! How dare you accuse my household of some malevolent conspiracy against the youth Antinous," Sabina proclaimed for all to hear. "It may not be known to you, but the youth Antinous acted as a useful balm between my husband and I. He was attentive to communication between our households and regularly performed the duties of an appreciated herald between contending parties with great distinction. He is a great loss to our continuing rapport. His rare diplomacy in these activities will be sorely missed. You err in your assumptions, scandal-monger historian!"

The assembly hushed. Clarus by now was alarmed for his own safety. Sweat trickled down his forehead and across his jaw.

Hadrian again interrupted.

"I instructed you, Special Inspector, not to involve the empress in your enquiries. You have no authority there; my wife is above your station, yet you have heard her view. What are you trying to say, Tranquillus, tell us or I must dismiss you immediately!"

Suetonius's internal machinery shifted its grinding cogs towards some other purpose.

"Great Caesar, there is a pattern to this Court's behavior which impacts upon the events of the past few days," Suetonius explained. "A climate exists among us which leads to these possibilities. But I'll move elsewhere in my presentation if it is your will."

His voice softened to a less accusatory tone.

"Another among us is the freedwoman, Thais of Cyrene. Until a year or so ago Thais was the property of Antinous's household assigned as a language tutor. Prior to departing Rome on this expedition Thais's status as a slave was manumitted by *vindicta* before a magistrate. She was relinquished as his property. She is no longer a slave. She is a freedwoman.

Recently, some weeks after the dissolution of the lad's *eromenos* relationship at Alexandria, Thais and Antinous became intimate. Very intimate. No previous intimacy had been expressed between them ---"

While the biographer was introducing Thais, Hadrian had revived from his languor. His ears pricked up at the account of her involvement with Antinous.

"--- Thais believes she might now be pregnant due to the young man's attentions," the Special Inspector intoned quietly.

The assembly rustled in *sotto voce* while Thais was seriously discomforted.

"However, Thais has many reservations about the manner of Antinous's death. Perhaps she will tell us why. Describe your last words with Antinous, Cyrene."

Suetonius turned to the dark young woman standing nearby. With her eyes firmly planted on the figure upon the bier, Thais groped to stammer a response. Suetonius nodded encouragingly.

"Good sirs, my former master Antinous spent much of the night and morning prior to his death in my company. He and I were very close, if you understand my meaning, but he did not discuss any threat to his life. Nevertheless he engaged in actions which should have aroused my concerns and invited my greater curiosity ---"

"What were those actions, Cyrene?" Suetonius asked.

"Antinous endowed me with a great sum of treasure that day."

"Treasure? What treasure, Cyrene?"

"Coins to a considerable value, precious objects of jewels and gold, and the deed to a property in the city of Athens at Achaea. The total value is very considerable."

"Can you vouchsafe for this endowment, Cyrene? Do you have proof of ownership? Or have you acquired it illegally, perhaps by theft or worse?" Suetonius probed in the style of a prosecutor.

Salvius Julianus, the *quaestor*, spoke up from across the aisle.

"I can vouch for it, Inspector. My steward, our clerk, and I recorded the endowment in Antinous's company, notarized the records of transfer, and have stored the valuables in the Companions' coffers for security. All with proper receipts and seals. The endowment is legal and secure with all parties.

Antinous was to make a separate endowment the same day to one other person. Both endowments together may have been to the full value of his possessions."

"Is such a gesture so unusual, Thais of Cyrene?" Suetonius soothed. "Surely such gestures are understood between companions of substance?"

"No, Special Inspector, they are not!" a voice called from one side.

Arrian of Bithynia made the announcement across the assembly.

"Senator-Consul Arrianus? You wish to speak?" Suetonius asked. Arrian spoke anyway.

"The treasures you speak of were the Bithynian's total wealth. Coins, gold, jewels, and the deeds to two properties were Antinous's entire fortune. Unlike many at Court the youth hadn't sold favors or peddled his influence with Caesar for high prices. Though his wealth may have been comforting to a lad entering adult life, it was not excessive by the standards of this Court. I know, because I had been the securer of his treasures in my own chests prior to that very day."

"Why do you think the fellow withdrew his wealth and offered it elsewhere? Especially on the day prior to his death?" Suetonius asked. "Is there a connection?"

"He would not give me an explanation of the reason for his withdrawal," Arrian stated. "I begged him to leave his valuables where they were safe, yet it did not occur to me he was about to give his property away to others. I thought perhaps he'd been smitten with the *Chrestus* disease or fell under some other fast-talking inducement?"

Suetonius seized an opportunity while this matter was progressing. "Tell me, Senator, do you recall securing Antinous's *Abrasax* ring among those treasures?"

"It wasn't necessary; he was wearing it as usual. He treasured the jewel, a special gift from Caesar," Arrian replied. "He wore it always."

Suetonius made a special note of that comment in his memory. He continued.

"So why then, I wonder, did the lad transfer the remainder of his wealth to others that day? Thais ---?"

"I do not know," she quietly replied. "He didn't tell me of his plans. He simply said I was to use the endowment for my sustenance now that I was a free person. I was to rely upon Lysias should anything untoward happen to him. I did not realize how something untoward, something awful, would occur so very soon -- in fact later that very day."

Thais's eyes welled with moisture as they fixed upon the pale figure on the bier.

The biographer turned to the *ephebe* standing beside Thais. "Lysias, do you have anything to contribute to this mystery?"

Lysias picked up the refrain.

"Antinous endowed the remainder of his estate to me. It too was notarized by Julianus's stewards. Ant offered no explanation, but he was adamant I receive the gift.

We've known each other a long time, so I imagined I could return his property to him later when he came to his senses. Ant, like me, is a second son with a claim to only a minor inheritance. He will need this wealth someday. All of it. But that day will now never come, will it?"

"So the Bithynian gifted his entire wealth to others on the very day prior to his death?" Suetonius summarized. "Unless the youth was unhinged, this suggests to me he knew he was greatly at risk, or already knew of his forthcoming fate. This does not imply an accident, Great Caesar. It tells of suicide, murder, or madness.

With mortician Kenamun's opinion of the deep incision on his left wrist and his great loss of blood which would render him incapable of entering the river, we arrive at a disturbing scenario. Murder, pure and simple. So who among us was willing to see Caesar's former *eromenos* dead? And what was their motive? *Cui bono?*"

The entire assembly hushed. Clarus was fearful the presentation was speedily going nowhere and Hadrian's patience and interest would be in jeopardy.

Suetonius returned to his fishing expedition, desperate as it may have been.

"Senator Arrian of Bithynia, you deal extensively in other people's wealth or treasures?"

Arrian looked to the Special Inspector with a querying, startled eye.

"What can you mean, Tranquillus? Yes, I am a trader, an investor, and a securer of valuables, but I do not *deal* in other people's wealth, as you say. I *deal* only in my own.

I am also a commander of the Legions, a recent proconsul to Baetica at the Iberian Peninsula, and I sit in The Senate at Rome.

Trading and investing in speculation is to my own benefit as a businessman, but I do it with my own money. Securing valuables in safe storage is a service to those of my *clientela* who trust my integrity with their precious things or have no access to a temple's sanctuary for storing wealth.

Wealth is hard to acquire and even harder to retain. I offer protection against theft or misadventure to members of my *clientela*. But this is not *dealing* in other people's wealth, Suetonius Tranquillus, though some may become my partners in speculation. Many people benefit from my policies."

"You received a visitor late at night after Caesar's celebration on the eve of The Isia, the same night Antinous died. The visitor stayed overnight and departed the following morning. May I ask who was that visitor?"

Suetonius was going out on a limb again, and knew it. The investigating team hadn't seen the visitor's face, but Surisca's identification of his perfume indicated the *Western Favorite* was the likely candidate. The biographer was keen to explore any hidden motive for the pair's meeting on the very night Antinous died. He wondered whether either was party to some act of malevolence against the youth.

"Special Inspector, why would you ask such an impertinent question?" Arrian replied. "You've over-stepped your commission, Inspector. My visitors are my own affair. Those I receive are my own matter. You possess no mandate with a well respected senator of Rome,

Tranquillus! Yet because your intentions are honorable, on behalf of your investigation and our master's pain, and because I wish to relieve you of any suspicions you may hold, I'll respond to your questions nevertheless."

There was no *patrician* derision in his voice. The assembly focused intently on his reply.

"The visitor you talk of was Senator Lucius Ceionius Commodus of Rome. Commodus and I retired late after Caesar's celebration of The Isia to talk deep into the night on many issues. Senators are inveterate gossipers, as we here are all well aware. Senators have a great deal to discuss, to argue, and sometimes negotiate together.

Commodus reflects the views of a particular *patrician* faction at the Senate, I reflect an alternative colonial view. There are many other factions, some of who disagree with us both vehemently.

Do you think Commodus and I are intimately engaged in some way, Inspector? Do you suspect we're having a hot, passionate sexual affair? No, Inspector, Commodus has far more nubile people in his sights than a warhorse such as I.

Besides, Commodus is now a married man. His wife Avidia is with child at Rome. So he has other priorities these days. These aim to consolidate his career and his future political life, not the pursuit of gentlemanly pleasures.

Caesar has let it be known Commodus may be adopted as his legal heir. Therefore he may be a candidate to be Caesar someday. There are some senators who may resist this prospect, so Commodus and I share continuing broad-ranging discussions of policy and our roles in resolving them. We have interests to explore on behalf of our respective factions and the wider Empire.

All this is entirely innocent, Special Inspector, and does not lead to the murder of Hadrian's intimates. Does this satisfy your prurient curiosity?" Arrian ventured. "If not, ask Commodus yourself."

Turning to the former *Western Favorite* standing nearby still fumbling for signs of spoiling on his boots and toga, the biographer raised a single questioning eyebrow.

Commodus replied simply, if dismissively.

"It is precisely as Arrian says, no less, no more."

Chastened, Suetonius lurched into fresh, deeper waters of exploration.

"Senator Commodus, would it be presumptuous to infer that the death of Antinous may be a welcome contribution to the progress of the career of an Adoptee Designate?" he proposed, daringly risking Hadrian's ire in the process. "Especially as no love was lost between you and the dead youth, we're told? Could this be construed as a motive for pursuing the boy's destruction?"

Commodus sighed with weary disinterest and then raised sufficient energy to bat the accusation aside effortlessly in the derisive manner of his class.

"Antinous, good Inspector, was my benefactor's greatest joy. Despite my onetime jealousy of the young man's influence upon Caesar, I am not one to deny others their deserved happiness. Especially my Caesar. And definitely not by murder! Gold would probably be adequate encouragement to achieve those ends, I'd guess. You're barking up the wrong tree, Tranquillus. You'll have to search elsewhere for your murderer."

"Yet you are known to have once attacked that unarmed youth at sword point at Athens? You inflicted a wound on the fellow's face! Is Caesar aware of this assault, Senator?"

Commodus sighed tiredly and straightened a fold in his toga.

"That was many years ago. I was suitably chastised by Caesar some months later. But my impetuous nature has moderated over time. I do not harass Caesar's companions these days. Instead, I revel in his pleasure. His joy is my joy.

I am known for many petty foibles, Inspector, but murdering Caesar's chosen companion is not one of them. Besides, you have my alibi for the night in question, I was fully engaged with witnesses of probity throughout. You need not fish in my direction, Tranquillus. Am I such a fool I would jeopardize my future in such an unprepossessing venture?"

Clarus and Suetonius glanced sheepishly to each other. This line of enquiry was leading nowhere. Suetonius changed tack. It was now his palms which were sweating. It was time to return to the Egyptians.

"Priest Pachrates, you yourself have been identified by the two fishermen Ani and Hetu to be the man who was sailing the river at very earliest light when the body was discovered. Ani and Hetu described your temple's *felucca* with its identifying blazons and your temple colors. We possess a record of their words identifying these insignia."

The Egyptian wizard looked pained by this accusation. He drew himself to his full height.

"But that's not possible, Inspector. Not only am I never upon the river so early in my sacramental day, our sole river vessel is out of commission. It lies at dock awaiting repair. It was damaged a month ago in a river collision. We do not possess a river-worthy *felucca* at this time. So we hire other people's craft to travel."

"Allow me to read the relevant testimony," Suetonius responded. "Strabon, locate the transcript and read!"

The scribe declaimed the words loudly for all to hear.

"… The fisherman Ani speaks:- *We know all the fishermen and ferrymen at Besa and Shmun. We know their boats, their trade, and their daily habits. They're our neighbors, we know everyone well. Even though it was some distance away, we could see it was a different sort of boat to ours and of a different people. It was a strong wooden* felucca *of quality, well made and costly, not a boat of bundled rushes.*

Inspector Suetonius speaks:- *'And who would own such a boat at Besa or Hermopolis?'*

Ani replies:- *'I did not know either the boat or the two rowers. It could have been a new boat from Shmun we had not seen before, but I would still know the rowers. Perhaps it was a boat sailed by priests from upstream for The Isia, or a boat belonging to Pharaoh's people'.*

Suetonius speaks again:- *'Did the boat have any identifying features? Would you recognize it again?'*

Ani:- *'Yes, it was painted the color of the sky and possessed the ever-watching Eye of Horus at the prow. Its sail had no insignia."*

Whispers rippled the assembly. Suetonius looked questioningly at the priest.

Pachrates spoke with a gleam in his eyes.

"The field of sky-blue and the Eye of Horus are indeed our markings on the hull of our damaged boat from Memphis. Yet you say its sail had no insignia?

Great Caesar and Special Inspector, listen to me; the single craft we possess here at Besa, which has been out-of-commission awaiting repair for the past month, indeed possesses a sail. It is stored at this very temple for security from common theft. It's a sail emblazoned with the major emblem of our deity, the Ram's Head of Ammon. If the *felucca* had been our vessel, all three tokens of the Old Religion would have been visible to your fishermen, the colors, the Eye, and the Horns of Ammon. The vessel you describe simply is not ours."

Silence fell across the chamber. Surisca tugged at Suetonius's sleeve and raised a finger to speak. Clarus sharply waved an impatient dismissal.

"We're in the company of your betters, woman," he hissed. Suetonius nodded approval nevertheless. She whispered into her hirer's ear.

"May I ask, master, who translated the fisherman's words for you? I was not present at that time, and I doubt any fisherman among the population speaks Greek, let alone Latin."

The biographer blushed in recognition, knowing full well who the available translator had been.

"Strabon," he whispered, turning evasively to the scribe, "who was our translator?" Strabon nodded towards the detachment of troops standing at attention across the sanctuary.

"It was Centurion Quintus Urbicus of the Alexandrian Praetorians, yonder," he whispered.

Surisca's query shifted the enquiry's terms swiftly.

"It is possible, Caesar, that we can test this translation," Suetonius advanced. "I wish to call upon the testimony of a layman worker in our company here today. He is named Hetu, a fisherman. Hetu, come here!"

He waved to the clutch of six Egyptian workers hovering beyond the assembly with their cleaning materials, sponges, and brushes.

"Hetu the menial?! Hetu the serf?! Hetu the fisherman?!" Pachrates wailed.

Strabon, who had spied the man earlier, moved forward and waved at the quaking figure hiding behind other workers, peeping out hoping not to be seen. Strabon called him to the front of the assembly by his name.

"*Hetu!*"

The workman reluctantly shambled forward, his eyes darting about at the weapons, uniforms, and fine fabrics around him, as well as the temple guards' *assegais* glinting beneath the brazier flicker. He was ushered into the presence of the awesome notables of Rome and fell to his knees from sheer fright.

"Surisca, do you have sufficient command of the local dialect to translate for us?" Suetonius asked. "We should not leave it to the kind priests of Amun or the efficient Alexandrian guardsmen to interpret for us, don't you think?"

The Syri nodded affirmation.

"Firstly, we must ask him how he came to be here at the Temple of Amun. We were certain he'd been killed by renegades. Ask him for his explanation."

Surisca turned to the trembling worker and spoke patiently and calmly in the fellow's own language. Hetu listened intently. His surprise at being spoken to in his own tongue by such a high ranking lady of quality was evident on his features. He responded in halting bursts of his native speech. Surisca turned to Suetonius to offer her translation.

"He says he fled his attackers after witnessing the killing of his cousin Ani, and escaped here to take sanctuary at the temple. The priests here are customers of his fish and fowl, and pay too for laboring chores, so they know him well. He intends staying hidden from attack at the temple until *Pharaoh's Soldiers* have departed on their journeys."

"I see," Suetonius said. "He suspects his attackers were *Pharaoh's Soldiers* does he? Now ask him a simple question:- tell us about the vessel seen upon the Nile at earliest light on the day of his discovery of the water demon, Antinous. Ask him to describe it just as he and Ani described it to us two days ago."

Surisca began to speak to Hetu in a slowly-enunciated articulation of his tongue. His body responded sharply in fear at the mention of Ani's name. On hearing-out Surisca's query, and after a few moment's recollection, he replied in the sharp monosyllabic bursts of his native dialect. Surisca translated carefully to the assembly.

"The vessel was a dhow of fine timbers, a costly lateen-rigged craft from a foreign place.

It's hull was the bright color of the spring crocus, a vivid yellow, and its sail was painted with the many-pointed starburst of the Old Pharaohs.

It was large enough to carry six sailors, though only two were travelling that dawn.

They were having trouble controlling the vessel in the brisk morning breezes. They were amateurs not familiar with the Holy River's whims.

He and Ani were too far away to recognize by their faces, but they were known to be foreigners because of their clothing ...."

Suetonius looked to Pachrates and Kenamun for their confirmation of the translation. The two nodded acceptance.

He looked towards Urbicus. The centurion was standing-at-ease pointedly averting his eyes. A rustle of whispers swept across the assembly.

"Its sail was emblazoned with the many-pointed starburst of the Old Pharaohs," Suetonius repeated. "This is surely the eight-pointed star of Alexandria and its dynasty of the Ptolemies. This is the Alexandrine insignia of Rome's Legate Governor. The boat was from the fleet of river craft sailing with *The Alexandros*, the flotilla of Alexandrian vessels following in the governor's wake."

Governor Titianus immediately cast his eyes over members of his retinue around him. He looked to Urbicus and other officers of his auxiliaries. His glance fell upon Anna Perenna, who stood motionless by his side. He was seeking some acknowledgement of the use of his vessel two dawns previously. No one responded.

He spoke.

"Only two of our craft carry the Governor's star insignia, the others are indicated by their respective corps blazons. Tell us, what more do your investigations reveal, Special Inspector?" the Governor asked, intrigued.

"Hetu thought of the vessel's sailors to be *'foreigners because of their clothing,"* Suetonius emphasized. "Who could these foreigners have been, we wonder? To Hetu, of course, anyone not residing at Besa is a foreigner."

Governor Titianus spoke again.

"My chamberlain retains records of those who go to-&-fro from *The Alexandros* including, I hope, our service craft. I will order an immediate search of the records," Titianus declared, "but it takes time."

"This might not be necessary, Lord Governor," Clarus intervened enigmatically. "We have taken certain precautions which make a search unnecessary."

Suetonius interrupted the notion.

"Perhaps firstly, though, we should ask Centurion Quintus Urbicus how he managed to be so close to the place where Ani and Hetu uncovered the body at such an early hour two dawns ago? Is the centurion a regular sojourner at the river's edge so early in the day? Does he take the air with his fellow soldiers at first light?"

He turned to Urbicus at the head of the Alexandrian troop just yards to the side of Titianus. All eyes fell upon the guardsman. Urbicus cleared his throat.

"Special Inspector, I and my men had been on a drunken spree throughout the night, and we were returning to our tents in the early hours to revive. It was the first day of The Isia, so our previous night's celebration had been very festive, sir. We probably overdid the festivity a bit, I'd say. There was much wine, women, and pleasure to be had."

"Where precisely, Centurion, did this festivity occur?"

Urbicus hesitated momentarily.

"We had been at the guardsmen's party attached to Caesar's own personal celebration that night. It was at a courtyard close to the Imperial Household's tents," the Praetorian regaled happily. "It was a good party. A hundred officers and ranks from various corps mixing together at Caesar's behest. The wine and local beer flowed abundantly. Soldiers know how to enjoy themselves!"

"How long did this jolly event prevail, Centurion?"

"Why, it had begun in the late afternoon I'm told, but we arrived at dusk. We stayed until the very end in the wee hours, almost dawn. Soldiers' celebrations always survive until the booze runs out or everybody's rotten drunk. Or they've taken a woman or lad for their pleasure."

"So, you were the entire night at the Household's tents enjoying this trooper's party? From dusk until before dawn?" Suetonius probed. "That's a long night's partying?"

"True, Special Inspector. We're members of the Guard after all. We have our hell-raiser reputation to uphold."

The assembly chuckled with uncertain enthusiasm.

"Tell me, Centurion Urbicus, do you have a witness? Is there anyone here who can vouchsafe your drunken revel that night?"

Urbicus looked blinkingly around the assembly. His sight settled on Decurion Scorilo at the head of the Horse Guard brigade colorfully garbed in their Germanic ethnic uniforms.

"My friend and colleague Decurion Scorilo of Caesar's special Horse Guard can vouch for me, Inspector. He was there too. Ask him yourself."

Suetonius cast a questioning eye towards Scorilo, who responded haltingly in his Germanic-accented Latin.

"Yes, sir. We both enjoyed Caesar's party for the troops that night, sir."

"So you too, Decurion, partied into the night as well? Also until dawn?"

"Of course. That's what soldier's drinking bouts are for."

Suetonius turned to Salvius Julianus's group of *lictors* and grooms. Beside them was the jetty clerk of *The Alexandros* he had brought with him.

"Officer of the Watch," he called to the clerk, "you register traffic to and from *The Alexandros*, yes?"

The uniformed Alexandrian was prodded forward gently by Julianus to respond.

"I do, noble sir," he stammered.

"Tell us who you are, identify your unit, and describe your duties," the biographer said.

"Sir, I am Danaos, born at Tanis of the Nile Delta marshes. I am of mixed Greek and native descent. I am a *tesserarius* of the Alexandrian *Auxilia*. I supervise and roster the sentries of the Watch. During this imperial river tour I am the shore clerk at the jetty to *The Alexandros*, the Governor's barque offshore. I and my staff monitor and record all movement to and from that vessel."

"Do you read and write, *Tesserarius* Danaos of Tanis?"

"I read some Greek and some Latin, sir, with a little more in the local Demotic. I have not mastered the art of writing well. I can maintain records but not express myself."

"My fine scribe Strabon has acquired the traffic records of the past few days at *The Alexandros*. He has in his possession the record of the day and night, and the following days too, of two evenings ago. This is believed to be the time of Antinous's death," Suetonius announced for all to hear. "I want you, *Tesserarius* Danaos, to tell us if the record for the first evening is written in your hand?"

Strabon untied the ribbon bindings of the papyrus sheets and took the papers to Danaos to inspect.

"Indeed, sir," the clerk confirmed, "this first sheet is my own writing. I was the attending registrar that night. The next morning's sheet is written by one of my subordinates."

"Tell us, Danaos, had there been any unusual traffic that afternoon or evening?"

"Not especially that I recall, other than the Governor's group departing for an overnight celebration at Caesar's quarters. The traffic was of familiar faces at *The Alexandros*. The only unusual visitor was a guest of the Governor's consort, Anna Perenna, who arrived with a letter of authority from her. He arrived at dusk."

Titianus glanced slowly around at his consort at his side, whose eyes were firmly planted ahead of her. The ashen powdered face was unresponsive.

"Did the visitor have a name, Danaos?" Suetonius asked.

"The young noble's name and a note on his authority are inscribed on the sheet, sir. His face was not known to me. I had no recollection of a previous visit."

"Will you read your ascription of his name to us, *Tesserarius*," the Special Inspector asked. Strabon offered Danaos the sheet to read. Danaos cast his eye over the sheet.

"The letter of authority, an invitation written and sealed in the hand of Lady Perenna, introduced him as Lysias of Bithynia. It said he was attached to the *contubernium* of the Imperial Household, and was invited to a professional consultation with Lady Perenna. My notation confirms this to be so."

Thais and Lysias, standing not far from Suetonius's group, tensed in astonishment. Lysias grasped Thais's hand urgently, his features expressing utter astonishment. Hadrian's sight fell enquiringly across the couple in deep foreboding.

"How would you describe Lysias of Bithynia to us, *Tesserarius*? How tall was he? How was he dressed? What company attended him? And so on? Would you recognize him if you met him again?" Suetonius asked, his eyes narrowing to interpret the clerk's features. "Is he here among us now, for example?"

He knew full well Lysias stood close nearby accompanying Thais.

"Why yes, great lord, the fellow is with us here as we speak. I recognized him the moment I arrived. He is even wearing the same uniform of his visit at *The Alexandros*," Danaos burbled with helpful enthusiasm.

"Uniform? A uniform?" Suetonius called, turning towards Lysias who was garbed in the regular *chiton* tunic and mantle of a Greek civilian, not his hunting cuirass, helmet, and weapons.

"Yes, sir. There. Over there," the *tesserarius* burbled, pointing across the chamber.

The entire assembly turned their heads in unison in the direction of his gesture.

"On the bier. The body. The dead person. That's Lysias of Bithynia!" he declared with confidence.

A rustle of louder voices rippled across the gathering. Hadrian sat up abruptly to observe the clerk more closely.

"The body upon the bier?! You believe that to be Lysias?" Suetonius called aloud to confirm Danaos' statement.

"Yes, certainly. He's still wearing the same armor he wore at the jetty. That fair-haired young man over there. Fine looking fellow. I'd recognize him anywhere. It was him," the *tesserarius* confirmed. "He has died, has he?"

CHAPTER 32

'*T*essararius Danaos, are you sure the man lying upon the bier was the fellow who said he was Lysias of Bithynia three evenings ago? He was the man you permitted to travel to the governor's barque at Lady Perenna's invitation as recorded in your log?"

"Yes, sir. Indeed, sir. I am sure, sir. Am I mistaken somehow?"

Suetonius and Clarus looked to each other. Lysias had not been lying. He had not visited *The Alexandros* three evenings ago. It was just as he had protested earlier. The person presenting himself as 'Lysias' had been Antinous, impersonating Lysias for a reason of his own. He did so with a written invitation of authority from the priestess Anna Perenna inscribed in Lysias's name. What could this mean?

The Special Inspector asked a question aloud for all to hear.

"Look again at your papyrus sheet, Danaos. The visitor you know as Lysias was unaccompanied by others at the time. But will you read the name of the person or persons who preceded or followed him?"

Suetonius had already recalled the names from his earlier inspection of the records.

Danaos drew the sheet closer to his sight and fingered the column of names written in his own Greek alphabet scratchings. His finger paused at a name.

"Yes, sir. The youth Lysias was preceded by Quintus Urbicus, a centurion of the Alexandrian Praetorian Guard, the governor's security unit. They both travelled together in our runabout gondola to the *The Alexandros* to attend the Lady Anna Perenna."

A flutter of whispers swept the assembly. Suetonius raised a finger for quiet.

"And again, *Tessararius*, have you noted the name on your list following after the person you know as Lysias? Did he too travel to *The Alexandros*? What was this person's name and, and what time of day would it have been?"

The clerk returned his finger to the sheet and followed it down the column.

"Yes, the dead man over yonder was followed by a senior officer of the German Guard. One Scorilo, a decurion of the Horse Guard. The three were boated to the governor's barque together. The time, you ask? It was then dusk. Night was quickly approaching. I recall it well. My shift was to finish in only four hours."

The assembly shuffled in its place.

"Very well, Danaos, I wish you to now look over the sheets for that same night and the following day to tell me when these three visitors returned from *The Alexandros*?" the Special Inspector asked. He had remembered the discrepancies noted the previous day.

The *tessararius* pored through the subsequent sheets of papyrus. Several names were listed as coming or going, including the governor's party's return at high sun the following day, but Danaos could find no reference to either Lysias or Urbicus departing the vessel at the wharf. He then spied Decurion Scorilo's name on a second sheet recording his departure from *The Alexandros* four hours after dawn the following day.

"My subordinate has been a fool or greatly remiss, masters! Neither the youth Lysias nor Centurion Urbicus are listed as departing the governor's vessel, yet the German decurion is registered when he departed four hours after dawn the next day. My subordinate will be punished for his omissions, masters!"

"They might not be omissions, *Tessararius*. Your subordinate may have been quite accurate in his record. I think I begin to understand the situation," the biographer muttered. He turned to the gathering and its ruler. He now possessed a greater perception of the issues.

"We have several contradictions in these testimonies here, Caesar. Firstly, we have a clerk's record of a *'Lysias'* visiting *The Alexandros*. This turns out to be an impersonation by Antinous for a reason as yet unknown, and we have two guardsmen who accompany the youth to the barque. Yet neither Antinous nor one of the two guardsmen appears to have later returned from the vessel, unless our records are in serious error?

In the meantime we know some dire fate befell Antinous. He appears to have been seriously wounded and bled to death, and either fallen overboard or been placed in the Nile. Meanwhile the highly-regarded centurion who had accompanied him happens to be one of a troop of guardsmen who incidentally stumble upon two fishermen as they discover the body of the youth the following morning in the river's edge. These coincidences strike me as unlikely."

Suetonius allowed a few moments to pass to let that information settle in. He then raised further contradictions.

"Caesar, I need not remind us how both Centurion Urbicus and Decurion Scorilo has told us here only moments ago how they spent the entire night at a troops' celebration of The Isia from that same dusk until the following dawn. Yet the testimony here proclaims to us they were in widely diverse places at the very same time.

Centurion Urbicus says he was at an all-night party, while these papyrus records claim he spent the night aboard *The Alexandros*. He also managed to be by the riverside at the time Antinous's body was hauled from the Nile.

Separately, we have depositions taken from Decurion Scorilo declaring how he performed Guard duties at Caesar's welcoming banquet for Senator Commodus throughout that very same night. Yet he appears magically to have been in three places at precisely the same time – at an all-night party for the troops, onboard *The Alexandros*, and as a Guard officer attending the welcoming banquet. These competing facts are a great mystery and enigma, my lord."

Both Urbicus and Scorilo stood motionless, undisturbed by the sardonic observations. Urbicus eventually cleared his throat to speak.

"My lord Special Inspector, may I speak? These records are obviously a blatant forgery! Not only were we entertained all night at Caesar's party for his troops, those sheets from the jetty are inconsistent and bear poor witness. I piss on their inaccuracies and those who would slander senior, proven officers of Caesar's Guards. It's an offence against our honor! I will pursue the offender for blood satisfaction!"

The centurion's stern accusation shifted the atmosphere considerably. Suetonius became fearful of how the swiftness of judicial favor could shift ground so easily. He was determined to probe deeper before Urbicus or Scorilo wriggled off the hook.

"The letter of authority, the invitation from Lady Anna Perenna, was this retained, *tessararius*, to confirm at least one of these claims?" Suetonius asked, swiftly subsiding into desperation.

"No, great lord, only my notation was entered on the sheet telling it had been sighted. The youth Lysias, if that's who he was, took it with him. But the writing was definitely in the hand of the Lady. I have sighted My Ladyship's invitations often," the clerk confirmed. He was now confused about the real identity of '*the youth Lysias*'. Governor Titianus glanced to his consort at the unexpected implication of *many invitations*.

"The Lady Anna Perenna," Suetonius articulated rhetorically to the gathering, "just who is the Lady Anna Perenna? Tell us, priestess of Rome, who you are, what was your original name prior to adoption by your cult, and where were you born? What is your origin?"

Perenna smiled in a confident manner which disconcerted her interrogator. She responded in an untroubled, even disparaging, manner.

"My dear Special Inspector, why should you ask? I am who I am. I am Anna Perenna at Alexandria, nothing more, nothing less. Frankly I do not know the answers you seek."

Suetonius turned towards Geta the Dacian who had been beside Caesar's throne. The mess of Hadrian's discharges had been cleansed away by the Egyptian workers. Geta's clothing and personal bearing too were adequately restored to cleanliness.

"Geta of Dacia, tell us, does the woman Anna Perenna remind you of someone? Do you see a resemblance? Don't you feel you might know might this woman?"

The biographer was taking great risks punting upon such similarities. Geta stood apart with a quizzical expression.

"No, I don't Suetonius. I have no idea what you mean."

"Look at yourself and at Perenna. Don't you see a resemblance? Coloring, height, facial features, your accents, even the marks upon your cheeks? There are many coincidences. Too many coincidences. It screams at us."

"You see things I don't see, Special Inspector. Yes, there are accidental resemblances. But they are not substantial. What are you getting at?" the Dacian asked his interrogator.

Hadrian began to be aware of the biographer's meaning. He interrupted the conversation.

"Are you asking, Inspector, *is Geta related by blood to the priestess? Are Perenna and Geta somehow of the same family?*"

Suetonius nodded sheepishly. Hadrian turned to the Dacian.

"Tell him, Geta. Tell him of your past and your origin," the emperor encouraged.

"My lord, I don't know what you mean. My past is buried in my distant childhood. I've long forgotten it. I have difficulty recalling anything from my earliest years. My life and memory really begins at Rome when I entered your Household. What preceded that time is lost to a great degree."

Hadrian turned to Suetonius. He spoke tiredly but pointedly.

"Special Inspector, I shall tell you. Our friend Geta is of the royal line of Dacia. He's the son of the *Decebelus* who Trajan triumphed over when Geta was only a child. I served as a commander of Legions under Trajan. It was a hard fought, cruel war.

Geta's original name was Dromichaetes, Prince of Dacia, along with a long litany of native titles and splendid honors. If this is your intended implication, he had a sister of a similar age and appearance named Estia, who he now barely remembers. Estia and Geta were very alike in their features, being of the same parentage.

Geta and his sister were assigned to me as war hostages. Such hostages can be useful to Rome when re-establishing a sympathetic aristocracy in a conquered land. But I assure you, Tranquillus, Estia is not Anna Perenna, if this is your meaning?

Geta's sister Estia was entered into my sister Domitia Paulina's household to be educated as a proper Roman lady. Despite my sister's fond affection and care for Estia, the girl died of a child's ague before she was ten years of age. I supervised her funeral. We didn't tell Geta. What he didn't know wouldn't hurt him. So there is no blood relationship between Geta and the priestess Perenna, despite any physical similarities you may detect."

Caesar had put an end to that speculation.

The biographer was disconcerted; he was running now out of options. He looked across to the *Quaestor*, Salvius Julianus, for new inspiration.

"Senator *Quaestor* Julianus, you have something to show us. I think it's time to explore your discovery."

Julianus strode across to Clarus and the biographer. He was carrying a large globular shape under his cape. He lowered the object to the flagstones of the sanctuary and withdrew the cape. A sturdy terracotta urn with a waxed stopper stood upright before the assembly. Suetonius sensed how Perenna imperceptibly quivered at its sight. Urbicus and Scorilo stirred momentarily as well.

"*Quaestor*, please explain where you acquired this *amphora*," the biographer asked.

"At your behest, Special Inspector, I and my *lictors* representing my legal authority attended *The Alexandros* after those summoned here by Caesar had departed prior to dawn.

We approached the cabin assigned to Anna Perenna, who was already journeying with the Governor to Caesar's marquee. Her cabin was firmly locked, so we were obliged to break entry.

It appears to be a sort of workroom or apothecary's laboratory. I impounded the objects you requested on behalf of your investigation. One is this *amphora* containing an unknown substance which was high upon a ledge sanctified by a votive lamp. Another was a locket on a leather thong draped around the urn's neck. I've brought two other objects I felt were meaningful, which my *lictors* retain nearby."

Perenna whispered sharply into the Governor's ear. Her anger was audible.

Suetonius continued his questioning.

"My Lady Anna Perenna, priestess of Rome, do you recognize the objects which stand here before us? Are these your property?"

The priestess's reply was snappy.

"You have no right, Troublemaker, to break into my private quarters to steal my possessions. In Egypt we cut a hand, an ear, and an eye from those who thieve! You should have asked my permission first. I'm sure I would have been gracious to you in your search."

"As gracious as you were when we visited you only yesterday?" Clarus interjected. "You were barely gracious then, madam."

Anna Perenna seethed.

"My lady, we have before us here a terracotta *amphora*," Suetonius announced for all to hear. "It is thoroughly stoppered and sealed, yet I notice a small leak from one lip. It exudes a dark substance. A dark ruddy substance. May I ask what this urn contains, madam?"

Titianus turned to his consort with a querulous expression. She fumbled a hesitant response but soon resettled into her confident, unflappable manner.

"Special Inspector, I am a priestess of the ancient cult of Anna Perenna. We have a long history at Rome. We specialize in women's matters.

We offer poultices or pessaries to ward off the risk of pregnancy. We offer herbs and medicaments to maximize a woman's fertility or give pleasure. We act as midwives in birthing; we provide love philters and talismans to attract a desired lover; we mix lubricants which arouse partners during sex; and we create paints and pastes to enhance our beauty. We make *kohl* paint to outline the eyes and to deflect bright sunlight; we mix powders with rich color to apply as rouge or a dusting on our eyelids, cheeks, bosoms, or buttocks. We grind precious metals to scatter as pretty glitters; and we create lip paints in tones of scarlet to make women's mouths sensual and desirable to their menfolk," she explained.

"-- And so?" the biographer queried. "The urn?"

"You have in the *amphora* before you a preparation of secret ingredients which will shortly coalesce into a quantity of lip paint. It takes nine days to mature. Then it is ready to apply."

"What's in the preparation, priestess?"

"Why Inspector, that's a priestess's secret."

"What's in it, priestess? Tell us. We have no secrets here."

Perenna was slowly consumed with a rising vexation.

"It is a secret recipe of ochre, iron ore, and the *fucus* plant, with the extra coloring of tiny crimson bugs gathered from African cacti. It is all blended into the purified lard of an ass and perfumed with blossom oils.

Through its nine day maturation period my cult offers prayers and ceremonies to imbue the mixture with magical power in attracting admirers. That's why it was hallowed by a votive lamp and a *phylactery* talisman. My clients among the elite swear by the rich color of my lip paint and its power in attracting a lover."

The biographer looked limply towards Clarus and Julianus. He continued unabated.

"Why was this urn raised high upon a ledge, priestess?"

Perenna was thoughtful for only a fleeting moment.

"The fats of the mixture are attractive to rats. The *Alexandros* seethes with Nile water rats in the bilges, so we keep edible things high beyond their reach."

Suetonius felt stumped again. Surisca leaned across to Suetonius to whisper in his ear.

"The locket, my lord, the locket. It means something."

Suetonius swept the leather-thonged golden locket from Julianus's arm. Perenna's manner stiffened. Both Urbicus' and Scorilo's eyes became riveted to the bubbled case of beaten gold dangling from the thong's loop. It was an ordinary *bulla* locket of no distinction.

"And what is this, my lady?" Suetonius addressed the priestess. She hesitated briefly.

"It's nothing, just the special prayer that infuses the lip paint with its attracting powers. It is women's secret magic. You need not concern yourself with such fanciful trivia."

Once again Surisca whispered into the biographer's ear.

"She's being evasive. It's something special."

"Strabon, good scribe, read the locket's lip-paint prayer to us," the Special Inspector instructed. "We're not averse to women's magic here."

Strabon took the locket and flicked its catch open. Inside were a small furled square of papyrus and a lock of hair. The hair was light in hue and appeared singed by flame. The scribe also noted a single word scratched on the inside of the case. His eyes widened and he glanced nervously to the biographer for permission to respond.

"Well go on, man, read the prayer," Suetonius pressed. The scribe unfolded the paper. Again, he grew concerned. He had a catch in his throat as he read aloud.

"When the King of the Lionhearted
Plays with his man-cub no more
It's time for the lackey
To restore his own pride."

The assembly in the sanctuary rustled with murmuring.

Hadrian fidgeted uncomfortably on his Egyptian high chair, but remained seated. Geta gritted his teeth and clenched his fists. Arrian's head hung low in despondency. Balbilla and the *Augusta* exchanged meaningful glances. Lysias and Thais grasped each other's hand more firmly. Clarus displayed increasing alarm.

"There's a tress of hair inside, pale in color, and a name is engraved on the interior, sirs," Strabon weakly called.

"What name, scribe?"

"The engraved name is *Antinous*."

Minds across the chamber raced to interpret the cryptic quatrain and the Bithynian's relationship to it. Why would Caesar's retired *eromenos* retain such a quaint phylactery? Who was the King? Who was the lackey? What was it all about?

One particular possibility dawned on some in the assembly, something unthinkable, something utterly inadmissible. Was Caesar some form of *cinaedus*, they wondered? Surely not?

It is not feasible for an admired *Princeps* to be a *cinaedus*, these would reason. Such behavior is not within an *Imperator*'s lexicon of attributes. Great dishonor lies in that direction. *Cinaedi* are objects of derision for their lack of self-control. Surely Caesar is not a *cinaedus*?

Suetonius again recalled how so few of Hadrian's reported sexual exploits were with women. In fact, to his knowledge, not a single one he could remember. This was despite the tacit assumption an emperor has his unrestrained pick of life's more pleasurable opportunities, of any gender including the female.

Did this mean Hadrian's taste is strictly for his own gender? Fine. This has no real concern in Rome's *phallocentric* sexual code as long as the maturer contender is strictly the active partner in sex. They who penetrate are *virs*; those who are receptive are *femina* or *pathicus*. To take the passive role is a woman's, a youth's, or an adult *pathic*'s contemptible fate. Even a *fellator* with males, or a male *cunnilinctor* with women, are equally unmanly in this code.

For a man to prefer these roles is to invoke the *pathicus* status. As a *pathic cinaedus,* he is a shame to his gender and Roman custom.

Suetonius realized the quatrain had added a new elliptical dimension to Hadrian's profile, and done so in full public display. The prospect now tenderly arose that it may have been Antinous who performed the male phallic function, unless the relationship had been a mutually carefree *ride there for a ride back* in which sexual favors were reciprocated?

Once again Suetonius recalled how outsiders are unlikely to fathom the inner mechanisms of other people's relationships.

But now it was time to determine precisely what fate had befallen Antinous.

"Priestess!" Suetonius demanded, "Show us your lip paint! Open your urn before Caesar and our assembly!"

Macedo carried the terracotta pot to the priestess and pressed it into her unwilling grasp. Perenna looked around at the surrounding assembly of observers whose eyes were fixed upon her and her pot. Reluctantly, she grasped the *amphora* and strained at the wax-sealed stopper, her eyes gleaming in fierce resentment. The plug broke away after some effort. She held the open urn forward brazenly towards her interrogators for inspection.

Governor Titianus beside her leaned towards the mouth of the jar and peered inside. He withdrew smartly as its odor stung his nostrils.

"Blood. Rotting blood. Pints of it. Must be several days old. Goes off quickly in this climate. Smells of a battlefield or an arena's sands. Repulsive stuff!"

A mournful groan rumbled across the chamber while the priestess Perenna stood her ground in fierce feral belligerence. A defensive stoop descended upon her posture as her eyes blazed from behind their mask of ashen pallor.

"What blood, Perenna? Whose blood? The youth Antinous?" Suetonius called in an increasingly pained voice.

The priestess raised the jar high and hurled it bodily across the space towards him. The urn flicked splashes of wine-colored, viscous slush as it hurtled downwards and crashed to the flagstones at Suetonius's feet. Its terracotta shell fractured into a dozen shards as its contents splayed-out across the granite. Once again a ripely-sour stench exuded through the sanctuary.

Titianus raised a slight finger gesture to Tribune Macedo. The Praetorian commander nodded to his cohort nearby. The guards stepped forward and positioned themselves around the priestess.

"Whose blood, Perenna?" Suetonius repeated. "Whose is it?"

The priestess struggled and hissed vehemently at all around her but spoke no words. Julianus called aloud to his *lictors*. One delivered some objects which had been concealed out of sight. They were a bronze basin stained with a dark-colored dry scale, and a similarly stained bronze surgeon's scalpel. He held them before him to display to all.

"These were lying behind a curtain. They look recently used. There were two more terracotta *amphorae*, also containing fluid," he offered as he stared at the dark ooze spread across the flagstones.

Several in the assembly realized Antinous's very life itself lay spilled out onto the temple stones.

Thais and Lysias walked hesitantly to the pool of dark muck and lowered themselves to their knee at its edge. Thais was quietly weeping. Lysias was visibly mortified. He dipped one fingertip in the pool to examine its consistency. He fell to sobbing.

"Antinous?", he called aloud plaintively, his pain audibly startling the assembly. Hadrian raised himself from his seat, his eyes wide and fixed upon the pool of sludge across the granite.

"We have one further matter to address, Great Caesar!" Suetonius declared aloud.

"What could that possibly be, Inspector?" Hadrian replied in rasping tones redolent of abject despair.

"I wish you to ask one of your Guard for an inspection of their purse, Caesar."

"Their purse?" Hadrian asked impatiently. "Why so, Tranquillus? What's important about a purse?"

"I wish you to command Decurion Scorilo to open and empty the contents of his belt pouch to our view."

"Decurion Scorilo of the Horse Guard? Must I ask one of my most senior and best officers to degrade themselves here, Inspector? Your enquiry is getting out of hand, Tranquillus!"

"I believe I must ask, my lord. It is necessary. If I am mistaken in my reasoning you can dismiss me from your service and prosecute me for the insult, Caesar."

Hadrian faced toward Scorilo and gave the order.

The tattooed German was initially hesitant, but then unlaced the purse-pouch at his sword belt. The investigating team's hearts were in their mouths, with their eyes on the pouch. Had Suetonius erred in his gamble?

"Show us the contents, Decurion," Hadrian instructed. Macedo moved forward to have a closer view and announce the findings.

Scorilo poured baubles from the pouch onto his large, broad, warrior's hardened palm. He silently offered the items to view. Macedo read out the list of debris.

"One gold *aureus*, two silver *denarii*, some bronze coins, two ivory dice well-worn, a bone toothpick, a small ball of black resinous substance wrapped in a leaf, and a man's jeweled ring. The ring!" he repeated excitedly. "Quality silver; well worked; set with a deep blue *lapis lazuli* stone carved with the figure of the deity *Abrasax*, I think. It is surrounded by mystic symbols and antique inscriptions! We have seen this ring before!"

Hadrian rose bolt upright. His eyes had cleared, his stoop dispersed, and his physical energy was restored.

"Scorilo! My protector Scorilo! Where and how did you attain that jewel? How did you come by Antinous's special gift from me? You are no thief, are you? Surely not? That ring is a rare magical talisman of great value. Do you rob the dead? Account for yourself, Decurion!"

Scorilo remained firmly silent. Anna Perenna's voice began to rise to a shout from her guarded position. The priestess's cries were becoming feverish with recklessness.

"Scorilo! Brother Scorilo!" she crowed loudly. All heads turned abruptly from the decurion to Perenna and back again.

"Brother, the time for Zalmoxis has come! It is over! The oath is fulfilled! Zalmoxis will reward us for all eternity. The Iron King's loved one is sacrificed. His life blood was forfeit! We have tasted that blood. The God has absorbed his victim's *arete* from his gore. The gore is now putrid, it has been absorbed. It's over and done. We too can now go to the Underworld of Zalmoxis and join our ancestors at last!" The priestess was exultant.

The assembly broke into uproar.

"Will someone explain to me what is happening here!?" Hadrian bellowed over the cacophony. Geta stepped forward and assumed vocal command of the assembly.

"Silence all! Stand in place! Listen!" he commanded in the stentorian style of his father's distant memory. "The truth now comes to me! I see into my remote past as a child at Dacia.

The woman Perenna and the guardsman, Scorilo, are sister and brother. I see into my childhood days. These two are the daughter and son of the high priest of Dacia, old Dicineus *the Sacrificer*, who was my father's advisor. I see the woman called Anna Perenna when she was a child my own age. We were acolytes of Zalmoxis at the killing of Iron People captives. I forget her name but I recall her zest for the killings.

Her priestly father Dicineus and his family relished the sacrifices. She too had the marks of Zalmoxis tattooed on her face, the insignia of the priestly class and its bloodline. Her brother Scorilo was much older. He was already a young Wolf Warrior proven in combat. He was one of my father's fiercest bodyguards and has the victor's tattoos to prove it. He was one of the horsemen who escorted my father and mother, with my sister Estia and I, into the forests of Dacia to escape the pursuing Iron People.

Who are the Iron People? The *Iron People* are us, we Romans. I too am now an *Iron Person*. I too am a Roman.

My father discharged his guards to allow them to flee before the enemy could overtake us. But he demanded an oath of revenge, the oath to Zalmoxis. He sent my mother, his queen, and then himself to Zalmoxis. Before he killed himself he demanded we swear an oath to destroy the Iron People king's loved ones too, in reparation to Zalmoxis. It was a fearful oath of dire consequences!

I too swore it. I was very young. I swore to kill the Iron People king's loved one too, in vengeance. But I failed in my oath, I am pleased to say. The children of Priest Dicineus *the Sacrificer* did not! They killed the king's loved one, Antinous."

Geta slumped against Caesar's throne, exhausted.

Hadrian spoke in a disbelieving voice to Perenna and Scorilo.

"Is it true you are the children of Dicineus, that murderous priest?" Neither responded.

"The *Bastarnae* were one of the tribes of the Dacian Confederation, yes?"

Again silence.

"Is it true the blood on the stones here is that of Antinous?" he asked further. Again no response.

Hadrian grew gray with distress.

"Why, Dacians, why? Why would you bleed such a gracious man, such an innocent, for your pointless obsession?" Hadrian's eyes were riven with pain.

Perenna struggled ineffectually in her captor's grip, her eyes wild, her body writhing with feverish energy. The *kohl* lines had begun to melt down her cheeks in her body heat; the ashen powders of her face were corroding from her skin; the hue of her oiled lips was smeared across her mouth. In her disorder she projected the energy of a wild forest creature or ghoul seething with savagery, an alien demon bent upon havoc.

Suetonius, Clarus, Strabon, and Surisca whispered together as one, "The She Wolf."

"The oath is fulfilled!" Perenna cried aloud across the sanctuary, her haughty disdain resounding off the temple stones. "The loved one of the Iron People's ruler has been sacrificed to the god of the Dacians! His face was daubed in his own blood! We dipped our fingers in his gore to lick and taste his *arete*. We drained his carcass of its *arete* to offer to Zalmoxis the life-juices of the precious loved one of the Iron People's King!

Our priestly father's strangling at Rome is revenged. The *Decebelus's* honor is restored. The blood debt of our warriors in the arenas of Rome is paid. The faithful devotees of Zalmoxis have exacted bitter retribution!"

Perenna, or whoever she was, was spiraling into delirium.

"How did you persuade Antinous to participate in his own slaughter, priestess of Zalmoxis," Suetonius called to the deranged creature before him.

"The fool was a willing victim! His desire was urgent. He craved to exchange his lifeforce for the lifeforce of his *erastes*, this King of the Iron People. This king is diseased, he told us. The king is affected with a dropsy of the internal humors. He is dying, he bleated in tears. He wished to give the king renewed life, <u>his</u> youth's fresh life! He wished the *Imperium* to receive his hero's gift and to exchange his years of health for the king's declining lifespan!"

The assembly was enthralled by the escalating frenzy.

"The youth had witnessed those wizards who claim to revive a beheaded man. He knew how return from the Land of the Dead was feasible with the proper sorcery. At least that's what he thought. He was taught Queen Alcestis had been brought back from Hades' grasp by Hercules. He had been taught the heroes who sacrificed their lives in antiquity's wars live on eternally at the Isle of Achilles across the Black Sea. He learned how the followers of *Chrestus* revere their executed founder because he was magically reborn, resurrected to life again. And he saw with his own eyes how Great Alexander *Divus* lies intact still after four hundred years, preserved by a potent magic.

This year's Isia was his opportunity to become Osiris, restored from death to life. He took his opportunity. I used his need and his love for his *erastes*, and told him how Anna Perenna too can exchange the energies of one life for another by her incantations. I said she too can revive the dead. He believed me, the fool ..."

"Cease talking, Hagne!" Scorilo suddenly called to the priestess. "They'll indict you for murder or worse. The penalty is vile, Sister. Cease now!"

Surisca whispered to Suetonius and Clarus, "Is the Bastarni guardsman then the wolf?"

Perenna continued unabated. She was on a roll.

"The boy wanted it! He pleaded for it! He was impelled to exchange the surging lifeforce of a healthy youth with the fading energies of his imperial *erastes*. He wouldn't cease his pleading. He said he was so utterly indebted to Caesar and committed to Caesar's cause as ruler!"

Hadrian slumped heavily back into his throne, disconsolate. He was overwhelmed by her words.

"So you helped him to do it, *Hagne?*" the Special Inspector asked coolly as Strabon scribbled speedily at his notebook. Suetonius used the barbarian name Scorilo had called. "Tell us *Hagne*, how was it done, priestess of an alien god? Tell us all."

The woman began burbling with zealous, righteous enthusiasm.

"Brother Scorilo and Centurion Urbicus had befriended the youth for our purpose. They taught him tricks of swordsmanship and other warrior's skills. They persuaded him to come to *The Alexandros* to my sanctuary to effect the transfer. He was to come under another name to deflect attention. I wrote an invitation note in the name of one of his friends, Lysias, to ease him past the sentries without his real identity being noted. He suspected nothing, he was so trustful of us.

He was to wear his ceremonial uniform beneath his cloak, this was to be a formal rite of great majesty. He did so without fear. He believed how in nine days after his journey through Hades' domain he would be restored to life, but at the cost that his youth's lengthy lifespan would be exchanged with Caesar's shorter span. Meanwhile, Caesar would live and rule!"

The woman was trembling in exultation and fervor. She was triumphant.

"Why would Antinous believe such a thing? He is no fool!" Suetonius called.

"Fool? *Love* is a great persuader. Fools do remarkable things for the sake of *Love!*"

"And then?"

"We performed a ceremony honoring Rome's *Anna Perenna* of old, and the youth voluntarily drank my infusion of *opion* and *kannabis* in wine. He believed it to be my magical potion to effect the transfer of energies. He swiftly drifted to sleep.

My brother and I then performed a rite to Zalmoxis and burned a lock of the victim's hair for the God to receive as smoke signaling his impending spiritual presence.

I lanced his wrist veins, inserted a surgeon's bleeding spigot to siphon, and proceeded to drain him as our priests do when they slit the throats of offerings. With time, our basin collected enough blood for three *amphorae* jugs.

Blood is the food of Zalmoxis. Blood carries the *arete* of a man.

I anointed the victim's face with his own blood, the ultimate insult of the God. Over the following days Zalmoxis consumes his entire *arete* by fermenting the blood to an odious filth. This is our way."

The woman's delirium was assuming a dire *maenadic* aspect. There were vestiges of some ancient ritual frenzy betrayed in her behavior. She had become a wild creature.

"And, *Hagne*, what more ---?" Suetonius resolutely pressed.

Perenna/Hagne assumed a soberly circumspect demeanor.

"It was nothing personal, just honor's revenge," she smiled.

A crushing silence now weighed the sanctuary.

"The lad died. It was late at night. Pressing out the blood for Zalmoxis had taken much time. While it was still dark, Scorilo and Urbicus tumbled his body through a starboard port into one of the Alexandrine runabouts roped at the stern readied for sailing.

I stored the *amphorae* for consecration to determine if I had inherited my father's power of regeneration of the dead. Priest Diceneus, my father, had been a practitioner of *theogia*. He tested many victims, but with what success is unknown to me. I aspire to similar prowess. I was to devote nine days to the necessary incantations and rites. But now we'll never know, will we?

At the very earliest light we three pushed off to sail the craft downstream to an inlet close to Urbicus's tents. The two placed the body at the river's side where we knew it might soon be discovered. There was already movement about, so Urbicus stayed at the inlet to rejoin his detachment. Scorilo and I eventually maneuvered the runabout back to *The Alexandros*. The rest is known to you. Our victory was complete."

"You've told us about Scorilo and yourself, but why was Urbicus involved?"

Hagne of Dacia, nee Anna Perenna of Rome, laughed a raucous, quavering laugh whose shrillness spoke of triumph and insult. The She Wolf was savoring her kill.

"Urbicus is one of my *inamoratas*. The poor darling will do anything I ask. And all for a little bodily titillation. But I keep him on a tight rein, the dear. Those Mauritanians and Numidians, they'll do anything for sex. The desert wilds of Africa must be very lonely at night."

Suetonius glanced to Urbicus standing nearby. The soldier was flush with anger, but his restrained eyes stared straight ahead in impassive soldierly discipline. Escape from the sanctuary was not feasible; a Scythian archer would bring him down with a single shaft.

"Why you, Centurion? Why did you participate in this mad venture? You're a man of good sense," the Special Inspector probed.

Urbicus stood utterly motionless and silent.

Governor Titianus broke the intensity of the atmosphere. He had quietly distanced himself from his consort who was stooping in her craven, seething manner nearby.

"Macedo, take the Horse Guard decurion into custody. And take too the woman Hagne or Perenna or whoever she is, I no longer know.

Secure the brother and sister in the woman's chamber aboard *The Alexandros*. Make sure they're isolated, restrained, well guarded, and carry no weapons for self-harm. I will access them there for intimate interrogation. Afterwards, Caesar will decide what to do with them at his leisure.

Take Urbicus and strip him of his Praetorian regalia. Imprison him in the camp guardhouse. He will meet military justice in due course."

Suetonius noticed Titianus's eyes and Urbicus's eyes met for a fleeting moment. It carried a subliminal message, he thought. It was a message he sensed he might never interpret.

Hadrian slowly rose from his throne and stood silently, imperially, looking to the bier and its sad, pallid burden. It dawned on the entire assembly it was time to stand upright and be attentive under Caesar's presence.

The *Augusta* rose in silent respect, Geta stood tall, and the dispersed individuals returned to their protocol order. Only Macedo's officers were moving about as they stripped Scorilo and Urbicus of their weapons and strapped shackles to their wrists.

A hush settled upon the sanctuary. Hadrian spoke carefully, thoughtfully, as his words reverberated off the ancient stones.

"It is time to leave this dark place and this dark affair. It is to be formally recorded here under my authority how Antinous of Bithynia died by falling into the river. Nothing more. The subject of the method of his death and its perpetrators is under prohibition. They do not exist. Let our documents record nothing further of the matter. It is forbidden on pain of exile.

Suetonius Tranquillus and Septicius Clarus, you have fulfilled your commission. In return you will be awarded one hundred thousand *sesterces* each, as promised, and be absolved of the previous charge of *laesa majestas* against the empress, my wife Vibia Sabina.

For Suetonius Tranquillus a new indictment of *laesa majestas* against my honor will be raised. Its details will be formulated and addressed at my leisure. We move on. Hear all!

I proclaim my edict before you here at this dawn of the Third Day of the Festival of Isis. Secretary Vestinus, *Quaestor* Julianus, Prefect Governor Titianus, and officers of the Household hear my command and enact it immediately.

The honor of the youth Antinous of Bithynia is to be restored. The omen divined by the Priests of Amun of the youth's divine status as Osiris Reborn is to be written into law at Egypt and proclaimed to the Empire. As *Pontifex Maximus I* ordain Antinous to attain *Divus* status before the eyes of all the Empire. He is to be celebrated accordingly.

The priests of Amun are to honor his *Divus* status with appropriate rites. A sufficient endowment is to be assigned to this priesthood to institute his adoration in perpetuity as a Protector of Youth, a Guardian of Healing, and a Defender of Birthing.

Temples and shrines are to be erected across the Empire to celebrate his virtues and values. Statues and portrait busts, issues of coins and medallions, plus public festivals are to be created in his honor. Youth Games are to be announced in select cities in his name, and funded with desirable prizes."

A tear formed at Hadrian's eye. His lip trembled faintly. He continued.

"I announce here how the city at Middle Egypt we were to inaugurate today in my honor by the name of *Hadrianopolis* is now relinquished. It is cancelled.

Instead, I announce the inauguration of the new city of *Antinoopolis*. It is to be the liturgical centre of the cult of *Antinous Divus* at the place where he fell into the river and today's miracles have occurred. The new city is to be peopled with Romans and Greeks, mainly discharged Legionaries. They will be provided with free land and seed here. This will encourage immigration.

A mausoleum housing the eternal remains of *Antinous Divus* will be erected at Antinoopolis to be the focus of the new city and attract pilgrims to its miracles and rites. Memorial statues of *Antinous Divus* are to be crafted plentifully for dissemination across the Middle Sea.

His *arete* will be celebrated at Antinoopolis just as in life he had recommended Caesar's be celebrated at this place. *Hail Antinous! And hail to the foundation of Antinoopolis!*"

Hadrian collapsed to his chair to rest. A rumble of chattering voices swept across the assembly, slowly surging to burst into enthusiastic applause. Cries of *Hail Caesar!* and *Hail Antinous Divus!* were shouted. They were accompanied by stamping of feet, rattling of swords on shields, and shrill whistles by the troops.

The priest Pachrates strode across the stone flagging and struck the granite slabs loudly three times with his staff. A hush resumed. Pachrates was beaming. Things had turned his way at last.

"Great Pharaoh! Hail to you! We too hail Osiris Reborn, the youth Antinous reborn in the guise of Antinous-Osiris! Now, Caesar, witness the light of Amun-Re on this Day of Antinous, Divine Healer and Protector of the Young, risen like Apollo Phoebus as a sign of restored vigor to the Great Pharaoh Hadrian and his Empire!"

As he uttered his praises he thrust his ceremonial scepter high towards the eight high cedar doors arcing between pillars behind the sanctuary. The priests stationed by the doors began chanting a deeply sonorous incantation. At Pachrates' cue, united as one, they swung open the heavy cedar portals facing the chamber with a single mighty heave. It permitted a shimmering blaze of morning sunlight to flood into the stony interior.

During the debacle with Hagne and Scorilo the sun had fully risen beyond the eastern ranges opposite the temple. Its shining luminosity now swamped the broody gloom of the sanctuary with brilliant splendor. All eyes were enchanted by the intensity of the vision. Rows of priests rattled their *systra* and banged their cymbals or tambours to a crescendo as they completed their chant. Pachrates finalized it with a prayer of praise.

"Hail Amun-Re, the Hidden God who reveals Himself in Light and in all other deities, and reveals Himself in Antinous-Osiris Reborn!"

The central statue of Osiris as Serapis stood in sharp silhouette against the morning brightness. Its long shadow fell meaningfully through curling incense clouds across the bier supporting the dead

Bithynian. Pachrates and Kenamun threw their priest's staffs to the stones with a resounding clatter as each of the assembled clerics fell to their knees to prostrate themselves in reverence to the new incarnation of their deity lying upon the bier.

Hadrian rose slowly, tiredly, exhaustedly from his throne. He paused thoughtfully and muttered something half-voiced towards the assembled onlookers.

Many in the chamber missed his words, but Suetonius, Clarus, Surisca, and Strabon heard clearly. Thais and Lysias too caught the phrase, while Geta's response indicated he too had apprehended the remark. The *Augusta* turned in reaction while Arrian stood motionless in grave solemnity. They had heard him intone feebly, even reluctantly:

"Love is something to be pitied in a Caesar. Pitied."

Hadrian signaled to his retinue with his eagle-tipped baton of office to dismiss the assembly. He clasped his puke-soiled toga folds about himself and lunged unsteadily towards the entrance corridors followed by his staff and soldiers. He paused by the bier to look upon the face of his departed companion as the morning sunlight flared across the youth's calm features.

Caesar lingered for an instant seemingly frozen in eternity. He then averted his eyes to move speedily away. Duty called. The business of governance beckoned. The Empire waited impatiently. Sentiment will be postponed to some other time.

Suetonius again detected the glint of moisture at his eyes as the *Princeps* passed by.

Yet, the biographer wondered to himself, is it really true *love is something to be pitied in a Caesar?*

EPILOGOS

The first sounds I heard were calls of alarm and shouted voices. The camp lanes at the Nile's banks were alive with slaves and attendants scurrying to-and-fro, while passing members of the Household and its military drew closer for a better view. In the sweltering blaze of noon I saw leaping flames and roiling smoke. The Governor's barque was ablaze.

The She Wolf, Hagne, nee Anna Perenna, and her Wolf Warrior brother Scorilo had been imprisoned under guard in her witch's den at the stern of *The Alexandros*. They were both manacled to separate beams facing each other in that musty chamber of decayed detritus, razor-sharps, and ill omens, to await examination by torture.

Governor Titianus announced he would comprehensively explore the origin of the conspiracy which culminated in the distasteful murder of Antinous, and determine if the incident connected to other disaffected members of the Court, Horse Guard, or Praetorians.

The barque chamber had been cleared of the remaining residues of her sacrificial victim, Antinous. These included the two *amphorae* of his putrefying blood and half-burned locks of hair. The ooze which had splashed over the temple flagstones was respectfully scraped up and interred in an embalmer's canopic jar. Antinous's bier soon carried nine jars of assorted viscera or bloody slimes.

But the remnants of desiccated organic matter, lizards, frogs, spiders, beetles, a stillborn fetus, exotic herbs, wild grasses, and evil-colored fungi, remained aboard *The Alexandros*. They were stocked in their racks and chests surrounding the two prisoners. Titianus anticipated his interrogation might uncover what further mischief his consort had been entertaining during the four years of their lusty, if tempestuous, relationship.

But this was not to be.

I was told by a reputed witness how under some pretext the devotee of Zalmoxis, Hagne, found a way to shift her manacled limbs to strike at a candelabrum which happened to be close nearby. She toppled its lamps and their oil splashily to the cabin's floor. At least that's the story we were given.

The splashed oil and nearby hangings caught fire instantly, with the flames skimming from drape to drape across the den in a cascading rush. The blaze latched onto the parched timbers and other flammable materials of the old Governor's barque. It was soon sweeping around the chamber and taking grip of the vessel in a rapidly expanding conflagration.

Despite the efforts of staff trying to bucket water onto the flames, *The Alexandros* became engulfed in a raging firestorm. The gilded tinderbox confection became a searing inferno. Its few inhabitants at that time, male and female, scattered swiftly. Some leapt overboard into surrounding boats, a few hurtled less felicitously into the river's rush. All escaped the inferno. The grand Alexandrine allegory and its two manacled prisoners were abandoned to their fiery fate.

We were told how at the advent of the fire the shrill jibes of the She Wolf, shrieking insults in the guttural rasps of her original dialect, cut through the snarl of flames. Her gales of victory laughter rose above the holocaust in defiant taunts.

I am also told no sound emanated from her brother's lips. He journeyed to the Underworld of Zalmoxis without so much as an audible whimper.

After some moments the She Wolf's vocal barbs transformed to less-exultant, high piercing screams of anguish and pain. Soon, only the crackle-and-snap of the consuming flames radiated across the river's surface as the ornate craft burned spectacularly to the waterline beneath the hovering midday sun.

We four members of the investigating team recalled the words of the Oracle at Siwa, *"Fire purifies!"* Nevertheless it seemed a remarkably convenient accident or turn of affairs, we each thought.

So, does my secret history have a happy ending? Well no, if you consider our loss of the well-favored Bithynian youth. Yet these events possessed their own satisfactions for some.

Titianus's Iberian slave companion Sotira moved into tent chambers with the Governor within the encampment the very same day.

Vibia Sabina *Augusta* and her gentlewoman companion Julia Balbilla retired from social events during the remainder of the Nile tour. The revelations at the assembly in the temple had unsettled many at Court, including Hadrian's wife.

Instead Balbilla, a classicist poet of note, commissioned stoneworkers to inscribe flattering verses to her Imperial patron on the granite plinths of ancient monuments along the route of the Household's travels. She intends these public tributes in elegant verse to the *Augusta* to weather the long life of these monuments, perhaps as eternally as those to Antinous by her husband.

It seems devising ingenious ways to survive into eternity is an almost universal compulsion among us these days?

Curiously, later I learned at a distance how the Alexandrian Praetorian, the centurion Lucius Quintus Urbicus, didn't face a court martial. He didn't meet discipline and execution as might be expected. After all, to our view he was implicated somehow in the death of several people including that of Antinous himself. His role seemed as murderous as the Dacian brother and sister.

Instead I am told Urbicus has been quietly reassigned to the service of the Prefect of Praetorians, Quintus Marcius Turbo, at the grim Praetorium Fortress on Rome's Quirinal Hill. I haven't yet fathomed the implications of this unexpected gesture, but it seems to suggest a promotion?

Clarus simply raised an eyebrow charily when I mentioned it, but he diplomatically made no comment.

One wonders at the coincidence of so many of those of African origin involved in the matter, such as Urbicus, Titianus and, more remotely, Prefect Turbo himself. Did I, Clarus, and Surisca miss something?

My complete lack of success in engaging Surisca's professional charms continued. After three days of ineptitude in exacting a Roman male's customary prerogative with a woman, especially a woman well paid for the purpose, I finally desisted. *Fortuna* is telling me something? Several days in each other's company had changed the nature of the relationship. I became fond of her.

Perhaps it had been the Three Fates' way of telling me I should pursue other diversions so late in life than pursuing women young enough to be my granddaughter?

Instead, I endowed Surisca with half of my award of *sesterces* from Caesar. I did this because she contributed to our enquiry in ways far beyond her contracted fee. In fact, her perceptions had been pivotal to the crime's resolution. Even Clarus agreed to this, if grudgingly.

At first Surisca was wary of receiving my pledge of the fifty thousand *sesterces*, possibly thinking I possessed some gross intention upon her person in exchange. Once she realized my gesture was genuine and without strings attached, she became the joyful grand-daughter I had never given birth to, but vaguely hankered for. The donation, I suggested to her, might be a useful adjunct to her funds in starting her perfumes manufacturing workshop.

Even further, Geta the Dacian also approached her with warm congratulations. However he had far better fortune with her charms than I. Their memory of their playful week together at Shuni earlier in the year had lingered and prospered. In fact the two decided to retire together to somewhere like Antioch, Damascus, or Massilia at Gaul, where the huge quantities of blooms necessary for steeping in oil to create intense perfumes were more readily harvested. Geta intends to make Surisca his mistress or concubine, though I suspect Surisca has other goals.

Geta sought Hadrian's blessing for the liaison. Someday the two might marry in the traditional manner, though a woman of Surisca's independent lifestyle and Geta's noble heritage probably doesn't require such fancy formality.

Lysias and Thais too may follow a similar path. Arrian recently offered Lysias the post he once had in mind for Antinous as an officer in his administration. As the newly-appointed Governor of Cappadocia,

Arrian's offer was a remarkable opportunity for Lysias to be attached to his new administration, especially one which has been delegated the control of two additional entire Legions, not one – the *Legio XV Apollinaris* and *Legio XII Fulminata*.

This was the very target Arrian had been pursuing for several years to defend our eastern frontier against the Alans barbarians. Arrian regarded Antinous and Lysias to be major contributors to this happy outcome. So perhaps one day Lysias too will return to Bithynia in a role as a senior officer of the Imperium.

Thais is definitely pregnant. It's visible now. The birth is expected in early summer here in Alexandria. She will retain the child, if it is healthy. Though she has her own independent wealth, thanks to Antinous, she has accepted Lysias's offer for her to come under the protection of his household at least until the child is secured sufficiently in maturity. They will see how things stand between them afterwards.

Lysias, of course, is as keen to see a healthy child delivered as is the mother. Both have an emotional connection to the child, in different ways. The Greek word *arete* comes to mind.

Yet it's also possible Thais will accept Hadrian's invitation to assume the role of a priestess of Antinous-Osiris.

At Hadrian's vast palace complex at Tibur outside Rome, the one where Antinous had contributed plans and designs for artificial lakes, grottos, and a youths' *palaestra*, Caesar's architects are presently building an elegant shrine to the man based upon Hadrian's special design. Perhaps Thais is the appropriate resident celebrant at this facility, he has suggested?

Already some very fine statues of the Bithynian are in place. These are works which idealize the lad's features in the current fashion. They display a slight softness of muscle tone untypical of Antinous's sturdy tissues, plus a demurely-sized penis to represent his youthful age. There are no scars on his cheek or wrist.

The likenesses are remarkably faithful to his memory, to my eye. Perhaps strikingly so. Among other things, they depict the human animal at its most elegant magnificence.

The artist Cronon of the Fayum is commissioned to supervise all reproductions of the Bithynian's features on coins, medallions, tondos, upwards to busts and life-size statues. Cronon's remarkably lifelike painted portraits of Antinous act as authorized guides for artisans across the Empire who have never seen the living fellow. The result is statuary of the fellow is appearing in great numbers across the Empire.

Thais will more greatly appreciate Hadrian's offer when she realizes his Tibur *Villa*'s shrine houses the ashes of the father of her child. That's the rumor anyway.

It seems the public have been led to believe how the bodily remains of Antinous lie in state, carefully embalmed for eternal display, at the cult temple being erected in Antinoopolis at Middle Egypt. As with Alexander's cadaver at Alexandria, Antinous will be the focal point of the city and its community, in perpetuity. It supplies the glue which holds the diverse social elements together while providing a draw card for pilgrims from around the Empire.

Already tales of miracles at the temple involving healing and childbirth, as well as success in love, are circulating. Antinous's beauty has attracted a veritable stampede of adherents. Some rites and festivals are known to be carefree, if not downright uninhibited.

However, just between us, it is also whispered the recumbent figure on display behind the bronze grille within the rising structure is in fact an expertly carved effigy coated with a rare resin to replicate embalmed flesh. The model is toned in natural colors to seem believable, though it's sufficiently protected not to be manhandled by visitors. That's the gossip, anyway.

I am told on good authority Hadrian had the mortal remains and blood residues of the lad secretly retrieved from the embalmers and privately cremated under his aegis as *Pontifex Maximus*. They say it was a rite of extraordinary beauty. A pure white dove took flight from the pyre when the flames rose, indicating Antinous's pristine spirit soared to the heavens above. Was this yet another *resurrection* among the reputed litany of resurrections?

Hadrian has retained the ashes and personally interred them within a compact Egyptian obelisk at his new shrine at Tibur. This chapel will be known as *The Antinoeion*. It is only a few paces from the private apartments once happily shared by Caesar and his beloved *eromenos*. Yet it took the needless death of his companion for Hadrian to awaken to his own heart and acknowledge the depth of his feelings for another man.

Hadrian wears the miniature blood-jewel figurine of Osiris retrieved from Antinous's gut on a fine gold chain around his neck. It can sometimes be seen peeping out beneath folds of clothing as Caesar turns sharply to one side or leans forward at a certain angle.

Pachrates dramatically proclaimed this figurine was Antinous's bloodstream and life energy – his *arete?* – transfigured into a talisman suffused with his youthful potency.

It is true Caesar seems to have recovered a great part of his health in recent times, to the joy of us all. Yet I wonder if the figurine was yet another of that theatrical wizard's sleight-of-hand manipulations, just another oriental deceit?

On his left hand Hadrian wears the deep blue *Abrasax* stone. Its rich, dark hue with the finely engraved figure of the deity surrounded by arcane syllables seems striking upon someone who previously disdained jewelry. One wonders if the talisman will bring to Hadrian a similar future to the one delivered to its previous owners, Antinous or Basileus Alexandros? Fame eternal, yes, but at a high price.

I still await Hadrian's pleasure at Clarus's villa in Alexandria. It seems my offence at the Temple of Amun was that so much personal information about Caesar and Antinous was openly aired before the entire Household and its interminable gossip mill.

State secrets were made public; embarrassing personal minutiae were exposed to the view of all; the *erastes/eromenos* relationship was shown to have an unexpected polarity. For this I am charged again with *laesa majestas*, and my head may pay for it.

The Court meanwhile is forbidden to discuss the revelations at the temple or challenge the official decision on Antinous's fate on pain of exile. Antinous simply fell into the Nile. It happens. End of story.

However Septicius Clarus has intimated my head might not be forfeit after all. He has conveyed the impression Hadrian will accept as recompense my services as his editor in authoring his own autobiography, his *Memoirs.* Perhaps this is to ensure the precise facts of the past four years don't enter the public domain and history's muckraking record? Hadrian has his own reasons to prefer otherwise. I am already framing in my mind an elegant *Memoir* for Hadrian.

So if I am to edit Caesar's memoirs, this work before you is likely to be acquired for a suitable sum – a highly suitable sum, hopefully - to divert further copies and dissemination. It will simply disappear from existence.

Yet there are unanswered questions.

Are the Lion and its Cub now reconciled? Has the lackey's pride been restored?

Should a Caesar really be pitied for ordinary human sentiment?

There is nothing in life like love, I say, whatever its manifestation. As the Caesars themselves show, it may come in many differing varieties.

Among these, we ask, is it nature or nurture which gives a so-called *cinaedus* his, or even her, extraordinarily fertile, prolific, inspiring *daemon*?

Those of us familiar with these gifts salute such bounteous genius. Perhaps it begets progeny of the mind to replace progeny of the loins?

Our world would be desolate without them.

FINIS

Printed in Poland
by Amazon Fulfillment
Poland Sp. z o.o., Wrocław